Praise for the novels of
New York Times bestselling author
DIANA PALMER

"Diana Palmer is an amazing storyteller, and her
longtime fans will enjoy *Wyoming Winter* with
satisfaction!"

—*RT Book Reviews*

"The popular Palmer has penned another winning
novel, a perfect blend of romance and suspense."

—*Booklist* on *Lawman*

"This is a fascinating story…. It's nice to have a hero
wise enough to know when he can't do things alone
and willing to accept help when he needs it. There is
pleasure to be found in the nice sense of family this
tale imparts."

—*RT Book Reviews* on *Wyoming Bold*

"Sensual and suspenseful."

—*Booklist* on *Lawless*

"Diana Palmer is a mesmerizing storyteller who
captures the essence of what a romance should be."

—*Affaire de Coeur*

"Diana Palmer is one of those authors whose books
are always enjoyable. She throws in romance,
suspense and a good story line."

—*The Romance Reader* on *Before Sunrise*

"Lots of passion, thrills, and plenty of suspense…
Protector is a top-notch read!"

—*Romance Reviews Today*

A prolific author of more than one hundred books, **Diana Palmer** got her start as a newspaper reporter. A *New York Times* bestselling author and voted one of the top ten romance writers in America, she has a gift for telling the most sensual tales with charm and humor. Diana lives with her family in Cornelia, Georgia. Visit her website at dianapalmer.com.

Books by Diana Palmer

Long, Tall Texans

Merciless
Courageous
Protector
Invincible
Untamed
Defender
Undaunted
Unbridled

Wyoming Men

Wyoming Tough
Wyoming Fierce
Wyoming Bold
Wyoming Strong
Wyoming Rugged
Wyoming Brave
Wyoming Winter

The Morcai Battalion

The Morcai Battalion
The Morcai Battalion: The Recruit
The Morcai Battalion: Invictus
The Morcai Battalion: The Rescue

Visit the Author Profile page
at Harlequin.com for more titles.

DIANA PALMER

FOR NOW AND FOREVER

HQN™

HQN™

Recycling programs for this product may not exist in your area.

ISBN-13: 978-1-335-01348-4

For Now and Forever

Copyright © 2019 by Harlequin Books S.A.

The publisher acknowledges the copyright holder of the individual works as follows:

Dark Surrender
First published in 1983 by Dell. This edition published in 2019.
Copyright © 1983 by Diana Palmer

Color Love Blue
First published in 1984 by Dell. This edition published in 2019.
Copyright © 1984 by Diana Palmer

www.HQNBooks.com

Printed in U.S.A.

CONTENTS

DARK SURRENDER   7

COLOR LOVE BLUE   175

DARK SURRENDER

CHAPTER ONE

AUTUMN FELT GOOD. It made Maggie Sterline's heart quicken to see the bonfires late in the afternoon, to smell the faint scent of powdering leaves mingled with wood smoke. It brought back haunting tales of hobgoblins and magic and Indian campfires. Of course, the leaves in south Georgia were nothing like the glory in the northern end of the state, where ghostly mountains lifted their smooth peaks to be dotted with gold-and-red dabs of color against the sapphire canvas that was the autumn sky. But it was much the same in other ways. The Indians had once lived in this part of her native state, too, Maggie thought, and the moccasined feet of the Lower Creeks had left their imprints in local history. There were arrowheads and bits of pottery all around Defiance testifying to that early occupation.

Maggie had always liked the town's name: Defiance. It sounded as if it liked impossible odds, and if Saxon Tremayne caught up with her, she'd need some defiance. Some hope.

The thought of the big man made her shudder. She'd come very close to falling in love with Saxon in those weeks she'd spent in his company while she'd worked on an in-depth photo feature about the industrial giant for the regional magazine she'd worked for in South Carolina. It had been great fun. And she'd only been dimly aware that Kerry Smith was working on an exposé about some local cotton mill causing brown lung. If only she'd paid attention!

She perched herself on the edge of her cluttered desk. Maggie was a good-looking young brunette of twenty-six; not pretty, but slender and attractive, from her high firm breasts to her small waist and narrow hips. She had good legs, too, but today she'd wrapped them in long fashionable boots under a colorful gray-and-red plaid skirt over which she wore a white blouse and a knitted gray vest. She looked trendy, but not flashy, and the newspaper's owner, Ernie Wilson, liked the touch of class she lent to his modest operation—or so he said. The owner of *The Defiant Banner* had known Maggie's family since his grandfather bought the newspaper, and he was sometimes more of an uncle than an employer. He hadn't even asked questions when Maggie had come into his office looking for a job, her face drawn and haggard, her jade-green eyes hunted and afraid. Ernie Wilson never asked questions, and Maggie assumed it was because he had such a knack for reading minds.

She'd needed the job desperately. More than a means of support, it had meant a refuge from the furious textile magnate who'd blamed her for selling him out for the sake of a story. His subsequent battle with the environmental people and his plant's labor union had been a direct consequence of the accusing front-page story about the lung-damaging capabilities of his plant and his carelessness in not correcting the situation. In fact, the modifications to update the plant and install a new system to control the damaging cotton dust had been planned and were well on their way to being implemented. But the story didn't make mention of that fact;

it made it seem as if Saxon Tremayne was a money-mad businessman who put profits above safety. And he'd blamed Maggie for that piece of damning fiction. He'd judged her guilty without giving her the benefit of the doubt or an opportunity to tell him her side of it. He'd promised only retribution for her betrayal, and Saxon Tremayne was a man of his word. It was worth its weight in diamonds, and in the South Carolina textile town of Jarrettsville, it was law.

Maggie hadn't wanted to leave the graceful little town. She was innocent, and if he'd given her half a chance, she might have proved it to him. But he hadn't been in a listening mood the day the story broke. His voice had bellowed at her over the phone, deep and slow and as cold as a mortuary. He'd cut her off before she could put the blame on a mix-up over bylines, promising reprisals in that cutting tone he used best in a temper. He never raised his voice, but it was worse than being yelled at.

The worst thing of all was that her heart, so long untouched, had finally been his for the taking. She'd learned to love the big man in the brief period she'd spent with him, and if she'd just had a little more time, she might have been able to catch his eye. He'd been friendly, cooperative. But not once had he touched her or looked at her in any intimate way. People said he was still grieving for his late wife. But nothing he'd told Maggie gave the impression that he'd felt anything at all for the woman who'd shared his bed and board for eighteen years. Maggie had wondered at the time if he was capable of deep emotions. He seemed to be a loner, involved deeply in business but only casually interested in his family. There wasn't much of that either, she knew: a stepbrother, a mother and a few scattered cousins whom he barely acknowledged. She didn't even know where his family lived.

"Daydreaming again?" a light, teasing voice whispered at her ear.

Her dark-lashed eyes flew open, their emerald-green depths brilliant enough to shock as she met Eve's dancing gray ones.

"Sorry," Maggie murmured sheepishly, and blushed. "I was just going over some notes in my mind."

"About how to help the firemen raise enough funds to buy that new turnout gear Harry's got his heart set on?" Eve grinned. "Come on, Maggie, don't hold out on me. Who's caught your eye?"

Maggie smiled mysteriously. "A great, hulking creature with eyes like a tiger's—tawny and deep-set and mysterious," she replied, exaggerating only a little. "No, really, I was trying to decide which of the city commission candidates to call first for an interview." She sighed. "It's going to take me two weeks to wrap up this race." She moaned. "Pictures, interviews—and none of them will hit the issues on the head. I'm so *tired* of having men tell me they're running for office because the city *needs* them. My gosh, Eve, if they really cared about the city, at least four of them would never run for office in it!"

Eve patted the taller woman's shoulder. "There, there," she murmured. "It's all those years you spent working for a magazine that's done this to you. You'll get used to it."

"Why won't they answer my questions?" she asked wearily.

"Because the way you get elected in Defiance is to

say as little about yourself as possible. The less the voters know," she whispered conspiratorially, "the more of them will vote for you."

Maggie stared at the ceiling, as if she expected to find answers hanging from it. "Dad warned me not to go to college in South Carolina," she murmured. "That really was my worst mistake. I should have stayed in Defiance and gone into local politics."

"Run for office," Eve encouraged her. "I'll vote for you."

Maggie stretched lazily. "Personally I'm voting for Thomas Jefferson in this election."

"He's dead," Eve pointed out.

"Well, I won't hold that against him," Maggie said straight-faced. She ran a hand through her dark hair impatiently. "I guess I'd better hit the road. I'll swing by Jake Henderson's place and take a picture of that giant cabbage he's grown while I'm out. Have I got anything pending?"

Eve checked the big calendar on the wall, scribbled all over with a big red pen, and shook her head. "A luncheon tomorrow when they're giving out those student awards at Rotary, that's all."

"Okay." Maggie grabbed up her thirty-five-millimeter camera and an extra roll of film along with her purse and paused at the door. "Call if you need me."

"I'll come myself," Eve promised with a wry glance at the doorway leading into the makeup room. She raised her voice above the soft humming sound coming from the computer in the next office. "I need a break, what with all the hard work I do around here that goes unappreciated!"

A tall, gray-haired man with a slight paunch came to the door, scissors and a galley proof in his hand.

"If you want to do some work, Miss Johns," he told Eve, "get in here and start pasting up. I've got the front page and the editorial page done and twelve more waiting while you pass the time with Miss Big-city Journalist there."

"I don't associate with you backwoods journalists," Maggie informed him haughtily. "And I fully expect to get a Pulitzer with my fine feature on Mr. Henderson's twenty-five-pound cabbage that he raised from a tiny seed in his garden."

Ernie Wilson stared at her unblinkingly. It was the look he used on Tuesday, when they were making up the final pages and they were sitting on the deadline for the printers. It was a cross between despair, exasperation, and the threat of imminent alcoholism. It spoke volumes.

"'Bye," Maggie said quickly. With a wink at Eve she dashed out the door.

Professor Anthony Sterline was relaxing in the small living room with his afternoon paper when Maggie dragged into the house, kicking off her shoes in the hall.

"I'm here," she called.

"About time," her father replied dryly. "You're an hour late. Not that I expected you early, since it's Tuesday."

"I'll never get used to standing on my feet all day while we make up that…paper." She sighed, joining her father on the sofa. She leaned back and closed her eyes. "Oh, if supper would only cook itself."

"It has," came the amused reply. "Lisa's home."

Maggie's eyes flew open. "Already? I thought she'd be much later."

"Her flight was canceled, so she traded places with one of the other stewardesses and came home early. She's got engaged."

"Engaged? I didn't even know she was dating anyone," Maggie said with considerable interest.

"Randy Steele. Didn't she mention him? The family lives in Jarrettsville. Very well-to-do, she says," he said.

Steele. Steele. Somewhere in the back of Maggie's tired brain that name rang bells. But she couldn't quite place it. But Jarrettsville was one place she'd never forget.

"Maggie!" her sister cried suddenly, flinging herself through the door and onto her taller sister's prone body with a gleeful laugh. Lisa was fair and green-eyed, and nobody who saw them together would have suspected they were sisters. Lisa's features were delicate and sharp, where Maggie's were more muted. Lisa was small-boned, and Maggie was tall and statuesque. But the one thing they did share was the color of their eyes—the same bright jade-green of their father's eyes, unmistakable.

They began to talk all at once, exchanging greetings, asking questions, until the excitement faded for a minute.

"Dad says you're engaged," Maggie ventured.

"Tattletale," the shorter woman told her father, sticking her tongue out at him. "I wanted to surprise her. He's gorgeous," she added with a sigh. "Tall and sexy—and rich too—although that's not why I said I'd marry him. I'm so in love, it hurts," she added solemnly. "I never dreamed it would happen to me, and certainly not like lightning striking. We've only been dating for a month."

"When have you set the date?"

Lisa looked uncomfortable. "That's the hitch. Randy won't set the date until he decides what to do about his home problems. I'm going to fly up there this weekend and meet his mother and brother. I'd like very much to have you go with me. I'm going to need some support."

It was beginning to sound like a play. Maggie stared at her sister. "Support?" she prodded gently.

Lisa sat down in the armchair across from the sofa and looked preoccupied. "Randy's brother is blind," she said quietly. "There's only him and his mother in the big house in Jarrettsville, and Randy doesn't feel right about marrying and leaving the responsibility for his brother with his mother."

"A commendable attitude," their father said with an approving nod. "But is the brother a total invalid?"

"I get the feeling," Lisa said slowly, "that he's something of a tiger. He was a high-powered businessman before his accident, always on the go. Now he's just not able to live that fast anymore, and he's bitter about it." Lisa studied her pale pink-tipped fingers. "Randy says he won't even leave the house. He won't learn Braille, he won't get a Seeing Eye dog, he won't even try to adjust to it!"

Professor Sterline ran a restless hand over his thinning gray hair. "Perhaps it's just taking him a little time to adjust," he remarked, leaning forward. "I had a student in my history class who was like that. Once he was able to accept his blindness, he progressed rapidly."

"You don't understand, Dad," Lisa said gently. "Hawk's been blind for eight months."

"Hawk? Odd name," her father observed.

"It's a nickname, but I've never heard Randy call

him anything else," Lisa said with a wry smile. "Anyway it's not as if the accident just happened or anything. And he's gone through half a dozen nurses. Randy says he's a holy terror."

"A lion with a thorn in his paw," Maggie corrected gently, feeling a strange kinship with the unknown blind man. Her own trauma had begun about that same length of time ago. "He just needs someone to pull it out."

"How are you with a pair of tweezers?" Lisa teased. "You will come, won't you? Mrs. Steele's looking forward to meeting you."

"I'm not sure if my life insurance covers lions," came the dry reply. "And my memories of Jarrettsville are rather…unpleasant."

"We'll carry a chair and a whip to protect us from Hawk," Lisa promised. "But I didn't know you'd ever been to Jarrettsville…"

"What is his mother like?" Maggie asked, eager to change the subject.

"Long-suffering and patient, he says," her sister told her with a smile. "I've never met her. Randy says the house sits right on the edge of the Blue Ridge Mountain foothills, surrounded by huge live oaks. It was a plantation during the Civil War."

"It does sound interesting," Professor Sterline remarked, his eyes lighting up at any mention of his subject. "Magnolia Gardens is in South Carolina, you know, and there's a fascinating story behind it. It seems that…"

The girls weren't in time to stop him, so they sat quietly and listened with grave courtesy while Professor Sterline gave them the long history of the Civil War in South Carolina. Maggie didn't usually hear many of his lectures since she'd moved into her own apartment; she spent the night only when her sister was in town so the three of them could have some time together.

That night Maggie lay awake a long time, her mind full of Saxon Tremayne. The trip back to South Carolina was one she'd rather not have made, but she couldn't deny Lisa that small sacrifice. Besides, if Saxon hadn't come after her head in eight months, it was unlikely that he'd still be in the mood for retribution.

That had disappointed her in one minor way. She'd wanted him to come after her—for any reason, even revenge. In her mind she could see those tawny eyes watching her, studying her, in a face as broad and tanned as a Roman's, his size setting him apart as much as his air of authority. He was a striking man: rugged, commanding, with a voice like rich, dark velvet when he spoke softly. Not a day had gone by that she hadn't thought about him, missed him, wondered if he'd forgiven her for what he'd thought she'd done. If only she could write and explain. Perhaps now that his black temper had cooled, she could reason with him, tell him the truth. But if he was still angry, writing to him could be a monumental mistake. She'd never talked about her hometown; there had never been the opportunity. He knew she was from Georgia, but not where, and she was faintly glad. Saxon never hesitated to use his power. He wouldn't have batted an eye at buying out the newspaper to fire her. And there were other, less pleasant ways he could have chosen to get even with her.

She rolled over, burying her hot face in the cool pillow. Perhaps it was best this way. What did she have in common with a millionaire, after all? Even if she'd caught Saxon's eye, he'd probably have had no use for her past his bedroom. He wasn't a man to form permanent relationships; his mind was devoted entirely to business. If only she could forget.

This trip with Lisa would take her mind off it at least. And certainly being around Randy's fiery brother would keep her occupied. She smiled secretly. Hawk sounded like the bird of prey from which his nickname undoubtedly came, sharp and deadly. She was intrigued already by Lisa's description of him. How dreadful to have had so much, and lose it through blindness. She wondered idly if she might be able to get through that layer of fierce bitterness and help the poor lion find peace.

It was a tempting thought. She closed her eyes on it and drifted slowly off to sleep.

CHAPTER TWO

RANDOLPH STEELE WAS every bit the dish Lisa had described. He was tall, whipcord slim, with dark hair and an olive complexion, and blue eyes under impossibly thick eyelashes. He had a live-wire personality, and it was obvious from the moment he met them at the Greenville airport that Lisa had his whole heart.

He kissed her with gusto, then stood back to study her petite figure with eyes that spoke volumes before he turned to extend a hand to Maggie.

"You must be the big sister," he said. "As you have probably already deduced, I am the fiancé."

"I had a sneaking hunch you weren't a total stranger," Maggie replied, giving his hand a firm warm shake. "Nice to meet you."

"Maggie's a reporter, you know," Lisa burst out enthusiastically. "She writes for our local paper!"

"Will you be quiet?" Maggie groaned, whirling around in frustrated embarrassment with her hands clasped behind her head. "You know I don't like to talk about what I do!"

"Your guilty secret is safe with me," Randy replied, leading them out to the parking lot with a suitcase in either hand. "And, kidding aside, you'd better keep it a secret from Hawk. He hates reporters."

"Was your mother frightened by one before she gave birth to him?" Maggie asked with a grin.

Randy laughed at that. "Not my mother. Hawk is my stepbrother. In a sense he and his father married me and my mother. Steele Manor was Mother's, of course, but Hawk controls the family finances. Mother is a dear, but a bit frivolous, and she has no business head."

"Your stepbrother must be pretty smart," Lisa said.

"Brilliant," Randy corrected. He paused beside an elegant deep burgundy Lincoln town car and after the bags had been safely stored in the trunk, asked the women to come inside—Lisa on the passenger side and Maggie in the back—before he slid in under the wheel.

"What does he do?" Lisa asked.

"He's a businessman. Or he was," Randy corrected sadly. "When his father died, he took over all the family holdings, and there were a lot of them. He was constantly on the move up until the accident."

Lisa reached out and caught Randy's free hand as he pulled the car out into traffic and headed it out of Greenville. Maggie, who'd only been to Greenville once before, was fascinated by the blend of historical buildings and modern ones, the sprawling downtown mall and the unusual street signs as well as the surprising small-town look of the downtown area, all set against the distant backdrop of the Blue Ridge Mountains.

"What kind of business is the family in?" Maggie asked politely, her eyes roving everywhere as they moved out of town.

"Textiles," Randy replied, shooting a smile and a wink toward Lisa.

"What a coincidence," Lisa cooed. "Maggie used to

write about them a lot in her old job, before she came home. She was a—"

"Do shut up, darling," Maggie told her younger sister with a sweet smile, "or I'll tape up your mouth. Randy doesn't want to hear about my whole history. I'm sure he's much more interested in yours."

Besides, she added silently, *if his people are in textiles and he learns why I left Jarrettsville, he might know Saxon Tremayne and let it slip. And that kind of trouble I don't need!*

"You're so modest," Lisa complained. "Why don't you want people to know you write? Besides, Randy's family...almost," she added shyly.

He squeezed her hand. "Very almost. All we have to do is figure a way out of this mess my family's in." He sighed. "I just can't leave Mother here with Hawk. It would be like sacrificing her. His temper was always formidable, but since the accident he's been like a wild man. One nurse left the house at three o'clock in the morning in her nightgown. In her nightgown! The police stopped her, of course, and wanted an explanation. They called the house, and we cleared up the misunderstanding. Hawk gets violent headaches sometimes at night, he went to ask her for an injection, and she thought he wanted something quite different." He laughed shortly. "Anyway it embarrassed Mother to tears. She couldn't face her garden club the next day, and she's hardly been out of the house since."

Mrs. Steele sounded like a sparrow turned loose in a cage with an eagle. How hard it must be for her to live with her volatile stepson and retain her sanity, Maggie thought.

"Couldn't you find a former combat nurse?" Lisa teased.

"We did, don't laugh," he replied with a wicked, smile. "A crusty old ex-lieutenant who'd been in the WACs. She lasted a week. You think I'm joking. When you meet Hawk, you'll see that I'm not."

"Is there any hope that they might be able to restore his sight surgically?" Maggie asked gently.

"Not really. It would be much too dangerous. Hawk won't even talk about it."

"How did it happen?" Maggie asked softly.

"Hawk served two tours in Vietnam. He earned that nickname because he never missed with an M1 rifle. It's rather ironic that he didn't lose his sight over there when he caught the shrapnel in his head. The doctor explained to me that the shrapnel had lodged near the base of the frontal lobe of his brain, but didn't impair him in any way until it was dislodged eight months ago in that wreck and blinded him. The best he can hope for now is that the shrapnel will someday shift again and relieve the pressure on his optic nerve." Randy sighed. "If he hadn't been in such a temper, it never would have happened. He has monumental control usually. But he'd had a hell of a lot of pressure, what with the newspaper story and the union going out on a wildcat strike, and then the ultimatum by the environmental people. He'd just called a meeting on it and was rushing to the plant on a rain-slick highway when the car went into a skid." He shrugged. "The problem solved itself, of course, when the union and the state people realized that the solution was almost in operation. A tempest in a teapot, as they say. A quiet disaster."

Scandal. Environmental people. Story. Maggie went rigid in the back seat.

"Funny," Lisa murmured. "Maggie wrote a story about some textile company, didn't you, Maggie? Dad said something about it in passing…"

Randy laughed and shook his head as he turned into a side road. "Maggie wouldn't write that kind of story, I don't think. My God, Hawk went right through the ceiling over it. It was a pack of lies, and I'll never know how it got into print. Two reporters were fired over it, as I recall, but the main culprit got away. Hawk would have crucified her if he hadn't been blinded. He was out for blood."

Maggie felt as if she were smothering—choking, dying. It was like some horrible dream, and she couldn't wake up from it.

"What is your stepbrother's name?" Maggie asked in a husky whisper. "His real name?"

"Hawk? His name is Saxon," Randy told her matter-of-factly. "Saxon Tremayne."

Maggie's breath seemed to trap itself in her throat, so that it could neither back up nor go forward. She wanted to throw herself out of the car, to run, to escape. But the Lincoln was already winding up the long paved driveway to the Steeles' Victorian home, fronted by a garden that must have been glorious in the spring.

"Your mother's name…isn't Steele," Maggie said weakly.

"No, it's Tremayne," Randy agreed, missing the panic in his green-eyed passenger's face. "I kept my father's name, so lots of people assume that hers is still Steele too. What do you think of my home, darling?"

he asked Lisa, who was equally unaware of Maggie's buried terrors.

"I love it," Lisa sighed dreamily, studying the front of the massive house with its gingerbread woodwork, long front porch with white furniture, and neatly trimmed surrounding shrubs and trees.

"I hoped you would," he murmured softly.

A dainty little blonde maid opened the door for them.

"Is Mother home, Grace?" Randy asked her with a pleasant smile.

"Mrs. Tremayne is in the living room, sir," came the sweet reply, joined by a wistful glance as she watched him enter the wide hall with Lisa on his arm.

"Thanks," he murmured, leading the women to the entrance of the spacious Early American–style room with champagne-colored draperies and a huge stone fireplace with two high-backed chairs facing it. A fire was glowing brightly in the hearth, warming the room against the chill of autumn.

Maggie's hunted eyes roamed around as she searched wildly for a way to go home. She couldn't stay here. Not now.

Sandra Tremayne rose as they entered the room, a small, thin little woman with clouds of tinted blond hair and eyes the gray of a winter sky. She stood up to envelop her tall son in her arms, a cloud of delicious perfume drifting around her like the pale blue dress she was wearing with her white pearls.

"You must be Lisa," she said softly after she'd welcomed Randy, smiling shyly at the young woman at his side.

"I am," Lisa said, smiling back. "Randy's told me

so much about you, I couldn't wait to meet you. And I do love your home."

"I'm fond of it, too, especially in the spring. And this must be Maggie," she added with a smile in the brunette's direction.

Maggie extended her hand and found it gripped warmly. "I'm glad to meet you," she replied courteously.

"I've looked forward to this," Sandra confided. "Your rooms are all ready for you, and—"

"I can't stay," Maggie blurted out, ignoring Lisa's shocked expression. "I just remembered, I'd promised to cover a story tonight, and I really can't go back on my word. I'll have to fly back, and perhaps I can come back down tomorrow," she said in a panicky tone, her voice rising. "Randy, would you mind driving me back to the airport? Or if not, I can get a cab... I'm so sorry," she added quickly, thinking, *I'm going to make it, I'm going to get away before Saxon knows I'm here, before—*

"Surely you aren't leaving when you've only just arrived?" came a deep unmistakable voice from an armchair near the hearth, one of two with their backs to the hall.

Maggie had heard that velvety voice in her dreams. She'd missed it, feared it, agonized over it in the past several months. And now all her worst fears had come to pass. She'd run away, but fate had caught her and flung her back in Saxon's path with a relentless flick of its cruel hand. It was too late to run anymore.

Saxon stood up slowly, as big and imposing as she remembered him. He seemed a little paler—his shaggy dark hair was in need of a trim—but basically he was the same man.

He held on to the back of the chair with a big broad-fingered hand, a ruby ring glittering on a little finger, and stared in the direction of the voices. He wasn't wearing dark glasses, and he wasn't carrying a cane. And all his scars, like Maggie's, seemed to be beneath the exterior.

"H-hello, Mr. Tremayne," Maggie said unsteadily, wishing she had the back of a chair for support.

"Come here," he said without preamble, while three pairs of eyes watched the byplay, fascinated.

Licking her dry lips, Maggie walked gingerly to his chair and stopped just a yard away from him.

"You're not afraid of the blind man, are you?" he asked with a bitter laugh.

"Don't…" she whispered shakily, her eyes running over his broad, leonine face hungrily.

"Saxon…" his stepmother began nervously.

"You didn't recognize the name?" Saxon asked, raising his voice. "Surely I've cursed it enough! Maggie Sterline. Sterline, dammit!"

Randy whistled through his teeth, tossing a sympathetic look toward Maggie. "I thought the name sounded familiar." He groaned, drawing Lisa close. "Oh, Lord, love, we're in for it now."

"Poor Maggie," Lisa murmured, aching for her sister. "If only I'd known. She never said anything to me!"

"She probably didn't connect Hawk with Saxon," Randy said, sighing. "I never called him by name around you either. What a hell of a coincidence."

"Here on a visit, Miss Sterline?" Saxon asked her, venom in his deep voice, in the tawny, sightless eyes. "I hope you packed a bag, because you're staying for a while."

" I … am?" she echoed weakly. She wasn't easily in-

timidated, but there was something in Saxon Tremayne
that demanded obedience, and she gave it.

"You sound nervous, Maggie," he said, a giant cat
playing with its prey. "Don't panic. It's all worked itself
out, and I've got bigger things on my mind than stripping the skin from your lovely body. Pull up a chair and
sit down. Randy, Mother...close the door on your way
out," he added pointedly—not asking, telling.

Randy and Mrs. Tremayne visibly relaxed, and Lisa
sighed thankfully. They slipped out the door, closing it
gently behind them.

Saxon sat back down in his chair, and Maggie
perched on just the edge of the other one, watching him.
She couldn't help noticing how the faint gold specks
in his black smoking jacket brought out the gold in his
tawny eyes; how the fabric stretched sensuously over
his massive chest, which tapered to a flat stomach and
broad, powerful thighs. He was forty, but it didn't show
in that athletic body; only in the silvering at his temples
and the new lines in his hard face.

"Ironic, isn't it?" he asked shortly. "Your sister and
my stepbrother."

"Are you going to break them up?" she asked quietly.

"That depends on you, honey," he said in a voice she
didn't like. "Randy can't buy a shoelace without my signature until he reaches twenty-five. That's two more
years. Do you think they can wait that long?"

"That would be cruel..."

"I'm a cruel man," he said curtly. "Women like you
have made me wary. Why did you come here?" he added
bluntly.

"I didn't know who you were," she replied simply.

"You didn't connect Steele and Tremayne, I gather?

I don't suppose I ever mentioned it when we were together." He leaned back, his face going even harder in memory. "I was fascinated by you, Little Miss Journalist, did you know that? I could look at you and ache all over."

She gaped at him. She'd never realized he felt anything but courtesy for her.

"Tongue-tied?" he growled. "Don't let your imagination loose. I was attracted, I'd have liked to get you into my bed for a night or two, but that was as far as it went. Reporters weren't my cup of tea even before you sold me out to your scandal sheet."

"I didn't!" she protested, sitting straighter.

"Oh, hell, I don't even care anymore," he ground out. "It's too late for all that. I'm blind."

She closed her eyes on the flat statement. Blind. Blind. It echoed in her mind like a chant, "I'm sorry," she managed to say.

"Thank you," he replied coolly. "That helps a hell of a lot."

"I didn't make the roads slick," she cried.

"You wrote the story."

"No, I didn't, I swear I didn't. It was a mix-up in the bylines," she said, trying desperately to convince him.

"I hope you don't expect me to buy that," he replied. He drew a cigarette from his pocket and lighted it as smoothly as a sighted person; he was hardly fumbling at all, Maggie thought.

"You do that…very well," she remarked.

"The first time, I set fire to my sleeve," he recalled with a bitter laugh. "But eventually I got the hang of it."

"If there's anything I can do…" she began helplessly.

"Oh, there is," he replied smoothly. "Very definitely

there is. You can stay for a few weeks, Miss Sterline.
You can share this travesty of living with me until I'm
convinced you're genuinely repentant."

She chewed on her lower lip. "A whipping boy?" she
asked with dignity.

"A companion," he growled. "I need someone to lead
me around, haven't you noticed?"

"You had a nurse…"

"Had is right. Yes or no? But if you say no," he added
darkly, "I'll forbid the marriage and cut Randy off without a single dime. That wouldn't endear you to your
sister, would it?"

"What will it accomplish to keep me here?" she
asked uncertainly.

"Quite a lot," he said, his tawny eyes glittering men-
acingly across the few feet in her direction. "I owe you,
honey. You can't imagine how much I owe you until you
see how I have to live from day to day, through the end-
less nights, with my mind on fire with pain. I want you
to see what you accomplished with that damned story
you betrayed me for!"

"I didn't betray you!" she cried.

"Can't you even tell the truth when you're caught
red-handed?" he asked with disgust in his tone. "My
God, why hide behind excuses that won't hold water?
Don't you think I checked? They said there was no mix-
up—that the picture was yours, and the byline. The man
you accused of writing the damned story was the one
who denied it to my face."

"Because you probably went storming into the office and backed him up against a wall," she accused.
"Kerry was just a boy!"

"More like a rabbit," he scoffed. "He could barely talk at all."

"If you hate me so much, why do you want me here?" she asked wearily.

"Maybe I'm lonely," he said curtly. "Trapped. Tired of being patronized and pacified and pandered to. Tired of nurses who are too nervous or too belligerent to do me any good." He shifted restlessly, and his eyes closed momentarily. "When Randy told me his fiancée's last name was Sterline, I asked about her family. He mentioned you. It was Christmas, so it was a simple matter to lead him into inviting you with Lisa. I want you with me. You're going to be my eyes for a few weeks. Apart from everything else you might consider that you owe me at least that much—regardless of where the blame lies," he added when she started to speak. His huge shoulders lifted and fell. "I was stupid enough to believe I was the subject of a feature, not a character assassination."

Her eyes washed over him like rain, drinking him. Could she bear being in the same house with this man even for that short time? she wondered. Watching him, seeing him like this, hating his blindness and blaming herself for her small part in it...

"I'll be your eyes," she said finally, in her soft quiet voice, and she saw him visibly relax. "For a while. But I may do you more harm than good, the way you feel about me."

"You don't know how I feel, honey," he returned quietly, crossing one long leg over the other. "If it comes right down to it, I'm not all that sure myself. I've spent months blaming you for everything that's happened, because hatred is a powerful motivation for survival and I needed it. I still need it, in a sense. But I'll try to keep my resentments under control. It's…hard for me," he said hesitantly, "being like this. I'm not used to feeling…vulnerable."

He meant helpless, she knew, but he couldn't manage the word. It was like weakness, to admit it.

"At least two nurses would testify in court that you aren't vulnerable," she reminded him with a smile he couldn't see.

His dark, heavy eyebrows went straight up. "The night runner and the drill sergeant?" he asked innocently.

She laughed out loud, in spite of herself. "Is that what you called them?"

He shook his head. "I had Randy describe the runaway. He said it was pure conceit on her part if she thought I'd brave her bed, even out of desperation. And the drill sergeant…my God, I got tired of being ordered to drink my split-pea soup! Have you ever eaten hospital split-pea soup? That's what hers tasted like—no salt, no seasoning, no peas. Just thick, hot water with a drop of flavoring."

"How about the others?" she asked.

"A few assorted spinsters with Jane Eyre complexes," he said, dismissing them. "How can any woman expect a blind man to fall in love with her on sight? I'd have to feel them to do that, and I don't know many who'd take to being Brailled physically by a stranger. Would you?" he asked suddenly.

She flushed. "You know what I look like," she hedged.

"It's been eight months," he reminded her. "You may have gained weight, or lost it."

He'd teased her like this once before, when she'd been doing the interview, and it had promoted a closeness between them that she had had hopes for. But now she couldn't help but be wary of him after what he'd said. He might be trying to make her vulnerable just to get even with her for what he believed she'd done, and she didn't dare drop her guard.

"I might contaminate you," she returned with a sting in her voice.

"Temper, temper," he said with a maddening smile.

"You're a pirate," she grumbled.

"With patches over both eyes?" he baited.

"I don't want to stay here!" she burst out suddenly, as she realized the predicament she might find herself in with him.

"But you're going to," he said calmly. He shifted in the big chair, uncrossing his legs. "Would you like to go on salary?" he added. "We can call you a nurse-companion and I'll pay you what the nurses got. You can tell your father I'm hiring you."

"I have a job too," she said quickly, "with our local newspaper."

"You're taking a leave of absence for the next two weeks," he replied.

"My boss won't give me a leave of absence..." she began.

"He will if I tell him to," he replied with biting confidence, his whole look arrogant. "If he says no, I'll pay off the mortgage on his paper and fire him."

"How do you know he's got one to pay off?" she returned hotly.

One corner of his mouth went up. "Times are hard, honey, and unless he's thrown in with a combine, he probably has hell keeping the doors open. There's a mortgage."

She couldn't believe that he'd go to those lengths, but it was in every ruthless line of his broad face. He'd decided that he wanted her company, and he was going to get it no matter what lengths he had to go to. She understood now why he was so rich. It had been inevitable, with that raw, driving force in him.

"I'd rather you let me go back home and sent me letter bombs and threatening notes," she replied quietly.

"And I'd rather you stayed. So would your sister, I imagine," he added, reminding her of what he'd threatened earlier.

"Mr. Tremayne—"

"Go and tell the others they can come back in now," he said, ignoring the thought she was trying to voice. He looked weary all of a sudden, and one big hand rubbed at his eyes, as if they pained him.

"I'll have to call my father, and my boss," she began.

"Go ahead."

"Are you sure this is a good idea?" she asked very gently.

"I'd like to meet your sister, if you'd ever go and bring her here," he said impatiently. "And put this out for me," he added, holding the half-finished cigarette out in front of him.

"You don't want a companion, you want slave labor," she grumbled. But she took the cigarette and crushed it out in the ashtray beside his chair. "And to think, before I knew who you were, I actually felt sorry for you. Sorry! I might as well weep for a hungry lion!" she muttered.

He laughed softly, as if the words delighted him. "Go on."

"Yes, sir, Mr. Tremayne," she grumbled on her way out.

All three of them were sitting on the long sofa in the front entrance, as if they were afraid to move too far away because they might miss hearing her scream for help.

"It's all right," Maggie told them, watching with hidden amusement the way they got to their feet.

"You're still in one piece," Randy said, breathing a sigh of relief. "My gosh, I'm sorry I let you walk into that, but I had no idea who you were. I didn't even connect it."

"Lisa hadn't told us that you wrote, dear," Sandra Tremayne added gently, her eyes compassionate, not resentful as Maggie had feared they would be after her identity was revealed.

"I'm so sorry about Saxon—Mr. Tremayne," Maggie said earnestly, and the guilt was in her whole look. "It was a mix-up in the bylines. What I did was a feature story, but the bylines were switched, and I got the blame for what one of the new reporters had done on brown lung. I had too much respect for Mr. Tremayne to pull an underhanded stunt like that on him. I'm aware that some journalists don't think twice about how they get a story, but I'm not one of them. I hope you believe that, even if he won't."

"I do," Lisa said gently, moving forward to hug her older sister. "I've known you all my life, remember?"

Maggie smiled, her voice wavering as she replied, "Yes, love, I know."

"Nobody's blaming you," Randy said quietly.

"Hawk's had a rough time, and he can't come to grips with what's happened. But I know, too, that it could have happened anytime. He could have just as well been on his way to buy gas, or eat out. And for what it's worth, I think Lisa knows you well enough to vouch for you."

"Has he thrown you out?" Sandra asked, genuinely concerned. "I really won't stand for that, you know, it is still my home, and you're very welcome to stay."

"No, he didn't throw me out," Maggie said with a quiet smile. "Quite the opposite. I'm going to be his eyes for a few weeks."

"Or... ?" Randy asked knowingly.

Maggie smiled back in spite of herself. "Or he'll buy my employer's newspaper and fire him, he said."

"He probably meant it," Randy agreed with a heavy sigh. "He's paying you for the dubious honor, I hope? I imagine you have bills to handle just like everyone else."

"I have, and he is," Maggie agreed, stretching wearily. "At least he isn't having me stuffed and mounted. That's something. And I think I truly understand how he feels." Her eyes grew sad. "What a tragic thing to have happened. It hasn't been easy for him, I'm sure, as active and involved as he was. And to never get out at all... Why won't he?" she asked.

Randy's lips made a thin line. "He won't be led around like a dumb animal, he says," he told her. "That's the excuse I get anyway. We've both offered. He won't let us help him."

"He may let me," Maggie said thoughtfully. "As long as he thinks I'm being ordered to, at least," she added with a grin.

"And that," Sandra Tremayne told her son, "is why women will rule the world someday. We let you believe you have the ideas, but actually they're all ours. Right, girls?"

"Right," Maggie and Lisa chorused.

Randy only sighed. "Shall we go back in?"

"He wants to meet Lisa," Maggie murmured as Randy opened the door, and Lisa hesitated, but her sister grabbed her hand and dragged her over to the big high-backed chair.

"Mr. Tremayne, this is Lisa," Maggie said, placing her sister's hand in his big one.

He could be charming when he wanted to—and this, Maggie thought, was one of those times, "I'm very pleased to meet my future sister-in-law," he said with a voice like velvet, and a smile. "What does she look like, Maggie? Like you? Or is she fair?"

"She has short green hair and freckles," Maggie said helpfully. "Oh, and a wart on her left cheek."

He scowled, looking more intimidating than ever in his darkness, his bigness. "There went your Christmas bonus, Snow White," he told Maggie.

She laughed in spite of herself. He looked so ferocious. "She's very fair," she said relenting. "Not quite as tall as I am, much better figure than mine, with green eyes and delicate features. All right?"

"You're insolent, miss," he accused.

"Yes, sir," she agreed, winking at Lisa.

"Now I understand why Lisa is an airline hostess," he remarked. "She does it to get away from you."

"That was unkind," Maggie murmured.

"And probably true. You're both probably tired from

the trip. Why don't you rest for a while?" he added courteously. "Mother, are the rooms ready?"

"Yes, Saxon," Sandra assured him, relief showing in every soft line of her face. "Come with me and I'll show you upstairs. Can I have the maids bring you anything, dear?" she added.

Saxon shook his head. "No, thank you," he said quietly. "I'll sit here for a while longer. Maggie!"

She turned from the doorway. "Yes, sir?"

He hesitated. "When you feel up to it, come back and talk to me."

"Yes, sir," she murmured.

They said the longest journey began with a single step. And that invitation was the first for Maggie. She was smiling when she followed her sister and Mrs. Tremayne up the staircase.

CHAPTER THREE

"It's going to be just lovely having some women in the house." Sandra Tremayne sighed as she lifted her coffee cup to her lips after the elegant china had been cleared from the table.

"Reverse chauvinism," Randy remarked, lifting the remainder of his wine in a mock toast.

"You don't know how lonely it is for me," the older woman accused.

"It wouldn't be so bad if Saxon would stop chasing nurses out into the night," Randy remarked dryly, with a glance at his somber stepbrother, who was sipping his coffee at the head of the table without, to Maggie's amazement, spilling a drop.

"I don't think Maggie would run," Saxon remarked with a faint smile. "Fate has a way of tossing her back to me when she tries, doesn't it, Maggie?" he added with cynical amusement.

Maggie picked at her crumpled linen napkin. There was a bite in his voice, and if she hadn't realized it, before, it was beginning to dawn on her that he hadn't forgotten his resentments, as he'd called them. They were simply tucked beneath the surface of his abrasive personality, ready to manifest themselves at a moment's notice.

"I came under my own power," she reminded him.

"And if you'd known who I was?" he demanded coolly, his eyes faintly cruel. "Would you still have come to see about the blind man?"

"Don't look to me for pity, you black-hearted beast," Maggie shot back. "You aren't helpless!"

He threw back his head and roared with laughter, while his stepmother and stepbrother stared, started, and began to smile. So that was how the lion had to be handled! And they'd been sympathetic, almost pandering to him.

"You hard-nosed little cat," Saxon chuckled. "I'll bet you bleed ink."

"Coffee," she corrected.

He leaned back in his chair with a sigh. "I know. I live on it too."

"You drink far too much of it, dear," Sandra noted. "It's a miracle your skin hasn't turned. I read about a man who drank and ate only carrot juice and carrots," she added. "He died, and his skin was orange…"

"I'm not surprised." Randy laughed. "But, Mother, what about the time you went on that grapefruit diet? You didn't develop an acid personality."

"Cute, Randy." Lisa laughed.

"That's why you're marrying me, surely?" he returned.

"By the way, have you set a date?" Sandra asked seriously. "We have to decide on a gown for Lisa, and sent out invitations and arrange about the flowers…."

"How about Christmas Eve?" Randy asked Lisa. "I've always wanted to be married then."

"It would have to be in the morning," Mrs. Tremayne reminded them, "because of the midnight service. We're Presbyterian, you know," she added.

"So are we," Lisa said, laughing. "How's that for a nice coincidence?"

"Lovely!" Sandra burst out, and smiled. "Oh, it will be the most beautiful wedding. Let me tell you what I think about flowers. Since it will be Christmas, we could—"

"Just a minute, Sandra," Saxon said, pushing his chair back from the table. "Maggie, let's go into the living room. Talking about weddings gives me indigestion."

"Yes, go ahead, dear," Sandra said, subdued, watching them leave the room, the big man allowing himself to be guided by the slender woman. There was something akin to pity in her eyes.

Maggie positioned Saxon in front of his big chair before the hearth and took the seat beside it as he eased down into the soft cushions.

"Well, you've charmed my family," he murmured when he'd lighted his cigarette and crossed his legs to get comfortable.

"It's mutual," she answered quietly. The flames were hypnotic, their heat cozy and pleasant. To sit there in that room with him was like coming home, Maggie thought. She didn't understand why, but she found pleasure in it.

He shifted restlessly, his eyes staring straight ahead. "I wish to God I could see you," he muttered. "Have you changed? Are you thinner, heavier? Is your hair still long or have you had it cut? Come here!"

The whip in his voice startled her into movement. She stood up uncertainly.

"Here, in front of me," he growled, motioning her

down between his knees, his big hands catching at her pant-clad legs to coax her.

His touch brought back memories. He'd only done that when necessary, to help her out of cars, or through doors, but his fingers had sent wild chills down her spine every time he'd put them on her, and she'd never got over it. Now, with the months of missing him adding to the excitement, her heart went wild when he leaned forward and cupped her face in his warm, strong hands.

"This is the only way I have of seeing you now," he said quietly. "Do you really mind?" he asked gently.

"No," she whispered. "No, I don't mind."

"Your voice is unsteady," he remarked. "Are you afraid I might choke you?"

"No, sir," she replied, closing her eyes as his thumbs ran over them, over her thin eyebrows and down over her long patrician nose to her soft bow-shaped mouth and then around the outline of her oval face with its high, elegant cheekbones. His fingers were just slightly callused, as if he'd been riding lately, and they felt deliciously abrasive on her whisper-soft skin as he touched it, finally running his hands over her short dark hair. He sighed heavily.

"You've had it cut," he murmured.

"I—it got in my way," she lied, knowing full well she'd had it cut because he'd once liked it.

"I remember how it looked that day we walked through the park," he said gently, his voice deep and slow in memory. "It was blowing out of control, and I got you a piece of ribbon from the flower vendor to tie it with."

"And a bouquet of violets to go with it," she added, hurting with the memory. It had been such a bittersweet day, the last she'd had with him before the story hit the stands.

His hands tightened on her face. "Let it grow again," he said gruffly.

"If you like." She looked up into his sightless eyes, and she wanted to cry. They were sensuous, with chips of gold in their tawny depths, with lashes any woman would have envied, and lines at the corners. The brows above them were thick and dark, and she wanted badly to reach up and touch them.

"I'm not through," he said quietly, his eyes seeming to search her face as he held it in his big dark hands. "I want to know how you've changed physically, and this is the only way left to me. Will it offend you to let me touch you?"

Her eyes closed on a wave of pain. To feel his big hands touching her body was as close to heaven as she expected to come on earth. *Offend* her?

"No," she whispered unsteadily. "It won't…offend me."

He caught her by the shoulders and drew her to her feet as he rose, holding her in front of him. His fingers released her and began a journey of discovery that made her tremble with delight. They traced her arms through the silky Qiana blouse that was the same shade of dark green as her eyes, discovering that they were as thin as ever. They ran back up to her shoulders and traced them to her long, elegant neck, then down to her collarbone.

"You're very thin," he said gently, pausing at the V neck of the blouse.

"I—I always lose weight a little in the autumn," she faltered.

"Do you?" His fingers moved again, down over the

high, smooth slope of her breasts, and he felt her stiffen and jerk as they lingered on the beginning of the soft curves.

"I know, it's intimate," he said softly, scowling as his fingers traced tiny patterns through the fabric and the flimsy lace of the bra under it. "And you aren't used to letting a man touch you this way, are you?" Without waiting for an answer, he moved his hands completely over her high breasts, then down over her rib cage to her waist, her narrow hips, and finally to her thighs.

"You're so thin you tear at my heart," he said in a voice that puzzled her. "Did you eat supper?"

"Yes, sir," she told him.

"From now on see to it that you eat a big breakfast, and don't skimp on lunch. If I find out that you've been cutting meals, I'll feed you myself, is that clear?" he added shortly.

"Being thin is the rage right now," she said, defending herself, unwilling to admit that the reason for her slenderness was grieving over being away from him all this time.

"I don't want you thin," he replied. "I want you the way you were when I could still see. You had the loveliest figure I'd ever seen. High, firm breasts, a small waist, and hips that were utterly tempting. I want you that way again."

She flushed at the speech. "Doesn't it matter that I might not want to gain weight?" she managed to ask.

His hands slid back up to her waist and pulled her body close against his. "No," he replied honestly.

Her hands pressed patterns into his silky brown velour shirt, feeling the hard muscles under the softness of the fabric, warm from his big body. "Saxon…" she began nervously.

He bent. "I like the way you say my name," he whispered, his warm breath smoky against her lips. "Say it again."

This was getting too close for comfort, and she tried to make him let go. But he only held her tighter.

"Don't fight me," he murmured absently. "Pound for pound, I'm twice your size."

"Don't," she pleaded quietly, hating the sensations his careless caresses were causing. "You're just lonely, and you've been without a woman for a long time…"

"What makes you think so?" he murmured with a mocking smile. "I may be blind, but that doesn't stop the wolf pack from stalking me. Didn't you know? Randy's been running interference for months—or I'd be shaking them out of my mattress. They think the sympathetic nurse approach will touch my cold heart."

"How amusing," she muttered, laughing involuntarily.

"That's something I'd never expect you to do," he added solemnly. "Money never mattered, did it? You'd have spent time with me if I'd had nothing—as long as I was newsworthy," he added with sudden bitterness, and for an instant his hands were cruel where they gripped her.

"Saxon, I didn't betray you," she whispered, gritting her teeth against the bruising fingers. "I didn't!"

His mouth crushed down onto hers, finding it blindly, hurting as he took out the memories on her soft lips. It was like being tossed onto the rocks by storm-torn waves; he was brutal and tears welled in her eyes. She'd wanted him eight months ago with an almost shocking passion, and despite her nunlike upbringing, she'd have given herself to him joyfully in the throes of her growing love. But this was hardly worthy of her daydreaming.

As if he sensed the tears, he lifted his dark head and scowled. His heart was thudding roughly against his chest, his breath came hard and fast.

"I'm hurting you?" he asked curtly.

She licked her cut lip and managed to catch her own breath. "Please let me go," she said through her tight throat.

His big hands relaxed their bruising grip and he murmured something gruffly under his breath. His blind eyes shifted restlessly.

"I tasted blood on your mouth," he said heavily. "Are you all right?"

She swallowed nervously. "It was…just a cut. I'm all right. Saxon, let me go, please!"

"I used to wonder how it would be to kiss that pretty mouth," he said softly. "I didn't mean it to be like this though. Don't struggle," he said, subduing her effortlessly. "Let me have your mouth one more time. Let me…make amends," he murmured, bending again.

This time his mouth was exquisitely gentle, rubbing against hers with a slight teasing pressure that was as tender as a baby's touch. His big arms swallowed her like warm bathwater, coaxing her body to relax, to allow the touch of his, to soften and melt into him.

"You taste like a virgin," he whispered into her mouth, twisting her body sensuously against the length of his, and his lips smiled tenderly against hers. "Are you?"

"Are you?" she returned with what spirit she could muster, her voice sounding as wobbly as her legs.

"Not for half my life," he replied. "Can't you tell?"

She could, but she wasn't going to admit it. Her fingers pushed against his chest. "Saxon—"

"Don't you want to unbutton my shirt, Maggie?" he whispered sensuously, nibbling tenderly at her full lower lip. "Haven't you wondered what it would be like to touch my skin?"

Her face flamed. Her blood surged up in her veins and ran in full flood. Yes, she'd wondered, and she wanted to, but giving in to Saxon now would be a step toward emotional suicide. He wasn't sure himself whether he wanted her, or just revenge, and she wasn't sure enough of him to find out.

She was debating on how to tell him all that when the door opened suddenly.

Maggie ducked under his arms and got around beside him just as Mrs. Tremayne, Lisa and Randy walked in, talking and laughing and unaware of the undercurrents in the far end of the room.

CHAPTER FOUR

BLESSEDLY NOBODY SEEMED to connect Maggie's red face and Saxon's smug smile, and the conversation became general. She sat on the sidelines, watching Lisa smiling comfortingly at her, and felt herself relax. Her lip, where Saxon had bitten it, no longer bothered her.

She studied the big imposing man in the big chair beside the fireplace with covetous eyes. He was so good to look at, so good to touch. Part of her was disappointed that the others had chosen that moment to interrupt, while another part felt relief. He wasn't sure himself whether he hated her or not, and while she might enjoy the touch of his hands, she couldn't take the harsh accusation in his voice without reacting to it. He'd frightened her, shocked her, by turning out to be the man who blamed her for his predicament. But Maggie was spirited, and she had a temper. And she wasn't going to let any man—even Saxon Tremayne—walk all over her.

A comer of her full mouth turned up. So he was determined to keep her here, was he? She'd let him think he was bulllying her into staying. He was right about one thing; he did, very definitely, need someone to keep him from tumbling headfirst into a long bout of self-pity. The man she remembered had been obsessively athletic, enjoying horseback riding, polo, tennis, and handball. He was an excellent swimmer as well, and he was always restless, eager to be up and away. When she'd been working on the disastrous feature, she'd had to follow him around just to get any information at all.

The man sitting so quietly in his chair now was a stranger. He still barked as the old Saxon Tremayne had. But some of that magnificent spirit was lacking; the bounding self-confidence was gone. Remembering the way he'd been, it hurt her to watch him. She shifted in her chair, her eyes worried. Somehow she'd have to help him cope, if she could. She'd have to make him go out of the house, meet other people, learn to stand by himself again. And she'd do that, she told herself. Onc way or another she was going to help him—even if he didn't want to be helped—and she didn't kid herself that it was going to be easy. He had a magnificent temper, one that matched his towering physique, and it was going to take cunning as well as kindness to get him back on his feet.

"You're very quiet, Miss Reporter," Saxon called suddenly, causing an immediate lull in the conversation about the nearby mountains and the blazing beauty of autumn in the upstate this month.

"Am I?" Maggie asked. "I was wondering if you'd like to take a drive up in the mountains one day."

His face hardened, his eyes kindled. "What for?" he asked curtly. "Do you expect my eyes to be miraculously restored?"

"You don't have to see to appreciate beauty," she returned, watching him closely. "Of course, if you'd rather hide in here…"

"Hide?" he exploded, and his mother smothered a grin.

"Well, what would you call it?" Maggie asked reasonably. "You never leave the house, do you?"

He shifted angrily in the chair that just barely contained his formidable body. "I won't be led around like a half-witted child," he said proudly.

"You won't be," she promised. "You know, you really ought to be flattered. I don't offer my company to just anybody. And I certainly don't take men driving every day."

The teasing seemed to get through the armor around him. He pursed his chiseled lips and cocked an eyebrow. "How do I know you can hold a car in the road?"

"You don't," she agreed, and laughed. "You'll just have to trust me not to do you in. Besides, I'll be in the car too. I'll have to be careful."

He drew in a deep breath. "All right. In the morning if it isn't raining."

"What's wrong with rain? Do you melt if you get wet?" she asked him.

He lifted a bushy eyebrow. "Don't be smug, miss," he murmured with a glint in his sightless eyes. "I know very well what melts you, or don't you remember?"

She averted her red face. "You'll have to get Saxon to take you by the company while you're out," Sandra remarked, noting the color in Maggie's face and guessing the reason for it.

Saxon's face darkened, his big hands went taut on the arms of his chair. "That's out," he said firmly.

"But, dear," Sandra argued gently, "it would do you good—"

He got to his feet impatiently. "I'll decide what's good for me," he said curtly. "Where's that damned coffee table? I'm forever tripping over it. I can't understand why you people insist on moving it around!"

Maggie got to her feet, moved by Sandra's worried

face. "Stop growling at people," she told Saxon, moving close to take his big hand gently in hers. For a moment she was sure he was going to shake it—and her—off. But after a brief hesitation his warm fingers curled around hers and pressed them possessively, sending a warm current through her body.

"Going to lead me around, are you?" he asked sharply.

She winked at the others. "No, sir," she said pertly. "I thought I'd let you lead me."

"Oh?" He smiled faintly. "What would you like to walk into first? A chair, a wall?"

"How about the front porch?" she suggested. "The sun's come out, and the mountains in the distance are glorious."

"I wouldn't know," he replied.

"I'll describe them to you," she offered, tugging at his hand. "Excuse us while we argue in peace," she told the others, who laughed softly as the two went out the door.

"Are we going to argue?" Saxon asked when she seated him beside her in the glider on the long, graceful front porch.

She drank in the sweet, crisp autumn air, her eyes on the brightly colored leaves of the distant trees that covered the Blue Ridge Mountains. "It seems to be all you want to do," she replied.

"Like hell it is," he murmured, reaching out until he found her hand. He curled her fingers into his and leaned back with a hard sigh. "I've missed you."

"Have you?" She looked up at his hard face and something inside her melted. She wanted to admit just how much she'd missed him, but it might give him a weapon to beat her with, and she didn't know yet how far her trust of him would reach. His mood swings were too sudden.

He laughed curtly. "Don't believe me, do you? What's wrong, honey? Do you think I'm looking for weaknesses before I attack?"

"Aren't you?" she returned.

He shrugged his broad shoulders and released her hand to light a cigarette. He scowled as smoke curled up from the cigarette in his fingers. "I blamed you at first," he admitted. "My God, I've never hated anyone as much. I didn't expect that kind of betrayal from you. I thought we were close to the beginning of a very— different kind of relationship than the one we had."

Her eyes closed. She'd thought so too. The day before the issue had hit the stands carrying the story that had damned her in his eyes, there'd been one long moment when they'd stared at each other with all the camouflage removed; when his eyes and hers had echoed the same horrible hunger, the need that would almost certainly have been translated into fierce ardor if his office door hadn't been suddenly opened by a junior executive.

"Are you ever going to believe me?" she asked under her breath.

"I'm blind," he ground out, and took a vicious draw from his cigarette. "Have you any idea what it feels like to be without the sun, to live in shadow, to be totally dependent on other people? It's something that's never happened to me before, and I'm—" He stopped, chopping off the words abruptly to take another draw from the cigarette and blow it out. His heavy frame relaxed. "I'm not coping," he admitted finally. "Sometimes, at night, the pain is bad. I can't sleep, so I lie awake and brood. I can't run the company like this, not without eyes, so the whole burden falls on Randy, and he's not old enough or experienced enough to cope."

"What utter rot," she told him bluntly, turning in the seat to face him, warmed by the heat from his big body. "You can do anything a sighted man can do, if you'll just stop feeling sorry for yourself and try."

He stiffened, then exploded. "Feeling sorry for myself?" His face went rigid and his sightless eyes searched for her voice. "Damn you!"

It would have been less intimidating if he shouted, but that calm, cold voice had the cut of a sharp razor, and Maggie felt chills at the impact. But she wasn't going to back down, not one inch. Pity, despite the fact that she felt it, wouldn't help this proud, arrogant man to escape the prison he was making for himself. Only anger was going to do that.

"What would you call it, Mr. Tremayne?" she taunted. "You sit in the house all day and refuse to help yourself. You won't go near your empire. What's the matter? Won't you be able to take it if somebody opens a door for you?"

The cigarette shot off the porch and he caught her shoulders in his big hands with amazing accuracy, shaking her roughly. "Stop it," he shot at her.

The feel of his hands made her weak-kneed, but not from fear. "Aren't you just afraid of pity, Saxon?" she whispered, watching his face as it came closer. "Isn't that what's wrong?"

His jaw clenched, his eyes narrowed, and she could see the arrow had hit home. His dark eyes closed and opened again. "Yes," he breathed.

Her hands found his face, tremulous hands, taking a

liberty that once they wouldn't have dared. He flinched almost imperceptibly at the silken contact.

"How," she whispered, "could anyone pity a man like you? Don't you know that you're still more of a man, even without your sight, than most men are? Blind, lame, deaf or paralyzed—you're still Saxon Tremayne. If you'll believe in yourself, you can do anything you want to. Anything."

She saw the flickering of indecision under his thick lashes. His hands where they gripped her upper arms had become gentle; holding, not hurting.

"I can't bear pity," he said.

"I'm glad," she replied, her voice lighter than she felt, "because I wouldn't presume to offer it to you."

"I won't use a damned cane," he warned.

She smiled through tears he couldn't see. "You'll have me, for a while. Then you can replace me with a Seeing Eye dog. Don't you like animals?"

"I don't know," he said quietly. "I've never had time for them."

"Dogs make nice pets," she said. "They're very intelligent, and they're softer than a cane. There are even new devices that can be surgically implanted to approximate sight."

"No," he said curtly.

"You could at least speak with a doctor…"

"You could at least shut up," he murmured, and before she realized his intention, he bent forward and his mouth eased onto hers, his chiseled lips parting as they met hers, merging with them, opening them to the soft slow probing of his tongue.

Her hands on his cheeks hesitated for a second before they slid up into the thick silvered hair at his temples. Her own eyes closed, and her mouth yielded to his, wanting it, as the wind whipped softly around them, blending with the soft sounds of fabric sliding against fabric as he brought her closer.

It was heaven to be held like this, kissed like this. It had been so long, and she'd wanted him so during all the lonely months. She moaned softly at the force of the hunger. She'd never expected to feel such overpowering desire for a man; desire that made her ache in ways she never had, that made her legs tremble, her protests die before they ever reached the mouth he was devouring.

He drew back an inch, and his hand moved from her arm to the soft warm swell of her breast.

"No," she whispered, moving it up gently to her shoulder.

"I only want to 'see' what you look like," he murmured with a wicked smile.

"You already have," she reminded him.

"You've probably changed by now," he chuckled. "And I'm a poor blind man, without eyes to see."

"Pull the other one," she said, laughing. "You lechrous tycoon, you."

"I thought you were staying here to help me. My bed is quite large…"

"Not that kind of help, and you very well know it," she returned.

His fingers traced up to find her lips, teasing the soft lines into a smile. His eyes sparkled with humor, the way they had so long ago when they could see her. "Are you still a virgin?"

She studied his face. "How do you know I was?"

"I didn't. But you weren't very worldly, Miss Sterline," he reminded her. "And it still bothers you to be touched with any intimacy. I'm just curious. I'd like to know if you've been with a man."

Her eyes found his collar, watching the heavy pulse that leaped against it. She sighed. "It isn't exactly in vogue these days, and most people don't believe me anyway—so I just let men think I'm being almighty selective and let it go at that."

"I take that to mean that you've never said yes?" he asked, his eyes more intent than she'd seen them so far.

She drew in a deep breath. "Yes," she admitted wearily. "I'm not trying to bring back the Victorian age," she added. "It's just that, for me, sex means commitment. Utter commitment to one man. And I've never found a man I cared to make a commitment to."

"You are a very attractive woman," he murmured, reminiscence in his dark eyes as they stared blankly toward her. "Stacked, I believe the term is, and with a lovely face to match. There couldn't have been a shortage of offers."

"There hasn't been," she admitted. She smiled up at him; Maggie realized it was a smile he couldn't see, but it was in her voice all the same. "Yet," she added impishly.

He didn't smile. His fingers moved again, going over her delicate features lightly. "I want you," he said quietly, the words having all the more impact for their very softness. "I want the first time to happen with me."

Her breath caught in her throat. "Why?" she asked, drowning in his touch, in the soft words.

"Because some careless damned fool would hurt you. I wouldn't." His head went forward, his cheek drawing slowly, sensually, against hers, his breath warm at her ear. "I've never made love to a virgin," he whispered.

"I've never wanted to until now. Do you know what a priceless thing you are?"

Her fingers contracted at the back of his head. She wanted to stretch like a cat, to feel her body move sinuously against his, and her own longings were faintly shocking. She could hardly breathe for the pounding of her heart.

"Is this part of it?" she managed to ask, hating the words as she said them, but she was weakening, and she didn't dare. "Part of the scheme to make me pay for what you think I did?"

His body froze and tautened. He drew in a breath and moved away from her. All the old rigidity was back in his face; the tenderness had vanished from his cold brown eyes.

"You're sharp, aren't you?" he asked with narrowed eyes. "I'll have to be more careful from now on."

"You won't bring me to my knees, Mr. Tremayne," she said pertly, moving away from him. "But you're welcome to try."

"Don't you think I can, honey?" he asked, cocking an eyebrow. "This was just a minor skirmish. The battle is yet to come, and you're going to be here for a while."

"Only a couple of weeks," she replied firmly. "I do have a job that can't be held open indefinitely."

"We'll discuss that little problem some other time." He lighted another cigarette. "I thought we came out here to admire the view."

"So did I," she muttered, crossing her long legs. "What would you like to do about it? I could gather some leaves and toss them over you, along with a few pebbles, to give you the feel of the season."

"I could pitch you off this damned porch too," he chuckled. "Blind or not, it wouldn't take much effort."

She laughed with him, some of the tension gone. Her eyes drifted out toward the highway to the backdrop of blue mountains.

"How long have your people lived here?" she asked.

"In Jarrettsville?" he asked. "Oh, a hundred and fifty years or so. The Jarrett who founded the town was an ancestor."

"And your stepmother's family?" she asked.

He grinned. "Carpetbaggers." He chuckled. "I dearly love to tease her about it. Sandra's the salt of the earth. She can take a joke—even at her expense—and don't think she doesn't give it back. She isn't a fiery woman, but she's damned stubborn. Her people were Steeles from Chicago. Her grandfather settled here and went into the textile business, just as my people had. It's a major industry in this part of the state."

"And you had your biggest branch in Charleston," she recalled. "Not here."

He smiled. "My mother's people were from Charleston," he told her. "As a matter of fact, my grandfather's father—my great-grandfather—was town marshal there for a while until he was killed trying to arrest a man. I still have the old pocket watch he carried, with his initials carved inside the back. It's quite a treasure."

"I guess so," she agreed. She smiled and sighed. "I have a few treasures from my mother's side of the family. An old Confederate pistol, and some crystal and silver. Not very much, I'm afraid. My people weren't wealthy."

"Neither were mine, honey, not at first. They came over here from Scotland with the clothes on their backs, and a lot of determination to make some kind of better life for themselves."

"They seem to have done that," she commented.

"Not without some effort. It still takes a lot of effort to coordinate the plants and keep them going." He began to brood again, and she punched him in the arm playfully.

"All the more reason to get you back on your feet," she said with a laugh. "Now, how would you like me to walk you around the yard a few times and teach you how not to trip over the roots of the oak trees?"

His head tilted back. "It would be like you to lead me right into the damned tree."

"Who me?" she asked innocently.

"Yes, you, Snow White," he returned. "But you'd better keep one thing in mind before you trip me up."

"What's that?" she asked, rising with him.

"If I fall, I'll fall on you."

She stared at his bulk and sighed with theatrical perfection. "Oh, my, I'd better make sure you don't," she told him. "I'd be a little flat bit of color on the ground, wouldn't I?"

"If we fall," he murmured, bending down, "I'll have other things on my mind than leaving you flat."

"Well, I won't ask what," she promised, taking his hand. "I'm a good girl, I am, and I'm not letting any lecherous tycoon lead *me* astray!"

He laughed as she helped him walk down the steps. It was a beginning at least.

CHAPTER FIVE

LATER IN THE upstairs bedroom that Maggie had been given for the length of her stay, she and Lisa sat talking after they'd dressed for dinner.

"I thought you were a goner," Lisa said with a laugh, glancing at her older sister, who was wearing an emerald-green chiffon dress that matched her eyes.

"You weren't the only one," Maggie confessed. "I don't think I've ever had such a shock that I couldn't even fight back. When Randy mentioned that his older brother was Saxon Tremayne, I was sure my life was over."

"He's a dish, isn't he?" Lisa murmured unexpectedly, her eyes calculating.

"Who? Randy?" came the dry reply.

"You know very well I meant Saxon," Lisa said, pursing her lips.

Maggie's eyes fell to the floor, to the white shag carpet that set off the royal-blue velvet bedspread on the four-poster and the heavy matching curtains at the windows. "I thought he hated me. I'm still not sure that he doesn't. All this talk about helping him get his bearings might just be a cover-up, something to keep me here while he plots revenge."

"If the way he was clinging to your hand was any indication, I wish Randy hated me that way."

Maggie smiled. "He was making sure that if I ran him into a wall, I'd go too. What am I going to do about my job? You know they'll never be able to go two weeks without me."

"Everybody is expendable," her sister reminded her. "They'd have to do without you if you died. Besides, I have a feeling that Mr. Tremayne has already taken care of it."

She winced. "I never dreamed that it would be like this for him," she murmured, her green eyes troubled. "Lisa, what if it was my fault? What if his sight never comes back?"

Lisa touched her arm gently. "Stop that. All you have to do is concentrate on helping him get his confidence back. And if you care as much as I think you do, that shouldn't be very hard for you, should it?"

Maggie stood up with a sigh. "I know what I feel," she confessed. "It's what *he* feels that's going to keep me up nights. I won't worry about it right now though. We'll go down and have supper, and then I'll try to live one day at a time."

"A very practical solution, if you ask me," came the amused reply.

But Maggie didn't feel practical. She felt confused, hungry, and frightened. Sitting next to Saxon at the long table under the crystal chandelier, she had a crazy impulse to get up and run.

He was as sensuous a man as any woman could ever have wanted, she thought, watching his beige silk shirt strain across his massive chest under the tweed jacket. The thick, dark shadow of hair-roughened muscles was just visible through the thin fabric. Maggie had never seen Saxon without a shirt, but she was suddenly aware that she wanted to. She wanted to touch him...

Shocked by the force of her own longing, she dug into her food with a vengeance, keeping hidden the eyes that he couldn't see.

"You're very quiet, Maggie," he murmured gently.

She glanced up nervously and smiled, forgetting for an instant that he couldn't see her. "I'm just busy concentrating on this delicious food," she lied, adding silently, *which could be cardboard for all my taste buds are telling me.*

He cocked his shaggy head to one side, his dark eyes faintly amused. "Are you sure?"

"What do you think is the matter with me then?" she asked, taking the argument into his own camp. "That I'm sitting here mooning over you?"

He threw back his dark head and laughed, and Sandra and Randy stared at him, amazed. Apparently laughter was a rare commodity in the big dark man since his accident.

"Are you?" he asked. "Mooning, I mean?"

"If you must know," she muttered, "I'm worrying about what I'll do if you suddenly take a notion to drive when we go out in the morning."

That brought laughter from the other members of the family as well and effectively ended his pointed questioning.

The next morning Maggie donned a pleated green plaid skirt and a green sweater with her bone-colored boots before she went downstairs. She felt a strange new excitement at the thought of being totally alone with Saxon, having him all to herself even for a few hours.

It was something she'd dreamed about before the story broke and ruined things between them.

Saxon was already at the breakfast table, but the others were nowhere in sight.

"Maggie?" he asked softly, lifting his head when he heard her soft footsteps, and something in his tone made her blood run wild.

"Yes," she replied, seating herself next to him at the long table. "I thought you said to get down here by seven."

"I did."

"But where are the others?" she persisted.

"Still in bed," he murmured with a faint smile. "No need to rouse the whole household just because we're going out, is there?"

"No, of course not." She had to tear her eyes away from him. He was wearing a white turtleneck sweater under the same beige tweed jacket he'd been wearing the night before, with tan slacks, and Maggie thought he looked good enough to eat. "Would you like some more coffee?" she asked, lifting the pot.

"I haven't had any yet," he replied. "I was waiting for you."

She smiled secretly. "Should I be flattered?"

"That would depend on how hungry I was," he replied, "and I'm keeping that bit of information to myself. How about putting some eggs on my plate, honey? I sent Mrs. Simpson out to get the mail from our post office box."

She obliged him, reaching for the platter of bacon and country ham when she'd put the eggs down. "Bacon or ham?" she asked.

"Bacon, but try the ham yourself," he told her. "It came from the farm."

She studied him. The house was sitting on a lot of land, and she'd noticed the white-fenced pastures around it with curiosity. "Is this a farm?" she asked.

He grinned. "Very astute, Miss Sterline. Yes, it is a farm, and we raise most of our own meats and vegetables."

She sighed. He was apparently more of an outdoorsman than she'd even guessed. That would make his blindness an added burden. She added a huge, fluffy cat's-head biscuit to his plate and her own.

"Butter?" she asked.

"Please."

She buttered both biscuits quickly and told him where everything was on his plate, using the numbers of a clock as indication points. Surprisingly he didn't make any snide comments about her directions as he began to eat—and without losing a single morsel.

"You've gone quiet again," he mentioned after a minute.

"I was thinking that you must have enjoyed working around the farm...before," she confessed.

His dark face clouded, and she could have bitten her tongue for the hasty remark. "Yes," he said curtly. "I did a lot of riding as well."

She looked up. "You could still ride, couldn't you?" she asked.

"With a companion, I suppose so," he said noncommittally. "Do you ride, Maggie?"

"A little." She grinned. "I fall off if I have to go very fast, though."

That seemed to restore a little of his lost humor.

"You could ride with me," he suggested. "I could hold you on, and you could point me in the right direction."

She looked at him. Just the thought of being so close to him took her breath away. She could almost feel the warmth, the powerful muscles, against her. "Sure," she countered. "And if you fell off, you'd take me with you and crush me!"

He looked toward the sound of her voice, his hard face with its strong lines sensual, like his voice when he spoke. "I'd like very much to crush you," he murmured. "Under me. All of you."

She felt the blush that ran into her cheeks and lifted the coffee cup to her lips. She wouldn't have touched that line with a ten-foot pole.

"Won't play?" he murmured with a wicked smile. "We'll see about that. Finish your breakfast, honey. We've got a lot of ground to cover today."

She leaned forward. "Where are we going—besides for a ride?"

"To my office," he said with a rough sigh.

She smiled secretly. That would be the biggest step he'd taken since the accident, and she couldn't help feeling proud that she'd had a part in it. She lifted her fork and stabbed a piece of country ham from its platter.

When they finished breakfast, she held his arm, half guiding him out to the garage where the family cars were kept.

Inside were a Mercedes, a Fiat and a big black Lincoln town car.

"Which one is yours?" she asked uncertainly.

"Guess."

She studied his lofty face. "The Lincoln."

He cocked an eyebrow and smiled. "Should I be flattered that you know my taste?"

She laughed. "I don't know."

His arm reached around her shoulders, holding her close to his side. "I need a big car, honey. There's a lot of me to squeeze in it."

She nudged him playfully. "I'll vouch for that," she agreed, tugging him toward the car. "Well, I just hope I won't rip off the fenders getting us out of here. I drive a Volkswagen, you know."

"My God," he said, laughing. "You *are* going to have some adjusting to do. I'll trust you, though, Maggie. With the car at least," he added in an undertone that bothered her.

He paused as she was trying to put him in the passenger side. "Just a minute." His hands ran from her shoulders down to her waist, making her tremble with the unexpectedly sensual exploration. "What are you wearing? Describe it to me."

She did, her voice straining from the sudden contact with his big hands as he held her; Maggie realized their bodies were almost touching.

"What kind of sweater is it?" he murmured, and reaching up, traced the V neckline with one long, probing finger. "Soft skin," he murmured gently.

The exploring finger eased inside the neckline to trace the slope of her breast. "Very, very soft."

She caught his trespassing fingers and held them in her own. "Shame on you," she told him.

He only laughed. "Are you blushing? I'm sorry I can't see you, Maggie, I have a feeling your eyes are giving away the whole show." His face clouded suddenly, and he let go of her with a sigh. "We'd better get on the road."

She moved away from him, feeling both relief and disappointment. If only she could trust him not to hurt her. But she still didn't know if revenge was motivating him, and until she found out, she didn't dare let him get too close.

CHAPTER SIX

THIS PART OF western South Carolina was largely foot-hills leading to the majestic Blue Ridge Mountains. Now, with autumn painting them in carnival colors, the view was so breathtaking that his blindness seemed faintly obscene.

"It's cool out today," Saxon remarked, his sightless eyes facing forward while Maggie drove the big car down the highway.

"Yes, it is. I only wish you could see the mountains," she remarked gently. "They look as if some overeager artist has taken a palette of gold and red and orange and amber and flung each color at them with the tip of his brush."

One corner of his wide mouth curved. "You do that very well—the description. Where are we?"

She named the highway. "It's very long, and there isn't much traffic right now. The mountains are ahead of us in the distance and we're driving through what used to be hills. There's love grass curling down the banks."

"Love grass?" he asked with a cocked eyebrow.

"Truly," she said, and laughed, "that's what it's called. Our soil conservation people in Georgia plant it to keep down erosion on high banks, just as they put rock riprap on streambeds to keep the banks from washing away. I suppose your own soil conservation people are responsible for doing it here."

"We ought to be near Jarrettsville now," he remarked, changing the subject as he shifted in his seat.

"Just over the hill," she agreed, watching the small city come into view against the colorful backdrop of the mountains. "It's bigger than I remembered," she murmured. "But just as lovely."

"I've always thought so," he said. "It's not as big as Anderson or Spartanburg or Greenville, but it's still a formidable textile center."

"Your corporation is the most formidable member, I recall," she said with a smile.

"We started out small," he told her. "But we're still growing, despite the economy. Where are we?"

She told him. "As I remember, we turn right here," she said.

"Yes, and then left."

"But does that go behind the plant?"

"It goes to the computer center," he said. "Where my main office is. You've never been there."

She followed his directions in silence, recalling that period in her life that had ended in such tragedy. She remembered several visits to the gigantic Tremayne Corporation's mills, but somehow the computer center had never been on the agenda. At the time she and Saxon had been concerned mainly with the production end of the business. He'd mentioned the place where the corporation's nerve center was located, but she'd never really been that interested. She'd been far more interested in the man himself, and his publicity department had provided her with all the photos of the operation that she'd required for her disastrous story.

She parked the car near the entrance to the computer center and cut off the ignition. But when she started to get out, he was sitting rigidly in his seat, staring straight ahead with a scowl above his sightless eyes.

"Coming in?" she asked gently.

He drew in a deep, impatient breath. "I don't know if this is a good idea."

"Why not?" She eyed him mischievously. "Afraid of swooning female employees tripping over you?"

He looked startled for an instant, and then laughter burst out of him and washed away the taut lines in his broad face. "God, you're good for my ego," he chuckled.

"Anytime," she told him. "Now, shall we get out, or would you rather sit here and brood for the rest of the morning? Just think how suspicious it would look if any of your executives happened to see us sitting here."

"Oh, I don't think it would look suspicious," he murmured, and before she realized what he was planning, he reached out and caught her, jerking her across the seat and onto his lap.

"Saxon..." she breathed jerkily.

His face was somber, unreadable, as his warm fingers Brailled her face, lingering on the soft curve of her mouth. "Nervous?" he murmured. "There's no need. What could I do to you here?"

"Would you like a list?" she asked. "We'd better go in, hadn't we?"

"I don't want to go in yet," he replied. His fingers tilted her chin so that she could feel his warm, smoky breath against her lips. "I could eat you!" he breathed, bending.

She felt the hard crush of his mouth with a wild aching in the most improbable places. She didn't even try to fight. The feel of him was too exciting, like an aged wine that she craved. Her body lifted into his arms as if it was the most natural thing in the world. She'd never cared so much about another human being—not even members of her family. He was the light of her whole existence, and denying him was impossible for her. Blind or not, he was still Saxon.

Her mouth gave him back the kiss. Her arms reached around his neck, and she clung to him. She could hear the hard sigh of his breath, feel the rough hunger in his big body as he pressed her hips into his with a grinding motion.

"Oh!" She gasped into his mouth at the unaccustomed intimacy.

He heard the tiny sound and smiled against her lips. His hand pressed harder at the base of her spine, and he lifted his head, alert to the tiniest sound, the smallest movement.

"Why, Maggie, did you think blindness had made me impotent?" he asked outrageously.

She struggled up and away from him, aware all the time that she'd never have got away unless he'd wanted her to. He sat there, delighted with himself, and she glared at him from a face frankly red with embarrassment while he laughed softly.

"Will you hush?" she grumbled as she struggled to restore some kind of order to her appearance in the rearview mirror, uncomfortably aware of the lingering desire in his broad face that matched the desire she'd felt for the first time.

"I can't help it. I'm not used to dealing with nervous virgins. It's…intoxicating."

"I'm not nervous," she denied shortly.

"You're definitely unsophisticated," he returned softly. "You make my head swim with the possibilities."

"Just you forget about the possibilities and concentrate on being a successful businessman, will you?" she muttered.

"I think I'd rather be your lover, Maggie," he returned in a tone that made her knees wobbly.

"Can we go?" Was that tiny squeak really her voice? she asked herself.

He grinned. "If you're afraid to pursue this very interesting conversation, I suppose we can postpone it until later."

"That's what you think," she mumbled as she got out of the car and went around to guide him toward the building.

The Tremayne Corporation's main office sat on several acres of beautifully landscaped grounds and easily filled two tremendous buildings and two smaller ones. Maggie remembered the biggest as being the main mill, where fibers became fabric. The other large building was the sewing plant, where garments were made and finished. The two smaller buildings were the distribution center and the computer center.

She noticed the Tremayne Corporation logo on the computer center, with its distinctive oversize red *T,* and smiled. It suited Saxon, that bold color. If he'd been a color, he'd have been red, because he was so vivid.

His fingers tightened on hers as they went up the few steps and into the modern building. The lobby was filled with potted trees and plants, making it spacious and welcoming.

"I like this," she murmured as they walked toward the redheaded receptionist. "It's like an Oriental garden, complete with miniature waterfall," she added, noting the lush vegetation surrounding the small artificial waterfall against one wall.

"I had it designed that way," he said curtly. "The girl at the desk—is she about your age and a flaming redhead?"

"Yes," she agreed, watching amusedly the look of surprise on the redhead's face when she caught sight of the big dark man and his companion.

"Mr. Tremayne!" the secretary exclaimed, rising, her face smiling and excited. She rushed from behind the desk with an apologetic glance at Maggie and grinned at Saxon. "Well, it's about time you made an appearance," she teased. "All this work piling up, and Randy carrying it off and losing half of it."

Saxon chuckled softly, visibly relaxing. "He'd damned well better not lose any of it. How are you, Tabby?" he asked.

"Well, it's pretty dull around here without you," she sighed, winking at Maggie, who smiled back. "So peaceful. No shouting, no cursing..."

"It may not last long," he told her. "I want to know what's been going on. Randy's hardly forthcoming, and to be truthful I've had my mind on other things."

"I'd hate being called an other thing," Tabby told Maggie. "I'm Octavia Blake—Tabby to my friends."

"Maggie Sterline," she replied, shaking hands. She liked the tall redhead already. "Which way do we go?"

"I'll show you. Coffee, boss?" she asked Saxon.

He nodded. "Black and strong, and put some cream in Maggie's."

"Will do," Tabby said, while Maggie caught her

breath at his phenomenal memory. All these months, and he even remembered how she took her coffee!

Tabby left them in a huge immaculate office with a massive oak desk, leather furniture and what looked like a microcomputer on a table beside the desk.

Maggie helped Saxon to the chair, and when he sat down behind it, it was like old times. The first time she'd ever seen him was behind a desk—at the sewing plant one building over. He'd been visiting his plant manager when she came in to ask about doing the feature story. And afterward they always seemed to meet in one plant or the other, or in town. She'd never seen this particular office.

"It suits you," she said, watching him lean back in the swivel chair.

"What does?" he asked.

"This office. It's solid and dependable and a little overpowering."

He laughed. "I feel a little overpowered myself right now." He clasped his hands behind his head, and the shirt strained sensuously against the hard muscles of his chest. "I used to take my sight so much for granted," he murmured. "Can you imagine how it feels to sit here, in this chair, with the responsibility that goes with it—and be blind?" His face hardened; his eyes glittered.

She closed her eyes on a wave of pain. "You'll cope with it," she told him firmly. "You'll manage."

"Manage," he scoffed. "If it hadn't been for that damned article of yours, I wouldn't have to manage!"

"And if you hadn't been speeding…" she began hotly, but before she could get out the words, Tabby came in with a tray, stopping her in midsentence.

"Here you are," Tabby said, smiling, oblivious to the

dark undercurrents. "I filched a few doughnuts from the cabinet to go with them. I don't imagine you ate much breakfast—as usual," she said to Saxon.

"Efficient as always, Tabby. Maggie, will you amuse yourself for a few minutes while we talk business?" he added curtly, taking his coffee from Tabby after Maggie had picked hers up. "Turn on the computer, honey," he told his secretary, "and put in the file on the Bilings account. Randy said there was a problem."

"Problem isn't the word," Tabby murmured, taking out a floppy disk from its container. She turned on the computer, waited for the load signal, and slid the disk into its slot with a flick of her finger.

"Here you are," she said. "The biggest obstacle is their union. The workers are concerned about their jobs, and there's some crazy rumor that you're going to replace the older workers immediately so you won't have to pay retirement benefits. Isn't that incredible? The union is fighting the merger tooth and nail, threatening a walkout as soon as the papers are signed."

"Oh, hell," he said curtly. "It isn't the union, it's that vice president of Bilings's—he wants the presidency of the company, and he's stirring up trouble deliberately to blackmail me into putting him in the executive chair. If he's promoted, no strike—he laughs off the rumor to the union, assures them that the older workers will be retained if he's made president, and uses that against me." His face darkened, but his eyes sparkled with challenge. "There's only one thing he hasn't counted on. I don't like blackmail. I'll go down there myself tomorrow and call a meeting with the union on the spot, and I'll make damned sure the plant's vice president is there to hear every word."

"Going to fire him?" Tabby grinned.

"That's too easy," he replied, leaning back to sip his coffee. "I'm going to demote him to the ordering department and make his life hell for a few weeks. If he sticks it, I may give him the presidency. Read me the résumé on him."

Maggie, angry and frustrated at having to hold it all in, took her coffee and wandered around the room while Tabby read the file to her boss. There were photographs all around the room, showing every phase of the vertical mill operation from fiber to finished goods. Maggie recognized each phase of the operation from selection of fibers through carding, combing, the forming of the sliver (which, she remembered, rhymed with *diver),* drawing and roving. It was fascinating to watch the fibers—either cotton, nylon or polyester or blends of each—formed into the sliver, the loose rope made from the fibers, and then to watch the slow narrowing of the sliver through each process until it became yarn or thread. The sewing plant held as much fascination. It reminded Maggie of puzzle pieces: Each seamstress was responsible for a different operation as garments were slowly assembled from pieces cut in the cutting room to finished garments inspected by quality-control people.

Other photographs showed early days at the cotton mill, with wagons full of just picked cotton being unloaded in bales.

Finally, when she'd looked at each one twice, and Tabby was still reading, Maggie paused by the window, which faced the mountains. But she wasn't looking at the autumn splendor. Her mind was still on Saxon's unfounded accusation. She wanted to hurt him, as he'd hurt her.

She wasn't even aware that Tabby had finished speaking, or that Saxon had been barking out orders in his deep quiet voice, until he called her.

"Maggie, have you gone deaf?" he growled.

She jerked at the sound, turning. "There are times when it's better not to hear," she returned pointedly, joining him at the desk. "Are you ready to go?"

He tilted his head, aware of the bite in her tone. "What is it?" he asked.

Tabby murmured something and left them alone, closing the door behind her.

"Well?" Saxon persisted. He stood up, one big hand resting on the desk. "Maggie?"

She glared at him. "I've told you until I'm blue in the face that I didn't write that article," she said harshly. "What do I have to do to convince you?"

His face relaxed, but only a little. "Come here."

"We need to go—"

"For God's sake will you come here?" he ground out. "Maggie, don't make me stumble all over the room trying to find you!"

She hesitated, but only for an instant. She didn't really want to humiliate him. She moved forward.

He seemed to feel the heat of her body before she ever got to him, because he reached out and caught her shoulders, pulling her against him.

"I told you at the beginning that I tend to get impatient and short-tempered," he said quietly. "It won't get better, especially when the headaches come, so if you want to back out of the agreement and go home, I won't stop you."

The statement shocked her. It didn't sound like a man after revenge. She stared up into the unseeing dark eyes with her heart in her own—and all her resentments fell away. It wasn't fair, she thought bitterly, that he could undermine her resistance this way, just by being humble. And it was so obviously a false impression, because when had Saxon Tremayne ever been humble?

She sighed. "I've got a temper of my own, and I lose it far too often," she murmured. "Shouldn't we go?"

He drew her forehead against his chest with a sigh, holding her gently, rocking her in his warm arms with his cheek against her dark hair. "Bear with me," he whispered at her ear. "I'm doing my damnedest not to hurt you."

It was quite a confession for the rigid, uncompromising man she remembered. She had a feeling that he never apologized.

"Said the wolf to the lamb." She laughed.

"You've got teeth yourself," he reminded her with a laugh. His arms tightened for an instant before he released her. "You wouldn't last long around me if you were one of those meek little angels most mothers want their daughters to grow into. Let's go home, honey. I've got to rout Randy out and talk tactics with him."

"You're the boss," she said, taking his hand to walk him out the door.

Tabby met them in the outer office. "Want me to pack up some of these little nagging problems and let you carry them off, boss?" she asked, tongue in cheek.

"What kind of little nagging problems?" he asked.

"Well, for example," she rattled off, "there's the soft drink machine that masquerades as a one-armed bandit. There's the coffee machine that gives coffee but no cups. There's the computer repairman who promised to be here Monday and hadn't shown up Friday. There's the dogged apparel fastener salesman who wouldn't listen when I tried to tell him we were contracted to another supplier. There are the three girls who can't sew but want to start at twice the salary we pay production workers…"

"Get me the hell out of here," Saxon told Maggie with a loud laugh. "Take care of it, Tabby," he called over his shoulder.

The redhead stuck out her tongue as they left the building.

CHAPTER SEVEN

"WHERE TO NOW?" Maggie asked when they were back in the car.

"That's up to you, honey. You're driving," he said with a smile.

"Want to ride up in the mountains and have a picnic?" she suggested, feeling elated and adventurous. "We could stop and get some cheese and crackers and cookies."

"Childhood revisited?" he chided.

"Something like that," she admitted. "Lisa and I used to go fishing with Dad, and we'd always stop at some little country store to get something to snack on. I'd all but forgotten what fun it was."

"I haven't been fishing since I was twelve," he recalled.

"What do you do for relaxation when you're not working yourself to death?" she asked after she'd cranked the car and pulled out onto the highway.

"The corporation has been my vocation and my avocation for years, Maggie," he said quietly. His hands dug for a cigarette and he lighted it with careless ease. "I haven't had time for anything else."

"It sounds rather narrow," she observed.

"Does it? What do you do when you're not working on the newspaper?"

She sighed. "Not a lot," she confessed. "We only have two reporters, and the other one is just part-time, after school. I'm on call twenty-four hours a day. If anything happens, I'm expected to cover it, regardless of what time it is."

"That doesn't sound very safe," he remarked. "What if there's a night robbery?"

"I get my camera and go," she said simply. "It's part of the job. News doesn't take holidays."

"Blind dedication," he scoffed.

"We're the public's eyes and ears," she argued, warming to battle. "We're writing history as it happens. Who's going to record important events for posterity if we don't?"

"I fail to see what difference it's going to make if a small-town bank robbery is recorded for posterity," he said shortly. "And does it really matter if you get the facts at midnight or at seven the next morning?"

She drew in a sharp breath. "You just don't understand."

"I never did. You give a hundred and ten percent to the job, and who cares? Not the people who read the stories. They knew everything before the paper went to press. They just read it to find out who got caught."

"You're oversimplifying."

"No, I'm not. You're overstating the importance of what you do. I've noticed that about dedicated journalists," he continued. "They see the job as a holy grail. It's nothing more than an overglorified gossip column, which sometimes causes more problems than it solves. I've seen radical groups parading for the benefit of television cameras."

"We do a lot of good," she muttered, executing a turn.

"Name something," he challenged.

"All right, I will." And she proceeded to rattle off projects the paper had supported—programs to benefit the needy, the homeless, the aged, the underprivileged, the uneducated, the bereaved, the blind, the victimized, the multiple-handicapped—and only when she paused for breath did he stop her with an upraised hand and an amused laugh.

"Okay, I get the picture," he admitted. "Maybe small-town papers accomplish more, and I won't argue that you do some good. But," he added, "will the world end if you give it up?"

She thought about that. "Not for the subscribers," she confessed. "Because there's always somebody who can replace you on a newspaper staff, and probably do a better job than you did yourself. But I don't know if I could live without it, you see."

"Why not?" His head lifted, as if her answer seemed to matter intensely to him.

"It's not a dull job, and it's never routine," she replied. "There's always something going on, either a project you're following, or a big story beginning to break under wraps. You can't get bored, because you don't have the time." Her face lit up with the memories. "You get to go in the front door of places you couldn't get in the back door of if you were just an average citizen. You get to meet extraordinary people, do exciting things. I love it," she concluded. "It's…everything."

"A man should be that, to a woman," he said quietly.

"No man is ever going to be everything to me," she replied, easing the car onto the highway that led to the distant mountains.

"I wouldn't be overconfident if I were you," he advised. "Very often, none of us are as self-sufficient as we convince ourselves we are."

"Speaking from personal experience?" she challenged.

"Yes," he admitted, surprising her. "I never thought I'd live to see the day when I'd have to be led around by the hand like a child, Maggie. I'd have bet money that it could never happen."

"It won't always be like this for you," she told him with more conviction than she felt.

"Won't it?" He laughed bitterly. "That's not what my surgeon told me."

"Circumstances may change," she reminded him.

"Whales may drive cars some day," he retorted.

"Saxon…"

"Leave it, honey. Tell me where we are."

He wasn't going to discuss it any more, that was obvious. She sighed wearily. "We're heading out of Jarrettsville going west, and there's a highway leading off to our left across the Tyger River. Which way do I go?"

"Straight ahead. We should be in the foothills of the Blue Ridge Mountain chain by now."

"We certainly are." She laughed, noticing the hilly countryside, the open country and the occasional cabin nestled among the glorious foliage.

He named two highways and added, "Where they intersect, take the left fork and about three to four miles along, there'll be a small country store on the right. We can stop there and get some snacks."

"You've got a good memory," she remarked.

"I do my best. Are you familiar with mountain driving?"

"Not as used to it as I'd like to be," she admitted,

"but I won't panic if the brakes get hot and start squealing. I've driven in the Georgia mountains up around Blairsville and Hiawassee. And believe me, that's good training!"

"I know what you mean. The curves are quite a challenge." His face hardened, and she knew he was remembering his racing days.

"Would you like to hear the news?" she asked, and before he could refuse, she turned on the radio, grateful for the small diversion that might keep him from brooding.

Minutes later they were climbing around some hairpin curves, and she wasn't nervous at all with Saxon beside her. Oddly enough he made her feel secure. She'd stopped at the little country store and stocked up with canned sausages, crackers, cookies and soft drinks and some old-fashioned hoop cheese.

"It's beautiful here," she said, stopping at a deserted roadside park that overlooked the mountains.

"Deserted?" he asked.

"Oh, very. Shall we unload and stay awhile?"

"Suits me."

She helped him out of the car and, ignoring the cement tables and benches, they sprawled under a spreading maple tree, finishing off the cheese and crackers and sausages before they relaxed with soft drinks and cookies.

"It's so beautiful here," she said with a sigh, stretching back to close her eyes. "Cool and sweet-smelling and so peaceful."

"You're years too young to need peace," he observed.

"We all need it at times," she returned.

"Remind me to have a wheelchair brought in for

you, Granny." He laughed, finishing off his soft drink. He lay back on the crisp leaves beside her with a sigh. "God, I needed this. The silence, the mountains, you…"

She rolled over on her side to study him. Close up like this, he was a different man from the high-powered tycoon she'd glimpsed in his office earlier.

"A loaf of bread, a jug of wine…" She grinned.

"And thou," he murmured. He reached out to find her arm, and his fingers stroked it gently, sending little darts of sensation through her. "Come here, Maggie," he said softly.

"It's public." She hesitated.

"I'll hear a car before you will," he said quietly. His fingers tightened. "I—I need it, can you understand that? I need to prove to myself that I'm not half a man as well as a blind one…"

What an unfair argument that was, she thought miserably, going to him without reservation. But it was out of love, not pity—something he couldn't know. The feel of his long hard body against hers was a foretaste of heaven, and all she wanted out of life at that moment.

"I've wanted this all day," he murmured, nuzzling his mouth against her soft face until he searched out her warm lips. His hands pressed her toward him; the scent of him filled her nostrils. "I've wanted the taste of you, the feel of you against me—things I haven't had a lot of since you came back."

Her eyes closed, and she forced herself to relax, to yield to his strength. "You're very strong," she murmured, letting her hands trace his broad shoulders.

"And you're very soft," he replied. His hands moved up her rib cage to savor the high full curves of her breasts. "Especially here…"

She started to protest, but his mouth was working magic on hers, as expert as she remembered, and just as dangerous as it mocked her faint protest at the intimacy of his fingers.

"Don't fight me," he murmured against her lips. "I'll confine my attentions to this very interesting territory, if that's what you want. Where are the buttons?"

She tried to concentrate, but he was stroking her lips with his tongue and her mind was somewhere in limbo, not on the unusual pattern of the buttons that were located under her arm.

"So," he murmured, finding them, and his fingers went to work, easing them apart. "And this little wisp," he whispered, unhooking the fastening of the bra that was little more than decoration. "Ah," he breathed as his hands found sweet, living warmth and felt her sudden stiffening, heard her wild gasp. "Maggie, you're like silk to touch," he breathed, "and so sweet that I could eat you!" He brought his mouth down against the taut, swelling rise of her body and savored the lightly scented skin with something rivaling reverence. "You taste of flowers," he whispered as she arched and bit her lip to keep from crying out, letting his hands lift her up to his gentle, searching mouth. He tasted her, nibbled at her, until a sharp cry burst from her lips with the force of the pleasure he was giving her.

"Maggie," he moaned softly, and moved his hands back down to cup her, stroke her. His mouth slid up to hers and took it roughly. His fingers contracted suddenly, and she cried out.

He stiffened, lifting his head, his hands quickly easing their rough grip, "I'm sorry," he said gently, "that was unforgivable. Did I hurt you badly?"

Maggie licked her dry lips and watched his sight-less face, frozen with concern. She felt the air chilling her taut bareness where his warm, moist lips had left it vulnerable. "You didn't hurt me, Saxon," she confessed softly.

The hard lines of his face relaxed, and his hands swallowed her again, feeling her body tense and arch up to him as he explored it. "Still, I won't be that rough again," he promised. "Do you like the feel of my hands, Maggie?"

She fought for sanity, but he was creating unbeliev-able tension in her—new pleasures, exquisite pleasures. "Please," she breathed, reaching up to catch his head, to coax it down to her hungry body. "Like this…"

"Yes, darling," he breathed, easing his mouth against her, "like this…" He drew his forehead across her, his eyes, his cheeks, in a caress like nothing she'd ever imagined. For all her age she was remarkably innocent when it came to intimacy. Not because she was a prude, but simply because no man had ever stirred her blood the way Saxon was stirring it.

His lips touched her, adored her, in a silence that was intensified by the rustle of leaves in the breeze, the crispy sound of the leaves under her back as she writhed helplessly beneath his hands, his mouth.

He moved then, easing up to let her feel his full weight, from breast to thigh, and the unfamiliar differ-ences between his male body and her own. She caught her breath at the sensation of oneness.

His mouth savored hers as his body moved sensu-ously over her own, faintly rocking, softly grinding, and she moaned helplessly.

"Nymph," he breathed into her mouth, his hands

going under her slender hips to lift, gently, to press her to him. "Sweet little seductress, feel the effect you have on me."

"Saxon," she whispered achingly. "Oh, Saxon, what are you doing?"

"Don't be embarrassed," he whispered soothingly. "I know all too well how new this is for you. Just lie still, honey, and let me show you what to do. I'm going to be very, very slow, very tender…" His hands moved and she bit off a tiny cry as she felt them easing the skirt up her smooth thighs.

"The road," she choked, feeling her crazy body yield to his, her legs cooperating with him, her hands clinging when they should be pushing, when his intention was too clear to mistake even for a novice.

He caught his own breath as he moved, creating a new, almost unbearable intimacy between them. Her body felt as if it were going to stiffen into oblivion, to die of the tension, arching endlessly upward, her fingers digging into his hips.

"Now," he breathed shakily, and his fingers found the buttons of his own shirt, opening it so that her breasts flattened under the warm, prickly weight of his hair-roughened chest. His body moved again, his hands touching her in unbearable ways. "Now, Maggie, help me…"

It was the last straw. She gave in without reservation, loving him, wanting him, tears rolling down her cheeks at the painful hunger he was creating while she waited to give him everything, her body, her heart, her very soul…

The sound of an approaching car barely penetrated her screaming mind, but Saxon heard it. Sensitive to the least interruption, despite his own staggering involvement, he lifted his head and froze. He was dragging at air, his body shuddering with mindless necessity, damp and faintly trembling, his heart shaking him.

"Oh, God, no," he ground out, and she watched his face contort as he dragged himself away from her to lie rigidly on his back. He looked like a man in unholy torment.

"Saxon, are you all right?" she asked quickly, dragging herself up hurriedly to rearrange her clothes, her eyes fearful as she stared at him and the car approached rapidly.

"What do you think?" he ground out.

His voice sounded ragged. She wondered at the wisdom of trying to fasten his shirt, but he was already doing it himself even as a carload of tourists came snaking past them on the highway. A woman in the passenger seat waved merrily, apparently oblivious to the blazing tension of the comfortable-looking people under the big maple tree.

"They're gone," she murmured unnecessarily.

He drew in one long final breath and sat up, his face dark and drawn. "Damn," he growled huskily. "Maggie, I almost took you, do you realize that? Right here, in plain view of the highway, and I was so far gone, I didn't even realize what I was trying to do!"

She studied his broad, hard face with faint awe. It was strangely satisfying to know she had that effect on him.

"You've been a long time without a woman, haven't you?" she asked haltingly.

His eyes began to glitter narrowly as he sat there, stiff and unyielding. "Is that what you think?" he asked sharply. "That I was so desperate, all I needed was a woman's body?"

"Wasn't it?" she asked, and held her breath for the answer.

The glitter got worse. "You really believe that I could use you like that, knowing you're a virgin?" He got to his feet. "Thanks for the character reading, Maggie. It's been fascinating. Let's go home."

"I wasn't trying to stop you," she reminded him quietly.

He laughed bitterly. "Of course not," he said with contempt. "Why should you? If I got you pregnant, I'd be wide open for a lawsuit. You'd be on easy street for life."

Her face went bone-white, but she didn't say a word. She started picking up the picnic things and loading them into the car, putting the trash in the trash cans. And she didn't say one word to him all the way back home.

When they got back, he was even worse, roaring around like a cyclone, growling about business, complaining about Maggie's lack of cooperation when she tried and failed to get a businessman he wanted to talk to on the phone for him. Finally she lost her temper and slammed out of his study, leaving him alone with his bad temper.

CHAPTER EIGHT

THAT EVENING SHE was careful to sit beside Lisa at the supper table and encouraged her to talk so that no one would notice her unusual quietness. At the head of the table Saxon looked no more disposed to conversation himself, brooding and darkly oblivious as he picked at his food.

Maggie escaped upstairs at the first possible minute, despite the fact that Saxon had gone straight to his study when the meal was finished. She couldn't face questions about the day she'd spent with her new boss without blushing, and that would have led to some interesting comments.

She sat in front of her mirror for a long time, brushing her hair with slow strokes while she relived every minute of his bruising, compelling ardor. It had been a long time since a man had tried to make love to her, and not once had she responded to another man the way she'd responded to Saxon. If the other car hadn't come barreling down the road, she'd have given in to *him* completely there under the trees, without even the thought of protest or modesty. She couldn't remember feeling such a blazing inferno of hunger. She still ached with it, burned with it. Just the memory of the afternoon made her body tingle with excitement. She'd loved the touch of his warm hard fingers on her skin, their expertise so evident that she bristled with envy for the women he'd learned it with. She closed her eyes and trembled with a silvery longing to be back in his arms again, to be cherished, to be…tutored. What would it be like to share his bed? she wondered hungrily, and her eyes flew open. She was going to have to get herself firmly in hand. An affair with Saxon Tremayne was a dead end, and she had the rest of her life to think about. Experiencing him as a lover would ruin her for any other man, and she didn't dare risk that. Life without him was going to be hard enough anyway, without that.

She thought ahead to the day she'd leave Jarrettsville, leave him, to go back to her job in Defiance. It was as bleak as winter to her mind. Just to sit and look at Saxon was pleasure enough for an entire day. To be touched by him was heaven itself.

She stood up, hating her weakness even as it washed her in yearning.

A sound caught her ears. She paused. It came again, louder, from the room next door that was occupied by Saxon. She hesitated for an instant before she went to it and stood listening.

It came again. A groan. A hard, rough groan, like that of a man in horrible pain, penetrated the thick wood.

She started to knock, then thought better of it. She opened the doorknob and pushed. It was unlocked.

She stepped into the brown-carpeted room, her eyes falling hungrily on Saxon's big body spread out on the thick quilted coverlet that was done in creams and browns to match the Mediterranean decor.

"Saxon?" she called softly.

He turned his head in the direction of her voice,

and she could see harsh lines of pain carved into his pale face.

"Maggie?" he whispered huskily.

"Yes." She went to him, compassion softening her voice, and sat down gingerly on the bed beside him, feeling the warmth of his body radiating to her thigh. He was wearing trousers and his shirt, the jacket and tie thrown on a chair and his shoes sitting beside the bed.

His fingers felt across her thighs for her hand, in her lap, and he grasped it tightly. "Stay with me," he said in a taut tone. "I need you. God, I need you…"

"I'll stay," she said soothingly. Her hand, unbidden, went to his broad forehead to brush back the disheveled silver-splintered darkness of his hair. His brow was hot to her cool fingers. "I'm right here. I won't go anywhere. What can I do to help? Is it a headache?"

"Damnable headache," he corrected, wincing. "Tablets—in the top drawer of the bedside table."

She let go of his hand and found the prescription bottle, reading the directions before she asked if he'd already taken any of them. When he shook his head, she toppled two of the white tablets into her palm and went to fetch a glass of water from the bathroom.

After he'd taken the tablets, he lay back heavily on the bed, his hair dark against the cream-colored pillowcase.

"It will take twenty minutes or so," she murmured. "I'm sorry, it must hurt abominably."

"What a tame word for it," he growled.

She smoothed his hair again, remembering his vicious words as they left the roadside park. Probably the headache had started then, and caused him to react to her the way he had. It was pain and frustration, not hatred, that had caused him to be so hostile. Now she understood, and the sting went away.

"I was damned cruel to you, wasn't I?" he asked curtly, as if he could hear the thoughts going through her mind.

"Yes, you were," she told him, not pulling her punches.

He managed a wan smile. "I wanted you," he said quietly. "The last thing in the world I expected was a carload of tourists to roar by."

She felt herself tingling at the thought of just when those tourists had interrupted them. "It was a pretty public place," she murmured.

"I didn't know where I was at the time, and don't pretend that you did either," he muttered. "You were just as involved as I was, and if they hadn't happened along, we'd have—"

"I'd have come to my senses," she replied curtly, trying to convince herself.

"Like hell you would've," he taunted.

She tried to smother a smile and lost. "Leave me a few illusions, will you?"

He laughed softly and sighed, pressing a hand against his forehead. "It was delicious, wasn't it?" he asked. "Just the two of us, no distractions, the wind blowing and the leaves rustling, and the taste of you in my mouth..."

"If you're trying to embarrass me, forget it," she told him, fighting the urge to throw herself on him and kiss the breath out of him. "I'm twenty-six years old, and I don't think I can be shocked anymore."

"Do tell?" he murmured. "When I finally get you in my bed, we'll see about that. Or do you still have doubts that I'll manage that before you leave here?"

"I don't want to have an affair with you, Saxon," she said quietly. "That doesn't come under the terms of our agreement. I'm here to help you cope."

"And that's all?" He caught her fingers and raised them to his mouth, teasing their tips with his tongue, his lips, until she felt again the fiery longing to lie with him.

"How's your head?" she hedged, trying to ignore the sensations he was arousing.

"Getting better by the minute," he murmured. He pressed her palm against his mouth and traced its delicate lines with the tip of his tongue.

"You need rest…"

"I need you," he breathed, tugging on her wrist. "Lie with me for a minute. Let me touch you the way I touched you this afternoon."

"We shouldn't…" she protested.

"Maggie, we're both adults," he reminded her. "Grown-up people, not children playing with fire. We both know the risks, but I'm not going to take you like this. I'm far too tired to do you justice, and my head aches like hell. I just want to hold you against me. Is that so outrageous?"

"You make me sound like an adolescent prude," she grumbled. "And I'm not. I'm just cautious. I'm stupid about men and women in beds, hasn't that occurred to you? I don't even know how to protect myself, because I've never had to!"

"You don't have to now," he returned, glowering. "Not yet, at any rate. I won't seduce you tonight. Would you like that in writing and notarized?"

"I'd like to pour a bucket of hot oil over your head, that's what I'd like," she muttered venomously.

"It feels as if someone already has," he returned, and looked it.

She melted. It was diabolical of him to use his pain against her, but she couldn't refuse him.

"I can't believe this is good for you," she murmured as she eased down beside him on the bed.

He seemed to tense as he felt her body sliding alongside his, but after an instant, his arms slid around her and he moved, pillowing his heavy head against her warm breasts.

He sighed wearily. "Oh, God, that feels good," he whispered achingly.

Yes, it did, she thought, relaxing herself as the weight of his head made her feel the most exquisite pleasure. If it gave him peace, it was so little a sacrifice for her.

He relaxed there for a minute without moving, but almost inevitably, his lips began to inch forward, burning through her thin blouse as they found the slope of her breast.

"Saxon," she whispered.

He ignored the soft plea. "Don't talk," he murmured against her. His teeth nipped at her sensually through the layers of fabric that separated them. His hands under her lifted, pressing her body hard against his mouth, and it became suddenly hungry, demanding.

She caught her breath. *Fool,* she taunted herself before she felt the first sensuous waves hit her. *Fool. You knew this would happen!*

He rolled over, taking her with him, so that she was lying on her back with his massive body above her while his mouth played relentlessly with her soft curves through the fabric.

"Help me undress you," he whispered against her

throat. "I want to touch every inch of your skin with my lips."

"I want it too," she managed unsteadily. "But not like this—not now. Give me time, Saxon!"

"Why should I?"

Her eyes closed. "Because I've got to walk in with my eyes wide open," she said simply. "I've got to be willing to take the risks. I—I don't do things on the spur of the moment. I can't."

He laughed softly against her silken skin. "I told you not more than a minute ago that I wasn't going to seduce you. Didn't you hear me?"

"What would you call taking my clothes off?" she muttered.

"Exciting," he whispered wickedly. "Gloriously exciting. But I wasn't going to undress all of you, baby. Only the upper half—so that I can feel these," he whispered, brushing his lips maddeningly over her breasts, "deliciously bare."

She wanted that, too, with a surge of hunger that knocked her right off balance. Her body trembled slightly, and he felt it, along with the almost imperceptible lifting of her body.

"We both want it," he breathed, halfway removing his weight so that his fingers could find the buttons.

"What are you doing to me, you sorcerer?" she accused with weak humor as she lay perfectly still and let him slowly, sensually, unfasten the buttons.

"Preparing you," he whispered just above her lips. "Getting you used to me, so that when the time finally comes for us, you won't be afraid to give yourself freely."

"Will the time...come for us?" she asked through

taut lips as she felt his expert fingers toying with the front clasp that held the lacy wisp of her bra together.

"Inevitably," he replied in a slow, tender tone. "It's been building since the day we met. You haven't missed me any less than I've missed you."

Her eyes went liquid. "Have you...missed me?" she asked.

"More than I can tell you," he replied. He unfastened the clip and slowly eased the fabric away, so that she was bare from the waist up, so that the faint chill of the room washed over her, emphasizing her lack of clothing. "But not," he breathed, his fingers poised over her, "more than I can show you. God, Maggie, I wish I could see you," he ground out.

"There's very little to see," she whispered lightly, aching for his touch on her body in a warm, sweet yielding.

His fingers lowered, and she trembled as they made contact with the taut peak, very tenderly tracing it, and the softness surrounding it, while his face seemed to harden and go rigid.

"You want this very much, don't you?" he asked, confident of her response because of the things the reactions of her traitorous body were telling him.

"Can't you feel that?" she asked on a gasp.

"I can feel it," he agreed tautly. "But I want to hear it. I'm not used to making love blind, Maggie. This is the first time I've touched a woman since it happened."

"Is it very different from being in a dark room?" she asked unsteadily.

He bent over her, and his mouth smiled against her lips. "Maggie," he breathed as he took her mouth, "I've never made love in the dark."

Before that soft taunt could register, he was kissing her, and touching her, and her body was lifting in unholy torment to beg for the slow, lazy fingers that were introducing it to such exquisite pleasure.

She wondered how a human body could survive this kind of torture—aching with hunger, burning with a fever that no amount of ice could soothe, wanting. Wanting!

"Don't cry," he whispered, holding her still against him, his hands at her back, soothing, his mouth gently touching all over her face as he brought her down from the wildness of the plateau they'd reached together.

She couldn't seem to stop trembling, and pressed closer, drawing his strength into her. "Saxon," she moaned.

"It's all right, honey," he whispered softly. "Calm down now. It's all right."

Her arms clung around his neck. "Is it always like this?" she asked with a ghost of a laugh. "Do people go crazy like this, until they're on fire and burning up?"

His fingers smoothed back her wild hair. "It usually takes a lot more than what we did to cause that kind of reaction, Maggie," he said at her ear. His lips brushed the lobe. "I barely touched you," he breathed.

"I know." She laughed nervously.

His arms contracted, swallowing her closely. "God, you're sweet," he ground out, rocking her roughly. "Sweet, like honey, to taste, to kiss. You make me want to curl up with the pleasure."

She sighed into his thick hair. "There couldn't have been much of that, for you," she murmured. "I don't even know how to touch you."

His breath seemed to catch. "It boggles the mind," he murmured.

She nuzzled her face against his. "How's your headache?"

"What headache?" He chuckled.

She smiled, closing her eyes. They seemed to fit together beautifully, despite the disparity in their sizes, as if she had been created for him.

"Sleep with me," he whispered, tightening his arms. "Go and put on your gown and sleep with me, all night."

She wanted to. Her body screamed for it. But her practical mind reared its ugly head.

"No," she said gently.

"Why?"

She smiled wistfully. "Because we wouldn't sleep."

He chuckled at her ear. "Probably not. But, honey, it's going to happen. The only question is when, not if."

She knew that too. If she stayed here, it was inevitable. And how could she possibly leave him? It had been agony the last time; she'd never have the strength until he actually sent her away. And no matter what his motives were, it wouldn't make any difference. She was too hungry for him to care—that was the really frightening thought.

"Then not tonight," she whispered.

"All right," he agreed after a minute, and his arms tightened for an instant before he let her go. "Not tonight."

She sat up, putting herself back together. "Can I get you anything else before I turn in?"

He shook his head. "I'll be all right now. I want you to drive me down to Bilings Sportswear in the morning," he said suddenly, his face faintly brooding. "I've got to clear up that mess before I do one other thing."

It was good to see him involving himself in business again, she thought, and felt a stirring of pride at having been partially responsible.

"All right," she said. "What time would you like to leave?"

"Nine o'clock," he said. "I'll see you downstairs at seven." He grinned. "I'll touch you downstairs at seven," he amended.

"Why, you lecherous thing," she gasped.

He cocked an eyebrow. "You let me touch you up here. What's different about downstairs?"

"I'm going to bed before you compromise my principles," she informed him, rising.

"That might be wise. Maggie!" he called as she opened the connecting door.

"Yes?" She turned expectantly.

He started to say something and apparently thought better of it, because his face closed up. "Nothing. Good night, honey, sleep well. And thanks for the…sympathy."

"Not at all," she said, and grinned. "Thanks for the…instruction."

"As the saying goes," he murmured, "you ain't seen nothin' yet."

"That's what scares me," she murmured, and with a soft good-night, quickly closed the door.

He was cheerful and pleasant at breakfast for a change, looking rested and sexy and altogether too attractive in a brown pinstriped vested suit that gave him a tigerish appearance. Probably that was deliberate, too, she thought, but wondered absently how he'd picked out the color when he was blind.

"It's simple," he returned when she asked him, "I had Mother buy some of those plastic puzzles for infants. I put a different shape on each color. Square is gray." He chuckled. "Triangle is brown, circle is blue, and so forth."

"You," she said, "are a genius."

His white teeth flashed for an instant. "I try, baby, I try. What are you wearing?"

"A gray skirt, a white blouse, and a navy-blue blazer with black accessories," she replied.

"What does the blouse look like?" he asked with a raised eyebrow. "Is it low-cut?"

"I'll have you know, I'm dressed very conservatively," she returned. "The blouse has a modest V neck slashed to the waist, and the skirt has a slit all the way up to my thigh."

He chuckled delightedly. "Try again."

"Well, actually the blouse has a jabot collar, and the skirt only has a kick pleat in back," she told him. "But my wrists are shamelessly exposed," she added in a whisper.

"Brazen hussy," he accused.

"Only in bed with sexy men," she retorted.

"Only then if they teach you what to do," he accused.

"Well, I'm learning," she said defensively.

"Whew!" he said wickedly. "Are you ever!"

She grinned and picked up her fork. The ham and eggs looked delicious.

Bilings Sportswear was located on the outskirts of Spartanburg, a nice medium-sized company with over two hundred employees. It was strictly a manufacturing company, not a vertical-mill operation like the Tremayne Corporation. But it boasted a level of quality that any corporation would be proud to claim.

Its neat cutting room featured a conveyor belt to carry the huge bales of cloth to the stockroom, and long tables where spreaders and cutters worked to produce the pattern cloth pieces that were assembled on the shirt and pants lines by hardworking seamstresses. Everywhere there was the sound of sewing machines, a loud hum that drowned conversation. Conveyor belts were installed in both divisions, running between the sewing machine operators to carry piece goods in baskets as they passed through each operation in their assembly into clothes.

The office was a bright cheerful place with smiling women who did payroll and reception work and nattily dressed executives in suits who worked at administrative tasks and public relations.

Maggie was fascinated with the plant. Textiles had been one of her interests long before Saxon Tremayne stormed into her life, and the process of clothes-making had never bored her.

She clung to Saxon's big warm hand as the plant vice president Gordy Kemp escorted them through the operation. He was a tall man, very slender, with small green eyes and a thin smile that was all too ready.

Maggie couldn't help remembering what she'd heard about the man in Saxon's office.

"I'd like to have all the workers assembled in the shirt line now," Saxon said curtly when the tour was finished and they were standing at the swinging doors that separated the plant from the offices.

"Now?" Kemp burst out.

"Right now," was the cold reply.

Kempt shrugged, looked vaguely uneasy, and went into the office to have the announcement made over the plant's intercom.

Saxon's fingers tightened on Maggie's. "Stay right beside me," he said in her ear.

"What are you going to do?"

"Wait and see." His dark eyes gleamed with challenge and something else.

The sewing machines gradually came to a halt and the employees slowly grouped into a semicircle facing the doors where Saxon, Maggie and the young Kemp were standing.

Kemp looked more nervous than ever. "They're all here, Mr. Tremayne," he told the older man.

Saxon nodded. "Good morning," he began, addressing the workers, raising his deep voice so that it carried with a faint echo through the cavernous plant. "For the benefit of those who don't know me—and very likely that means most of you—I'm Saxon Tremayne. My corporation is in the process of absorbing Bilings Sportswear, as you've no doubt heard by now."

There was a low murmur among the employees that sounded faintly antagonistic.

"I understand," Saxon continued calmly, "that some of you are under the misconception that my immediate priority is the dismissal of the older employees here on some kind of trumped-up excuse."

That almost brought the house down. Kemp tugged at his necktie. "Mr. Tremayne..." he began in a strangled whisper.

Saxon raised a curt hand, stopping him. "I also understand," he added, "that this misconception has been promoted by certain management personnel within this organization."

Kemp stiffened, and Maggie glanced away before he noticed her interest.

"I want you all to know that we have no intention whatsoever of trying to cheat our older employees out of their well-deserved retirement benefits," Saxon said firmly, lifting his face as if he were staring straight at the onlookers. "Indeed, you may expect an immediate raise in salaries, increased insurance benefits and paid holidays. All of which I was amazed to learn that you *weren't* already getting. How does that sound?"

There was a loud roar, a lot of laughter, and some whistles. Saxon grinned. "I thought you might like that. And you senior employees will be interested to learn that we also plan to increase your retirement benefits.

"Here's what's going to happen within the next two weeks. Our administrative people have been working with Bilings's executives to formulate some new company policies. One of them is going to include monthly listening sessions—bull sessions, if you prefer. Two days a month you'll have the opportunity to sit down and talk with a designated executive if you have any complaints or suggestions for improvements. We're also installing a suggestions box, so that you can gripe and suggest improvements between listening sessions. Any improvements we implement because of an employee's suggestion will result in a nice bonus for the employee who suggested it.

"We're also going to update the operation here— add some new equipment and replace some of the older machinery."

There was a hush in the big room, and Kemp looked as if he were searching out a hole to jump into.

"Any complaints so far?" Saxon asked dryly.

"No!" several employees chorused, followed by another roar of laughter.

Saxon grinned. "That's just the beginning. I'll have more to say on the subject of changes later, and notices will be posted on the bulletin boards. When we get some of these improvements going, we'll have another plant-wide meeting and review what's been accomplished. Meanwhile if any of you has any reservations about the takeover, I want to know it. And from now on," he added darkly, "if you hear any rumors, bring them straight to me. I'll get to the bottom of it, and the perpetrator is going to find himself in a hell of a fix.

"One more thing," he added, "I'm not offering you any handouts. These added benefits aren't a bribe to keep you sweet. They're an advance against your continued attention to detail and your pride in production of a superior line of clothing. I understand that the quality-control people here are bored to death because they can hardly find enough seconds, thirds and wash garments to keep them working. That says a hell of a lot for you people, and I appreciate it. That's why you're getting raises. And if you keep putting out that kind of work, the raises will keep coming. If I make money, you make money, and later on we'll even discuss some stock-sharing programs. Now let's all get back to work."

With a rumble of happy, startled conversation the employees began to disperse, while Maggie watched with a faint smile and shook her head in bewilderment.

"Kemp?" Saxon asked curtly.

The young executive cleared his throat uncomfortably. "Yes, Mr. Tremayne?"

"Come into the office with me. You and I have a little business to discuss."

Saxon allowed Maggie to help him into the office and seat himself behind the big desk. "Okay, honey," he told her, "go read a magazine or something. I'll only be a few minutes."

"Okay." She grinned.

It was several minutes before the door to the office opened, and Kemp came out, his face pale. Maggie put down the magazine she'd been reading and went inside to help Saxon find his way back out.

"Now take me down to the cutting room," he told Maggie. He looked big and confident and faintly triumphant, and not the least embarrassed about letting her guide him around. It was such a change from their first encounter since his blindness that she smiled.

"What did you do to him?" she asked as they walked down the long, wide aisle past the smiling women on the assembly line. "He rushed straight out the front door."

"I put him in charge of the order department," he told her, "and sent him off to lunch. The cutting-room foreman has been here for twenty years, and he's been consistently passed over for promotion because of a disagreement he had with management over salaries. Apparently he's the only department head on the place who wasn't afraid to complain about the low pay."

"Going to pat him on the back?" she teased.

"I'm going to give him Kemp's job," he said, smiling. "I need a man I can trust running things here, and he's the shop foreman's friend as well. Always remember, honey, if you delegate, be damned sure of your choices. A bad manager can cost you an arm, figuratively speaking."

"Is there a union here?" she asked. "You mentioned a shop foreman, but—"

"There's a union forming," he replied. "The employees got desperate enough to vote it in, and even though I'm in management, after reviewing the operation here, I can't honestly say I blame them."

"Will Mr. Kemp stay on, do you think?"

"I don't know. He's been here for six years, Maggie, I couldn't just boot him out the door without giving him a chance. He's young yet, and making mistakes, but he's got the opportunity to learn if he takes it." He frowned. "Are we anywhere near the cutting room?"

"Just about. I've got homing pigeon instincts," she added with a grin, squeezing the big hand she was holding as they turned the corner into the cutting room. "Trust me."

"I'm beginning to see one of the benefits of this damned shrapnel," he said with a faint smile. "I get to hold hands with you all the time."

"You could do that if you weren't blind," she said.

"Could I really?" His voice was quiet and deep. "Or would you pack up and run if I regained my sight? You're a lot less nervous of me now than you were when I could see, Maggie."

She moved closer to his side, feeling a surge of warmth that made her want to throw her arms around him and hold tight. "When you had your sight," she reminded him, "you could have had any woman you wanted."

He drew in a sharp breath. "My God, you don't think I'd want you if I could see? And you say *I'm* blind!"

She looked up, wanting to pursue that, when a big, husky man with red hair came walking toward them from the office nearby.

"Morning," he said pleasantly, going to pass them.

"Good morning," Saxon replied. "Can you tell me where to find Red Halley?"

The other man, every bit Saxon's size, grinned. "You just did."

Saxon stretched out his hand toward the man's voice, "I'm Saxon Tremayne."

"Glad to meet you," Red said with a firm handshake. "That was a nice speech you made."

"It wasn't just a speech," Saxon said quietly. "I meant every word. How would you feel about ram-rodding this operation for me?"

Red looked as if he'd tried to swallow a watermelon. "Me?"

"Mr. Kemp has just accepted the position of head order clerk. I'm offering you his old job."

"Why?" Red burst out.

"Because you're a fighter," he replied. "I admire courage, Mr. Halley. I like executives who don't dive under their desks when I start raising hell about production. I don't think you will."

"But I never finished technical school," came the protest. "I lack three quarters—"

"There's an excellent technical school less than ten miles away," Saxon said, unabashed. "I'll foot the bill while you complete your training at night school."

Red sighed. "I'll have to accept now, won't I?" he asked with a sheepish grin.

"Don't bother to thank me," Saxon interrupted when

the other man started to do just that. "You'll earn every penny you get."

"When do I start?"

"How soon can you get to the office?" Saxon asked. "Hand over your job to the man you feel is best qualified to replace you. Now I've got to get going. I've a pretty full schedule. Good luck."

Red shook hands with him again and went off looking thunderstruck.

"Shall we go, Maggie?" Saxon asked after a minute.

She caught his hand and led him off toward the rear exit of the building. "I just stand in awe of you, Mr. Corporation Executive," she told him. "Talk about grit."

"You're not exactly lacking in that department yourself, wildcat." He chuckled. "Shall I wave goodbye to the girls as I go out the door?"

"It wouldn't be good business," she assured him. "They're already drooling over you, you gorgeous hunk. If you give them any encouragement, you'll be mobbed on the way out."

He cocked an eyebrow. "Oh? Are they pretty?"

"Every last blessed one of them," she grumbled, and meant it—even the plumper employees had attractive, smiling faces.

"Hmmm." He laughed delightedly and put his arm around her, drawing her close. "Jealous, honey?"

"Murderously," she agreed, going along with him.

"I wish that was the truth," he said quietly, and his arm contracted. "But I suppose I expect too much. Take me home, Maggie," he added before she could ask him what he meant.

"Have you ever considered writing a book on textile management?" she asked on the way home.

"A book? I've done articles," he admitted. "But not a book."

"It might be an interesting project," she suggested. "The market isn't flooded with them, and you've been in the business for quite some time."

He leaned his dark head back against the seat with a frown. He felt in his pocket for a cigarette and lighted it. "My God, you're full of surprises," he murmured. "I seem to have come back to life since you got here."

"I'll agree with that," she said. "But all you needed was a prod. You aren't the type of man to sit down and go to seed."

"Are you so sure of that?" he asked. "If you'll remember, I've done very little for the past few months."

She stopped at a traffic light on the outskirts of Jarrettsville. "Perhaps it was all that concerned kindness that clogged you up," she teased. "You just needed a nurse who'd hit you over the head with a brick twice a day."

He laughed. "What a way to treat a poor blind man!"

"You? Poor? Blind?" she exclaimed.

"A man at least, surely," he murmured.

She grinned, watching the light go green. "I've never had any doubts on that score."

"Especially at certain times?" he murmured.

She was glad he couldn't see the color in her cheeks. "You ought to be ashamed of yourself," she commented. "Trying to seduce innocent women in public places."

"As I recall, I almost made it too."

"I can't deny that," she admitted quietly. "I was more than willing. And I hope you aren't going to take advantage of that," she added. "I can't help the way I respond to you. I'm too new at it to be very good at restraint.

Especially when you're offering me a kind of pleasure I've never experienced."

His hand felt across the seat to catch hers and clasp it warmly. "That's one thing I've always liked about you," he said gently. "Your total lack of guile. You never lie to me, even when it embarrasses you to tell the truth."

"Wouldn't you know the difference?" she asked warmly.

"I think I would," he murmured. He sighed and squeezed her hand. "All right, I'll do my best not to back you into any corners. But I want you desperately. Surely you know that?"

"Yes," she said. "I know."

"Men are notoriously shrewd when their emotions take over. I wouldn't consciously make you give in—but I can't promise that I won't ever lose my head. You've already had blatant proof that I'm not always in perfect control of myself."

"Do you really want…just me, and not just a woman?" she asked, needing reassurance.

"You asked me that once before, and I blew up," he recalled. "No, Maggie, I don't just want a warm body. And even if I did, I've too much respect for you to use you that way. Satisfied?"

"I reckon," she drawled. Her eyes slid sideways to study his face. If his life was changing, so was hers. She felt a part of him, a very necessary part. He wasn't the kind of man who'd ever need another human being when he was all in one piece. He was self-sufficient and stubbornly independent. But now, without his sight, he was necessarily dependent on Maggie, and she loved being necessary to him—even in a small way.

"How are you at taking dictation?" he asked suddenly.

"Oh, I think I can keep up with you," she assured him, "if you still dictate the way you used to."

"Are you willing to stay with me until I finish the book?" he persisted. "I'd hate to have to break in a new typist after the first chapter or two. It wouldn't be good for the continuity."

She thought about that. Her newspaper job was important to her—it had been the most important thing in her life. But now there was Saxon. And if it came down to a choice, there really wasn't one. She'd call her boss and explain and hope he'd hold her job. If he couldn't, well, there was always nearby Ashton. She could find another job doing something...

"I'll stay with you," she said quietly.

He lifted his cigarette to his lips and looked darkly relieved. "We'll start today then. It'll give me something to do."

That had been her plan at the outset, but she wasn't going to admit it to him. It was enough that he'd snapped up the bait, Maggie thought.

They spent the afternoon in his study while he got his thoughts together and outlined the basic proposal for her. They decided between them what information would be needed besides his own expertise, and she took dictation for letters to be sent out to acquire the additional information.

Lisa waylaid her on the way upstairs as they went to clean up before supper.

"How's it going?" she asked Maggie. "I haven't heard him yell all afternoon."

"He hasn't," Maggie said, and grinned. "Oh, Lisa, if

you'd seen him this morning at the plant! He was just fabulous. Took over the place, charmed the employees, displaced a scheming executive—he was wonderful!"

"He seems a lot different these days," her sister replied softly. "Of course, you've got a long way to go."

"Don't remind me!" Maggie laughed. "But I've made a start. At least now he's got something to do besides brood."

"That's a fact. By the way," Lisa added, stopping at the door to Maggie's room, "did you know that Sandra's invited guests for supper?"

Maggie's eyebrows lifted. "Who?"

Lisa sighed. "The girl next door and her brother, I'm afraid," she said gently, watching Maggie's face fall. "She's not very happy about it either. They stopped by and practically invited themselves. There was nothing she could do—graciously—except agree to it." Lisa's eyes clouded with anger. "The girl's name is Marlene Aikens, and her brother is Bret. He's okay, but she's a fourteen-karat pain in the neck."

"Does Saxon know?" Maggie asked.

"I doubt it. Sandra said Marlene chased him relentlessly until he all but threw her out the front door. But she's getting brave again. Figured that absence would make the heart grow fonder." Lisa grinned. "Sandra doesn't think so though."

Maggie only nodded. But she had a strangely disquieting feeling about the dinner party—as if it might develop into something that would drastically affect her happiness.

CHAPTER NINE

IT WAS JUST as well that Saxon couldn't see, Maggie thought miserably, sitting across from Marlene Aikens at the long elegant table. She'd only have felt more dowdy than she looked, compared to the elegant blonde's simple and wildly expensive black sheath dress. Maggie's plum-colored pantsuit was like something off the rack by comparison, and the older woman's sophisticated smile let her know it.

But Bret Aikens was a pleasant man, just Maggie's age, with dark hair and eyes and an easygoing personality—nothing like that of his rather flamboyant sister. Maggie found herself seated next to him at the table, and they had an immediate rapport.

"I hear you've become Saxon's eyes," he murmured over the salad.

She smiled. "In a manner of speaking," she confided. "And not totally. There are times and places when he has to make a guess…"

He grinned. "Say no more. You're from Georgia?"

"Sure am," she said pleasantly. "But I enjoy your state. It's beautiful country up here."

"We think so," he said, nodding. "Of course, the low country is the most densely populated, and with Charleston and Myrtle Beach and Hilton Head and those resort places, it tends to draw more attention.

But our chamber of commerce is trying to devote more time to promote the upcountry now."

"The history is what fascinates me," Maggie said, sipping her coffee. "I was never all that interested in the Revolutionary War, but since I've been here, I'm getting curious."

"You'll find that more Revolutionary War battles and skirmishes were fought in South Carolina than in any other state," he told her. "Around a hundred and thirty-seven of them, if memory serves."

"So many?" she exclaimed.

"You bet. And did you know that General Frances Marion—the so-called Swamp Fox—was from South Carolina?"

She laughed. "How could I forget? He's my father's hero. My father," she added, "is a history professor at our local college. Which helps to explain my interest in the subject. It was self-defense!"

He smiled across the table at her, and there was pure male interest in his eyes. "What a dull subject for such a pretty girl," he murmured.

She pursed her lips. "What a silver tongue you have, sir. Do you polish it daily?"

He tossed her a roguish wink. "Twice every day," he agreed.

Down the table Saxon was being treated to a breathy recital of Marlene's "utterly boring" week. He didn't seem to mind though. His broad face was smiling as he listened.

"The worst part of it all has been missing you, darling." She was sighing, putting a well-manicured hand on his broad one where it was resting on the table. "Why wouldn't you let me visit you?"

"I've been busy," Saxon replied. "And now that Maggie's here to help me get around, I'm going to be even busier. We're working on a very interesting project together."

"Oh?" Marlene asked with a venomous look in Maggie's direction. "What, darling?"

"That," Saxon murmured dryly, "would be telling. Wouldn't it, Maggie?"

"Yes, it would," she said, nodding, and gave Marlene a fearless grin.

"Well, how mysterious." Marlene laughed coldly. "But could I borrow you tomorrow, Saxon, for an hour or so? I've been so lonely..."

"Sorry, Marlene," he replied without hesitation. "I told you, I'm going to be on a tight schedule for a while."

"Business, always business." The blonde pouted. "You never let yourself have any fun."

"Don't I?" Saxon murmured with a tiny smile, and Maggie fought to keep from blushing.

The conversation drifted inevitably to the coming holiday season, and Sandra elaborated on her plans for Lisa and Randy's Christmas wedding.

"If you have time later this week," Bret murmured to Maggie, "I'd love to drive you over to Spartanburg and show you the Price House and the Walnut Grove Plantation. They both date back to the eighteenth century. In fact, the Walnut Grove Manor House dates back to seventeen sixty-five and was the home of a female scout for the Revolutionary War generals at the Battle of Cowpens. Come to think of it," he added with a beaming smile, "we could drive over to the Cowpens National Battlefield while we're at it and see where the Patriots gave the Redcoats their worst defeat..."

"I'd love to," she said, interrupting him. "What day?"

"Friday? About eight thirty, and we'll make an early start?"

She nodded. "That will be fine. And—uh—don't mention it to Saxon just yet, will you? I'd rather tell him myself."

He studied her and glanced down the table to the big dark man. "He won't like it," he sighed.

"I know," she murmured with a mischievous smile.

"He doesn't even make you nervous, does he? He frightens most people."

"The bigger they are, et cetera," she assured him.

"If you say so," he said, grinning. "But just in case, we might see if we could get one of those old cannons in my trunk... say, did you know that the old Confederates used walnut hulls to dye their uniforms gray? They took the—"

"—those black walnuts in the big yucky hulls that dye your shoes black when you walk over them?" she interrupted.

"The very same," he agreed, and proceeded to tell her how the dyeing process was accomplished.

She listened with obvious interest. He was so different from his snobby sister. She liked him. And she had a feeling that she was going to need that day away from the house. It looked as if Saxon were planning to put a lot of work into the book. That would mean a lot of work for her, she thought—not that she minded. It was just that she dreaded the enforced proximity with him. She was uncertain of her powers of resistance if he began to put on pressure. She didn't think she could survive an affair with him. Bret, on the other hand, was a nice safe man with no evil intentions who could be her shield against Saxon's ardor. At least she hoped he could. And she had a feeling that she was going to need one.

The next two days went by smoothly and with surprising speed. Saxon dictated, Maggie wrote and typed, and work on the manuscript progressed nicely.

On the third day they worked right through supper, eating on trays in his study, where they locked themselves so that they wouldn't be interrupted by the rest of the family.

"Getting tired?" he asked after they'd finished eating and Maggie had taken ten more pages of dictation.

She stretched lazily. "Not terribly. Are you?"

He leaned back in the swivel chair behind his desk, his powerful chest muscles emphasized by the long-sleeved beige silk shirt he was wearing as he lifted his arms. "I very rarely feel the need for rest this early," he confessed. "I enjoy working. I like what I do."

"And that's probably why you've made such a success of it," she remarked. Her eyes studied his hard, deeply lined face. "Saxon, haven't you ever wanted a family of your own?" she asked suddenly.

He laughed shortly. "What brought that on?"

"I don't know," she admitted. "It's something I've wondered about, that's all."

His eyes darkened as his head turned toward the sound of her voice. "I could ask you the same question."

She smiled wistfully. "Yes, I'd like a home and children of my own. It just never happened for me. I'd have to love a man very much to consider living the rest of my life with him."

"And you've never loved anyone like that?" he probed.

She shrugged. "I've thought I was in love once or

twice," she said softly, not adding that one of those times was with him, and that she still felt that way.

He sat very still, his whole posture attentive. "And?"

"It didn't work out" was all she'd admit to. "And you?"

He leaned back in his chair. "I found the woman I wanted," he said harshly. "I just couldn't keep her."

She was suddenly and violently jealous of the faceless woman, but she schooled her voice not to show it. Her hands clasped each other tightly in her lap.

"Did it…have something to do with your blindness?" she asked quietly.

"Everything," he growled.

And for that, he blamed her. He didn't have to say it; it was in the hard lines of his face, in his sharp half-angry tone. And what could she do? Nothing would restore his sight, according to what he'd told her.

"Have you thought about going back to see your doctor?" she asked after a minute.

"What for?" he asked wearily. "The problem is a piece of shrapnel, Maggie. Unless it miraculously shifts from its present position, there's nothing to be done. They've already told me that." He got up from the chair and felt his way around the edge of the desk and to the sofa where Maggie was sitting rigidly on the edge of her seat.

"Where are you?" he asked, reaching out a big hand slowly.

She caught his fingers and curled hers around them. "I'm right here," she said, and her eyes adored him.

His own fingers moved, wrapping themselves warmly around hers, and he smiled. "How long has it been since I've kissed you?"

"Oh, a lifetime or so," she returned lightly. But her heart was racing, her breath was catching, and her eyes were on his broad mouth with an aching hunger.

"Too much work and too little play isn't good for either one of us, you know," he said softly.

"So they say," she replied in a breathless tone.

His fingers tightened. He leaned back against the sofa. His free hand flicked open the buttons of his shirt lazily, and a slow, sensual smile touched his mouth.

"Suppose you come here," he murmured deeply, "and I'll give you a refresher course in basic lust?"

She laughed helplessly. "Why, you lecherous old tycoon, you!"

He sobered, his eyes narrowing. "Maggie, do I really seem old to you?" he asked suddenly, and as if it mattered.

Her heart ached for him. She felt a tinge of regret for the thoughtless teasing. "No," she said softly, easing down into his warm, hard arms to pillow her cheek against his hair-roughened chest. "No, you don't seem old to me at all. Just mature and sensuous, and quite deliciously masculine."

He caught his breath. His hand pressed her cheek against the warm muscles, moving it slowly, rhythmically against him. His breathing quickened at the feel of her skin; his heart thundered at her ear. "Sensuous?" he murmured huskily.

"Very," she admitted, and felt her own breath becoming ragged. She liked the feel of the curling hair, faintly abrasive at her eyes, against her nose, against the corner of her mouth. Her lips parted and she moved, turning them against his chest, enjoying the tangy scent of soap and cologne and pure man in her nostrils as she breathed him. His hands caught in her hair, tangling in it as if he enjoyed its silky texture, and he brought her lips against him in a slow circular pattern.

She let him guide her mouth, tasting him as she felt the hard edge of his belt against her cheek, her hands enjoying the rough warmth of his chest in a silence that burned with sweet sensation.

Her fingers tangled in the wiry hair over the warm muscles, testing its strength as she drew back to look at him.

His hand touched her face, long fingers tracing her eyes, her eyebrows, her nose and cheeks and chin and the soft line of her mouth.

"I wish I could see you," he murmured softly, his voice deep and quiet in the stillness of the room. "You're very quiet when I hold you—your voice gives away nothing until I arouse you completely."

She buried her face in his warm throat, touched by the words, by the softness of his voice. "Can't you tell that you please me?" she whispered.

"I don't want to know what you're feeling," he murmured. "Your body tells me that. I want to know what you're thinking."

"Why?"

His fingers moved down to her neck, catching in the softness of her hair to ease her head back on his chest, arching her throat.

"Your heart's going faster by the second," he remarked quietly. His fingers slipped down to the soft, firm roundness of her breast and cupped it as if she were already his possession.

"So is yours," she whispered back shakily.

He bent, his mouth brushing hers gently. "Lie with

me," he whispered, easing her down with him on the sofa. "Let's make love to each other and forget the world and the darkness. Let's forget everything...except this..."

His mouth took hers, warm and hard and frankly hungry, his arms bending her into the hard contours of his body while the kiss went on and on.

Vaguely she felt his hands under the soft T-shirt she was wearing, lifting it, finding the small clasp that held her bra together and unfastening it with slow deft hands.

"Saxon..." she protested weakly.

"Let me," he whispered, finding her with his hands. "You know you want to."

Of course, she did; that was the whole trouble, Maggie thought. Denying herself the magic of his touch on her bare skin was as impossible as denying she loved him.

His mouth brushed lazily, teasingly, across hers. "Take it off," he murmured.

"The family—"

"The door's locked, remember?" he whispered, half amused. "And I can't see you..."

What good did protesting matter anyway? she wondered dimly as his hands went to work, easing the top and the bra from her before he laid her gently back down on the soft cushions.

He started to move down, but she pushed gently at his own shirt with hands that should have been protesting, not helping him.

"Do you want it off?" he asked tautly, his usual control oddly faltering.

"Please," she whispered.

He stripped off the shirt and tossed it onto the carpet,

and she caught her breath at the size of his chest and shoulders, the huge muscular arms and the arrowing of dark hair that ran down surely past his belted waist.

"Do you like what you see?" he asked under his breath as he eased down so that she could feel only the warmth of his torso but not its touch.

"Oh, yes," she whispered, and her eyes worshipped him. "Yes, I like it very much."

"I wish I could look at you," he breathed gruffly, easing slowly, slowly down so that she felt him first as a whisper then, with tormenting pleasure, felt the abrasive masculinity that teased and stirred her body until it told him blatantly how much it wanted his.

His mouth was tender on her face while his fingers, softly touching and exploring textures, sought and found the proof of her arousal.

"Do I feel as good to you as you feel to me?" he asked in a curt undertone.

"Yes," she breathed into his mouth.

His hands moved down to her narrow hips, bringing them sensuously against his, grinding them against him slowly. She moaned softly, and he caught the tiny sound under his mouth, smothering it. His tongue teased her lips and darted into her mouth; she felt her body go rigid with desire and wondered how it could bear the tension of wanting and not having.

He whispered barely intelligible words into her ears, endearments mingled with remarks that made her skin burn and her body tingle.

"Am I shocking you?" He laughed breathlessly as his body moved completely over hers, letting her feel the powerful contours crushing her down into the soft cushions.

"Yes, you beast, you are," she gasped, trying without success to catch her breath as his hips moved against hers with shattering intimacy.

"Don't just lie under me," he ground out. "Help me."

Her nails dug into his powerful arms. "Saxon, don't," she pleaded shakily as the unfamiliar intimacy made her tremble. "Please, don't."

"I want you," he replied tautly. "And what's more, you want me. Do you think I can't feel it, taste it?"

"Not…like this," she pleaded, knowing that if she didn't reach him soon, she never would. "Please!"

His breath was coming heavily and hard. He hesitated, his sightless eyes looking down as if trying to see her. "Is it the setting that bothers you?" he growled. "We could go up to my bedroom, or yours."

"You know why," she whispered.

His jaw tautened. "I know you're a virgin, if that's what you mean. I won't hurt you, Maggie."

"You only want me because you're blind," she shot at him, desperate for ammunition, and hated the words when she felt him stiffen. "That's all it is, Saxon. You want me because I'm a woman and I'm handy!"

His face darkened angrily. He pushed himself away from her and sat up, so sensuously attractive that it was all she could do not to throw herself on him. But she gritted her teeth and put her bra and blouse back on, avoiding looking at him.

"Hand me my shirt," he said curtly, as if he hated having to ask her even for that.

She put it into his outstretched hand and turned away when he pulled it back on.

She heard the click of his lighter as he lighted a cigarette and smelled the acrid smoke a minute later.

"You wanted me enough that night in my room," he said with biting sarcasm. "What happened, Maggie? Did you suddenly get turned off by my loss of sight, or did your dinner partner have something to do with it?"

"Dinner partner?" she murmured, remembering Bret and the invitation she was going to have to own up to.

"Bret Aikens," he reminded her.

"He's very nice," she said noncommittally.

"Mother said you and Bret had a lot of common interests," he said shortly.

She sighed. "Well, we both like history," she admitted. "In fact, he's taking me to Spartanburg tomorrow to see some special points of interest there," she added defiantly.

His face went livid. She could see miniature explosions in his eyes. "Like hell he is," he said. "You've got work to do!"

"Not tomorrow I haven't," she told him. "I'm going."

"Not while you're working for me!"

She threw back her hair and started toward the door. "I'm either going to Spartanburg tomorrow or I'm going home to Georgia tomorrow," she shot back at him from the safety of the doorway. "And there isn't one thing you can do to stop me!"

She went out, slamming the door noisily behind her.

Saxon wasn't up when Bret came to pick her up promptly at eight thirty the next morning, and Maggie breathed a sigh of relief. She'd really been prepared to pack her bag and go home if she'd had trouble about the trip, but she was secretly glad that she didn't have to carry out the threat. Leaving Saxon now was going to be worse than having a tooth pulled without anesthetic, and no doubt it would hurt for a long time.

But she schooled herself to forget the future and concentrate on one day at a time. Bret was good company, keeping up a pleasant, undemanding conversation as they headed down to catch one interstate going east and another going south.

"We'll bypass Spartanburg on the way down to Woodruff," he explained, "to see the Price House, but we'll go back that way through Roebuck, where the Walnut Grove Plantation is located, and we'll swing through Spartanburg before we go home. Okay?"

"Sounds great," she told him. "You must know your way pretty well."

"I do," he agreed. "I've been there several times. I like history," he added with a grin.

It was a beautiful drive, through some of the prettiest country Maggie had ever seen, although it seemed to take a long time. But when they got to Woodruff, it wasn't quite time for the towering brick house to be open to the public, and they had to go to a nearby restaurant and drink coffee until eleven o'clock. When they got back, other tourists had gathered.

Bret paid the admission, refusing Maggie's offer of money, and then she forgot all about money as they toured the historic Price House. It had a steep gambrel roof and inside end chimneys, an acutely unique style for the Deep South. The bricks for the house with its flat face were made on the premises and laid in Flemish bond. It sat on what was once a two-thousand-acre plantation and was built in 1795—to serve as an inn as well as a home. Thomas Price, whose brainchild it was, also ran a post office and a general store. Period furniture graced the house, and Maggie felt the pull of the past strongly in its gracefully aging confines. The county historic preservation commission had obviously been active in the restoration.

When the tour was over, they climbed back into the car and headed north to Roebuck to tour Walnut Grove Plantation.

Maggie fell in love with the house, with its graceful front porch and chimneys at each end. It was clapboard over log construction with Queen Anne mantels and fielded paneling, and featured antique furnishings and accessories which portrayed living conditions in Spartanburg County before 1830.

The separate kitchen featured a collection of eighteenth-century utensils. There was a blacksmith's forge, a meat house and a barn. And the office of the first doctor in the county.

All in all, it was fascinating. But Maggie found herself drawn to the grounds with their ancient oaks and walnuts, and the Moore family cemetery where Margaret Katherine Moore Barry was buried, along with other family members, slaves and Revolutionary soldiers.

"She was a scout for General Morgan at the Battle of Cowpens," Bret remarked, nodding toward the grave, "and the daughter of the house."

"She must have been quite a lady," Maggie reflected, closing her eyes to drink in the delicious autumn air. "I wonder if she minds all these people tramping through on floors that she swept with her own hands, and staring at her grave?"

"I doubt if she had to sweep floors," he murmured.

"I'm sure there were servants," she agreed. "But a woman brave enough to scout for the army would hardly be afraid to pick up a broom if she needed to. I'll bet she was something special," she added with a smile. "One of the first liberated women."

He laughed. "I've always thought that myself. The past is always with us, isn't it?" he mused, sticking his hands in his pockets to stare back at the house. "We're always curious about those who came before us. How they lived. How they survived. How they loved and hated, and how they died. The same as someday future historians will be curious about us, and our time."

She shivered delicately. "I don't like to think about that. We'll be dead."

He turned back. "What a profound thought. Are you afraid to die?"

She sighed. "Yes and no. I'm a good Presbyterian, you know, and I try to live my religion. But I'm not always as good as I wish I were," she added with a laugh.

"None of us is. I just live one day at a time, myself," he told her, "and do the best I can."

She smiled at him. "Which is all any of us can do, I suppose. The leaves are going," she added, nodding toward the partial bareness of some of the trees behind the house.

"We'd better be doing the same," he told her, checking his watch. "My gosh, I didn't realize it was so late. We're not going to have time for Cowpens today, I'm afraid. As it is, we'll be going home in the dark once we stop for supper."

"My fault," she said, apologizing. "I was so fascinated that I couldn't leave—"

"I enjoyed it," he said, cutting her off and grinning. "I like to see people appreciate history. Especially in my own state. Ready?"

"Whenever you are. It's been a great day," she added. "Thank you."

"Thank you," he returned. "We'll have to do this again."

She murmured something, not committing herself, because she was already dreading going back to the house. Saxon was going to be out for blood, and she knew it.

Lisa and Randy had gone out when Maggie said good-night to Bret and walked into the silence of the house. But Sandra was still up, pacing the floor. She stopped at the sight of Maggie and went quickly out into the hall to meet her.

"Thank goodness you're home," she said with evident relief, a worried frown between her worried eyes. "Oh, Maggie, will you go up and see if Saxon will talk to you? He's locked himself in his room and hasn't eaten anything… He won't let Randy in, he won't let me in—it's just so unlike him," she concluded helplessly. "Something must be wrong, and I'm so worried. Will you… ?"

"Of course," Maggie said gently, knowing what was wrong. It would have been amusing in other circumstances—a grown man throwing a tantrum because he hadn't got his own way. But as she mounted the stairs she began to think about how very vulnerable his blindness made him. Sighted, he'd have forced her hand about Bret. They'd have fought it out verbally, or he might have come after her, but he'd never have locked himself away out of pique. He was blind, and it made him helpless in a new and frightening way. He couldn't deal with the world as he used to.

She sighed as she paused in front of his door before she knocked.

"Saxon?" she called gently.

There was no response. None at all.

She knocked again, louder. "Saxon!"

This time there was a muffled sound. "Go away!" His voice sounded strangely slurred.

"It's Maggie," she called again. "Please let me in!"

There was a long pause, during which she really worried. Then there was a thud and the sound of furniture and the door being knocked. A key turned. The door opened.

She gaped up at him, catching her breath. He was pale; his hair was tousled, his face unshaven. And he was standing there absolutely nude, without a stitch of clothing on his big, hair-roughened body.

CHAPTER TEN

MAGGIE GASPED, BUT she couldn't drag her startled, fascinated eyes away. He was as appealing as a delicately carved Greek statue, not an ounce of flab or fat on him, all muscle and blatant masculinity.

"If you're coming in, come on," he growled, turning to weave his way back toward the bed.

She followed him, closing the door behind her, and watched him collapse into the rumpled brown sheets with a groan.

"You're ill," she burst out.

"I'm something," he said weakly. "Get me something cold to drink, will you, honey? God, I'm burning up!"

She had to steel herself to move closer, but she finally gathered enough courage to stand beside him and touch his broad forehead. It was blistering hot to the touch.

"Flu, I'll bet," she mumbled. "I'll be right back. And you should be under the covers."

"Then cover me up," he growled huskily. "God, it's hot…"

He was rambling. She pulled the covers gently over him and went downstairs to tell Sandra, who in turn called the family doctor. He'd just arrived and gone upstairs when Lisa and Randy came in.

"What's going on?" Randy asked quickly.

"It's Saxon," Sandra said. "Maggie says he's burning with fever."

Randy shook his head. "Boy, that's one for the books," he remarked. "I can only remember half a dozen times I've ever seen him sick. How about some coffee while we wait for the verdict?"

"Maggie and I will make it," Lisa volunteered, leading her sister off into the kitchen.

"How bad is he?" Lisa asked as they filled the pot and made four strong cups of coffee.

"I don't know," Maggie mumbled. She put cups and saucers on a tray with cream and sugar. "I feel like it's my fault. He didn't want me to go out with Bret, and I did it for spite…"

Lisa touched her arm gently. "It's probably just a virus. He'll be all right, really he will. He's so strong."

Tears misted the older woman's eyes, but she managed to smile through them. "I hope so."

Lisa hugged her. "Come on, let's go drink our coffee."

The doctor was back down in a few minutes, shaking his head. "Stubbornest man I ever knew," he grumbled, refusing Sandra's offer of coffee. "It's a virus, one of those forty-eight-hour things that I've seen a dozen cases of so far this week. I gave him an antibiotic and wrote a prescription for some tablets." He dug it out of his pocket and handed it to Sandra. "Give him those twice a day until they're all gone, keep him in bed, give him plenty of fluids, have him take aspirin for the aching. If he isn't better in three days, call me."

"Thank you, Doctor Johnson," Sandra said gently. "I hated to ask you out at this hour of the night."

He grinned. "No trouble. It was a change from delivering babies. That's usually what I get called out at night for. Night."

"Good night."

Sandra escorted him out and started upstairs, leaving the rest of them to follow.

Saxon was under the covers, thank goodness, Maggie thought as they filed into his bedroom, but he looked like death, and he was still hot with fever.

"He needs sponging," Sandra remarked, wringing her hands nervously. "Randy…"

"Maggie," Saxon called huskily, holding out his hand. "The rest of you go watch television or something. I only need Maggie."

"But, darling…" Sandra protested gently.

Saxon's dark eyes opened threateningly, as intimidating without sight as they had been with it. "I said I want Maggie," he repeated hotly. "No one else!"

"We'd better humor him, Mother," Randy said with a wicked smile at Maggie. "He has good taste in nurses, after all."

"Are you sure you don't mind?" Sandra asked Maggie with a worried look.

"I don't mind at all," Maggie lied as she realized what staying with him was going to mean, and she still wasn't quite over the shock of seeing him au naturel.

"If you need us…" Lisa began.

"I'll scream and run up a flag, okay?" Maggie teased. "I've nursed you and Dad through flu and viruses. I know what to do. But I sure could use another cup of coffee."

"I'll bring you one," Lisa promised. She followed the others out the door and closed it behind her.

"My cold drink," Saxon added, reminding her.

"Oh, my gosh!" She ran to the door. "Lisa, will you bring Saxon a tall glass of something cold, please?" she called to her sister.

"Sure thing!" came the reply, drifting back up the staircase.

"Top reporter," Saxon chided when he heard her approach the bed. "Photographic memory."

"I was worried," she excused herself, reaching down to hold his big hand in her own. "Do you feel any better?"

"Why do people always think that having a needle stuck in their arms will improve their complaints?" he growled. "Now my arm hurts as well as the rest of me. Dan put the damned needle through the bone!"

"Shame on you," she scolded gently. "Here he comes all the way out here in the middle of the night to see about you, and all you want to do is complain about the way he gives shots. I ought to call him up and tell him how ungrateful you are."

"You would, too, you little headache," he muttered, drawing in a hard breath. His eyes closed. "Maggie, I feel like hell. Don't leave me."

Her fingers tightened in his. "I won't. I won't."

He drank every drop of the iced soft drink that Lisa brought up with Maggie's coffee and then dozed off. But he woke again not two hours later, tossing and turning, and the fever was blazing.

The rest of the family had already gone to bed, but Maggie remembered what Sandra had said about sponging him down. It would certainly help to bring the fever back to normal while the antibiotic had time to work.

She got a basin and a soft sponge and, gritting her teeth, pulled back the covers and began to draw the damp sponge over his feverish body.

He stiffened at first at the unfamiliar touch, and then relaxed and lay back with a hard sigh, his eyes closed, his limbs barely stirring. She lingered over him, feeling his skin cool, watching the expressions that drifted over his broad, hard face. He needed her. For a few hours, he actually needed her.

She finished and drew the covers back over him, and he slept again. She sat beside him in an armchair, watching him, drinking in the sight of him, until the small hours of the morning. She could just barely keep her eyes open, and suddenly she couldn't keep them open at all. Her body slumped sideways in the chair and she slept.

He was still asleep when she woke and leaned forward to touch his face. It was cool, thank goodness; the fever had broken. She left him long enough to freshen up and change into a pair of brown jeans with a beige pullover top, and to get a tray to take back upstairs. Sandra had a meeting that morning with her church group, and Randy and Lisa were going downtown to start shopping for furniture for their new home.

"Do you mind if we all desert you?" Sandra asked. "If he'd let us sit with him, I'd certainly do my share."

"I know that," Maggie said with a smile. "I don't mind, really."

"A labor of love, my dear?" Sandra asked in a tone soft with understanding.

Maggie, unembarrassed, nodded. "I'd better get this upstairs before he wakes," she said, indicating the tray. "I hope I can get him to eat something, even if it's just a piece of toast."

"Well," Randy remarked, "if he'll do it for anyone, it'll be for you."

"I hope you're right," she returned. "See you all later."

She fitted herself into the big armchair by his bed and nibbled at a piece of toast while she drank her coffee. He began to stir, his powerful legs flexing, and the covers went flying as he stretched.

"Maggie?" he murmured, turning his head toward the chair.

"I'm—I'm here," she managed to say, fighting to keep her eyes on his face.

One corner of his mouth turned up. "What color is your face?"

She cleared her throat. "How about some coffee and toast? I brought a pot and several buttered slices, and some jam."

He tugged the covers back up to his waist and sat up, propping back against the pillows. "I'd love the coffee, and one piece of toast, but without jam. I still feel a little weak. Have you been here all night?"

"Yes," she said, fixing his coffee and putting it within his reach, along with a piece of toast. She told him where it was and went back to her chair to watch him sip and nibble. "Randy's going to get your prescription filled and bring it back at lunchtime. The doctor said you didn't have to start them until tonight."

He finished his toast and swallowed his coffee. "I feel rusted," he remarked with a hard sigh. "Run me a tub of water, Maggie, and help me into it. And have the maid change these sheets, will you?"

"I'll change them," she said. "If you could wait until Randy gets home."

He lifted an eyebrow. "Embarrassed? There's nothing left that you haven't already seen. You're a big girl."

"Yes, I am, but—"

"Haven't you ever seen a man without his clothes before?"

"In books," she grumbled.

"Not in the flesh?" he teased. "My God, what a shock it must have been."

"Saxon, can't you wait until Randy gets back?" she asked.

He drew in a slow breath. "Maggie, I feel as if I haven't bathed for weeks, can you understand? I just want a tub of water. If you're too damned inhibited to help me, I'll manage alone."

"You make me sound like a prude," she grumbled. "All right, I'll help you. I don't suppose I could be any more shocked than I already am anyway."

"There's nothing shocking about nudity," he said. "Anyway God must not have thought so, because he made us originally without complete wardrobes."

"I suppose so," she admitted reluctantly. "But people can make something disgusting out of it."

"Like pornography?" he asked. "Yes, I know. They take an act of love and make an act of degradation out of it. But between people who love each other, Maggie, it becomes an expression of something more than desire. Just as bodies become more than objects of depravity."

She got up, smoothing down her T-shirt. "I'm shy with you," she confessed. "It's something I can't help, I don't have the experience to pretend sophistication."

"I'm glad you haven't," he said quietly. "I don't want you to get that kind of experience with any man except me."

She cleared her throat. "I'll run the water."

His soft laughter followed her like a relentless wind.

When she'd filled the big tub and turned on the whirlpool, she arranged towels and washcloths and went back to get him, her heart in her throat.

He tossed aside the covers and stood up, unembarrassed even when she hesitated, and he must have known that she was looking at him.

"Care to get close enough to lend me your hand?" he teased.

"Of course." She took his fingers in hers and led him into the big blue-tiled bathroom. "Sorry, I was just reviewing an anatomy lesson," she added with a mischievous smile.

"Disappointed, Maggie?" he asked softly.

She lowered his hand to the side of the big tub. "I'll bet they absolutely swoon when you undress," she murmured.

"Why don't you climb in here with me?" he asked after a minute, his voice taut and coaxing all at once.

"Well…"

"It's a big tub," he remarked. "You couldn't have had time to bathe this morning…"

Just the thought of being that close to him took her breath away, but she had just enough sanity left to refuse.

"I'll...have mine later," she breathed. "I—I had one before I left yesterday anyway."

"Coward," he accused silkily. He climbed into the tub and stretched out. "God, that feels good! Maggie, how about soaping my back, since you won't get in with me?"

She took the cloth and lathered it, sitting on the edge of the tub and trying not to feel the sensuous maleness of his muscular body as she drew it over his broad back and shoulders.

"Here," he murmured, drawing her hands around to his chest, leaning back with a contented sigh to let her soap it as well. Somewhere along the way, the cloth got lost, and her fingers were drawn to him like moths to a flame. Her breath caught; her heart seemed to be trying to climb up her throat as she explored the hard contours of his torso in a silence that blazed with excitement.

"Come in here with me," he breathed roughly. "I won't do anything you don't want me to do."

Her mind rebelled at the suggestion, even as her fingers were fumbling with her top and her jeans, and she was telling herself that this was insane, insane! But her body trembled with wanting, asserting itself for the first time in her life, demanding what it needed to survive.

She eased down into the warm water with him, feeling her skin slide against him, his powerful, hair-roughened thigh against her own, his arm reaching out to draw her close at his side.

"You see?" His voice was rough, ragged. "Maggie, you see?"

The words didn't make sense, but then they had nothing to do with what was happening, and they both knew it. Inevitably he turned, turning her with him so that her body was drawn fully against the length of his, and she felt the silken brush of flesh on flesh for the first time in the smooth warmth of the bathwater. Her legs entwined with his, trembling, her body tautened as her arms went around his shoulders and her breasts flattened against the soapy hair on his chest.

"Now," he groaned. His arms trembled as they drew her closer, and his mouth moved down to crush hers. The water swallowed them up to their necks, and under its churning surface she could feel his hands touching her as no man ever had before, exploring her, gentling her for what was surely to come.

"But…but we can't," she managed in a choked, half-whispered moan, trembling all over at the long sweet contact with his body.

"Why not?" he breathed, his tongue probing, darting past her teeth into the dark softness of her mouth, his hands gently lifting her hips and touching her thighs.

"Here?" she cried, but she was clinging, arching, and all at once there was such a terrible urgency as she felt him move her, ease and surge against her, and her mouth bit into his, her nails wounded, her voice cried out wildly in the sudden silence as the world darkened and reddened and spun away in a shimmer of fiery explosions around her and pain became a kind of terrible sweet necessity…

Maggie had always heard that men lost interest once their appetites were satisfied, but Saxon held her and brushed soft, tender kisses all over her face until she was calm once more. His fingers moved against her cheeks, her mouth, her neck, and he murmured things she barely heard at all, her body still racked by the aftermath of a pleasure that defied description.

"I thought…it was supposed to hurt," she murmured into his shoulder, feeling a little chill, as the water was just barely lukewarm.

"It did," he murmured at her ear. "You just didn't care," he added with a smile in his voice.

She drew back a little, embarrassed. "It's so strange, that you can want, *need,* pain in small doses. Why?"

"I don't know either, darling," he confessed quietly. "I only know that in all my life, there's never been anything like this, with anyone. I'm only just beginning to understand why the French call lovemaking 'the little death.'"

"It was that, wasn't it?" she breathed, leaning forward to brush her mouth softly against his, loving the hard warmth of it, loving the feel of his body next to hers.

He drew in a deep breath, his hands going to her shoulders, an odd kind of concern in his scowling expression. "Maggie, we'd better get out of here. The water's going cold."

"Oh, yes—yes, of course," she stammered. She struggled out, grabbing up a towel to wrap around herself and handing a larger one to him. They dried themselves in a stiff silence, and she walked back in the bedroom ahead of him to get a pair of pajama bottoms. She handed them to him and turned away to dress herself. When he finished, she led him back to his bed.

"I'll dry your hair, if you like," she volunteered in a dull tone.

"No," he sighed. "It's all right, I've gotten most of the water out of it. You'd better dry your own."

"I—I'll do that." She searched for something to say, but she was oddly shy with him now; she felt nervous, uncertain. He seemed to regret what had happened, and she turned away, still trying to reconcile her body's demanding hunger with her own reticence. She hadn't believed people could lose control of themselves so easily, so completely. Now it had happened, and the thought suddenly occurred to her that she could be pregnant. She hadn't even thought about the consequences—not once! All her upbringing, all her principles, had fallen to the wayside because of her unquenchable desire for a man who'd wanted nothing more than a body. And now he was regretting it, and so was she, but it was too late.

She dried her hair and spent several minutes in her room, trying to compose herself enough to go back. But the longer she waited, the more impossible it seemed. How could she face him after that wild abandon? *In the bathtub!* How could she ever face him again? Her eyes closed. Her body was already beginning to feel bruised from the porcelain. They must have been out of their minds!

Well, at least Saxon knew now that he was still a man, despite his blindness, she thought bitterly. And since he had what he'd wanted from her since she came back here, he probably wouldn't want her again. Had it been desire? Or had he been jealous of Bret—so jealous that he felt he had to assert his mastery over her? Or were there deeper, darker reasons? Was it revenge for what that misplaced byline had caused, revenge for the blindness that his subconscious blamed her for causing?

The thought paralyzed her. At the time she'd thought it was out of love. She'd convinced herself that the endearments he'd whispered, the ardent commands that led her into the sweet wildness of emotion, had been purely out of love. But now she had doubts. Couldn't any woman have pleased him, despite what he'd said? Couldn't he have attained that pleasure with anyone? After all, Maggie thought, men were structured to enjoy sex regardless of their partners—weren't they?

The longer she hesitated, the bigger the doubts grew, until she convinced herself that what had happened was nothing more than a sordid excursion into animal pleasure, a mistake that never should have happened.

She moved out into the hall just as Randy came down it.

"Randy, would you change the sheets for Saxon?" she asked hurriedly. "I've got to go out for a few minutes…"

"Oh, sure," he agreed with a pleasant smile. "Did you get any rest?"

"I slept a little, I just need some fresh air, that's all," she assured him. "Thanks a million."

She darted down the staircase, grateful that there was no one in sight, because she was crying.

She wandered around out on the grounds for hours, brooding, hating herself, hating Saxon. There was only one thing to do. Go home. Now. Before, out of some horrible circumstance, she wound up in his arms again. Once could be excused on the grounds of temporary insanity, but twice would be unforgivable.

She wrapped her arms around her, feeling the cold as

never before. She went back into the house and up the staircase, feeling like a prisoner going to the guillotine.

She knocked at Saxon's door, jumping when she heard the harsh "Come in!"

She opened the door and moved hesitantly into the room. He was under the sheets, smoking a cigarette, his face dark and lined heavily.

"Who is it?" he asked.

"Maggie," she said hesitantly.

A remarkably elated expression crossed his broad face; his eyes seemed to kindle as they turned toward the sound of her voice.

"Maggie!" he breathed. He held out his free hand. "Honey, come here."

She moved closer, but she wouldn't take the outstretched hand. She avoided it as if it were a red-hot poker.

"I've—I've been thinking," she said.

"So have I," he admitted, reluctantly drawing his hand back to clench it on the covers. "Maggie, we'd better get married."

Of all the things she'd expected him to say, that was the last, the very last. She stood gaping at him as if he'd offered to eat one of the curtains at the window.

"Why?" she blurted out.

He took a draw from the cigarette, looking impatient and terribly irritated. "Because you could be pregnant," he said bluntly. "Or hasn't that occurred to you? I was too far gone to think about protecting you."

She caught her breath. "That's not the best reason to get married," she said quietly, forcing her voice to be calm, to deny what she wanted most in all the world— to be Saxon's wife.

"What would be a good one then?" he asked harshly.

"Love," she returned. "On both sides, Saxon, not just one."

He seemed to freeze, to become rigid. His hand on the bed clenched until the knuckles were white, but her eyes were on his face and she didn't see them.

"You don't think love could come naturally?" he asked after a minute.

"I think we'd be crazy to take such a chance," she said sadly. Her eyes closed.

"And then, too, I'm blind," he ground out. "Not the greatest prospective husband in the world."

"That has nothing to do with it!" she protested. "Saxon, if you had your sight, none of this would even have happened, don't you realize that? You wouldn't have been jealous enough of Bret to seduce me, or so hungry for a woman that you lost your head. You wouldn't have—have wanted me!" Her voice broke, and with a tiny cry she whirled and ran for the door.

"Maggie, you crazy little fool!" he burst out. "Maggie!"

But she didn't stop, couldn't stop. He didn't love her. It was only guilt that made him suggest marriage, because he thought she might be pregnant. She couldn't let him trap himself into a marriage he didn't want. Without love it would never be enough. And if he fell in love with someone else, and found himself tied to her, it would have been more than she could bear.

She ran down the stairs, her eyes blinded by tears, vaguely aware of footsteps behind her. She stopped on the bottom step as she heard Saxon calling her.

She looked up to see him on the top step, his hand clutching at the banister.

"Saxon, no!" she screamed as his hand missed. "No!"

But the warning came too late. He went headfirst down the stairs with a horrible thud, tossing and pitching. She rushed toward him, but she wasn't in time to break the fall. She felt her own head knock against a step as she helped to stop his descent, but she held on, praying that it would be enough to spare him more pain.

They came to a tumbled heap at the bottom of the steps, sprawled over each other. She dragged herself up and looked at him. He was unconscious; his eyes were closed, his face white and devoid of expression, and there was blood at his right temple.

CHAPTER ELEVEN

THE NEXT FEW hours went by in a blur. Maggie must have screamed because when she looked up, Randy and Sandra were bending over Saxon, and Lisa was holding her close to keep her from throwing herself on Saxon's unconscious body.

She could barely tell them what had happened, her voice incoherent through tears, her eyes riveted to Saxon, her hand clinging to his until the arrival of the ambulance, which seemed to have taken an eternity. She rode with him in it, never leaving his side until they took him into the emergency room.

Finally Dr. Johnson came out to speak to the family, with a long technical description of what had happened.

"The most important thing," he concluded, holding Sandra's trembling hands tightly as the others gathered around him, "is that, because of the fall, the shrapnel has shifted. It's still not operable, but—with any luck at all, my dear—when Saxon recovers, he'll be able to see again."

Sandra caught her breath, and Maggie's face lighted up. He might be able to see! If that happened, perhaps he could even forgive her for this, for putting him in the hospital...

Tears rolled down Maggie's cheeks. If only. If only! She wouldn't mind giving him up if it would mean having him sighted again. She wouldn't mind losing him forever, as long as he could feel whole again. It would be worth anything!

Sandra turned toward her when the doctor had gone, promising to advise them of every new development.

"You see?" she whispered tearfully, holding Maggie close for an instant. "Everything always works out for the best. You were blaming yourself, my dear, but if he hadn't taken that fall…he may see again! He may see again."

Randy reached out a brotherly hand and ruffled Maggie's hair. "Will you calm down now?" He grinned. "It's going to be fine. Honest it is."

Lisa added her own enthusiasm to Randy's, gathering Maggie to her side. They stayed all through the long day until Saxon was finally conscious and able to receive visitors. They had to go in one at a time, so Maggie let the others go first—not so much out of consideration as pure cowardice. Finally it was her turn.

Maggie had never been as nervous as when she paused at the door of his room. She was wearing a simple green shirtwaist dress in a soft wool blend, beige boots, and her hair was soft and freshly washed and curling around her face. It had grown a little, but it would take a long time for it to grow as long as it had been when she first met Saxon, Maggie thought. She wondered how long it would take his thick hair to grow out again.

She pushed open the door and went in, surprised to find him sitting up in bed. The room, Maggie noticed, was dimly lighted.

He turned when she walked in, and his pupils seemed to dilate as they looked at her. They traced every line of her face before they fell to her body, lingering lovingly on every soft curve of it. He smiled faintly, his face mirroring masculine appreciation.

"Several days too late to do me much good," he murmured enigmatically, and caught her eyes just as the statement made blatant sense in her whirling mind.

She colored, and he saw it and laughed gently.

"Come in and sit down," he said.

She moved to the chair by the bed and sat on its edge, her purse held tensely on her lap.

"How—how are you?" she asked hesitantly. "How do you feel?"

"Sore," he murmured with a wry smile. "Tough as nails. Delighted. Able to conquer the world. A lot of things. Maggie, how do you feel?"

"Guilty," she replied without thinking, and her eyelids flinched as she looked at him. "Saxon, I'm so sorry!"

"For what?" he burst out. "For making it possible for me to see again? You crazy woman!"

"For making you fall down the staircase!" she corrected. "You could have broken your neck!"

"But I didn't. And it was worth it." His eyes searched hers and narrowed. "You were wrong, you know," he added quietly. "You don't seem to believe what I say, but it was you I wanted that morning, no one else."

She dropped her eyes. "Please, let's not talk about it. I only want to forget."

There was a potent silence before he spoke. "Was it that bad?" he ground out.

She swallowed. "How long will you have to be in the hospital?" she asked.

"Stop hedging," he said, watching her. "I want you to tell me. Was it that bad?"

She looked up, and the memory of lying in his big arms lighted a candle inside her, making her face glow with remembered pleasure. "No," she admitted.

With a long sigh he leaned back against the pillows, and his eyes closed for an instant. "I can see a distinct advantage in being sighted with you," he muttered. "You can hide things from me if all I have to go by is your voice."

She stared at the purse in her lap. "How does it feel—to be able to see?"

"There aren't words enough," he said simply. "We take sight for granted, you know, until we don't have it anymore. A simple thing like staring at the ceiling takes on mammoth proportions." He smiled faintly. "I'll never take it for granted again, I promise you."

"What will you do now?" she asked gently.

He shrugged. "When they let me out of here, I'll go back to work," he said. His head turned and he stared at her through narrowed eyes. "Still feeling guilty, or are you just wondering whether or not I'll be willing to part with your 'services' now that I can see again?"

It was like a slap in the face. *Services*—as if she were a common prostitute. She stiffened, but years of reporting had taught her to conceal her deepest emotions behind a mask, and she did it now.

She laughed shortly. "You'll hardly need me, with all those very eligible beauties vying for your attention, will you?"

"Missing your job?" he said, taunting.

She shrugged. "I always have," she said with a cool smile. "I haven't found anything yet that could replace it."

"Not even in that tub with me?" he asked abruptly and studied her delicately flushing face with eyes that missed nothing. "You might be interested to know that, of all the places I've had encounters with women, that was a first."

She tried to look sophisticated and failed miserably. "Oh, don't," she managed to say, turning her face away.

"You little prude," he scoffed, his voice deep and faintly amused. "Did you blush all over when you looked at me?"

She drew in a shuddering breath. "Yes, I did," she admitted. "Are you enjoying yourself, Saxon? Would you like to stick pins in me too?"

He studied her for a long time, dissecting the emotions chasing each other across her averted face. "I wasn't kidding when I asked you to marry me," he said out of the blue. "We both know that you could be pregnant."

She nodded, her eyes on her hands. "I could be. But there's just as much chance that I'm not. I still think it's crazy to get married without…without being sure."

He sighed, his eyes closing. "Maybe you're right," he said in a weary tone. "Maybe it is crazy. But, Maggie, I'm forty years old. You're—what? Twenty-six? How much longer have both of us got to go looking for a mate? We're compatible—we're damned compatible physically. Could you do better, all conceit aside? I can give you most any material thing you want. I'll… I'll take care of you, Maggie," he added, and she felt the hesitation; it was as if he'd meant to say something quite different but had thought better of it.

She felt like getting up and running. It wasn't something she should even consider. Despite the risk of pregnancy, it was crazy to let herself be coerced into a marriage like this, when she knew that he didn't love her—not in the way a man should love a woman to consider marrying her. Marriage was so permanent!

She looked up at him with all her uncertainties in her wide eyes. "What if you fall in love with someone else?" she asked quietly. "What if—what if I do?" she added, knowing the chances were billions to one, but too insecure to admit that she loved him and to risk rejection.

He flexed his shoulders. "We'll cross that bridge when we come to it. Well?" His dark eyes bored into hers, and one heavy eyebrow arched up toward the bandage around his head. "Still doubting? Come here, Maggie, and I'll convince you in the best possible way."

She really should have left while she was ahead, she told herself. But she wanted him so, loved him so. Her mind was overruled by her rebellious heart. She got up out of the chair, aware of the faint shock in his expression when she went unresisting to him and sat gently on the edge of the bed.

"Are you sure you're up to it?" she asked quietly, searching his drawn face.

"With you?" he asked in a deep, hushed tone. "My God, don't you know that I could get off my deathbed to make love to you? Come down here…"

His hand caught her upper arm and jerked her down against his broad chest. His mouth found hers in one smooth motion, his lips probing and demanding, his tongue invading her yielded mouth.

His fingers caught in her short hair and thrust her face hard against his, urgency in the sudden pressure of his mouth.

"No," she whispered shakily.

His nostrils flared as he let her draw away, but his eyes promised retribution. "I want you," he ground out, holding her gaze relentlessly. "Any way I can get you. And you want me. Won't that do, Maggie? Do you have to have promises of undying love as well?"

She touched his broad face with fingers that adored it, testing the texture of his cheeks, his lips. "No," she sighed miserably, "I suppose not." Her eyes searched his quietly. "At least I'm walking in with my eyes wide open, so to speak. I won't be expecting a saint."

"That's a good thing," he said, "because you won't be getting one. God knows, I'm not perfect."

Her lips pursed in faint mischief. "Oh, maybe in one respect…" she murmured suggestively.

He caught his breath and drew her fingers to his mouth, nibbling at them with his lips, his teeth. "Did you like it?" he whispered sensuously.

Her breath began to catch in her throat. "Yes," she admitted.

"Next time," he whispered huskily, holding her eyes, "it's going to be in a bed, with the lights blazing. Or in broad daylight so that I can see you, really see you, while we make love."

Her body tingled wildly, her heart ran away. "Saxon, would you want to have a baby?" she asked in a stranger's voice.

"Oh, God…" He groaned, dragging her mouth down to his. He kissed her wildly, roughly, his mouth frankly hurting in his sudden ardor. "Of course, I'd want to have a baby," he ground out, his voice shaking, his hand trembling as it held her mouth down to his.

"A little boy with dark eyes and big hands," she breathed into his open mouth.

"A little girl with green eyes and long legs," he corrected, biting at her lips, his breath ragged.

"One of each," she promised as he kissed her again, letting her feel the soft, slow pressure in every aching line of her lips before he increased it.

Neither of them heard the door open or the nurse's aide's discreet clearing of her throat until she did it loudly for the second time.

Maggie drew back, red-faced. "Oh!" she cried. "Uh, do you need me to—to step out into the hall?"

The older woman, a redhead, was grinning. "Only if you need the exercise," she said. "I knew he was dangerous the minute I laid eyes on him in the hall."

He grinned at her. "Well, there isn't a lot to do in here," he remarked. "I had to import my own toy."

The older woman laughed, winking at Maggie. "Listen to him! Don't you let him corrupt you, my dear. I know his type!"

"You're too late," Saxon informed her. "She just agreed to marry me."

"Poor thing," the nurse sighed, patting Maggie on the shoulder. "You make him treat you right, now, you hear? I'll just fill up your ice jug, Mr. Tremayne. Would you like some juice?"

"No, but I'd love a cup of coffee, if it's possible," he said with a smile that could have charmed a charging cow.

"I'll get you one," the aide said. "For you too?" she added, lifting her brows at Maggie.

"I'd love one," came the smiling reply.

"Back in a jiffy," the aide called over her shoulder.

Saxon grinned up at her, his face relaxed, his eyes

soft and dark. There was something different about him but something vaguely familiar in the look...

"Don't think so hard, you'll hurt yourself," he murmured. He touched her cheek with the backs of his fingers, his eyes sketching every line of her face. "When?" he asked.

"When what?" she murmured.

"When will you marry me? Suppose we make it a double wedding with Lisa and Randy. Would you mind?" he asked.

She caught her breath. "It's barely six weeks away..."

He put his finger over her lips, and his eyes were solemn. "I can wait six weeks—just. If you put me off any longer than that, quite frankly you aren't going to be able to keep me out of your bed. I want you desperately."

She drew in a steadying breath, melting under the fierce hot gaze. "All right," she agreed hesitantly. "Six weeks."

His chest rose and fell heavily. "Get me out of this place," he said curtly. "Bake me a cake with a file in it or something."

She laughed. "I'll smuggle in a helicopter at the first opportunity," she promised, and didn't resist when he pulled her back down and kissed her again.

The rest of the family was delighted when they heard the news. Lisa wept with her sister, and Sandra immediately started adding to the Christmas wedding plans by ordering another batch of invitations for Saxon and Maggie. Randy, grinning, remarked that his stepbrother was finally getting some good sense in his old age, but that it was too bad that it had taken blindness and a fall down the staircase to get him to the altar.

Maggie spent her days with Saxon as he continued

his recuperation at home. She had accepted the true nature of the wedding, knowing that he didn't love her, but too hungry for him to refuse. At least he wanted her. And perhaps when children came along, he'd learn to love her. She had to keep believing that; it was the only thing that made it bearable. And meanwhile she delighted in Saxon's company and the caresses that were becoming so deliciously familiar.

"What about your book?" she asked him a few days after he came home, when they were sitting in his study with the door closed while a cheery fire burned in the fireplace.

"The book?" He smiled. "Well, I might finish it someday. But since I don't need it to keep you here..."

"I wouldn't have left you," she admitted, curled up on the sofa with her feet tucked under her jeaned legs under the blue T-shirt. "It was nice to be needed."

He turned from the fireplace. "I still need you," he said quietly.

"Do you?" She stared down at her legs in the faded jeans.

He moved back toward her and sat down beside her. "I haven't made love to you since I've been home," he said gently, "because I wasn't sure that I could stop."

Her eyes darted up to his, and she caught her breath. "Oh," she said.

He smiled faintly. "Were you worried?"

She lifted her shoulders. "I'm not sure. I—well, I wondered if you were having second thoughts, that's all."

He caught her hand and held its soft palm to his mouth. "No, honey, I'm not having second thoughts. Are you?"

She smiled up at him. "No."

His eyes dropped to the low neckline of her T-shirt and darkened perceptibly. For several seconds his breath seemed to roughen before he let go of her hand and turned away to lean back against the sofa beside her and close his eyes.

"It's getting late," he said after a minute. "You'd better get some sleep."

Disappointed, she sighed deeply and started to get up.

He caught her shoulder as she started to rise and turned her, searching her face. "Maggie..." he whispered unsteadily.

Helplessly, she dropped down into his lap, her arms looping behind his head to tug it down. "Kiss me," she whispered shakily. "Oh, Saxon, kiss me very hard!"

His mouth crushed down against hers, and they kissed as if it had been weeks instead of days. She felt the rapidness of his heartbeat, like that of her own, drowning in the pleasure of being close to him, kissed by him, wanted by him. It had been far too long already.

She felt him shift, so that they were lying side by side, and one big warm hand slid under the T-shirt to rest against her waist.

"Is that all you're going to do?" she whispered under his mouth.

"What do you want me to do?" he asked with a wicked smile as he propped himself up on an elbow to study her.

"I thought I was the one who needed teaching," she murmured dryly.

"In this," he said, letting his fingers move slowly up

her rib cage, his eyes holding hers, "we're both beginners, Maggie."

"Beginners?" she breathed.

"Uh-huh," he murmured. His fingers easily disposed of the clasp of her bra, moving up to find the satin skin that firmed under his light touch. "Is this what you wanted?" he asked.

"Almost," she admitted, her breath catching as she responded unashamedly to the sensations he was causing.

His eyebrow jerked, and he smiled mischievously. "Then how about this, little one?" he murmured, slowly teasing the hem of the T-shirt up her body, exposing first her waist, then her ribs, and finally the soft curves of her breasts. And there he froze, the smile vanishing as he looked at her for the first time, seeing the vibrant flesh that he'd only touched before.

"Are you...are you disappointed?" she asked hesitantly when he didn't move.

His breath sighed out through taut lips. His eyes moved back up to hers. "No, I'm not disappointed," he said in a deep, husky tone. He bent again, and she watched his mouth open as it caught the taut peak between his lips and found it with his tongue. She arched helplessly, her hands holding him to her, her breath trapped in her throat as the magic began working on her.

His fingers bit into her, hurting, as his mouth grew more demanding. With a harsh sound he moved back to her mouth, poising just above it, his eyes fierce as they looked down into hers.

"Maggie—" he bit off. His hands took her body as his mouth took her parted lips, and she sank into the soft cushions under his formidable weight, accepting it joyously, without a semblance of protest.

She stretched under him, sensuously, feeling the powerful muscles of his legs brushing against hers in the silence that lengthened between them, punctuated by the sounds of harsh breathing and material brushing material, with the angry hiss of the fire close by...

His shirt was off, his bareness touching hers, when he drew back, his body shuddering with the effort of stopping. He rested his forehead against hers and fought to catch his breath.

"Oh, baby, you go to my head like bourbon," he murmured roughly.

She touched his broad shoulders gently, feeling the taut muscles contract.

"You're so strong," she whispered shakily.

"And you're very soft," he whispered back, his lips smiling as they touched hers. "Want me?"

"Yes," she said honestly. Her fingers brushed against his mouth. "Saxon..."

He shook his head. "Not tonight." He kissed her once more and sat up, refastening her bra, tugging her shirt back in place with slightly unsteady fingers.

"Why?" she asked softly.

He drew her into a sitting position and brushed a kiss against her forehead. "Because what happened in my bathroom was an accident—something I never meant to happen. The next time we make love, it won't be on the spur of the moment or because I happened to lose my head. It's going to be because we both want it, and with my ring on your finger."

"You really didn't mean it to happen?" she asked quietly, curious.

He let her go long enough to light a cigarette, and drew her beside him as he leaned back to smoke it. "No," he admitted. "At first I was teasing. Then, when I felt you against me, I lost sight of everything except how much I needed you. And from there, my darling," he laughed gently, "it was all downhill. I couldn't even manage to get you out of the tub first. I couldn't wait."

"Neither could I," she admitted on a sigh. "It was so beautiful, even like that… I hadn't realized that people could go so crazy all at once. I wasn't even thinking, I was only feeling, and it was so delicious that I couldn't stop."

"It's always going to be like that," he told her. "As long as we live."

She looked up at him with quiet, adoring eyes. Yes, she thought, they'd always be good together in bed. But how would they survive without love? Would her love for him be strong enough to keep the marriage together? Perhaps when there were children…

"Get Sandra to go shopping with you tomorrow and find a wedding gown," he said suddenly.

"I suppose I'd better," she sighed, nestling closer. "It isn't that far away. I thought something beige…"

"White," he corrected shortly, tilting her face up to his darkening eyes. "You came to me a virgin. White, Maggie."

Her lips parted on an intake of breath as she looked up at him.

"As far as I'm concerned," he said softly, "the marriage ceremony is a formality after the fact. When I took you, that was the beginning. I feel just as wed to you right now as I will when we put our signatures to the license and I place the ring on your finger." He took her left hand in his and kissed it. "What kind of ring would you like? A diamond?"

"I'd like an emerald," she replied. "A small one, set in white gold, with a band to match. How about you?"

He smiled. "You want me to wear a band?"

"Well, if you don't want to, I don't mind." She was lying, and avoided his gaze. "Some men would rather not, I know."

"Do you want me to?"

She shifted restlessly. "It's up to—"

"I said," he whispered, making her look at him, "do *you* want me to?"

She drew in a slow breath. "Yes," she admitted, throwing caution to the winds. "Yes, I do, I want those swooning women to know that you belong to me."

His fingers spread out against her throat, easing her head back on his shoulder while something dark and wild kindled in the eyes looking down into hers. "Say that again…"

"What?"

"That I'm going to belong to you," he murmured.

She flushed and tried to hide her eyes, but he wouldn't let her. "You'll…belong to me," she managed as his penetrating gaze made her knees feel weak.

"And you'll belong to me," he whispered back. "Body and heart and soul?"

"Body and heart and soul," she breathed. Her fingers reached up hesitantly to touch his face, his broad forehead, his eyebrows, his nose, his mouth. "All of me."

"Do you know the words of the marriage ceremony?" he asked against her forehead.

"Love, honor and cherish…"

"And with my body I thee worship," he whispered

fervently. His hands brought her against him, and he folded her into his body, his big arms swallowing her against his still bare chest, so that her hands were crushed into the thick mat of hair over the warm muscles. "Did I please you that morning?" he asked huskily. "Did I give you the kind of pleasure I meant to?"

"Yes," she whispered, clinging. "Oh, yes, Saxon. You gave me pleasure."

"And if there wasn't the possibility of a child," he continued quietly, "if I hadn't lost my head...would you still be marrying me at Christmas?"

She hesitated. He was asking her to make an admission that she was afraid to make. She could bear loving him in silence, but could she bear his pity if he knew the truth? She hesitated, frozen against his warm body.

He tipped her chin up, watching her quietly, intently. "I need to know," he said. "I have to know. Am I blackmailing you into a relationship you don't want?"

"I—I want you very much," she said.

"I know that. But it isn't what I asked." He pushed the wild hair away from her cheeks, her temples. "Maggie, I can force it out of you. You know that, don't you? All I have to do is strip you and start touching you. You'll tell me anything then, won't you?"

She swallowed. "Probably," she admitted. "But I'd despise you."

"Then don't goad me into it. Answer me."

Her eyes closed. "Are you going to strip me of pride too?"

"There isn't much room for pride in a good marriage," he reminded her. "Marriage is a compromise. It takes two people and an equal amount of give and take on both sides. Come on, Maggie, tell me. If you weren't afraid that I'd made you pregnant, would you still marry me?"

"Would you want to marry me if you weren't concerned about the possibility of a child?" she threw back.

He bent and touched her mouth very gently with his. "I would want you," he said in a deep, harsh tone, "if you were barren forever. I would want you if you were blind and deaf and helpless." His arms tightened. "I want children with you, but they don't have anything to do with the reasons I want to marry you."

She caught her breath at the tone of his voice. Her fingers speared into the hair over his broad chest and tangled there, pressing and pulling sensuously as the words began to penetrate her mind.

"Why do you want to marry me?" she asked.

"I asked you first."

She reached up and pressed her lips softly, warmly to his, opening them to coax his mouth into following suit. Her tongue traced the thin upper lip, the slightly fuller lower one, and his hands dug in at her waist under the tormenting pressure.

"What are you doing, you little witch?" he growled huskily.

"I'm showing you why I want to marry you," she murmured impishly. "I adore you. I love your body. I love your eyes and your nose and this little frown between your eyes. I love the way you look without clothes and the way you kiss…"

"Say the words, Maggie," he ground out. "Oh: God, say the words… I need them so!"

"I love you, Saxon," she breathed into his mouth, feeling with wonder the tremor that ran through his big body, the surge of possession in the arms that swallowed her completely. "I love you until I ache with it."

"Baby," he breathed, bending. His mouth opened against hers, fitting itself exactly to the bow of her parted lips, taking slow, sweet possession of them.

She felt him move, laying her down on the couch, his body following hers, melting down over it as they kissed slowly, tenderly, in a way they never had before.

"You only call me baby...when we make love," she whispered against his mouth.

"I can find other words, if you want me to," he whispered back. "Darling, honey, my heart, my own...my love."

"I—I like that last one," she murmured.

His nose rubbed against hers. "Do you want to hear it too?" he whispered. "That I love you?"

"Do you?" she breathed, barely able to breathe as she looked up at him, waiting, hoping against hope, needing.

"Hopelessly," he admitted softly, searching her eyes as everything he felt began to glow in his own. "Helplessly. Like a boy of fifteen. Since the day I opened my office door and found you standing outside almost a year ago."

"Oh, Saxon," she ground out, closing her eyes as she pressed against him, hiding her face in his throat.

"I haven't had a woman since that day," he whispered into her ear. "Not until that morning in the tub. I didn't even try, Maggie, there was nobody for me but you. Nobody. I've loved you for so long..."

"And I've loved you." She groaned. "I went through the motions of living, but all the while I thought you were hating me. And when I found out that you were

Randy's stepbrother, I was convinced that you'd gotten me here for revenge."

"When I found out that Lisa was your sister, I went crazy trying to think of ways to get you here," he confessed, holding her closer. "When I finally got Randy to think of asking you up here with Lisa for a visit, it was all I could do to sound indifferent. But I encouraged him every step of the way. I wanted you with me until I could taste it. And then, pretending to want revenge was the only way I could think of to keep you. Blackmail, intimidation, guilt…my God, the underhanded things I've done to stop you from leaving me!"

"Seducing me," she added with a sigh.

"I didn't plan that," he said, laughing. "But it seemed so completely natural at the time, so right. You were my first virgin, did you know?"

She shifted, drawing back to look up at him with smiling eyes. "I don't know whether to be jealous of all those women you got your experience with, or grateful to them. You made it so incredibly good for me."

"It was the same for me," he said, smoothing back her hair, "I'd never made love to a woman I was in love with, until then." He laughed softly. "I could have protected you, but I didn't. I wanted the threat of a child, I wanted a child with you. So I thought, What the hell, and just went ahead. I hoped that the risk might coerce you into saying yes when I asked you to marry me. And it did."

She shook her head. "No, it didn't," she corrected. "If I hadn't loved you, I'd have said no in spite of that risk. But you were offering me paradise. How could I have refused?"

His big hand went to her stomach, flattening out

on it possessively. "Will you mind being pregnant so soon?" he asked gently.

"We aren't sure yet," she reminded him.

He brushed her mouth with his. "I'm afraid that by Christmas we will be," he whispered sensuously, moving against her so that she was made blatantly aware of his hunger. "I could stay away when I wasn't sure of you. But now that I am, I want you more than ever. And you already know that I'm not going to take no for an answer, don't you?"

Her breath caught in her throat as he eased her shirt back up, and began to remove it. "The door…"

"I locked it when we came in here," he murmured against her parted lips. "Relax, darling. This time it's going to be everything either one of us could want. It's no spur-of-the-moment thing, no impulse. You're going to be mine for the rest of our lives."

While he was whispering, her shirt was being gently pulled over her head, leaving her bare from the waist up. He looked down at her with frankly worshipping eyes, learning every line of her, every curve in the static silence that followed.

"The lights…" she protested, flushing at the intensity of his gaze.

"Do you remember that I once told you I'd never made love in the dark?" he murmured, bending to brush his mouth slowly, agonizingly against the soft slow sweep of her breasts.

Her hands tangled in his hair, and she caught her breath at the new sensations, the slowness that hadn't been possible that wild morning.

"And I'd never made love at all," she whispered.

"And I couldn't wait," he recalled with faint amusement. "I was so hungry for you, so much in love with you. I used to lie awake thinking about how it would be, how I'd draw it out and make it so sweet for you the first time…"

She nuzzled against him, loving the thickness of his hair against her chin as he traced patterns on her bareness with his lips, his tongue. Her body lifted invitingly.

"It was sweet," she whispered. "Even though I had bruises all over."

"So did I," he murmured. "Help me. Here."

He moved her fingers to his belt and watched her flush and fumble with wicked eyes.

"On the sofa?" she whispered unsteadily.

"It's softer than the floor," he observed. "Unless…" He glanced toward the thick rug in front of the fireplace and cocked an eyebrow suggestively. "Well?"

The thought of that softness under her bare skin made her tingle all over. She caught her breath, and he read the answer in her eyes. He got up, shedding the rest of his clothes before he eased her out of her own and carried her to the rug.

She sank down into it, moving sensuously as she felt the furry thickness surround her, and watched him as he moved to poke up the fire in the fireplace before he came to her.

He smiled, half amused at the open curiosity in her gaze, the pleasure revealed in her misty eyes.

"Another first?" he murmured as he eased down beside her to prop himself up on an elbow, his body touching hers gently, making her want more than the light contact. "I gather that nude men weren't on your list of familiar things."

"I thought I mentioned that once before," she murmured. "Oh, Saxon, you have to be the most magnificent man…"

"You could pass for a particularly lovely Greek statue yourself," he replied, looking at her long slender body with a lover's eyes. "Maggie," he breathed, lifting his hand to run it slowly, lingeringly, down every soft inch of her, "I want you more than I can find words to tell you about it. I want to grow old with you. I want your children to be mine. I want to spend the rest of my life loving you, cherishing you…"

"I feel the same way about you," she replied. Her legs moved as she pressed her body softly against his, smiling at his involuntary response, the sudden tautness under the warmth of powerful muscle. "Make it last… a long time," she whispered softly, lifting her hands to tangle and tug gently at the mat of hair over his chest. "Make it last forever this time."

His breath came harshly, jerkily. One powerful leg insinuated itself across both of hers, and his hand flattened on her belly before it began to move in new, unfamiliar ways on her body.

She cried out involuntarily, trembling, her wide, awed eyes meeting his as her nails bit into him.

He smiled slowly, triumphantly. "Suppose I tell you exactly what I'm going to do to you," he whispered, bending to nip at her mouth with a slow, teasing pressure. "And how I'm going to do it," he added, laughing softly when she arched and moaned wildly. "Oh, yes, darling, it's good, isn't it? And this is just the beginning, just the tip of the iceberg."

"Saxon," she bit off, her hands clinging, pulling, her eyes pleading, her body on fire from head to toe as he teased and tormented. "I love you, I love you!"

"I love you," he whispered back. "I love every inch of you, every curve, every line. With my body I thee worship. This is where our marriage begins, here, now, as surely as if the marriage contract were already signed, the rings in place, the vows spoken. You're mine, and I'm yours, and this is our time."

"To love and to cherish," she breathed brokenly, her eyes wild and blazing with ardor. "In sickness and in health…all the days of my life. My darling. My darling!"

He soothed her, gentled her, drew her back from the summit, and when she was calm, he began all over again, his voice deep and slow and ardent, his eyes almost black with passion and love as he whispered—explicitly—what he was going to do. And then, with incredible patience and aching thoroughness, with his hands and mouth and his body, he brought her to the point of utter madness, to completion. And she felt her body lifting, rising, flying into the naked sun as the room and the world and reality all exploded into the joy of loving and being loved.

Minutes later, still trembling, she clung to him, her cheek pillowed by his warm, damp chest; his arm holding her; his mouth gently soothing her as it brushed her eyes, her nose, and the curve of her smiling lips.

"I never understood total commitment until you came along," he murmured lazily. "Now it all makes sense. One woman. Children. A home. All of it."

"Don't they say that good girls usually get pregnant the first time?" she asked drowsily, stretching.

He laughed. "You're good, all right," he muttered, turning to loom over her. "Damned good. Come here…"

"But you can't—" she began, until he moved, and she realized that he most certainly could.

"I don't know what kind of books you've been reading, honey," he murmured as his mouth broke hers. "But yes, it's most certainly possible—as you're about to find out. Touch me…yes, just…like…that! God, Maggie!" he ground out, and she yielded immediately as he guided her, prepared her, teased and tormented her in a long, leisurely loving that drove even the time before right out of her mind, until she could do nothing but cling and bite back the urgent cries that whispered hoarsely into his demanding mouth. And she understood finally why the French called it the little death—the most beautiful death imaginable…

The double wedding was a fantasy of white and lace and candlelight, with the church's gorgeous Christmas tree to the right of the altar when Maggie stood with Saxon's ring on her finger, and her sister and new brother-in-law beside them. Tears streamed down her cheeks unashamedly as she acknowledged her husband before the world, her fingers clinging warmly to his, her eyes adoring him.

The organ played, they walked briskly back down the aisle behind Randy and Lisa, and Maggie waved to her father, who was sitting with Sandra, as they left the small church.

"Run for it," Randy told his stepbrother as the well-wishers crowded around and a group of young people moved forward with streamers and tin cans, and the inevitable rice storm began.

Saxon, laughing, prodded Maggie toward his new Ferrari and put her in the passenger side, getting in quickly himself. They barely had time to wave goodbye to Lisa and Randy before they were heading out toward Charleston and their honeymoon.

He clasped her hand warmly in his after he'd turned onto the interstate and they were well out of the thick traffic of the city.

"Happy?" he asked softly.

"Deliriously," she breathed, looking up at him with all her happiness in her face, her eyes. "I love you."

"I love you, my darling. Merry Christmas."

"Merry Christmas." She leaned back in the seat, smiling.

His thumb caressed her palm. "Maggie, it's been six weeks," he reminded her with a laughing sideways glance.

"Yes, I know."

"Well, you little witch?" he prodded. His fingers contracted. "Tell me!"

She turned in the seat and curled one leg under her white satin dress, "I'm sorry, darling," she said gently. "I honestly don't know yet."

"I thought women were supposed to be able to tell."

"Yes, but you're counting your six weeks from the hot tub," she murmured, "I'm counting mine from the rug in front of the fireplace," she added with a blush, remembering that one furious lapse, after which they'd both struggled to keep apart until the rings were in place.

"Ah," he breathed, glancing at her with a wicked light in his eyes. "Talk about stamina. I think I proved mine that night."

"You may very well have proved your virility as well," she said, laughing. "Something that should have happened, hasn't, and it did just after your fall down the staircase."

"You didn't tell me," he accused.

She smiled. "Darling, a woman has to use all her weapons," she reminded him. "I loved you, but I was afraid if I told you, you'd back out of the wedding. At least until that night in the study…"

"You little witch," he accused again. "You seduced me!"

"Pot calling the kettle black," she said smugly. "I needed some insurance of my own."

His hand brought hers to his mouth. "Just wait until we get to Charleston," he threatened lovingly.

"I'll do my best, darling," she promised demurely, and her smile held all the promise in the world. "Oh, Saxon Tremayne, I love you shockingly!"

"I love you just as shockingly, Mrs. Tremayne," he replied gently. "What a great many blessings we have to count this Christmas."

"A duke's ransom," she said. She smiled contentedly as she watched the long highway run into the horizon and felt her husband's large warm hand strongly about her own. She wouldn't need presents under the tree this year, she thought joyfully. She already had the best one of all—love.

* * * * *

COLOR LOVE BLUE

CHAPTER ONE

THE WIND WAS STRONGER, but Jolana didn't mind. She liked the feel of it in her long, thick blond hair as she walked. She was a tall girl, and she liked her height, and the strides her long, slender legs made as she walked down Fifth Avenue. Country girl she might be, but she'd lived in New York long enough to match the pace of the city. She blended into the crowds of restaurant-seekers as yellow cabs filled the streets with lunch traffic.

Her face lifted, and she smiled. It was good to be alive and twenty-seven and at the beginning of a promising career. She was having a one-woman show at an elite art gallery in the city very soon and was making more money selling her paintings than she'd ever had in her life. She smiled, and her black eyes sparkled at the thought of her friends back home in Georgia who'd laughed at her ambition to become an artist. If only they could see her now, walking around in an Anne Klein dress wearing a knee-length suede coat with leather boots... Wouldn't they just grind their teeth?

She bumped into someone, because she'd been gloating over her success instead of watching where she was going, and two large hands caught and held her. She looked up into a face that arrested her apology even as she opened her mouth.

He had a face that she'd love to paint. Very Italian,

Roman, in fact, with curly black hair and a broad face, a straight nose and chiseled mouth, high cheekbones running down into an arrogant, square jaw. He towered over her, but he had an air of authority that didn't need great height or size to work. He was wearing a blue pin-striped suit with a leather overcoat, and he looked very well-to-do as well as arrogant.

"I'm not sure I like having myself critiqued," he said, and his voice matched his face. It was dark and deep and smooth.

"I'm…sorry," Jolana said. "I didn't mean to stare. It's your face."

His heavy eyebrows arched up. "I don't imagine anyone else has a prior claim to it," he returned. "Do you always walk around in a daze, or are you making an exception today?"

"I was gorging myself on vengeful thoughts," she admitted with a twinkling smile. "Heady with success and not looking where I was going. I'm sorry I collided with you, and even sorrier if I embarrassed you."

"I don't think anyone's managed that since I was six," he replied. He didn't smile. In fact, he didn't look like a man who did much smiling.

She cleared her throat. He intimidated her with his clipped speech and the impatient glance at his watch.

"Excuse me, I have an appointment to get to," he said. "Pay attention to where you're going, country girl, or you'll wind up under the wheels of a cab."

She glared at him. "I'm not a country hick, mister," she said shortly. "But where I come from, manners count. You seem to have misplaced yours."

And before he could reply, she moved away from him and stomped off.

Arrogant, rude, impatient man, she thought angrily as she made her way through the crowd and into her apartment building. A Roman gladiator might have looked like that, or a centurion off to war. She tossed back her hair with an impatient hand. Most New Yorkers were kind, thank God, and not the cold people she'd once thought. They were warm and friendly once you got to know them.

The doorman grinned at her as she went through the revolving door.

"Nice day, Miss Shannon," he said pleasantly. "Like autumn."

"Yes, isn't it lovely?" she replied with a smile. "And they said it was going to snow. How silly!"

She waved to the desk clerk, a young man with whom she'd become friendly over the months of her residence, and walked straight into the empty elevator. The doors closed, and she sighed as the elevator hummed to the third floor.

Her apartment was big, with a sunken living room and a decor done almost entirely in white and yellow. They were sunny colors, and she liked the cheery atmosphere of the white-carpeted room. It was stupid, of course, to have a white carpet. But she always took off her shoes at the door and made her visitors do the same. Even now, she was in her stocking feet and feeling warm and at home. The house where she'd grown up in rural south Georgia was nothing like this, she thought, grinning as she looked around at her elegant, very expensive surroundings. It was nice to have money.

She caught her breath. Money! Where was her purse? She checked her pockets—it was only a small clutch bag, and surely she'd brought it from the gallery when she came! She remembered having it in her hand. But where was it?

Frantically, she searched the room, the hall, even the elevator, backtracking to the revolving door. But it was nowhere in sight. The doorman hadn't seen her carrying a purse, he mentioned. And then she remembered two things. That she'd collided with that horrible man and probably it had fallen to the pavement. And that she was standing out on the street in her stocking feet and the pavement was cold.

The doorman was trying not to grin. He put a gloved hand to his mouth.

"I like going barefoot," she told him, grinning momentarily. She sighed. "Oh, what am I going to do? I know it dropped on the sidewalk, and probably it's long gone by now. All my credit cards were in it, my driver's license…"

"Maybe somebody will find it, Miss Shannon, and bring it to you," the doorman suggested helpfully.

Maybe Superman will fly down and ask me out to lunch, she thought miserably. But she only smiled and walked back toward the elevator.

A matronly lady in a gray wool suit and hat glanced at her disapprovingly.

"The latest fashion," Jolana said with a sophisticated smile. "Early primitive. It's all the rage in Paris."

And she walked into the elevator, pushed the button and smiled again as the doors closed.

She grimaced when she got back to her apartment as she glanced down at her ruined hose. They weren't made for walking on pavement, of course, but they'd cost quite a lot. She sighed as she stripped them off and tossed them in the garbage. Next time she'd know better, she supposed. But what was she going to do about her purse?

She phoned the police station around the corner and reported it to the officer on duty, but he told her what she already knew, that it was highly unlikely that anyone would give it back. He advised her to call her credit-card companies and report the loss of her cards and to apply for a replacement driver's license. She thanked him and put the receiver down slowly. Well, it was her own fault. Whom could she blame? That was easy, she thought darkly as she picked up the phone again. That tall, arrogant Italian. He was probably a member of the mob, she thought angrily. Probably a hit man. With all that arrogance, he was definitely no ordinary businessman, that was for sure.

She finished reporting the loss of her cards and went into her studio to stare distractedly at her unfinished canvas. It was one she was doing as a favor for the gallery owner, a present for a friend of his. A Greek landscape with fallen columns in the foreground and Mount Olympus in the background. It was a faintly trite scene, she'd thought when the owner asked her to do it, but he wouldn't hear of changing the subject. So she'd worked on it in her spare time, and now it was almost finished. Well, today was as good a time as any, she told herself. She might as well work instead of sitting around brooding.

She put on her worn, baggy jeans and a paint-covered smock with nothing under it. She lived alone and there was no one to see her, so she often dressed the way she felt most comfortable.

She was well into the painting, lost in dreams of ancient Rome, when the intercom buzzer interrupted her.

Her eyes sparkled as she went to answer it. She'd had some problems lately with a man who had bought a few of her paintings and saw himself as a lady-killer. She'd already refused three invitations to come over and see his collection. A lot of the men she met assumed that an artist must have a Bohemian streak and tried to take advantage. Little did they know that she had been raised in a Puritanical atmosphere and considered sex more than a party favor. In fact, she had made love to only one man in her life. Oddly enough, it had sent him running in the other direction. He'd assumed that she'd want commitment in return for her body, and he was dead right. She'd ached over his absence, but in time she'd realized that it was all for the best anyway. She wasn't geared to brief affairs. She wanted love.

She walked to the door and pressed the intercom button. "Yes," she said warily.

"Miss Shannon, there's a gentleman here who's found your purse," the doorman said.

"Fantastic!" she called into the intercom. "Please send him right up."

A few minutes later the doorbell rang and she ran to answer it.

"Miss Shannon?" the Italian-looking man asked, staring down his Roman nose at her. He held out her purse. "Not a bad trick, but I don't like being manipulated."

He looked angry and faintly menacing, and she blinked as she took the purse, feeling relief mingle with apprehension.

"Thank you, I was afraid..."

He cut her off brutally. "Taking your phone off the hook was a professional touch," he said maliciously.

"But you might have saved yourself the trouble. I don't have a weakness for call girls. Amazing how you got into the business," he added bluntly, letting his eyes run over her. "You're not that much to look at, frankly. That body—" he indicated it with a distasteful gesture "—wouldn't set any fires in my blood."

By now she was slowly reaching explosion stage. She tossed her purse over her shoulder onto the couch and glared up at him with pure hatred in her eyes.

"Mister, if I were your size, I'd throw you out the window," she said coldly. "Get out."

"I'm not in," he reminded her. "And not likely to be lured in. You're not my type, lady. Next time you need a man, put an ad in a magazine. But not mine, if you please. I don't cater to that kind of trade." He turned on his heel and walked slowly back toward the elevator, bending his dark, curly head to light a cigarette on the way.

"Oh, sir," she called after him in her sweetest tone.

He turned. "Yes?"

She made an unmistakable gesture, still smiling sweetly, walked back into her apartment and slammed the door.

"I told you," his voice came through the door, "no, thanks!"

And his footsteps died away. She picked up a vase and threw it at the wall, watching it break into a thousand pieces. If only that had been his arrogant head!

Later, she was horrified not only at his accusations, but that uncharacteristic lapse of hers and the terrible gesture she'd made. It shocked her that she could be that uninhibited. Why, she hardly ever even cursed! That man had a nasty effect on her, she decided finally as she went back to work on the painting. Thank God she was done with him! And she did, after all, have her purse back. That was a mixed blessing. She'd have to call around all over again to undo what she'd done when she thought it was lost. And it was all *his* fault.

The next day, she took the painting, wrapped up in brown paper, to the gallery on her way to buy a dress for the cocktail party the owner was giving that night.

"Here it is," she said, handing it to him. "All done."

"Jolana, you're a marvel." Tony Henning grinned. He looked faintly Italian himself, she decided, with his dark hair and eyes. "Nick's going to love it. I think," he added, laughing. "Putting Mount Olympus in the background is going to needle him good."

She cocked her head. "The painting is to needle him?"

"Well, he does occasionally come on like a Greek or Roman deity," he sighed. "You don't know him. If you did, you'd understand. We kind of had a disagreement over—" he cleared his throat "—your show."

She felt herself going weak. "What does he have to do with it?"

"He's my partner," he confessed. "He has a half interest in the gallery."

"You never said…!"

"It only just happened a few weeks ago," he told her. "As you're well aware, the art world is not exactly noted for its financial security. I've made a few bad decisions about shows that ended up costing me plenty. Besides that, I've had some losses in the stock market, and to tell you the truth I was in one hell of an economic mess until Nick pulled me out of the fire. He's my cousin, and I don't know what I'd have done without him."

"But my show… What about my show, Tony?" she asked nervously.

"It's still on," he assured her. "I told Nick that we had a contract, and we will have," he added, "as soon as you sign this."

The contract was dated two weeks before, and she lifted her eyebrows at him.

"Is this legal?" she asked.

"Sure, sure, just sign it and everything will be fine," he said, handing her a pen.

She hesitantly scribbled her name on the signature line and Tony quickly picked up the paper and nodded.

"Fine, fine. Now just relax. Everything will be okay, honest it will."

Her eyes searched his guilty face. "Why doesn't your cousin want me to exhibit my paintings here?"

"He thinks I arranged the show for you because we're lovers," he admitted, avoiding her gaze. "He hasn't seen any of your work… Well, I didn't have even one painting to show him. They all sell out the minute I put them on display. You've got a lot of fans in the city, at least three of whom still fight over your stuff."

She stared straight into his eyes. "Did you tell him we were lovers?"

"No," he admitted. "But I do live in hope," he added, leering theatrically at her. "There's a bed in back, you gorgeous woman, and I strip down nicely even at my age."

"Your age!" she scoffed, laughing now. "You're not old."

"Almost as old as Nick," he told her. "He's forty. Ancient. Of course, he looks it these days," he sighed.

"Poor old Nick, he's been pretty damned unlucky in his love life. Pretty damned unlucky."

"Is he ugly?" she asked, curious.

"Not by a long shot," he said. "He publishes a magazine all about the news of the financial world. It's one of the most respected publications in the field. Women just swoon when he walks into a room, but he won't even look back."

"A woman-hater?" she asked.

"Not quite," he told her. "He just doesn't get emotionally involved, that's all."

"I can hardly wait to meet him," she said drily, her black eyes twinkling as she looked up at him. "Will I get to, tonight?"

"I imagine so," he sighed. "You'll fall, just like all the others, I'm afraid. But let me introduce you, please. He may be ready to bite after he sees this painting. That will give you time to see if you'd like to escape before he starts chewing on you. He doesn't like artists, you see. He thinks they lead a licentious and parasitic life."

"I'll find something suitably decorous to wear tonight," she told him. "Or—" she grinned "—how about if I come nude?"

"Fine," he agreed quickly. "I'll cancel all the other invitations…"

"Crazy man. Tony, thanks for all the trouble you've gone to on my behalf," she added softly. "This will be my first really big show, you know."

"I do know. That's why I took on Nick," he said, as if it were really a sacrifice. "See you at seven."

"I'll be there!"

Several hours later, she was admitted to Tony's elegant apartment and shown into the shag-carpeted living room. She was wearing a gold lamé dress, the perfect foil for her blond hair and black eyes, with spaghetti straps and a bodice that dipped precariously in front and had hardly any back at all. It was chic and sophisticated and she already regretted the impulse that had made her buy it. She was already angry at Nick what's-his-name for trying to cheat her out of her exhibit, and this was her way of living down to his image of her. It was probably a mistake, anyway, she thought as Tony came forward, grinning, to take her hands.

"Just the girl," he said, kissing her cheek. "Oddly enough, Nick was impressed with the painting, Mount Olympus and all. He wants to meet you."

That was good news indeed. She followed him through the crowd of sophisticated art lovers and dealers and somewhere along the way she acquired a glass of champagne. Then they stopped, and she lifted her eyes from a black dinner jacket and white silk shirt and black tie to a face that was horribly familiar.

"Domenico Scarpelli, this is my latest find, Miss Jolana Shannon," Tony said proudly.

Jolana stared at the arrogant Roman face with undisguised anger, and it was returned full force.

"You'll understand if I don't shake hands?" she asked him with cold venom.

His eyes went up and down her body in the sheath of gold lamé. "I don't recall offering to," he said arrogantly. "So, you're Tony's artist. How sad that he never mentioned your name."

Jolana gave Tony her glass of champagne. "Lovely party. So sorry I have to leave," she told her host with a forced smile. "I feel a violent headache coming on. Must run."

"Take one step toward that door," Nick said coldly, "and you can forget your one-woman show."

She froze midstep with her back to him. "I thought I was already expected to do that," she laughed bitterly. "There are other galleries, Mr. Scarpelli, and I'm a determined woman. I can always wait on tables if things get too tough. Good ni—"

Nick took her arm firmly and guided her past Tony's stunned face into what was obviously a bedroom. He closed the door firmly behind them.

She backed away from the big Italian, coming up against the curtained window, her eyes wide with dread.

"Don't flatter yourself," Nick advised. He pulled a cigarette from his pocket and lit it. "I'm not that desperate."

She glared at him. "Why did you bring me in here, then?"

"To talk. It wasn't possible out there." He moved into the room and sat down gracefully in a chair by the king-size bed. "Sit down, for God's sake, I won't bite."

She moved hesitantly to a chair on the other side of the bed and eased down into it.

"Some call girl," he scoffed. "Why wear a dress like that when you're terrified of bedrooms?"

"To get even with you," she managed unsteadily. "Tony said…you didn't want to let me have my show, and that you didn't like women…"

"Tarts," he corrected. "Yes, that does figure. What you were wearing at your apartment was hardly provocative gear. I didn't think about the paint on you until later, and even then I didn't make the connection. There are a lot of Sunday painters in New York."

"I'm not a Sunday painter," she said with dignity.

"No, you're not," he agreed. "You have a great talent. Despite Tony's disgusting use of it in that painting," he added.

"He said you wouldn't like it."

"But, I did." He leaned back in the chair and smoked his cigarette quietly. "How long have you been painting?"

"Since I was old enough to hold a crayon," she said simply. "Mr. Scarpelli, I'm sure you didn't bring me in here to hear the story of my life."

"That's right, I didn't." He studied her quietly. "For reasons I won't go into right now, I need an escort for a party in Manhattan next Friday night. Come with me and I'll forget about challenging that flimsy contract Tony made you sign."

Her face flamed. "I told you, I'm not a call girl!"

"And I told you that I know that," he replied coldly. "I need a woman. Not in my bed, just on my arm, for a few hours. Yes or no?"

She caught her breath and considered all the angles. He had her right where he wanted her and they both knew it, so why pretend?

"All right," she sighed, weary of the whole thing.

"It's going to involve a little acting on your part," he added, pressing his advantage.

"How?"

He studied the tip of his cigarette. "I want you to act like a woman in love with me."

She stood up. "That," she told him flatly, "is it. I'd rather peddle my paintings on street corners…"

"Better them than your body. You'd earn more," he interrupted coolly, rising from his chair. "Now shut up and listen to me."

"Have I got a choice?" she asked, affronted.

"There's going to be someone at that party who thinks I'm carrying a torch for her," he said quietly. "I want to disabuse her of the notion, you understand?"

"Then ask one of your girlfriends," she replied.

"I am, as the saying goes, between women," he said curtly. "And the kind of woman I usually associate with wouldn't convince anybody that she was capable of decent emotional involvement. I don't want to take a hooker to my mother's home."

"You have a mother?" she asked with mock surprise. "Will wonders never cease?"

He glared at her. "You irritate me, Miss Shannon."

"Thank God I don't attract you," she said matter-of-factly.

"I'll pick you up at five on Friday afternoon," he told her. "And you won't tell Tony anything about the arrangement."

"Is that an order, Your Worship?" she taunted. "My, my, you do bear a resemblance to pictures of Roman centurions I've seen."

"My ancestors were fond of taking slave girls into their beds," he reminded her.

"I'd rather be thrown to the lions," she said with a sweet smile. "Are you through talking? I'd like to leave."

"No more than I," he assured her with a hard glare. He opened the door. "After you."

She lifted her head proudly and walked out of the bedroom ahead of him.

"By the way," he murmured, "where did you learn that interesting gesture you showed me in the hall yesterday? I thought well-brought-up young Southern ladies were more reserved."

She blushed to her blond roots and couldn't look at him. She walked away stiff-backed and melted into the crowd.

Although she'd planned to leave the party to get away from him, he solved that problem for her by leaving himself. And the minute he was out the door, Tony was after Jolana.

"What was that all about?" he asked quickly, drawing her over by the punch bowl.

"I lost my purse yesterday," she muttered. "He found it."

"And?" he prompted.

She shrugged wryly. "He thought I was a hooker."

"You!" He burst out laughing, and shook his head. "Boy, did Nick have a wrong number!"

"I told him as much," she said shortly. "Has he always been that horrible, or is it an acquired characteristic?"

"Nick's had a hard life, honey," he said. "But he doesn't usually go off half-cocked." He lifted his chin and pursed his lips while he studied her. He smiled slowly. "You must have made an immediate impression."

"I guess," she sighed. "He asked me out."

"He did? My God, that's a new one. I thought he was going to moon over…never mind, that's none of my business. But watch your step," he cautioned, unusually solemn. "Don't get too involved with Nick. He could hurt you badly."

"I've been hurt by experts," she replied lightly, but she meant it. "Don't worry. He won't get close enough to do any damage."

He frowned slightly. "You are going out with him voluntarily?"

Sure, and the Sahara was going to freeze over any day now, she thought.

"Of course," she replied with a cool smile. "And now, I think I'd better go home. It's been a long day, and I'm rather tired."

"What long day?" he burst out. "You haven't done anything except come here!"

"That's what I mean," she responded.

He chuckled. "Oh. I see. Nick does act a little like a steamroller, I guess. When am I getting the rest of those canvases for the show?"

"By the end of next week, okay?" she asked, knowing it was going to mean working half the night every night.

"Fine!"

"But I may ask for a slight extension. Until 1998?" she teased.

He snorted. "Tell me another one. Go home. Sleep."

"Anything you say."

"If only I believed that," he sighed. "Good night."

She waved her hand and left. But once she got outside into the cool night air, all she could think about was Nick Scarpelli. No man she'd ever met had made such an immediate impression on her. And that odd request... Why would a man who looked like that need a woman to pretend to be in love with him?

She walked back to her apartment as people around her hailed taxis and caught buses. It was comforting to have companionship, Jolana thought, even that of people she didn't know.

It was a brisk walk from Tony's apartment, and she let herself in with a sigh. It was going to take her a while to figure out Domenico Scarpelli's motive for the polite blackmail. Meanwhile, she had an exhibit to prepare for and no time to lose. She changed into her working clothes and got out her brushes.

her life. There was just enough room at the bottom of her jacket cover for his signature. Gregorio. The name was precisely French.

[...text obscured...] and him [...]

CHAPTER TWO

As JOLANA HAD EXPECTED, the paintings kept her up late for the next several nights. But Friday morning, she delivered them to Tony.

"Beautiful," he exclaimed as he sorted them. "Beautiful. This, especially."

He held up a landscape with Van Gogh-ish overtones and smiled at it. "Now, where have I seen that style before?" he asked, lifting an amused eyebrow.

"Sorry," she laughed. "I couldn't help it. The others are all my own style, though, aren't they?"

"Most definitely. I think you'll be pleased with the results of this show," he said.

"Oh, I hope so," Jolana responded, a small note of anxiety in her voice.

"I'll send them over to the framers today."

She smiled. "Fine! I can't wait to see what they look like matted and framed."

"You look beat, honey. Better go home and sleep for a few hours."

"That's exactly what I plan to do," she told him. "Talk to you later."

"You bet you will, you gorgeous creature."

She walked slowly back to the apartment, remembering and dreading what was coming later in the day. That terrible Italian would be on her doorstep at five sharp to take her to the party. She didn't know what to wear, she didn't feel like going. If it hadn't been for his threat about the show that she was killing herself to get ready for, she'd have locked him out and ignored him.

But that was impossible. So she napped for two hours and sorted out her closet. Would it be formal or not? She sighed over two dresses. One was long and risqué. The other a dream of an original in a soft, white sweater knit with long sleeves, a modest V-neckline and a princess waist. It would be a safe bet, since it would do for most any formal occasion without being overly dressy.

She put it on, liking the way it complemented her fair complexion. It made her black eyes blacker, her long, thick hair blonder. She added white accessories and the effect was dynamite. It might even turn Domenico Scarpelli's head. Although, of course, she wouldn't want to, she reminded herself.

At exactly five o'clock, the intercom buzzed and the doorman announced that Nick was on his way up.

If Jolana was hoping for any reaction from Nick, it didn't come. When she answered the door he gave her a cursory appraisal and checked his wristwatch.

"You're ready, I assume?" he asked politely.

"Yes." She had her purse in hand. She turned out the lights and locked the door behind her, oddly irritated that he hadn't even commented on her choice of clothing. He was wearing dark evening clothes, which made him look darker than ever. And more formidable. He wasn't a heavyset man, but his height made him seem wider than he was. That, and the set of his broad shoulders and his thick, curling hair.

"You just bubble with bright conversation, don't you,

Mr. Scarpelli?" she asked sweetly as she followed him into the elevator.

"I don't see any need to put on false fronts, Miss Shannon," he replied coolly.

Which puts me precisely in my place, she mused, glancing toward him.

He seemed restless on the way to the party, as if his nerves were suffering. If he had nerves. Jolana had her own ideas about that. She remembered what he'd told her about the woman who thought he was carrying a torch for her, and she wondered if it had something to do with her. Steamroller he might be, but he was an attractive man as well as a very wealthy one. She could see why women would chase him.

"Where are we going?" she asked when she was seated beside him in the plush interior of his white Jaguar.

"Not far," he said quietly, easing into traffic. "But I thought you might prefer driving to walking, in those."

He nodded toward her shoes and their three-inch heels.

"You're very courteous," she said politely. "But I've walked in them before."

"And gone barefoot the rest of the evening?" he murmured.

She thought she'd heard a note of amusement in his tone, and she remembered that the second time he'd seen her, in her apartment, she'd been barefoot.

"I don't really like shoes, you see," she admitted.

"Why?"

"I can't feel the carpet through them," she said, tongue in cheek.

He glanced at her, and his dark eyes sparkled with

humor. It changed him, made him younger and more companionable. His complexion was olive and smooth as silk. She wondered if it felt like silk, with that shadow that obviously meant he could grow a heavy beard if he wanted to.

"Where does your mother live?" she asked.

"An apartment in the East Eighties," he said quietly.

"Is it some special kind of party?"

"An engagement party, for the daughter of some friends of ours."

"Will there be a lot of people?" she persisted.

He glanced at her again. "Afraid of crowds?"

"Yes," she said bluntly. "Terribly."

His heavy eyebrows went up, as if he hadn't expected that. "No, there won't be a crowd. Just my mother and stepfather, my brother and some friends. And they don't bite, even if they are Italian."

She looked out the window. "Is that how I sounded?"

"No," he said after a minute. His dark, elegant hands gripped the wheel hard. "I'm on edge. It doesn't happen often, and I don't like it."

"Why did you bring me?" she asked quietly. "And why…"

"You should have been a reporter, lady, you're nosy," he said quite frankly. "I'm through answering questions. All you need to know is that your exhibit depends on how well you pull this off tonight."

"I've never been much good as an actress," she said.

"You'd better learn. Look loving."

"Cling to your sleeve, bat my eyelashes and breathe, 'Oh, Domenico,' in my sexiest voice?" she volunteered.

"Everyone calls me Nick, except my enemies."

"What do they call you?"

"Guess."

She laughed softly. "I fell right into that one," she said.

"Where are you from? Somewhere in the South, judging from that molasses accent."

"That isn't a good way to get acquainted," she told him with a hard glare. "And you're one to talk about an accent!"

"Don't start bristling. I like the way you talk."

"I'm glad you like something about me," she answered darkly.

"Are you?" He sounded surprised. "I didn't think I was your type."

"You aren't."

"I wonder."

She wouldn't look at him. Her life was complicated enough, and she remembered all too well the perils of getting involved with a man. It was a mistake she'd already made one time too many, and she wasn't making it again.

"No comment?" he prodded.

"I'm not in the market for a man, Mr. Scarpelli," she said quietly.

"Nick," he corrected. "You've got to sound the part as well as act it tonight."

He pulled into the underground garage of an old, elegant apartment building.

"Is this where your mother lives?" she asked to divert him.

"Yes. She and my stepfather have been here for over fifteen years." He parked the car and led her to the elevator. "My father died when my brothers and I were kids and my mother's been remarried twice since then."

"You're the eldest?"

"Yes. My brother Rick and I jointly own the magazine. He's in charge of advertising and sales and I handle the general management. My youngest brother, Marc, is the black sheep of the family. He's trying to make it on his own, but I hope that someday he'll join us at the magazine."

"It's a good publication," she said with grudging praise. "It's the only financial magazine I can read."

"Why do you like it?" he asked, interested, as they rode up on the carpeted, paneled elevator.

"Because I can understand it," she said honestly. "The stories about the mergers and company failures and renovations are fascinating. They're very much about people instead of about just facts and figures. And the way they're written makes them come alive for me."

"High praise," he said, hands in his pockets as he looked at her, really looked at her for the first time. "I never liked blondes in white until tonight. That," he said, gesturing toward her elegant dress, "is sexy as hell. On you," he emphasized.

Why did her heart have to take that wild leap? Surely he could see the reaction in her widening eyes, her restless movements, but she couldn't help them. She clutched her purse as the elevator door opened.

"Just getting some practice in," he said, smiling slightly as he took her arm. "Don't look so frightened of me."

"I'm trying. You're very big, aren't you?" she asked nervously.

The hand on her arm tightened and she felt him stop, felt his breath in her hair as he towered over her. "Would you like to find out for yourself?" he breathed.

She caught her breath, and he laughed lowly, wickedly. She tried to draw away, but his arm slid around her and riveted her to the muscular length of his side.

"I'm going to enjoy this," he murmured as they paused in front of one of the apartments. He pushed the button. "How old are you, anyway? Over the age of consent?"

"I'll never consent, and my age is none of your business," she answered sharply.

Before she could move, he tipped up her chin and bent, kissing her hard on the mouth. "Now," he said, watching the reaction darken her eyes, redden her cheeks. "Now you look like my woman."

The door opened and a tiny, dark woman embraced the big man while Jolana tried to get her breath and her composure back, all at once.

A long, rapid-fire exchange in Italian followed the greeting, and the little woman turned to Jolana and smiled widely.

"I am Nick's mother," she said in faintly accented English. "And you are Jolana, yes? Very pretty. You could be Italian, except for that glorious hair."

"Actually," Jolana confessed, "my grandmother really was Italian."

The old woman brightened immediately. "So." She nodded. "Yes, I could see it in the eyes. So dark and so fiery. Come. Meet my husband and my youngest son."

She was propelled along by the elegantly dressed and coiffed little woman, while Domenico sauntered in behind them, looking pleased.

"This is Paulo, my husband," she said, introducing a tall, thin, white-haired man. "And this is my son Marcello... Marc! Come say hello to Nick's girl!"

Shivers went down her spine at that introduction.

Nick's girl. She smiled wanly at the young man who held out his hand, noticing his astonishing good looks with forced interest. He was about her own age, and charming as well as handsome. But somehow he came off a bad second when compared with Nick.

"Introduce her around, Nick," his mother said, shooing them away. "I'll see if the meal is ready."

"Tyrant," Nick shot after her, and she grinned.

"They're very nice, your family," Jolana said quietly.

"I won't ask what you were expecting," he answered. His hand on her arm tightened as they approached a group of people about Nick's own age, and Jolana saw his expression become grim.

"Nick!" A gorgeous brunette came forward. Her soulful black eyes searched his for a long moment and she smiled faintly as her eyes went to Jolana. "A new girl? She's…very pretty," she added, forcing her smile to remain as she turned to Jolana.

Jolana felt sorry for her. She smiled genuinely. "I'm Jolana Shannon," she said.

"I'm Margery Simon," the dark-haired woman replied. "This is my husband, Andrew."

Jolana smiled at the tall, blond man at her side. He nodded his head curtly, glared at Nick and walked away.

Margery looked pained. "Andrew doesn't like parties, I'm afraid. Excuse me."

She walked after him, and Jolana noticed the half-full glass in her husband's hand. Obviously, he wasn't having his first drink of the day.

She glanced up and found Nick watching with cold, hard eyes as the man and wife went into the next room, where the food was being laid on the table.

"Have they been married a long time?" she asked.

"Ten years," he said curtly. "I was best man at their wedding."

"She seems such a nice lady," she said.

"No sympathy for poor Andrew?" he mused, glancing down at her curiously.

"He looks as if he has enough of his own without borrowing," she said. She gazed after the other man. "He reminds me of someone I used to know."

He cocked an eyebrow. "Recently?"

"A hundred years ago," she corrected.

He didn't pursue that, but she felt his eyes as he introduced her to three more couples, including the engaged pair. They went into the dining room a minute later, so there was no more opportunity for conversation.

The food was Italian, and delicious. Jolana ate far too much and barely had room for the delicate cannoli they had for dessert. When they retired to the living room for brandy and after-dinner coffee, she found herself sitting with Margery while the men and some of the other women congregated in small groups.

"Have you known Nick long?" Margery asked lightly, but her hand tightly clutched her brandy snifter.

"It seems like forever," Jolana muttered, glancing toward where he was towering over his stepfather and brother, deep in conversation.

"Yes, I know the feeling," came the soft reply, and the dark eyes that followed Jolana's gaze were wistful. "He's very handsome, our Nick. I've known him since I was fifteen, when we moved next door to his parents. He was seventeen, and I had my first date with him." Her eyes clouded. "How much we've changed, since then."

"Do you and your husband have children?" Jolana asked, changing the subject.

Margery nodded and smiled. "One son. I'd like more but Andrew never wanted any. Now, Nick," she said, nodding toward him, "would like a houseful."

"I can see what a flaming rush he's been in to start a family," Jolana said, tongue in cheek.

Margery laughed gently. "Yes, I know what you mean. But Nick's been busy. And I suppose he hasn't found the right woman, at least not until now. He'd hardly bring you to a family party if you were his usual type, would he?"

Jolana grinned. "You might be surprised."

"About Nick? Never." Margery sighed. "I married the wrong man ten years ago. I've been living with my mistake ever since."

Jolana felt embarrassed, but she could hardly walk away. And changing the subject seemed to be impossible.

"I'm sorry, I didn't mean to cry on your shoulder," Margery said impulsively and laid a slender hand on Jolana's wrist. "Forgive me. Andrew drinks heavily, and he frightens me when he drinks. I'm rambling, but it's simply nervousness."

For the first time, Jolana saw the woman's fear and sadness, and she felt oddly sympathetic.

"Can't he stop?" she asked softly.

Margery shook her head. "We've tried. When he graduated from alcohol to drugs, the damage began. Now he combines them..." Her eyes narrowed as Andrew turned, noticing her, and his face darkened. "Excuse me."

She got up and went to her husband. There was a

quick, sharp exchange. He caught her by the arm so tightly that it would probably leave a bruise, called good-night to their hosts and propelled Margery out the door.

Jolana watched with blazing dark eyes. She was hardly aware of Domenico's approach.

"What did you say to her?" he asked coldly, jerking her to her feet.

Her eyebrows went straight up. "Mr. Scarpelli, I was listening to her, not talking," she said, her icy tone matching his.

"Then why did he drag her out like that?" he demanded.

She pulled free of his grasp and glared at him. "I don't know, frankly. Nor do I know why she tolerated it. I wouldn't stay with a man who tried to wrestle me around in public like that."

"Tough lady, huh?" he chided.

"Yes, I'm tough," she agreed, pursing her lips as she studied his face. "So what?"

He glanced toward the closed door. "With his past record, he'll probably beat her."

"You might have stopped him," she suggested. "From what she told me, she was practically part of your family when the two of you were kids."

"Yes," he muttered darkly and sighed. "Damn Andrew," he growled. "Damn him."

"She doesn't have to stay with him, you know," she returned, moving away. "We're victims only if we allow ourselves to be. I feel sorry for her, too, but I don't have a martyr complex."

He started to say something, and she was frankly glad when they were interrupted. The look in his eyes had been predatory. Why did the woman matter so much to him? She shrugged. Probably he thought of her as a younger sister and felt naturally protective toward her. But she still wondered as she looked around the room which of those women was the one who was after Nick. The only one who seemed wildly flirtatious toward him was his sister-in-law, Deborah. Perhaps that was the woman, after all, she decided at last. He wouldn't want his newly married brother to be jealous of him and thought Jolana's presence and its obvious implications might put Deborah off.

With that in mind, she stuck close to him every time he went near his brother and sister-in-law.

But as they left the apartment at last, around midnight, he seemed irritated.

"What was that all about?" he growled, glaring down at her as they got into his car.

"Well, you said I was here to protect you from some woman. Wasn't it Deborah?" she asked calmly. "She was flirting outrageously with you…"

"You thought…?" He laughed softly as he started the car and pulled it out of the garage. "Deborah is a flirt, all right."

"Very pretty, too. I liked her. I liked all your family."

"I'm glad. Because you're going to see a lot of them in the weeks to come."

She turned in her seat. "Now just a damned minute…!" she began.

His eyes ran the length of her body and he smiled slowly. "We'll talk about it when we get to your apartment."

"No, we won't! You said tonight. Okay, I came with

you, but that's as far as you're going to blackmail me. I have a contract with the gallery!"

"Which my lawyers could break in about five minutes flat," he replied calmly. "Sit back and relax, Miss Shannon. We'll talk later. Right now—" he punched in a tape of Dvořák's New World Symphony "—I feel like some music."

She sat back with an angry sigh. She should have known she couldn't trust him. But what was he up to?

CHAPTER THREE

HE PARKED THE car in the underground car park and led her by the elbow as if he expected her to try to escape on the way up to her apartment. She might not have disappointed him, either, but he was strong and she wanted her exhibit. Well, she wanted it if it didn't mean something extreme.

"Stop looking at me as if I'm leading you to your execution," he remarked as the elevator stopped on her floor. "I just want to talk, all right?"

She sighed. "I don't seem to have a choice, Mr. Scarpelli, since you deal in such potent blackmail."

"That show means a hell of a lot to you, doesn't it, lady?" he asked shrewdly.

She glared up at him with flashing dark eyes. "I've worked toward it all my life. I won't give it up without a fight."

His dark eyes narrowed thoughtfully. "It isn't all fluff, is it?" he replied thoughtfully. "There's a lot of mind under that blond hair."

"Being blond isn't a joke," she said shortly. She opened the door to her apartment and stood aside reluctantly to let him enter.

He stared around him as if he were looking at the expanse of gold and white for the first time. He nodded. "Yes, it tells a story, doesn't it?" he asked, turning to stare down at her.

She blinked. "I don't understand."

"Don't you?" He gestured toward the white carpet and brass and glass coffee table, with the gold-toned furniture and drapes. "White and gold. Indicating a background that was black and poor?" he asked suddenly, looking down to catch the wild shock that widened her eyes.

She felt as if the floor had dropped out from under her. How did he see so much?

"Would you like something to drink?" she asked nervously.

"Why? Do I look as if I might faint?"

She glared up at him. "You're very presumptuous."

"I'm very perceptive. Why do you think I'm so successful?"

She made a rude sound. "You probably make a prosperous business of blackmailing people," she returned shortly.

He laughed, a deep, soft, rich sound that made tingles run along her spine. He rammed his hands into his pockets, stretching the fabric of his close-fitting trousers and unwillingly drawing her attention. She looked away, embarrassed by her own curiosity.

"I don't need to blackmail women," he remarked. "On the contrary. Some of them have tried to blackmail me."

"Without success, I'm sure," she said. "Would you like a drink?"

"No. Sit down, please."

He'd added the "please" when she gave him a hot,

belligerent look. He seemed to be oddly amused by her as she took a seat as far away from him as she could get.

His dark eyes went over her slenderness in the white knit dress, and she felt as if he were actually touching her with those dark, long fingers.

"You're beautiful," he said after a minute. "Really beautiful. Black eyes, long, thick blond hair, a complexion like the inside of a seashell. Firm breasts, smooth lines... Yes, you'll wear well. With only a few more lines, you'll look very like you do now when you reach sixty."

The personal remarks made her uneasy. She wasn't used to being discussed this way. Unfortunately, it showed.

He lifted a dark, heavy eyebrow and a corner of his mouth, as he slid his big arm over the back of the sofa and stared at her. "Do I embarrass you, Southern Belle?"

"That's a telephone company," she returned coldly.

"You're damned sensitive about your background, aren't you?" he asked. "Are you ashamed of it?"

"My background is none of your business," she snapped.

"What did you do, before you came to New York?" he persisted.

"I worked, of course."

"At what?"

She hated him, she hated his unrelenting interrogation. "I was a prostitute," she said with a sweet smile. "And on the side, I painted."

Surprisingly, he shook his head. "No, I don't think so. What did you do?"

She stared down at her dress. "I waited tables," she

spat, wondering why she'd told him that, when she'd told no one else, not even Tony.

"There's nothing to be ashamed of in that," he said quietly. "My God, I was a busboy in half the restaurants in the city before I started up the ladder."

Her eyes widened. "You?"

"I'm still a little rough around the edges, honey, haven't you noticed?" he asked with amusement.

"I would have been much too polite to say so," she admitted.

"Someone taught you the social graces with a vengeance. Who?"

"My mother," she said, smiling at the memory. "She was a lady. A true lady, in the best sense of the word. I was only ten when she died, but she left a lasting impression."

"And your father?" he asked, quite naturally.

She closed up. "What did you want to talk about?" she asked.

"Confession time is over, I gather. Too bad. I thought we were getting somewhere." He leaned back and crossed one long leg over the other. "All right. I want you to spend some time with me."

She looked up toward the ceiling. "All I want is to show my paintings to the world, and look what you do to me!" she moaned.

"Will it make a difference if I promise there'll be no blackmail this time?" he asked surprisingly. "You'll get your show, regardless. I'm presuming on our short but fervent acquaintance to ask a favor."

He was a puzzle like none she'd ever encountered. "You think I might feel like doing you a favor out of generosity?"

"No, I don't," he admitted. His eyes searched hers. "But I can guarantee you some unforgettably unique meals, and you won't have to clean up the plates afterward."

She had to muffle a laugh. "And you promised you wouldn't blackmail me."

"Scout's honor," he said, crossing his heart.

"Were you really a Scout?" she asked suspiciously.

"Sure. For one week. Until they caught me with little Mabel, trying for a merit badge of a different kind."

She did laugh that time, helplessly. "Oh, you are a devil," she said.

He grinned, and it softened him just a little. "Be a sport, Jolana. I'll show you a good time, and all you have to do is hang around with me. Just temporarily." He studied her narrowly. "Tony says there's no boyfriend?"

She shook her head. "No. There's no boyfriend."

"The way you look speaks volumes, lady, did you know?" he asked. "Somebody left a few scars, huh?"

"Stop being so...inquisitive, will you?" she asked restlessly. "You're making me nervous."

"I did that the day you walked into me," he reminded her. "Don't be self-conscious. I make a lot of people nervous."

"I know. I read your editorials, too," she confessed.

He chuckled. "What do you say?"

She shrugged, sighing. "I ought to have my head examined. But, okay." She looked straight at him. "But just for a little while, and only if you don't make passes at me."

"One kiss is a pass?" he asked, eyebrows arching.

"It hurt," she said shortly.

"Did it? I must be losing my touch. Come here, baby, and I'll kiss it better."

She jumped as he reached for her, but she wasn't fast enough. She wound up in his arms and on his lap, smelling the subtle scent of his cologne, drowning in the sudden warmth of his body. He was enormous up close, and his eyes filled the world. She stiffened, went rigid, like a cornered cat ready to claw.

His eyebrows edged together as he watched her. "All fur and claws, aren't you?" he asked softly. "Talk about repressed women...!"

"Let me go, please," she said unsteadily.

"Why? Will I break something if I kiss you?"

"Let me go!" She pushed at him wildly, but he only held her more firmly.

"That's enough," he said quietly. "I'm not into brutality. I won't hurt you, or force you. What happened?"

"I don't like being dominated," she burst out, her dark eyes glittering with fear and anger. "Not by anyone!"

He lifted his head and watched her calculatingly. "Tell me why."

"You don't have the right to ask!"

He sighed heavily, letting his eyes slowly wander along the smooth lines of her body. "Not yet," he agreed. His eyes went back up to catch and hold hers. "But someday I might. And someday you might like being dominated...by me."

The thought sent a surge of panic through her slender figure, and she felt herself tremble. Would he be rough with her, or was he capable of tenderness? Her only experiences of intimacy had been fleeting and unsatisfying, and no man she'd ever dated had made her want to lose control. But this man affected her differently from anyone else, and she was afraid of him.

"Will you let me go?" she pleaded weakly.

"Of course." He loosened his arms all at once, grinning when her skirt rode high up her thighs as she lifted her legs away. "Nice," he sighed.

She stood up, a delightful picture with her hair flying and her eyes flashing. "I hate you!"

"Do you? How exciting." He stood up, too, and smiled down at her from his much greater height. "But you'll sleep with me one of these days, in spite of it. And you'll like it."

She could have slapped him. She wanted to. But she was afraid of what his reaction would be.

"Good night, honey. I'll call you in a day or two. When you're a little calmer." He winked at her from the door. "Finished the paintings for the exhibit?" he asked suddenly.

"Yes," she managed. "They're at Tony's gallery."

"Mine and Tony's," he reminded her. "I'll drop by in the morning and take a look. I have an interest in you these days."

And she could take that any way she liked, his eyes added.

"*Ciao*, Jolana." He closed the door, and the apartment seemed less colorful.

She slipped out of her clothes and took a quick shower, dousing herself with expensive bath powder before she pulled on her gown and climbed into bed.

Domenico Scarpelli bothered her. He was the kind of man she usually avoided like the plague, because that kind brought back memories she could hardly bear.

There had been another such man in her life. An

uncle, who'd taken her in after the death of her mother. A bachelor, he hadn't wanted the bother of a young girl, and he'd never shown her any affection at all. But he'd been overbearing and sometimes brutal when she disobeyed. And once, after he'd been drinking heavily, he'd beaten her. Despite the fact that he was obviously remorseful about it the next day, the incident had left deep scars. Shortly thereafter, she'd run away, to stay with a distant cousin north of Atlanta. The cousin, a feisty lady in her sixties, had threatened to go to court to keep Jolana and threatened the uncle with the police if he tried to take her back. He'd been glad to be rid of her. So the next few years had been pleasant. But Jolana had been wary of men ever since, suspicious of them, distrustful. Many men were brutal, and she wanted no more part of brutality. So she'd spent her free hours, the few she had between college art classes and her job, with men who were very different from her uncle, men who were kind and soft and made no demands on her.

None of them had appealed to her physically, oddly enough, but at least she wasn't afraid of them. She was afraid of Domenico Scarpelli. And not solely because he was such a mountain of a man, and so strong. When he had pulled her body against his she had felt the oddest, most terrifying sensations. And the threat he'd made, about taking her to bed, had excited even as it frightened. Men dominated in bed, as so many of them did in everyday life. She was afraid of any kind of domination, and she knew that was the real reason she had never gotten serious about any man. Jolana was full of secret terrors, and she dreaded sharing them with anyone.

Tony called her the next morning, just as she was getting ready to run out to do some shopping.

"Nick loved the paintings," he said without preamble, and sounded smug and cheerful.

"Did he?" she asked.

"Especially the landscapes. He said they reminded him of the place he grew up," he added.

She was pleased about the praise, but she couldn't manage to express it. "How strange," she said instead, "I don't remember painting hell."

"Shame on you! Nick's going to be your biggest booster," Tony chided.

"Okay, I'm sorry," she laughed. "Uh, where did he grow up?" she asked, because the landscapes were Caribbean ones, inspired by a trip to the Bahamas.

"Nassau," he said. "His father had business interests there. They spent his childhood commuting between Nassau and New York."

"I thought he grew up poor," she said.

"He did. His father died when he was ten, and his mother married a, let's face it, a gigolo. The guy went through everything she had in a year and left her on the street. Nick had to go to work to keep them from starving. His mama waited tables and he was a busboy. But, honey, it was a hard life. She got sick... Hey, this is something Nick should tell you. He's a private kind of guy, doesn't like being gossiped about."

"I'd never tell him," she said, oddly touched. She could picture the proud Domenico Scarpelli as a busboy, and it hurt. Why, she wouldn't even contemplate. "But it explains a lot."

"Yeah, doesn't it? But don't waste time feeling sorry for him. He does okay."

"So I've noticed. He's like a steamroller, all right."

"Try working for him," he chuckled. "Once a month, one of his editors gets me drunk and cries all over me."

"I can believe that," she said. "Well, I need to eat lunch. I'm starved."

"Go! I'll talk to you later."

"Thanks for calling, Tony. 'Bye."

She hung up and had started for the door when the intercom buzzed. Frowning, she answered it and found that Nick was downstairs.

Puzzled and vaguely apprehensive, she told the doorman to send him up. A few minutes later she opened her door to find Nick grinning at her. "I'm hungry, are you? How about a nice, big steak somewhere ritzy?"

She couldn't keep from smiling. He looked big and very European in the expensive dark slacks and suede jacket he was wearing with a white turtleneck sweater. She shouldn't have been glad to see him after last night. But she was.

His eyes swept down her body in its gray flannel slacks and purple-patterned silk shirt. "You look nice," he murmured. "But you'll need a jacket."

She had a corduroy one, and it took only a minute to put it on, grab her purse and follow him out the door.

"Does it have to be somewhere ritzy?" she asked. "I feel more like a McDonald's hamburger, in this getup."

"You don't think McDonald's is ritzy? Shame on you," he said.

She laughed in spite of herself. "I guess it depends on your definition, doesn't it? I thought you were going to stay away for a while."

"Oh, that." He dismissed it with a gesture as they

left the elevator. "I was afraid you'd cry. Missing me, you know."

She shook her head. This was a totally different man from the taciturn, arrogant one she'd met on the busy city street. And she found she liked this one very much.

CHAPTER FOUR

EVEN HAVING LUNCH at a fast-food restaurant with Nick
was an experience, Jolana learned quickly. He told her
wildly amusing stories that kept her in stitches as they
ate.

"You're nothing like the man I bumped into on the
street a few days ago," she said after a few minutes.

"I was completely wrong about you, too." He studied her over his coffee cup with appreciative dark eyes.
"Are you as innocent as you seem?"

She shrugged and shook her head, "I'm not sure. I
had a bad experience right off the bat. I was eighteen
and in love for the first time." She sighed, remembering, her eyes wistful and sad. "He was thirty-two, a
salesman, of all things. He used to come into the restaurant where I worked. He fed me a line and I was
swept right off my feet. He talked me into his bed and
that was when I found out why he wasn't married and
how he really felt about women." She shifted restlessly
in her seat; the memories were painful. "Can we talk
about something else?"

"He hurt you?"

"Oh, yes," she laughed bitterly. "The next day, I
moved to another apartment, where he couldn't find
me. I literally hid out. It broke my heart, too, because
I really loved him. But he was one of those men who

just aren't capable of loving, I suppose, and I was too stupid to know it. Love hurts at that age."

"It hurts at any age, honey," he said with a bitter smile. He took a long sip of his coffee. "So what then? Did you give up on men entirely?"

"Except for the occasional friendly date, yes. I couldn't trust my own instincts anymore, you see," she explained, wondering even as she spoke how it was that she trusted him with things she'd told no one else.

"How old are you?" he persisted.

"Twenty-seven."

He cocked an eyebrow. "If you wait many more years to make a commitment, it's going to be too late. Don't you want a husband, a family?"

"No," she said. "I prefer my life as it is."

"A vacuum?" he asked.

"It beats having your heart torn out," she said with a smile.

For a moment he appeared lost in thought, almost as though he had forgotten she was there and was remembering something unpleasant, almost painful. Abruptly coming out of his reverie, he finished his coffee in one quick gulp. "Come on. Let's go walking."

"What a nice way to spend the morning. Freezing to death."

He glared at her. "It's unseasonably warm for January," he reminded her. "And walking is healthy."

"Do I look sick?" she replied.

"Don't get me onto that subject," he said as he cleared away the debris on their table, a tiny smile on his mouth. "I could go on for ten minutes about the way you look."

"That bad, huh?" she sighed. "Well, I've been working pretty hard lately, and keeping terrible hours…"

"That wasn't what I meant." He moved in front of her as she stood up. He was intimidating, sensuous. "You look gloriously beautiful."

She met his eyes and froze. They were so dark, and there was a glitter in them that both attracted her and terrified her. Domenico had an intense sexuality that left her weak-kneed. Her eyes searched his in the sudden silence, and she couldn't have moved to save her life.

"I'm beginning to thank fate for making you bump into me on the street that day, Jolana," he said deeply. "You fascinate me."

Her breath was coming too quickly for comfort. She didn't like the powerful reaction he caused in her and she felt completely vulnerable. She deliberately moved past him with a nervous little laugh.

"Well, where are we going?"

"How would you like to see my offices?"

She whirled, her face glowing with excitement. "Really?"

Her enthusiasm seemed to puzzle him. "It's only a magazine office," he said.

"Yes, I know. I've never been in one before," she confessed, smiling.

A slow smile spread across his hard face. "I've never seen anyone quite so enthusiastic about seeing an office before."

"I'm that way about most things, I'm afraid," she sighed, swinging around to rush out onto the street ahead of him, her hair flying in beautiful disarray around her flushed face. "I love seeing and doing things I've never done before."

He didn't answer. He was looking at her, watching the way the sunshine shimmered on her hair, making it seem a halo around her lovely oval face. His dark eyes dropped to her mouth and lingered there while he felt an odd sensation not unlike hunger.

She smiled at him over her shoulder. "Which way do we go?"

He blinked, coming out of his momentary trance. "This way."

His offices were on the fourteenth floor of a building near Rockefeller Center, very modern and up-to-date and neat. There were word processors everywhere and people doing layouts and pasting up copy. He showed her through the entire process, from the writing of an article to the making up of the magazine, and from there to its printing.

"Since we publish monthly," he explained when they were in the spacious confines of his private office, "we have to keep up-to-date with every facet of the stock market, and changes or coming changes in major corporate structure. It can get hairy," he added with a faint smile. "Especially when a corporate executive is going to get the ax, and we know it, and he doesn't."

"I can imagine!"

She moved to the wall, where she found his degrees—two of them, one in business administration and one in political science. She glanced at him, perched carelessly on the edge of his desk with his arms folded, watching her.

"These must have taken a long time," she observed.

"Mama always believed in education. She only finished grade school and was determined that her children would have more than that."

"Do you have a photo of Rick?" she asked, curious.

He picked up a framed portrait on the desk and offered it. She moved to stand in front of him. It was a photograph of Nick, his two brothers and their mother, fairly recent, too. Rick looked to be about two or three years younger than his brother, slight and slender and balding.

"Not a lot of resemblance, is there?" he asked, taking back the framed photograph to give it a cursory glance before he replaced it on the desk. "Rick is like our father. Marc is like Mama. I take after my grandfather."

"Was he a pirate?" she teased.

His hands shot out, catching her waist to draw her between his powerful thighs and hold her level with his dark, piercing eyes. "No," he said thoughtfully, holding her gaze. "He was an amazing man, though. He sired his last child at the age of eighty. He was Greek, you know, not Italian."

That explained the painting Tony had hired her to do for Domenico, of Mount Olympus.

"Was he…big, like you?" she asked nervously. The feel of his chest under her hands was making her uneasy, along with the masculine scent of cologne and the threat of powerful muscles surrounding her slenderness.

"No," he said softly. "He was small. Wiry. Very tough. My father was big like me. They called him 'Big Rome,' and he had a small textile empire in my boyhood. He died and Mama remarried, and in less than a year there was nothing left."

She couldn't admit that Tony had told her that, so she searched his hard face and asked, gently, "Why?"

His hands contracted, bruising her waist. "Mama married a fast-talking little rat. He liked to spend money and he liked to play the horses." He shrugged. "It didn't take him long to spend her into debt, and then he ran out."

"Lovely man," she muttered. "What happened to him?"

"He disappeared one day and we never heard from him again. Personally, I believe he ran afoul of some gentlemen who took exception to his welching on a bet." He drew her closer. "Don't stiffen up like that, baby, I won't hurt you."

Her hands spread, pushing. "Yes, I know. But, Nick, let's not start anything," she pleaded, knowing her voice, like her traitorous body, lacked conviction.

"I've lived my life starting things," he murmured, bending his head. "And I want very much to start something with you. You're like champagne, and I want the taste of you in my mouth…"

She felt his hard lips against her own, and involuntarily she jerked her head back. He only smiled. His hands moved up to frame her face and hold it steady.

"Don't panic," he whispered. "Satisfy my curiosity and I'll let you go."

"I… I don't want…to get involved," she breathed. It was a lie. Of course she wanted to get involved. He was like heady wine.

"Baby, you're already involved," he whispered back. His mouth touched hers gently, parting her soft lips, and an odd sound rolled up from his throat like thunder. His arms around her tightened, and all at once the kiss became deep and insistent and persuasive.

Her fingers clenched against his chest, she felt her body going rigid. And then it was like honey, like warm honey, flowing through her body. She let herself rest totally against him, her soft breasts crushing gently against his powerful throbbing chest, as her hands spread and began to explore the heavy, hard muscles.

Her breath sighed out wildly, her mouth opened voluntarily, her tongue probed hesitantly at his.

His hands moved down from her face to cup her high, taut breasts with tender, caressing movements, and he smiled against her mouth.

"No bra," he breathed. "I like that, I like feeling you. How the devil does this thing fasten?" he growled softly, searching for fastenings on the blouse she was wearing.

It was too far, too fast, but she couldn't resist him. "Here." She guided one of his hands to the buttons under her arm and stood watching his dark face helplessly while he unfastened them with torturous slowness.

"Yes," he breathed. His hand moved under her arm, up and over, stroking, soothing, until he found her breast. She trembled as his fingers moved delicately over its smoothness and touched the hard peak.

The smile had long since left his face, and there was a wild glitter in his eyes. Under her hands, his chest was shuddering with the force of his heartbeat.

"What color are you, here?" he whispered huskily. "Are you dark or light?"

She felt hopelessly naive despite her age. "I… I'm light."

His eyes had darkened to coal, and his face was rigid. "Show me."

He did something to the blouse and she felt its upward movement with a sense of helplessness, wanting his eyes there, wanting his hands.

He parted the edges and let his gaze drop to her body, and he caught his breath visibly. "My God," he breathed.

Incredibly, his hands were trembling, and a surge

of pure pride went through her slender body at that re-action.

"Baby," he whispered shakily. With his eyes still locked on her body, he bent and put his mouth slowly, reverently, to her breasts, nibbling at the taut peaks, smoothing them with lips and tongue, until she arched and threaded her fingers into his hair to hold him there, to make him come closer.

He lifted his head with a sigh. "Just a minute," he whispered unsteadily. He moved her to one side and went to the door to lock it. Then he picked up the phone and in a deceivingly casual tone told his secretary that he was in conference until further notice and to hold all calls, regardless of their importance.

Jolana stood watching him without even trying to protest or get away. He was teaching her a pleasure she hadn't known before, and she wanted more. Much more.

"Now," he said with a slow, hot smile, "let's try that again."

He stripped off his jacket and the sweater, baring a hairy, muscular, bronzed chest with muscles that seemed to ripple when he moved. He fascinated her, so unlike the men she saw on the beach or in art classes, who were usually pale and thin or flabby.

"Like what you see?" he taunted, pausing in front of her. "So did I." He eased her out of her jacket and the blouse and ran his big, warm hands lightly over her breasts, nudging the hardened peaks gently with his thumbs. "You were eighteen, you said. Has there not been a man since?"

"No," she whispered.

"There's about to be," he told her, smiling slowly. "Me. Here. Now. Lie down."

"Nick…" she began.

His hands swallowed her breasts. "Hush," he whispered, nudging her back against the long leather sofa. "Lie down. I want to touch you all over like this. I want to feel that silky skin against me, under me. I want to bury myself in you…"

"But we're strangers…!" she moaned.

"I knew you a thousand years ago, and you knew me," he growled. He caught her waist and tossed her down onto the sofa, laughing as he threw himself down on top of her and let her feel the full, delicious weight of his big body. "My God, I want you!"

"Nick, don't," she whispered, trying to sound convincing. "No, not like…this!" Her voice broke as his hands moved under her hips and ground them into his, letting her feel what had happened to him.

"Like this," he whispered at her lips, "I'm going to strip you, and touch you, and stroke you, and run my mouth over every inch of you. And then I'm going to invade you like a conquering army—and make you scream my name."

"I'm afraid," she moaned. She was. Not of him, but of the bad experience she'd had so many years ago.

He nudged her legs apart with his. His mouth opened hers softly. "You want me, too. Let me show you what a delight lovemaking can be. Let me give you the pleasure you don't think exists."

He eased down and the sudden intimate contact brought tears to her eyes. She gripped his arms tightly, her eyes opening, looking straight up into his as her jaw clenched on a rush of pleasure unlike anything she'd ever known.

"Touch me a little," he whispered. "Stroke my body."

She'd never touched a man before, but there was silk in his deep voice, and she was curious about him. Her hands smoothed over his shoulders, down into the thick hair over his chest and stomach. Her fingers paused at his belt, and his lips brushed tenderly over her closed eyelids.

"Go ahead," he whispered gently. "Touch me there."

"I...never have."

"Don't you want to?" he chided. "Aren't you curious?"

Her eyes opened and searched his, her face flushed, her hair in glorious disarray around her head. "It's so sudden..." she whispered.

His chest was rising and falling roughly. He lifted himself just a little and shifted, letting her feel the abrasive touch of his chest against the hard tips of her breasts. He smiled hotly when she gasped and arched up, begging for a closer contact.

"Think about how it would feel," he dared. "All of me, against all of you, naked, my body over yours. My lips here...and here..." His mouth opened on her breasts as he slid down against her, and the world seemed to catch fire. She felt his fingers opening her slacks so that he could kiss her flat stomach, her hips, her thighs. He had every stitch of clothing off her before she realized it, and he was doing things to her that she'd never imagined possible.

Her voice broke and she cried out, muffling the sound by biting her lower lip. The passion was so feverish, so unexpected, that she could hardly bear to be silent.

"Go ahead," he whispered roughly. "Scream. No one but me will hear you. Let me hear what I'm making you feel, baby. Scream for me," he taunted, and put his open mouth against her body in a way that made her arch in a wild, sobbing moan.

She thought she couldn't live, would never breathe again. She wanted him with an unexpected passion, wanted to take him, take possession of him. She cried and moaned and twisted under the passionate torment of his mouth and hands until, finally, he eased down on her and took her mouth again. But that was all he did. And he was still wearing everything except his turtleneck sweater.

Her eyes opened, drowsy with passion and hunger, black as coals, looking up into his dark ones. "Take me," she whispered softly.

He shook his head, smiling down at her with something like tenderness. "Not yet. I want you to think about it first. I won't offer you commitment, or marriage, or anything except this, until it pleases me to leave you. You understand? I'm offering nothing permanent. Because you are…the way you are, you have to walk into it with both eyes open. This—" he sighed heavily "—is pure seduction, and I've long since lost my taste for it. Ten minutes after I finished, you'd hate me."

Her head was just beginning to clear. She searched his dark face with a quiet frown.

"Not all men are out to hurt you," he whispered, bending to kiss her one last time before he arched himself away and got to his feet. He stood, stretching his powerful body, looking down at her with undisguised desire and appreciation, her slender pink nakedness highlighted by the dark burgundy leather she was lying on. "My God, I could get drunk on just the sight of you!" he said.

She stretched, too, feeling luxuriously feminine and bristling with the power to make his eyes burn like that.

"That," he murmured drily, "will get you in trouble. Here." He tossed her her clothes and turned his back. "I hate being a gentleman, so hurry up, will you?" He moved away and lit a cigarette. He felt drunk on the feel of her satiny skin; the exquisite contours of her breasts and hips lingered like a beloved memory on his fingertips. It had never been that intense before. The feelings had frightened him, although he wasn't letting her know that. He'd pulled back because he could feel himself falling into a bottomless abyss with her and it was as unwelcome as it was unexpected. He'd thought he could take her and forget her, but it seemed he couldn't. Otherwise, how could he have drawn back?

She was watching him as she dressed, still tingling from the contact with his long, dark fingers and recalling the exquisite pleasure he'd given her. She wanted him desperately. If one night was all she could have, that would be enough to live on. He was a dark sorcerer, and thank God he had scruples, because if he'd insisted, she wouldn't have been able to stop him. She needed a little time. But she was afraid the outcome was preordained. He appealed to her in impossibly sweet ways, and she'd been alone too long. But she wasn't sure she could survive an affair with him. He wasn't the kind of man a woman could easily forget, and he was making the rules.

When she was dressed she stood up and he turned toward her, his cigarette smoldering as he ran a hand through his thick curly hair. He smiled ruefully as his eyes wandered slowly down her body. "God, you're sweet to love," he murmured. "Honey and spice and silk, all woman."

She smiled. "You're not bad, either," she laughed. "Do you have to shake the women out of your sheets?"

"Occasionally." He moved forward, studying her with appreciation. "You look glorious when you're aroused. All dark eyes and peachy skin and a voice that makes me tremble with hunger. I could make love to you for days on end."

"You'd starve," she reminded him.

"I wouldn't care." He bent and kissed her mouth softly. "Who taught you to kiss?"

"A boy in my biology class who married my best friend." She smiled. "I won't even ask where you learned. That's ancient history, I'll bet."

"Pretty much." He lifted his head. "I meant what I said," he continued after a minute. "I want you. I'll go slow. You can have all the time you need. But I want a few nights with you like I want water when I'm thirsty."

"No bribes?" she asked with a quivering smile.

"I wouldn't insult you by offering, Jolana," he said honestly. "You aren't mercenary enough to be tempted. You'd have to want me enough to take what I could give you physically. No strings. No offers. Just sex."

Her eyes searched his quietly. "What you'd do to me wouldn't be just sex," she said.

He nodded, as if he understood. "Yes, I know. If it had been only a physical thing, I wouldn't have stopped just now."

She studied her shoes with eyes that only half saw them, thinking.

"Hey," he said, tilting her face up to his. "Don't make such heavy weather of it. There's no hurry. You don't

have to make up your mind in the next five minutes."
He grinned wickedly. "You can have ten, if you want."

She burst out laughing, and the tension was broken.
"What am I getting myself into?" she asked, shaking
her head.

"Just a little education, that's all. Anyway, why such
soul-searching? I thought all you wild artists were uninhibited."

She sighed. "Well, I used to think I was, until you
came along. Now all my inhibitions are back full force."

He touched her face lightly. "Yes, I know. I like you
that way. Come on. We'll walk for a while. You like to
window-shop?"

"I love it!" she agreed.

"So do I." He herded her out of the office, where no
one even looked up. Jolana wondered if it was a common occurrence for him to lock himself in with an attractive woman. Probably seducing women was part of
his lifestyle. She tried to remind herself that it was going
to be suicide, letting herself get mixed up with him. But
she wasn't listening to her own counsel. All she had to
do was look at the size and sensuality of that big, dark
body and she wanted him to the roots of her nerves.

He didn't pressure her. They walked companionably
down Fifth Avenue, gazing in shop windows, and she
laughed as he seemed as fascinated by jewelry windows as she was.

"I used to do this when I was a kid," he told her.
"Stand in front of toy stores and jewelry stores, and I
always swore when I got grown, I was going to have
an electric train set and a diamond ring."

She touched his broad, dark hand. "You got the ring,
I see," she stated drily, eying the diamond in the cen-

ter of a majestic gold ring on his right-hand ring finger. "How about the train set?"

He shrugged. "I wouldn't have time to run it," he said ruefully.

"Maybe Santa Claus will bring you one next year."

"I never believed in him," he said absently. "Times were so damned hard, and presents were a luxury we couldn't afford. Mama waited tables, I cleared them. Between us, we managed to keep food on the table and not much more." His eyes darkened and he jammed his hands deep in his pockets. "Mama saw to it that I graduated from high school. And, honey, you'll never know how she paid to keep me there. She hasn't been in good health for a lot of years, so I took over the burden when I got old enough. I got Rick and Marc through school by myself, and I managed college by playing the stock market." He glanced down at her with a thin smile. "Even then, I had a facility for it. I took advantage of that and bought up stock in a magazine that was about to fold. Where we went today is what I built from the ashes."

"My gosh," she whispered.

"Money is where it's at, didn't you know?" he asked. There was ice in his voice, pure ice. He stared at the diamond in the window, an engagement ring, with eyes just as cold. "Mama remarried, and on the third time she got lucky. This one got rich all by himself, and I respect him, and I call him 'Papa,' because it's what she wants. But if I'd had money, my mother might not be in such bad health today, and I might have married the girl I loved."

"Did she marry somebody who did have money?" she asked, curious.

He took a slow breath. "She married another man

because I'd had her, and she thought she was pregnant," he said bluntly. "I couldn't handle a wife, with all the burdens I had at the time, and she knew it. So she didn't tell me, and she married that…" His shoulders hunched and fell. "By the time I found out the real reason, it was far too late. She wasn't pregnant, but a few months later, she was. She had his baby and gave him a hold on her that she was never able to break. He beats her and abuses her, and there isn't a damned thing anybody can do, because he's threatened to take the child if she leaves him."

"I'm so sorry," she said gently. "You still love her."

"I don't believe in love," he said gruffly. He turned away. "Let's walk some more."

By now Jolana knew without having to be told that the woman Nick had loved was Margery. She remembered the longing way Margery had looked at him at the party and sadly realized that their love was still as strong as ever.

Nick was a strange man, complex, moody. But she felt a kind of kinship with him. Her own life had been a hard one, with a foundation of poverty and hopelessness. Her fingers reached out and touched his as they moved down the windy street to the sound of loud horns and the never-ending stream of yellow taxicabs.

He stiffened for a minute. Then his fingers wound into hers, linking with them, and tightened, palm to palm. A shiver of remembered passion tingled down her slender body and she felt alive as she never had before.

They went out that night, to an exclusive restaurant overlooking the city, and she ate prime rib and drank expensive imported wine and enjoyed flaming desserts. Nick laughed at her enthusiasm.

"Surely you've done this before?" he teased.

"Yes, but it never gets old," she sighed. She leaned back in her chair, holding the delicate china cup of coffee in her hand, and smiled at him. "I had a hard life myself as a child. No money, no close relatives except an uncle who was good with his fist. I got knocked around a lot."

His expression hardened as he studied her face in its frame of wildly beautiful golden hair, her dark eyes, the silky complexion of her skin against her emerald-green dress. "I can't imagine a man doing that to you," he said honestly. "You must have been a beautiful child."

She sipped her coffee. "I was ragged and dirty and I worked all the time. It would have taken a team of beauticians to make me look human, much less beautiful."

"Where were your parents?"

"My mother died when I was about ten. My father left me with his brother and went off to enjoy himself," she laughed. "I never saw him again, so I assume he's still enjoying himself somewhere."

"And the uncle?"

She stared into the coffee. "I don't know. Or care. I ran away to live with an old woman who was distantly related to me when I turned sixteen. Then I lied about my age to get a job in a restaurant in Atlanta. That way," she added, smiling slowly, "I could see the exhibits at the High Museum of Art, and in galleries. I even found an artist who was willing to work with me for the little sum I could pay. She was a lovely lady, elderly, but quick and talented. What I know, she taught me."

"She taught well," he said, and meant it. "You have a great talent. Someday you'll hang in the Louvre and I'll be able to say that I knew you."

That meant, she knew, that he was looking ahead to a time when they wouldn't be together. She had to keep that in mind.

But it wasn't easy. Dancing with him kept reminding her of the wild, sweet interlude on the couch in his office, and the ways he'd touched and roused her. He was so big that the top of her head came only to his chin, and being held against him was warmer than hugging a blast furnace. He moved gracefully for all his size, and he was light on his feet.

The band had been playing a moderately fast tune, but when they paused and began to play again, the music grew slow and sensuous.

"Finally," Nick murmured on a smile. "My kind of dancing music."

He lifted her arms around his neck and slid his own hands down her sides to her hips, holding her there while he moved with exquisite slowness among the throng of dancers. "Isn't this nice?" he chuckled softly.

She was aching in the worst possible places, feeling as if her trembling legs were going to dump her on the floor any minute. Her fingers tangled lazily in the hair at the back of his neck, feeling the soft coolness of the crisp curls there.

"Closer," he murmured, pulling at her hips. "I want to feel your thighs against mine when we move together."

"Don't do that," she whispered shakily. "I'll faint."

His cheek nuzzled hers. "Isn't it fascinating, the way we react to each other?" he whispered deeply. "I touch you, and we can't get close enough together. We tremble and ache and strain to join our bodies, even when we're only dancing."

"No fair, you said you wouldn't rush me," she pleaded.

"Did I? How stupid of me." But he released his tight hold with a sigh and let his hands slide up to her waist and rest there. "Perhaps you're right. A little time won't hurt. Probably," he murmured softly, bending his lips to her ear, "the waiting will make it much more intense when we come together for the first time."

Her nails contracted in his hair helplessly. She loved the feel of him, the light scent of his cologne, the warmth of his big hands against her skin. She remembered how she felt lying naked in his arms, and she wanted that.

Her eyes looked up into his, smoldering with passion, and he looked back for a long time without blinking, without speaking. One big hand trespassed to the very base of her spine and moved her against his hips with a slow, thoroughly explicit pressure.

"Can't it be tonight?" he breathed.

But she was just barely sane. She leaned her forehead against his dark jacket. "I want to. But I need…a little time."

He sighed long and hard and his hand moved again. "Jolana, you'll put me in an institution. For years, I haven't felt like this."

"I find that hard to believe," she murmured, forcing herself to say the words that were surely true.

"Honestly," he contradicted. "There have been other women, of course. But with you, my blood runs hot and wild. I want to do insane things with you."

"Like what?" she asked, lifting her dark eyes to his.

"I want to make love to you on tables," he said, his face mirroring the amusement in his deep voice. "Moonlit beaches. In the backseat of a car. Standing up," he added, holding her fascinated eyes. "In ways and places that I never wanted it before. At my age, a bed is more comfortable. But when I picture you, it's on a sandy beach with crashing surf and the moon gilding your skin as you move beneath me."

She pressed against him hard, trembling. "Nick!"

His breath came heavy and rough. His hands moved on her back with sensuous pressure. "I know of such a beach. In the Bahamas. We could fly down there tonight or tomorrow. I have a house on one of the out islands, an isolated place with an isolated beach. Look at me, Jolana." She did, and he held her eyes. "We could make love on the beach in broad daylight," he breathed roughly. "You could look at me while it was happening…"

Her breath caught and her mouth opened. Unable to resist the temptation, he bent and kissed her softly, warmly, as the music came to a close.

"Come," he whispered.

She followed him to the door and waited while he paid the tab. With mixed emotions, she let him lead her out to the car.

"Not tonight," she said as he climbed in beside her. "Give me two weeks. Just that. And I'll give you an answer. I promise."

He considered that for a long moment, looking as if he'd have liked to insist. He could have, and they both knew it. Her resistance was nil when Nick put on the heat. "Two weeks, *amore mia*," he agreed softly. "And then I take the choice from these delicate, talented hands."

Living through those two weeks hadn't seemed quite so hard at the time. But as the days wound by, and Nick began to insinuate himself into her life at an alarming rate, she felt as if she were going wild with hunger. He seemed to deliberately tempt her, in ways so subtle that she couldn't protest. He'd lean over her to serve her a drink, to ask a question, his lips poised just over hers. And when she was dying for the kiss he was threatening her with, he'd draw away with laughter and triumph in his dark, wicked eyes. Or he'd sit beside her to watch television or at a movie, and one big hand would travel slowly up and down her side, teasing at the edge of a breast, or just above it, until involuntarily her body would lift toward his fingers. And then he'd stop, abruptly, as if his movements hadn't been deliberate at all. They were little things, but maddening things. And all the while, they were talking, playing, having fun, learning about each other.

She found that he was an avid chess player, very deliberate with his moves, darkly concentrating. She, on the other hand, was haphazard, thinking only halfway through a move. He liked to jog. So did she. Often, she tried to picture him in shorts. She'd have bet that he had gorgeous dark, strong legs. She remembered that his chest and arms were darkly tanned. Sensuous. Very, very muscular.

He liked to work out in the gym, and one day she went to watch, feeling awed at the muscles in his arms as he lifted weights. He was wearing a T-shirt, and under it the unleashed power of his splendid physique made her sigh with admiration. He wasn't muscle-bound as a lot of weight lifters were, but he looked formidable enough. He caught her watching him and threw back his dark, curly head and laughed gloriously. He was so uninhibited. He fascinated her. She saw him cry over a particularly sad movie, unashamedly. She watched him with his mother on the occasions when they went to see her, and saw the love shining in his eyes. He was an emotional man, all arrogant pride and rough charm, but he appealed to every insecurity she had. He was strong and forceful and able to charm or demand whatever he wanted from life. Within days, she was head over heels in love with him and helpless to escape his pull. She knew she was going to give in, because she had to have something of him to remember when it was over. And if a few nights in his bed were the only way she could really get close to him, she'd agree to it gratefully.

Love like this was incredibly rare. It wasn't like the greedy, selfish infatuation she'd had for her long-ago salesman. No, this was a giving thing. She liked to do little things for Nick. She liked to make him special desserts when they ate at her apartment. She liked to give him presents. She'd found out that he was crazy about crystal, and she bought him a tiny lead crystal swan and presented it to him with bursting pride. She'd glowed when he became enthusiastic about it, turning it over and over in his big hands, fascinated. She didn't tell him about the portrait she was doing of him, a splendid painting of his torso with storm clouds behind and an aura of mystery about it.

The only irritating habit he seemed to have was making frequent references to Margery. As he and Jolana spent more and more time together, it began to grate on her nerves.

It seemed that they couldn't even have a meal together without some memory leaking out of Nick's past with a potent reminder of the woman he had cared for for so many years.

"I love eating out, don't you?" he asked one evening when they were enjoying a spaghetti supper at a nearby restaurant. He grinned at her. "I especially like leaving the dishes behind."

She laughed, too. "I like not having to remember four orders at once and not worrying about fouling up at least one of them."

He sighed, finishing his meal, and leaned back with his coffee cup in his hand. "Oh, the good life. Enough food, enough clothing, enough money. A car. A place to live where I don't have to fight to get into the bathroom." He shook his head. "It wasn't always so good."

"Yes, I know." She toyed with her dessert, a rich pudding. "I've still got a long way to go, but it's nice to be able to afford things."

"Margery always wanted a diamond watch," he recalled. He laughed. "I gave her one, for Christmas a few years back. Andrew raised hell."

His mention of Margery hurt Jolana, but she was determined not to let Nick know.

"Doesn't he mind your giving his wife presents? I gather that he isn't wealthy?"

"Andrew would drink up any profits he made if he were in business for himself," he scoffed. "He works for my stepfather, if you can call it work."

"People don't drink without a reason," she began.

"He beats her," he growled, glaring across the table.

"My uncle beat me," she returned, glaring back. "I got out. So could Margery if she wanted to."

He didn't like that. It showed in his eyes. "You don't know anything about it."

"Nobody really knows anybody else. Not deep down, behind the masks we all wear to protect us. You don't know what it's like between Margery and Andrew. You only know what she tells you."

He put his cup back on the table. "How's the pudding?" he asked, changing the subject with apparent friendliness. "Want something else?"

She started to protest, then let him have his way. Perhaps he didn't realize how often he mentioned Margery. She wasn't going to make an issue of it. Not yet, anyway.

Nick liked to sit with her while she painted, bringing along work that he couldn't find time for at his office. He wore reading glasses when he worked, and she couldn't help thinking that the dark-rimmed frames suited him, made him look even more masculine.

She poised at her easel, studying the fluid lines of his big body where he was sprawled on the studio couch with a sheaf of papers in one hand. He sensed her scrutiny and looked up, grinning.

"Painting me?" he teased.

She was, but not on the canvas before her. She was painting him in her mind, in indelible colors. "Sort of," she hedged. "You do a lot of work in the evenings, don't you?"

"I have to. I spend most of my day answering the phone and seeing people," he confided. "I can't get through paperwork and do that, too." He took off his glasses with a sigh. "I get sick of it sometimes. I'd like to fly off into the sun."

"To Nassau?" she probed.

He looked up. "How did you know?"

"Tony told me you liked my island landscapes and

when I asked why, he said you grew up in Nassau. I went there once, for several days," she recalled with a faint smile. "It was beautiful."

"Yes, I always thought so. When I was a boy, I used to hang around Prince George wharf watching the ocean liners dock, or wrangle invitations to go out on the fishing boats." His dark eyes grew dreamy. "Pirates were all over the islands a couple of centuries or so ago, you know. Woodes Rogers drove them out when he became the first governor of the Bahamas, there's even a statue of him…"

"…in front of the Sheraton," she added, grinning. "I used to come in by it every evening while I was staying there. And the old cannons… Aren't they something?"

"As you might imagine, I spent a lot of my boyhood playing pirate," he murmured drily. "Rick and I had some good times." Then the smile faded, and she knew he was remembering the end of it, his father's death.

"You loved your father, didn't you?" she asked quietly.

"He was some kind of man." He laughed softly. "I wanted to grow up and be just like him."

"Haven't you?"

He shrugged. "Sometimes I like to think so." He glanced up at her. "What are you working on?"

She stared at the canvas, at the pastel colors overlayered with vivid dark ones. An outline of a man and a girl was just beginning to take shape. "Something Impressionistic," she confided. "I don't often get to paint just for myself. I have to paint what people are buying, and landscapes have been very popular in recent years. That, and portraits. I've done several, but I don't like to. I have to paint what I see. And people don't like truth on canvas."

"Warts and all, so to speak?" he chuckled. "I understand. Margery did a drawing of me once, when we were teenagers, and I tore it up. She cried and cried..." His eyes darkened. "She's so sweet, so helpless, and now she's stuck with that damned drunk, and there isn't a thing I can do to help her. Nothing!" He shifted and glanced down at the papers in his hand while Jolana did a slow, furious burn. Margery. Every other word he spoke these days was *Margery*! It was a habit that she'd accepted at first, but as she became more emotionally involved with him, it began to grate. And tonight he'd outdone himself. "I can't get into this tonight," he said after a minute and tossed his work onto the floor, along with his glasses. He studied her with pursed lips and began to smile slowly. "Come here," he said in a deep, sensuous tone, patting the sofa beside him.

Just like that, she thought furiously. He could praise Margery to the high heavens, and then expect Jolana to fall into his arms. He was carrying that schoolboy protectiveness to impossible heights. Margery had been another man's wife for ten years now, but Nick didn't seem to appreciate that. She felt jealousy wash over her, along with a burst of pure hatred for the "helpless" other woman. How deeply did Nick still care for Margery?

She turned, staring at him with cold eyes. "Why?" she asked. "Would you like me to substitute for the beloved Margery?"

He paled. His expression changed and for an instant he looked murderous. He bent, picking up his papers and his glasses. He put the glasses in his pocket, slipped on his jacket, and stood up.

"Margery is none of your business," he said with icy formality.

"She should be," she laughed bitterly. "I hardly hear anything else from you but the wonder of her. You talk more about Margery than you do about your own mother."

"Are you jealous?" he taunted, letting his eyes wander over her insolently. "I don't sleep with her."

"You don't sleep with me, either, honey," she said sweetly, "and you're not likely to. I won't be a poor second choice for any man. If it's sweet little Margery you want, go for it. Just don't expect me to fill in in the meantime."

"Do you think you could?" he scoffed. "My God, you're all ice inside, with just an occasional meltdown. For days now, I've kept my distance, waiting for a single invitation. All I get is supper around here."

"What do you expect, for God's sake, when you spend the evening talking about other women? If you want to talk about Margery, go to a bar. I've got work to do!"

"Work seems to be the only thing you have any passion for," he said, turning. His big body seemed rigid, and a twinge of regret made her shift uneasily. But she didn't want Margery's leftovers, she told herself. If he couldn't give her anything but his body, then it was better that she never see him again.

"I'm looking for a man who wants me," she returned, glaring at him. "Just me, for myself. When I find him, I'll give him everything he needs or wants from a woman. But I'm not passing out samples."

"I can't imagine that doing you any good," he replied from the door.

"You seemed to like the taste you had," she returned, lifting her chin and smiling at him regardless of the cost. "I know you've had more than just a taste of Margery, Nick. And how does her poor fish of a husband like having you thrown in his face like an Olympic gold medal?"

For an instant she thought he might hit her, there was such fury in every line of his body. But, of course, he didn't. And without another word, he reached for the doorknob and stormed out of the apartment. The walls actually shuddered behind him.

It took a while for what she had done to sink in. She'd lost her temper and Nick, too. That was probably for the best, she tried to tell herself, because she was losing control of her life and her heart and even her body. But her life felt suddenly empty and impossibly lonely.

She hadn't realized just how involved she was getting with him. Even her apartment had begun to reflect it. There were ashtrays everywhere, for his cigarettes. There were magazines he liked, there were special desserts in the freezer that were his favorites, there were sketches and the unfinished painting of him. It was for the best, she told herself, and now he could go and moon over Margery.

The show at the gallery was just two weeks away, and already Tony was running an announcement in the *Times* about it. She'd worked so hard to make it this far. Nick wasn't going to ruin this for her, he wasn't!

But she cried for hours as it sank in that he wasn't coming back. She'd hoped and prayed that he'd call, or come. But three days went by, and she didn't know if she could bear it. Twice she picked up the phone to call him, and put it right back down again. Her pride was as strong as her feeling for Nick. She couldn't crawl to him. She couldn't!

Her eyes went to a letter on the coffee table, from Maureen de Vinchy-Cardin. She and Maureen had gone to college together. Jolana had graduated with a bachelor of arts degree and Maureen had majored in business administration. The young woman, daughter of an Irish mother and an aristocratic French father, was a countess, of all things, and she had a madcap brother named Phillipe who had frequently escorted Jolana when he came to see his sister. The three of them had enjoyed each other so much, and Jolana often thought that Phillipe would someday make some lucky woman a fine husband. He was such fun to be with. But there had never been the time, or the inclination, to get serious about him. Jolana's career had always come first and still did.

Maureen had invited her to come and spend a few weeks in Paris, and Jolana was tempted to go. She could get away from Nick and maybe forget him. Yes, it would be a good idea after the exhibit. She sat down, and with a breaking heart, she wrote and told Maureen she'd be in touch shortly about her arrangements.

The next morning, she was just returning to her apartment after airmailing the letter to Maureen, when she saw Nick climbing out of his Jaguar at the curb.

Part of her wanted to run. But the other part stood quietly and watched him, magnificent in his leather coat, towering above people around him, as he spotted her and walked toward her.

She felt sick. She couldn't go through it again, she couldn't. *Oh, Nick, go away, she prayed. Go away be-*

*fore we get involved, I couldn't bear to let you go once
we were involved...!*

"Hello," he said quietly, pausing just in front of her,
far too close.

"Hello," she said. Her hands stayed in her pockets.
"Passing by?"

He shook his dark, curly head. "I came to see if you'd
go to a party with me tonight."

"Do you need a bodyguard again?" she asked, laughing bitterly.

He shrugged. "I need you."

Her eyes closed and she bit hard on her lower lip.
"It's only physical," she said. "It will pass."

"No. I don't think so. Come with me."

"I'm going to Paris," she said simply.

"Not tonight."

"No, not tonight, but soon." Her wild eyes searched
his. "I don't want..."

He caught her shoulders and held her roughly. His
eyes blazed down into hers. "I don't want it, either, but
the past few days have been hell. So I'll stop talking
about other women, all right?"

What difference would it make, if he was still emotionally involved with Margery? she thought in anguish.
But he was close to her, and she loved him, and all her
resolutions melted when he bent and put his cool, hard
mouth to hers.

"Nick," she protested.

"Nobody's around," he murmured, ignoring the
amused looks of passersby. "Kiss me."

She did, helplessly, hungrily, with her whole heart.
She reached up and held him, and tears ran down her

cheeks in the cold wind and she thought she might die of the joy and relief.

"So soft," he whispered, cupping her face in his hands to study its subdued beauty. "So lovely. I look at you, and I can't believe how beautiful you are... *Amore*," he whispered.

His mouth touched her wet, closed eyelids, and his tongue traced the thick spiky lashes. "*Amore*, no more arguments, please. I've caused one of my reporters to resign, just to get away from my temper. Much more, and I'll have no staff left."

She laughed softly, through her tears. "No more arguments," she agreed. She drew away and looked up at him with soft, loving eyes. "Come on, let's go inside."

"I have no time," he sighed regretfully. He touched her lips with a warm finger. "Tonight, we talk, all right? Mama is giving a dinner party, she wants us to come. I'll pick you up at five thirty."

"All right," she agreed quietly. "Tonight."

He smiled. "I missed you, Jolana."

"I missed you, too."

He kissed her briefly and went back to his car with a careless wave of his hand. Jolana danced through the lobby to the elevator, feeling happier than she'd been in days.

CHAPTER FIVE

JOLANA KNEW NO one at the party except for Margery and her husband. And although Nick's mother and the other three couples did their best to make Jolana welcome, she was uneasy at best. Nick was attentive, as if he were trying to win her all over again. But Margery was eying him covetously, obviously. And as she expected, eventually, Margery managed to finagle a dance with him. And, minutes later, they disappeared.

Without knowing why, Jolana found herself standing beside Margery's thin husband, Andrew, at the punch bowl.

"Nice party," she murmured drily, lovely in her strapless white gown, with her hair loose.

"Is it?" Andrew scoffed. He looked down at her with a sigh. "You're very beautiful. Why is it that Nick can't see it?"

"See what?" she asked hesitantly.

He lifted his glass to his lips. "Never mind. Doesn't matter." He sighed heavily. "Not anymore, it doesn't matter. How do you compete with a guy like that, when he gets thrown up to you every day, every night?" He took another swallow from the glass. "Damn Nick!"

She knew just how he felt, but there was nothing she could do. And anything she said would only make it worse. "Does that help?" she asked quietly, nodding toward the drink in his hand.

He stared at her. "No. It makes it worse. But I've fallen on hard times and bad habits," he said ironically as his eyes wandered over her face. "Is there any chance that he'll marry you?"

She smiled sadly and shook her head. "No, I shouldn't think so. He isn't a marrying man."

"You couldn't really believe that," he asked.

"But I do," she replied. She poured herself a small glass of punch and sipped it. "Have you known him a long time?"

"Since we were teenagers. I took Margery away from him." He laughed coldly. "But although I won the battle, he won the war. He's as cold as ice, your Nick, except where Margery is concerned. But don't let that stop you from trying. Who knows? Maybe you'll succeed where all the others failed. At least you've got some brains. That alone sets you apart." His eyes held hers. "Don't let him get you caught in the middle. Look what it's done to me."

She started to pursue that, but Nick was suddenly back. "Hello, Andrew," he said coldly. "Let's dance, Jolana."

He tugged her onto the dance floor, and she frowned as she saw the look on his face. He seemed pale, and tense, and oddly taciturn. Nick, who usually laughed and talked incessantly. She looked around for Margery, but the woman was nowhere in sight. Perhaps she'd been wrong. Perhaps they hadn't gone off together, she told herself, grasping at straws.

"What were you saying to him?" he asked coldly.

"Just party talk, Nick, that's all."

Unthinking, she pressed close to Nick in conciliation and was shocked to find his body already aroused. His hand contracted around her waist, holding her to him, and his legs trembled.

"Nick!" she whispered, shaken by the sudden force of his passion, by a need that she'd never felt in him before. She looked up, seeking his face, and found torment in it. Everything in her that was womanly reached out to him. She touched his face gently, tenderly, and his jaw tensed even at the whispery caress. "Nick, come home with me," she whispered, so that no one could hear. "Come home with me, and I'll give you what you need so desperately."

His breath shook as his chest rose and fell. "Jolana…"

"It's all right," she whispered. "I know you won't hurt me. I'll give you my body, Nick. I'll lie with you in my bed and…"

"God," he broke off, shuddering, as his arm crushed her against him. "Jolana, I can't tell you…how I hurt!"

"I can feel it," she said gently. She felt full of her own power. She moved away, catching her hand in his. "Let's go."

She led him past his mother, pleading a splitting headache, and looked the part until they got into the elevator. She laughed softly. "Well, I have had splitting headaches before, so it wasn't a total lie," she said.

He still looked pale, and so flushed with hunger that she hardly knew him. The car was in a corner of the deserted garage, all by itself, and she remembered that the seat reclined all the way back. Her face flushed as she thought how easy it would be, at how vulnerable he was. The way he looked, the way he was trembling, he'd never make it to her apartment.

With a sense of pure witchery, she got into the car with him, thankful for the darkly tinted windows all the way around. Not that anyone was likely to come here. There was only one parking attendant, an old man, and he never left his office. She smiled slowly.

Nick hadn't said a word. He got in beside her and started to put the key in the ignition.

"No," she breathed, touching the back of his hand lightly with hers. She reached under the long gown, easing it up around her hips, and slid out of her silky briefs while Nick watched incredulously with eyes as dark as black flames. She dropped the briefs onto the carpeted floorboard and turned to him.

"What are you doing?" he asked unsteadily.

"Seducing you, darling," she whispered back. Her hands went, trembling, to his belt buckle. Seconds later, she moved over him, facing him, and her heart went as wild as his own when she eased down.

"I don't know how to do it this way," she whispered against his shaking breath, "so you'll have to help me."

His big hands found her hips and guided her, helped her, and his face hardened, his jaw tensed, his eyes narrowed as he sucked in a harsh breath.

"It's going to be too quick," he whispered hoarsely. "I'm burning up."

"I don't mind," she whispered back, smiling. "You can make it up to me when we get home. Come on, Nick. Take me."

"Oh, God!" he ground out. His mouth fastened onto hers as if he'd never tasted anything so sweet, and his fingers hurt where they dug into her soft skin. She felt him against her, hot and hard and hungry, and she let him fit her body over his with a sense of awe. It had been a long time, and it hurt a little, but she didn't make a sound. She clenched her teeth and leaned her forehead against his dark hair.

"Does it hurt?" he whispered shakily.

"Just…a little," she whispered back, easing into a slow rhythm with him. "It's been so long…you see. Nick… Nick…"

Her voice was rising. It shouldn't be happening for her, it shouldn't…but it was! She moved with him, hearing her breathing become as ragged as his, feeling his hands hurting, his hips moving roughly under her, his voice groaning at her ear.

"My God…in a car!" he burst out, and then his voice splintered, and his hands crushed her into his hips, and she felt the ferocity of movement build into a climax like nothing she'd dreamed of as they spent their urgency together and her voice echoed with his harsh groan.

A long, shuddering minute later, he kissed her as softly as a whisper. His lips moved over her face in tiny, soft caresses while her body was still fused to his.

"I'll never…never be able to make this up to you," he whispered tenderly. "You can't know how much I needed you!"

"I did know." She kissed him back, tender, soft kisses, and smiled against his lips. "Are you satisfied now?"

He lifted his head and looked into her eyes in the dim light. "No, Jolana. Are you?"

She shook her head. "All night?"

He nodded. "All night. In a bed." He touched her thighs lightly, smiling. "It won't be quite as frantic as this, either. Here, honey, we'd better make ourselves decent. This is hardly the place for making love."

She eased away from him and tugged her briefs back on, laughing. "Artists are unconventional, didn't you know? Besides," she added, glancing at him wickedly, "I didn't think you'd last until we got to my apartment."

"I wouldn't have," he agreed, something dark and violent in the way he said it. He sighed roughly, glancing at her. "Are you sure?"

"I'm very sure," she said solemnly.

He studied her as he finished arranging his slacks. And he smiled. "Okay. Let's go."

It took only a few minutes to get to her apartment.

He locked the door and began stripping off his clothes, and when he was through, he undressed her, slowly, tenderly. He led her, dark and gloriously naked, into the bedroom, and her eyes never left him. She was as on fire for him as he seemed to be for her. She searched his dark eyes for a long moment. Slowly she began to see how obsessively he wanted her. Perhaps, if she grabbed the opportunity, she could fight Margery. She could make him see that his obsession had no future. That he could love her, too.

He lifted her in his big arms, his eyes warm and glittering with controlled passion. "Now," he said, letting his gaze run over her as he tossed her gently onto the coverlet. "Now we have time to really become lovers, and enough room and comfort to do it right."

She trembled a little as he joined her on the bed, but his big hands smoothed over her softness and calmed her.

He bent, biting at her mouth, his passion immediate and uncontrollable. Her body burned at the first contact with his, and her hands seemed to belong to someone else, because they were doing things to his body that she'd never dreamed of doing to a man.

"Yes," he laughed gruffly. "Yes, touch me like that. Bite me, claw, scream. I want a wildcat under me, not a sweet little flower, you understand? I want a woman whose passion is as hot as mine, a woman to match me... Jolana!"

He groaned as she arched, twisting her body against his in a way that she knew would arouse him, while her searching fingers teased and tormented.

"Witch!" he protested, his eyes shining with passion, his hands hurting as they grasped her hips and pulled her under him. "Jolana, if you don't stop...!"

"Take me," she whispered, twisting, reaching up for him with trembling hands, a body racked by insatiable hungers. Her dark eyes were misty with desire, her lips parted under the force of her breath. "Yes, like that, take me, now... Come on, Nick, come on, come on, yes, yes!"

He shuddered as his hard, heavy body invaded hers, and she welcomed him. Her body eased into the helpless urgency of his rhythm, feeling the raging need in him, wanting only to please, to satisfy that terrible hunger.

She bit his earlobe softly. Her hands held him at the base of his spine, urging him even closer, her body moving softly, gracefully, under his weight. "Yes, darling," she whispered as he moaned harshly. "Yes, darling!"

"Jolana...!" He whispered her name over and over again as his body moved. His lips slid back over hers. His tongue penetrated her mouth deeply, his breath rasping as the motion of his body became suddenly cruel, his great strength unleashed in the convulsive throes of fulfillment. And his helpless groan went into her mouth and into her bloodstream, and her legs contracted to hold him as she felt the full force of his strength.

She soothed him when, finally, he collapsed, his body slick with perspiration, shaking with the force of his heartbeat. Her hands tenderly wove in and out of his hair and she kissed his drawn face softly, all over, with exquisite tenderness.

"You'll have bruises," he breathed unsteadily. "I wasn't gentle."

"You needed me," she whispered. "I won't mind a bruise or two. Satisfied?"

He laughed softly, delightedly. "No."

She stretched under him. "I'm glad. Because neither am I. Yet."

"Give me a few minutes and you will be," he promised. "My God, what an explosion! I never felt like that with a woman."

That pleased her. She brushed her mouth over his closed eyelids. "Really?"

"Really. Except, maybe, in the car. In the car, for God's sake!" he laughed softly, brushing the damp hair away from her face. "Twice, and still I want you!" He lifted his head and looked down at her. "You said there'd only been one man, one time, and he hurt you."

She touched his chiseled mouth with her fingertip, tracing it. "He wasn't like you. Nothing like you. I love you."

She hadn't meant to say that, but the look on his face was worth the temporary loss of pride.

"You don't have to say anything," she said, smiling. "It wasn't a question. Just an involuntary confession. I love you, I love everything about you, and I love the way you make love…"

"What I've done to you wasn't making love," he said after a long moment, shadows playing in his dark eyes as he looked at her.

"But this time, it will be. Rouse me again."

He rolled over onto his back, staring at her, with the hair-darkened expanse of bronzed muscles open to her, along with his formidable masculinity.

She stared down, fascinated but hesitant.

"Don't you watch movies or read books?" he murmured, smiling slowly.

"Well, of course. But I've never actually done it before."

"I'll tell you. And show you. And teach you how." He drew her hands down and his voice was like dark velvet as he told her, explicitly, how to arouse him, how to touch and tease his dark body. And she did, with hands that were fascinated by the textures of him, by his sudden responses to her exploration. He fascinated her as much this way as he did with the force of his personality, the exuberance with which he lived life.

"Now," he whispered, "lie down and let me excite you. And then I'll let you take me, the way you started to earlier." He eased her onto her back, smiling. "It's exciting for a man, to be taken by his woman. And you are that," he breathed as he bent to her taut breasts. "You are, very definitely, my woman."

She felt his open mouth on the swelling rise of her body with a sense of fatality. She couldn't imagine ever letting another man touch her this way, possess her this way. He was every woman's dream of what a lover should be, tender and demanding and wildly exciting to make love to. He kissed her all over, in ways and places that shocked her, and all the while he whispered to her, whispered intimate things that he was going to do, ways of pleasing her that made her tingle with expectation.

When she was crying aloud with the tormented, exquisite pleasure of wanting him, he shifted onto his back and lifted her over him. And helped her.

The feeling was almost painfully exquisite. And he watched her, and laughed even through his raging desire for her, his eyes possessive on the rise and fall of her slender, exquisite body, her breasts swollen and hard-tipped as his hands reached up to touch their warm beauty.

"I never wanted…a woman…so much," he whispered huskily. "Jolana," he groaned, holding her hips with his big hands, shifting her. "Like…that, baby."

"Yes," she whispered, shaken, "I love you," she told him on a sharp breath, her eyes black with passion as she rocked softly. Her hands held his to her body. "Help…me."

"Now," he murmured, knowing the signs. His body rose with expert sureness, and he guided her. "Don't be afraid…to let it happen. I can…make it happen. Like this…yes, now…"

She followed his lead, doing what he told her, and he watched it happen for her, watched her eyes dilate, her body arch and shudder, her throat stretch as she cried out his name and her nails dug into his body. And then, finally, he knew he could lose control of himself and feel her around and over and consuming him. He gave himself freely for the first time to something he'd never experienced before. Always, he'd held back at the last minute. His mind had refused to participate fully in lovemaking. But now, he relinquished control entirely, and his own body throbbed and burst and flew up into the sky, and he heard himself cry out helplessly, his voice deep and splintered, echoing in the sudden silence of the room. He seemed almost to lose consciousness then, the rigidity actually painful until that, too, vanished. He cried out something and then he collapsed, and she cried from the beauty of what they'd shared.

It wasn't until much later that Jolana realized how careless they'd been. Of course, the odds were that she would not get pregnant. At any rate, it was past time to worry about it now.

"Jolana," he whispered, holding her close. "Jolana, it was so beautiful. So beautiful. *Adore mio, che bella. Che bella!*"

"You said something," she murmured. "At the last. I didn't understand."

"It's just as well," he laughed softly. "It was something explicit and not too nice. I thought I was going to die."

"So did I, actually." She nuzzled close with her whole silky body. "Oh, Nick, Nick, I never realized, never imagined, that it would feel like that to make love with a man. I don't think I could stay alive if you never wanted me again."

"I'll want you all my life," he said softly, and as he looked at her he suddenly felt the words, felt the truth in them. She was glorious, God, she was! There had never been anything like what they'd shared tonight, not even with Margery. That sounded traitorous, so he dismissed it. But he had an empty life to face, and Jolana was beautiful. Intelligent. Talented. He needed someone and he had finally found her. "Maybe we'll have each other that long, too. But right now I have to go back to the apartment."

"Tonight?"

"Tonight." He reached down and kissed her softly, warmly. "I have to think. Maybe, soon, I might want you to live with me. How would you feel about that, independent lady?"

"You mean, get married?" Her eyes adored him.

"Yes," he said quietly, as if the idea had only just occurred to him. "Yes, I mean get married."

"Would you make love to me all the time?"

He smiled. "Yes."

Her arms reached up. "In that case, I guess it would be all right." She buried her face in his neck, floating on pure joy, so happy that she felt nothing life ever offered her would equal this, now. He cared. He had to care, to be so tender and concerned about giving her pleasure. She sighed gently, giving in to drowsiness. Yes, there would be a future for them. And she'd make sure that he never regretted the commitment.

The next morning, he was gone, and she felt exhausted from pleasure. She showered and put on slacks and an overblouse before she went to work on the painting of Nick. Now she could do it so much better than before. Now she could put so much love into it…

She'd expected him to come, or call, but by afternoon when there was no word, she picked up the phone and called his office. His secretary seemed concerned when Jolana asked where he was. Mr. Scarpelli had phoned earlier, she told Jolana, and said he'd be out of the office for a couple of days, because of a family problem.

Jolana put the phone back down gently and chewed on her lower lip. Had something happened to his mother? She dialed his apartment and waited impatiently. Seconds later, a voice she recognized lifted the receiver.

"Hello?" Margery's thin voice asked politely. "Who's there, please?"

Margery. In Nick's apartment. So that was his "family problem"! Jolana put the phone down slowly and started to cry with mingled rage and frustration.

Surely, there was an explanation, she told herself. Surely there was…! But the evening passed without a word, and she spent a long, sleepless night praying Nick would call and tell her he loved her.

Nick, meanwhile, was in torment. He'd gone back to his apartment from Jolana's arms, looking forward to a wildly satisfying future, and found Margery waiting for him with her young son, Tom.

She'd rushed into his arms, weeping hysterically. "Oh, Nick, he threw me out," she wailed. "I had no place else to go. Your mama gave me her spare key to your apartment and I took Tommy and we came here. I hope you don't mind… Oh, Nick, I'm so sick, so sick. He broke the little china doll you gave me when I graduated from high school. He said… I never loved him and that I only cared for you, and if I wanted to leave, there was the door. He was drinking…"

"All right, honey," he'd said softly, stroking her hair while his dreams turned to dust. "It's all right. You know I'll take care of you."

And she'd relaxed then, clinging as she always had, while Tommy stood apart looking lost and frightened and hurt. After he'd settled Margery and the boy, he'd gone out for a long walk, trying to ease his conscience. He shouldn't have started anything with Jolana. Not feeling the way he did about Margery. But now Margery was leaving her husband, and he could have her, just as he'd wanted her for so many years. He closed his eyes against the cold wind. Yes, he'd wanted her. But now she seemed a pale shadow beside the image of Jolana. He'd never expected what had happened between them earlier that night. He'd wanted only a brief affair with Jolana, to get her out of his system. But it had turned into something much more. He loved her. But it was too late. His obsession with Margery had finally gained him what he thought he wanted. And now that he had it, he was more unhappy than he'd ever been.

There was still Jolana to tell, and that was going to be an agony in itself. He was too honorable to throw Margery out into the streets, and too proud to tell Jolana the truth. So he'd have to go to the woman he truly loved and make her hate him, so that he could cope with the woman he had. Fate was cruel, he thought. He wondered why he hadn't seen years ago what a clinging, helpless vine Margery really was. What a contrast to Jolana, who was headstrong and independent and full of fire, who could make his blood run hot when she smiled. He almost groaned aloud. If only he could turn back the clock and make Margery see that what they had had together years ago had died, but neither of them had realized it. Margery belonged with Andrew—poor Andrew, who'd had Nick thrown in his face for ten years now. Jolana had said that, and Nick hadn't listened. Now he wished he had. But it was too late. He sighed, feeling the cold wind in his hair. Later, he told himself. In a day or two, when he might be able to tell her without his voice breaking, he would go to Jolana.

CHAPTER SIX

ONLY TWO DAYS had passed, but Jolana felt as if it had been an eternity since Nick had gone. When the doorman announced that he was downstairs, she waited for him, calm and empty and expecting the worst. She'd given him all the love she had to give. And she didn't need to ask why he was coming here, not when Margery had answered the phone at his apartment. She knew already that it was over. She was only bitterly curious about how he was going to end it.

She didn't hold out her arms to him, as she would have done two mornings ago. She offered him coffee instead, and he shook his curly dark head, preoccupied. He dropped into an armchair. The suede jacket he wore was hanging open, and his white shirt was rumpled. He looked as if he'd hardly slept at all, yet it was late morning.

"Sit down. Please," he added quietly.

It was a good thing that she did, because her knees felt weak. She clasped her hands in her lap and stared at him out of sad brown eyes.

"Well?" she asked with quiet pride.

He held his face in his hands, as if that would help his mind to function. He raised tormented eyes to hers. "Jolana, I said a lot of things the other night, and did a lot of things, that I'm sorry about. You see, Margery and I..." He fumbled to light a cigarette, and took a long draw of it while Jolana waited in an agony of impatience. He got up. "Margery and I, we got each other hot in the kitchen that night," he said finally, turning away from the horrified look on her face, the shock. "I wanted her to the point of madness, and I couldn't have her. So I had you instead. When I got home, she was there. She and Andrew are calling it quits. She and Tommy are staying with me now. I promised they could move in with me, that I'd take care of them."

She laughed, but not out of humor. She laughed at the total absurdity of the situation. She sat there and laughed and laughed, her voice high-pitched and hysterical and building, until Nick realized what was wrong and slapped her lightly on the cheek.

"Stop," he ground out, shaking her. "God, don't make it any harder than it is!"

"Harder?" She wiped away the hysterical tears and tore away from him, still laughing from halfway across the room. "Harder? You leave here talking about marriage and come back telling me you're moving in with another woman and her child?"

"I love her," he growled, averting his eyes before she could see the truth in them. "I always have! Since we were kids. I've ached for her. And now, at last, she can be mine, don't you understand?"

She forced herself to breathe calmly. "I understand, all right," she said after a minute, and her eyes were accusing and dark with contempt. "I gave myself to you in love, in trust. If I'd known that it was all, all of it, because you were lusting after that woman, I'd have killed you first. Get out."

His jaw tensed and he stared at her, tormented. "I'm sorry."

"Is that supposed to make up for everything?" she asked with a cold smile. "Is it supposed to restore my pride and my self-respect? You used me, in the fullest sense of the word, and I let you. I'll hate myself for that as long as I live. And I'll hate you even longer."

"I'm not proud of myself, Jolana," he said. "I wish things had been different."

She walked to the door and opened it, her chin up, her eyes glistening but steady. "It's been an experience, Mr. Scarpelli. You'll understand that I'd prefer to be alone now?"

He started toward the door and paused. "It won't make any difference, to the exhibit."

"I don't care about the exhibit anymore," she said. "And there's something else I don't want. Just a minute."

She went into her studio and brought out the portrait she'd been doing of him. It was magnificent, even unfinished, flattering and obviously done by a woman deeply in love. She thrust it into his hands.

"Merry Christmas," she said. "You can give it to Margery. Now get out!"

He actually winced. "Jolana…"

"Get out!" she screamed, hysteria finally winning out. She saw his face pale through a blur of hot tears. "Get out, get out, get out!"

He moved just a fraction and she slammed the door and locked it, bolted it, chained it.

"Jolana!" he called.

But she didn't answer. He stared at the closed door in a desperate kind of quiet panic. He heard the sobbing behind the door and he wanted to do something violent.

He leaned against the wall, trying to think of something, anything to comfort her. But what could he do? Margery had made a mess of everything. And he had made things even worse by telling that lie about Margery getting him stirred up in the kitchen at the party. It had been thinking about Jolana that had done that. He'd had to think about Jolana to bear the urgent kiss Margery had given him. Urgent. He almost laughed. Margery's idea of passion was quiet kissing and comfortable sex. And today he'd killed any future he might have had with Jolana by telling her a deliberate lie. But he'd had to, he told himself. He couldn't have allowed her to go through life mourning him, hoping for a new beginning. His dark eyes closed. He'd wanted to spare her any more grief. He'd wanted her to hate him so that she wouldn't spend her life looking back. He'd promised to take care of Margery and the boy. He had no choice, no way out. He'd only wanted to spare Jolana the grief of knowing. And he'd caused her to have hysterics. Not only that…there was something worrying him, some nagging fear. It was too quiet in the apartment, and he was suddenly afraid. What if Jolana did something stupid? What if… His breath caught. She'd been so upset, and he knew that most of her strength was on the surface, a mask she wore to hide her vulnerability from people who didn't know her. It was his own strength that had attracted her in the first place. What had he done to her while trying to spare her emotions?

He tapped at the door but she didn't answer. Idiot, he thought, of course she wouldn't! Not knowing it was him. What could he do? Call the police? What would he tell them? He turned away. Tony! He'd call Tony! Tony could get to her when he couldn't. He stared at the painting in his hands as he waited for the elevator. That would have to go, he thought bitterly, turning his eyes away from the love he could see in every brush-stroke, or he'd go mad remembering her. He sighed as he lifted his head. He knew without doubt that he'd just made the worst mistake of his life. Despite all his good intentions and noble ideals.

Jolana went into her bedroom and slammed that door, too, and took the phone off the hook. He was knocking on the outside door, but she put the pillow over her head so she wouldn't hear it. *Go away,* she told him mentally as the tears burned hot in her eyes. *Go away and leave me alone!* She lay across the coverlet and cried until there was no emotion left in her.

She loved him. Nothing was going to change that. Not his treachery, or Margery's triumph, or her own bit-terness. Nothing would change what she felt. He'd taken her love and thrown it in her face, in the most horrible kind of way. She felt dirty. Unclean. As if she were no better than a common prostitute. She wanted to die.

For a long time, she lay there, thinking about the emptiness, about a world that held nothing for her. She'd done little else since she'd called Nick and Margery had answered the phone. She'd known all along, but she'd been holding out a tiny glimmer of hope that he might change his mind. She should have known better. She stared at the ceiling and thought about how it would be not to hurt anymore. Not to ache for a man who didn't love her. She got up and poured herself a drink. She gulped it down and had another. And another. And after a while, she began to wonder what it would feel like to give it all up and die.

To die. And afterward, she wouldn't care that Nick

didn't love her. She wouldn't care at all. She got to her feet, feeling very calm. She even knew how to do it. She had some tranquilizers in her medicine cabinet. There was more whiskey in the cupboard.

But that would be stupid. Nick wouldn't care. Nobody would care. With a long, shaky sigh, she poured herself another drink and took just a couple of tranquillizers with it, just enough to help her sleep before she lost her mind with grief. She was so hurt and anguished and so alone. She knew only that life stretched ahead of her like an empty page that she could write nothing on. And without Nick, it would be forever empty. How would she live without him?

She began to get sleepy in a few minutes, finally! She felt herself drifting off quietly. Somewhere she thought she heard a pounding, but it was probably just her own heartbeat. Just that. She took a deep, slow breath and let it out. And knew nothing more.

Her nose hurt. She began to realize as she regained consciousness that there was a tube down it, and belching sounds coming from some loud machine nearby. She gagged, but she was held down, and then the machine was cut off and the tube removed slowly. Her throat hurt, her nose hurt, she felt very sick. All around her were lights and people in white. *This,* she thought, *is a strange kind of heaven. Maybe it's hell.*

She turned her head and there was Tony, his face thin and white as paste as he watched. He came closer.

"Hey," he said, trying to smile, "you okay?"

"Why am I here??" she asked faintly, and her eyes closed again.

The next time she came around, she was in a hospital bed with a plastic name tag around her wrist. She blinked and Tony was still there.

"How did I get here?" she asked, and talking hurt her throat.

"I brought you," Tony said through his teeth. He stood over her with his hands in his pockets. "God, honey, he isn't worth it. Not worth your life!"

She looked up at him with wet brown eyes. "But I only had a couple of drinks and just a couple of tranquillizers, to make me sleep," she whispered as it all came back, the pain and the anguish of losing Nick too much to bear.

"Honey, you never mix tranquillizers with whiskey," he said heavily. "Didn't you know? My gosh, what if I hadn't gone to see about you? What would I do for a show next week?" he added, trying to smile. He knew he couldn't tell her that Nick had phoned him in a panic, pleading with him to make sure Jolana didn't do something crazy. Damn Nick! But if he hadn't called, Jolana would be dead now. As it was, she was just about gone when Tony got there and broke down the door, with assistance from two of the neighbors. It was a relief to know that she hadn't really meant to kill herself. But the doctor had said that if she hadn't been found, it would have been too late to save her.

She fought to control herself and wiped her eyes with the sheet. "I guess you'd just have to get someone else," she said with a forced smile.

"Listen to me, hotshot," he said, moving closer determinedly. "If you try anything stupid like this again, you'll need a doctor for a different reason! You're no quitter. Stop feeling sorry for yourself and look ahead, instead of backward. You're going to have a great career, and eventually you'll find a man smart enough to love you. Nick deserves Margery, if he's too damned stupid to see how selfish she is. She's just using him, the way she used Andrew until he couldn't take it anymore. But that's Nick's problem, not yours. He's digging his own grave. Don't dig yours along with him." He caught her hand in his and held it tight. "You hold on to me. I'll get you through this."

Her fingers locked with his, and she saw the strength in him for the first time, and the caring that was beneath all his wild banter. "You're a nice man."

"Sure I am," he agreed. "And I'm the best friend you've got right now. So how about living up to my faith in you?"

She studied his long fingers. "I loved him."

"You'll get over him."

"Not while I'm here," she said. "Not while I'm around you. I'm sorry, but that's how it is. You… You won't be able to help mentioning him."

He grimaced. "Yeah, I guess not."

She lay back on the pillow and her eyes closed. "I have a girlfriend in France, one I went to college with. She asked me to come and visit, and I'd already written to tell her I would." She laughed bitterly. "Isn't that ironic? It will be spring soon. Paris is so lovely in the spring."

"What about the show?"

"You'll have to do it without the artist," she said sadly. "I can't bear to stay here that long."

He pursed his lips. "I suppose I could say that you came down with beriberi or something. What about your apartment?"

"I'll sublet it. That will be no problem at all. I'll leave

Maureen's address with you, and you can send my check there," she added.

"The address, I gather, is confidential?" he asked shrewdly.

"He won't ask," she said, dropping her eyes to the sheet. "He has Margery."

"He won't have her for long," he said in a rough voice. "When she's free of Andrew, she'll be after fresh game. When Nick's had his heart wrung out, he'll probably be in the same shape you're in. No inclination to pick up the pieces, Jolana?"

"I'd burn them, if I could," she said, and meant it.

"If it's any consolation, he probably cared a lot to get himself involved with you at all," he said, searching her wan face. "That never happened before. He's been obsessed with Margery for years, too obsessed to see her as she really is. She's not a bad woman. Don't misunderstand me, I don't hate her. It's just that she's weak and clinging and she likes to be pitied. When Nick won't pity her, she'll find another Andrew who will. Nick would terrify her in any intimate relationship. It would be like trying to mate a tiger with a lamb."

"Life teaches hard lessons sometimes," she said. Her fingers let go of his and she sighed, "I'm so tired, and my throat hurts terribly."

"I'll see the nurse for you," he said. He patted her hand. "Get through one day at a time. It will get easier every day, until one day the hurting will stop and you'll breathe in fresh air. Try it, okay? For me?"

"One day at a time," she murmured. "It sounds easy enough. Okay. One day at a time."

"Good girl." He glanced at her one last time and left the room.

She left the hospital the next day, worn out, exhausted, and so ashamed of her own impulsive stupidity that she could have cried. Wouldn't that give Nick a thrill, she thought fiercely, to know that she'd loved him enough to take her own life just because he wouldn't be in it anymore, even if it was accidentally? Stupid! Well, that was twice she'd been taken in by sweet talk and charm.

Next time, she'd go into a relationship with her mind, not her heart. She'd never give her heart again.

The apartment was still full of Nick. Despite her weakness, she went around getting rid of every reminder, every single thing that had a memory attached to it. Even clothes. She'd buy more in Paris.

She arranged to sublet her apartment and packed up her canvases and supplies to take with her. She could paint in Paris. And she remembered vaguely that Phillipe liked racing cars. Perhaps they'd all be going to the Côte d'Azur. That would be nice. She'd enjoy the sun and sand and excitement of Monaco and Nice and Cannes. She and Maureen had always enjoyed adventurous pastimes, along with Phillipe. Perhaps they could recapture their youth. It would be lovely to feel carefree again.

Tony stopped by as she was closing the last suitcase. He looked around with quiet eyes as she put down the case and turned. She was dressed in a black suit with white accessories, looking very chic with her new short haircut and clothes.

"How you've changed," he sighed. "And so quickly."

"I just grew up all of a sudden," she informed him. A slight smile turned up her lips. "I was a case of arrested growth."

He studied her wan face closely. "Nick sent a message for you."

"Take it back to him," she replied, still calm, although the sound of his name made her want to cry. "I don't want to hear it." She kissed his cheek warmly, smiling. "You're my best pal, Tony," she said. "I'll really miss you."

"I'll miss you, too," he said. He sighed. "Well, I'll forward the check to you soon. I'm saying that you had to go to Europe on a family matter. An emergency. The paintings will speak for themselves." He hesitated. "Uh, the one you did of Nick…was magnificent."

She blanched. "Where did you see it?"

"He gave it to me," he said quietly. His eyes searched her narrowed ones. "I'm going to tell you now, so you won't be holding out false hope. He and Margery are getting married as soon as her divorce is final. He said he was sorry for everything, and he never wanted you to be hurt."

She laughed slowly. "He never wanted me to be hurt. Now that's a classic." She stared into his eyes. "Take the painting and burn it. If you're my friend, do that for me. And tell him someday that I asked you to. Tell him I hope he gets hurt the way he hurt me. Only double."

"Don't be bitter," he pleaded quietly. "You're the one who'll be hurt by it, not him."

"Sure." She looked around the apartment one last time. "Well, I'm off to the moon, Tony, my friend. Paris, mecca of art. Wish me good luck."

"You know that already." He lifted her hand to his lips. "Get well. Then come home. Maybe you and I could…"

"No. No false hope, remember?" She smiled to soften

the blow. "I don't ever want to see him again. If I got involved with you, I'd have to."

"I could have him bumped off?" he offered drily.

"His ghost would probably haunt us both. Take care, my friend. Thank you for my life. I wouldn't have it, but for you."

He almost told her about it being Nick's idea to check on her, but he held his tongue. What did it matter anyway, now? "My pleasure. Just remember," he added. "One day at a time."

She nodded. "One day at a time. *Ciao.*"

"Ciao."

Paris was cold and rainy, and all the trees were bare and stark against the city skyline where the Seine meandered past bridges that sang their history in cold stone and survival. Maureen and Phillipe de Vinchy-Cardin lived near the Seine in a fashionable and expensive Paris apartment.

Maureen, slight and dark and full of energy, met her at the airport with open arms and the smile that Jolana remembered so well.

"My old friend," Maureen laughed, "how long it has been, and how glad I am to see you. *Mon Dieu*, you are as beautiful as ever. More beautiful!"

"So are you," Jolana said fervently, smiling down into the almond-shaped dark eyes. "Thank you for letting me come. I needed so desperately to get away for a while."

"I know about the necessity for getting away, I must confess," Maureen laughed. "With me, there is always a love affair that has not gone right. But someday, *chérie*, I will meet the right man and all will be well. Are you hungry?"

"Starved!" Jolana confessed.

"I have left Phillipe at the bakery. We must pick him up on the way home." She climbed into a Renault, as red as lipstick, and waited for Jolana to put her art supplies and suitcase in the back.

"What a cute little car!" Jolana laughed. "It suits you."

"Not as well as my Lamborghini," came the lament, "but at least it was affordable. Times are hard here, even for the well-to-do. Phillipe was elated that you were coming. We have had good times together, *n'est-ce pas*?"

"Oui," Jolana murmured, leaning back against the seat as Maureen pulled out into traffic. *"Très bon.* How is Phillipe?"

"As always. Still the happy bachelor." Maureen glanced at her. "And as crazy in the head as ever!"

Jolana laughed. "Remember the night he put soap suds in the fountain? And tied a huge satin bow to the back of the dean's car?"

"He was incorrigible. He still is." Maureen turned a corner where people were strolling by huddled in overcoats. "Paris is so cold and miserable at this time of year. Soon we go to Monaco, for the motorcar rally. The Côte d'Azur is much prettier, and warmer. You will come with us, of course."

"I don't want to impose…"

"Chérie, if I did not want you to impose, I would not have invited you. It will be so nice to renew our friendship. I have wanted for many years to have you visit, but you have been so busy… Tell me about this one-woman show in New York!"

Jolana did, leaving out all mention of Nick. "I hope it goes well. I just couldn't stay in New York any longer."

"A man, *chérie*?" came the wise query.

She sighed. Maureen always had been astute. "A man."

"Here, you will heal. Phillipe and I will help. Oh, *là*! Look at the crazy fool!"

Phillipe was standing in the middle of the lane, waving two loaves of French bread like a seaman giving semaphore signals to a landing plane. Maureen slammed on the brakes, laughing.

Jolana opened her door and stepped out, grinning at the tall, tanned Frenchman with his lean body and blond hair and twinkling brown eyes. "Stop that!" she called. "We're not an airplane!"

"C'est vrai?" he laughed. "But, then, *chérie*, you have not seen me drive. Here."

He tossed the bread onto the backseat, grabbed Jolana and kissed her heartily in front of all of Paris. His mouth was cool and careless and his eyes twinkled.

"Jolana," he laughed. "Welcome to Paris."

He went around to replace his sister at the wheel, stuffing her into the backseat while traffic backed up behind them. He made a face at it. *"Allez-vous en!"* he called, and added something that Jolana hesitated to translate even in her mind.

"Phillipe, for shame!" Maureen chided. "Where are your manners?"

"In the back, with the bread," he replied, pulling smoothly into traffic. "Jolana, have you come to paint?"

"Yes."

"I do not think there is such a market for dead trees and cold water." He grinned. "We go to Monaco soon.

It will be a better subject for your talent. By the way, did my lazy sister thank you for the painting you sent last Christmas, of the villa in Nice?"

"Yes, she did," Jolana returned with a dry glance. "And stop picking on my friend, you animal."

"Moi?" he burst out. "You defame me."

"No. I flatter you." She laughed. "I just love animals."

He laughed uproariously. "Do you? Then this will be a visit to remember, I think."

"Definitely that," Jolana agreed, and tried not to think why. Nick was still too vivid in her mind, the hurt too fresh, the wounds too raw. She wondered if he even thought of her now. He'd given Tony the painting. Her eyes closed. It had hurt her deeply that he'd thought so little of it that he didn't even want to keep it. Or perhaps sweet Margery couldn't bear the sight of it, she thought venomously. Damn Margery!

Around her, Phillipe and Maureen were arguing merrily about which dish to have the cook prepare for supper. Jolana coaxed her mind back to the present. She had to live for tomorrow, not yesterday. And as she listened to the gay banter of her hosts, she began to believe that it was possible to look ahead. She was going to make it somehow. Nick was a closed chapter in her life. And from now on, she was going to treat him as one.

As the days lazed by in Paris, and she was pulled into the frantic lifestyle Maureen and Phillipe enjoyed, it was like their old days at college over again. They went to discos and stayed out half the night partying. They visited friends, some of them wealthy jet-setters who didn't mind the unconventional antics of the de Vinchy-Cardins or look down on them as café society.

Jolana noticed that none of the old French aristocracy would receive them, but she imagined it was because of their youth and unusual lifestyles. They weren't conventional at all. She began to think she wasn't, either, because she seemed to fit in with them so well. She refused to consider the possibility that she was adopting their wild lifestyle in an attempt to forget her broken heart. She simply drank champagne and danced and partied and never looked back.

Meanwhile, she and Phillipe seemed to find more and more in common as they spent time together. Riding around Paris with him became an adventure. He was just as likely to stop impulsively at some expensive shop and buy something he clearly didn't need as he was to forget that they hadn't had lunch and suggest a stroll through an art gallery. He drove his little black Ferrari as wildly as any taxi driver, but he never came close to an accident. He was fast, but not reckless.

"I drive in the Grand Prix, *chérie*," he reminded her, flashing his white smile her way, with blond hair falling carelessly over his deeply tanned forehead. His eyes twinkled, and he seemed to glow when he smiled. He had a Continental sophistication and a devastating charm. Jolana was almost glad that he didn't try to use it on her. She was vulnerable enough from her recent heartache and might do something stupid on the rebound from Nick.

"Do you?" she asked, picking up the thread of the conversation with difficulty. "Just in France?"

"Mais, non!" he protested, rounding another curve with graceful skill. "The Mille Miglia in Italy, the Monte Carlo road rally... I race all over the world."

"I'll bet you win all over the world, too," she said drily.

"I always try to come in first, *chérie*, just to save the other drivers from tiring themselves too much," he told her. "I would not want them becoming exhausted on my account."

"Oh, no."

"Besides," he said, "I would lose too many bets." He grinned. "I win more from that than I do from the races."

"You like to gamble, then?" she queried.

He shrugged. "I have a facility for it." He glanced over at her. "I will take you to Monte Carlo, to the casino, when we go there and teach you to play roulette."

"That will be perfect," she said with a grin of her own. "I'm really good at going around in circles."

Phillipe laughed and turned the car onto the street where they lived. "Home again, and all too soon. If it were only spring, we would lie under the trees and drink good wine and eat cheese and bread."

"And get fat," she suggested.

"Me?" He stared at her. "God forbid! My image would lie in the dirt!"

"You mean, women would stop chasing you," she teased. "Maureen told me how they cluster around you."

"It is a pity," he said, sighing theatrically. "But, what is a poor man to do? I cannot be so ungentlemanly as to force them away from me."

"Someday you'll be kissed to death, no doubt," she agreed. Involuntarily, her eyes dropped to his mouth. It was much more sensual than Nick's, but every bit as masculine. For two weeks, she'd hardly noticed just how much of a man her hostess's brother was. Now, he seemed to be becoming as aware of her as she was of him. He caught her puzzled gaze and held it for a long moment, until her spine began to tingle. *Watch out,* she told herself. *Watch out, you're very vulnerable right now.*

"So threatened, those great, dark eyes," he whispered as he stopped the car in the garage and sat watching her. "Afraid of me, *ma petite*?" he challenged.

"No," she returned.

He smiled slowly. "Now, why is it that I do not believe you?"

She turned and opened the door as quickly, and as unobtrusively, as possible.

"Phillipe likes you," Maureen said that evening after Jolana had showered. "I think it's because you're so different from the girls he knows."

"I like him, too. I always did," Jolana said gently. She smiled at her friend. "He's crazy, you know."

Maureen laughed delightedly, clapping her hands. "Ah, yes, it runs in the family, you see. Jolana, I am so glad that you came. Things had deteriorated here… No matter, it is changing now, it is all changing." She studied her friend carefully. "You are happy, too, I think. Except for that touch of indigestion." Her eyes narrowed. "It is better?"

Jolana frowned. "I'm not sure. I just feel a general malaise." She laughed. "Maybe it's the difference, in the food and the air."

Maureen nodded. "Perhaps so." But she didn't speak further. She only stared, her eyes falling to her friend's waistline, her lips pursing speculatively.

"By the way, did you come in while I was bathing?" Jolana asked. "I thought I heard someone…"

"No, it was not I. Perhaps Agatha." She grinned, naming the very formal maid who worked for the family. "She is stealthy, is she not?"

"Very!"

"I had asked Phillipe to stop by your room and mention that we were ready to eat," she said thoughtfully. "But he would have knocked. Very much a gentleman, is Phillipe. Jolana, you do like him?"

"Very much," Jolana said, and meant it. She stretched. "I'm so tired. Must be this winter chill that makes me sleepy."

"Just so," Maureen agreed, but her face was thoughtful. "You are not so sad as when you came," she added. "A good thing, too. That man, the one you left behind you, it is for the best. At least you did not become pregnant."

"At least." Jolana laughed at her friend's frankness. "I'm not even on the pill. How lucky that it was only one night."

"Yes, it is." Maureen took her arm, smiling slowly. "Come. We have an especially good dinner tonight. I am famished."

They walked into the elegant dining room arm in arm, and there was the slightest inclination of Maureen's head as her eyes met her brother's. Phillipe smiled, and for the rest of the evening, his attention was on Jolana. She began to feel that there was hope for her at last, that she might be able to forget Nick and start again.

CHAPTER SEVEN

THERE WERE STILL the nights to get through, however. The long, empty nights when she remembered how it had been with Nick and thought she couldn't bear one more sunrise alone. But she clung to what Tony had told her. One day at a time. Get through each day, as if it were complete in and unto itself. It was like putting one foot in front of the other to take a long walk. Eventually, it got to be routine.

She wondered sometimes if Nick would find happiness with Margery. There was an old saying that you couldn't build happiness on a foundation laid with the grief of others. But then, weeds thrived, didn't they? Flowers had one hell of a hard time of it.

Her mind would keep going back to the way it had been in the car, to what he'd said about never feeling that kind of pleasure with another woman. But she forced herself to remember their final meeting as well, the pain and anguish. What had hurt the most was not that he didn't love her, but that he'd used her to assuage the lust Margery had roused in him. Only a cruel woman could do such a thing, to tease a man that way. He wouldn't be happy with Margery, she decided. Eventually, he'd realize what she was. But by then, it would be too late. He'd be married, if he wasn't already. And trapped. Margery would smother him. Own him.

It could have been so wonderful, if Nick had loved her back. They could have shared so much, they had so much in common. She was hot-blooded, as he was, and adventurous. They were more than lovers, they were twin souls. But he couldn't see it. Perhaps he might realize one day what he'd thrown away so easily. But when he did, it would be far too late. She thought how it would be, to have Nick at her feet, to laugh in his face. For a moment, her heart swelled with the thrill of revenge. But soon the fantasy faded and she faced the reality of being alone in the dark. She turned over on the pillow and closed her eyes. But it was a long time before she slept.

Phillipe, as they grew closer, sensed her sadness, and one evening when they were walking in the small walled garden behind the apartment, he asked the inevitable question.

"There was a man, *n'est-ce pas*?" he said as they stood under a cold winter sky and bare tree limbs.

"There was a man," she said. Her dark eyes lifted to his in the semidarkness. "But I'm all right now."

He took her slender hand in his and studied it, and his eyes were kind. *"Pauvre petite,"* he said. "Life has its moments, does it not? We have all loved the wrong person at one time or another. But love is inexhaustible. You will find it again."

"If I do," she said with a flash of her old dryness, "I'll run like hell in the other direction."

He smiled slowly. *"Oui,* I have felt the same." He sighed, stretching his tall body as he stared out at the bare landscape leading to the Seine. "Winter. I hate it so. But soon it will be spring, and the whole world will be different."

"I can hardly wait," she said, smiling.

"Soon, we go to Monte Carlo, where there will be the motorcar rally and the opera," he said. "And we will sail on the Mediterranean, and go to the film festival at Cannes. We have a villa, you know."

She moved restlessly. "I hadn't thought that far ahead. I should go back to the States…"

"Why?" he asked, turning with his hands in his pockets to study her. He wasn't as blatantly masculine as Nick, but he had a sensuous, very sophisticated charm, and he was young and full of life and fun.

She shrugged. "Why, indeed?" Well, she had the check that Tony had forwarded from the exhibit—a very satisfying amount. It would do for expenses. She had nothing to go back to. Why not?

"*Petite*, in my way, I am as alone as you," he said in a surprising moment of gravity. His soft, dark eyes stared down into hers. "I have wealth and a title and, therefore, friends. But they are for the most part the kind of friends who would desert me if my fortune ever did."

"You have Maureen, at least," she said, smiling. "I have no family at all."

He took a hand from his pocket and drew it gently along her cheek. "The man from whom you ran—there is no chance that you will reconcile with him?"

"None," she said tautly.

"May I ask you something deeply personal?" he added, and there was an oddly calculating look on his face for a moment, an intense scrutiny.

"Yes."

"You were lovers?"

"For a night," she agreed, feeling safe with him, safe enough to discuss it. "He said that we would be married. But then the woman he loved agreed to divorce her husband and marry him." She laughed bitterly. "I was stupid enough to believe him."

"He was blind," he said, tilting her chin up to his smiling face. "Such beauty, such grace and elegance. Any man would want you, *ma petite*."

Her eyes searched his. She almost asked, Would you? But she kept her silence.

Incredibly, he seemed to see the question in her eyes. *"Oui,"* he said softly, bending. "I would…want you."

Theirs had been a casual relationship, full of fun. But all at once, it entered a different dimension. His mouth touched hers as lightly as a held breath. But when he felt her uncertain response, he smiled, and his arms drew her close. His lips parted slightly, parted hers, and he felt alive for the first time since she'd left the States.

"I will ask nothing that you do not wish to give," he whispered. "Relax. This is all I want right now, just a kiss."

She forced her taut muscles to give in, and she felt the strength of his body, smelled the spicy fragrance of the expensive cologne that he wore. He smiled at the acquiescence, bent again. And this time, the kiss was neither tender nor brief. He was experienced. Very experienced. He didn't rush her, or force her. He coaxed the response he wanted from her with warmth that surprised her into feeling passion. She hadn't thought she would be capable of it, after Nick. But she was. She was!

A tiny gasp went from her lips into his opening mouth. He lifted his head to look at her, finding the shock of his touch in every soft line of her face.

"It surprises you that you can enjoy this with me?" he asked gently.

"I didn't think I could," she whispered, fascinated with the pleasure of being held by him, kissed by him.

His fingers touched her face delicately, and his warm eyes smiled into hers. "He hurt you. But I can heal you, given the opportunity. I can make you whole again." He bent, touching her closed eyelids with his lips. "*Chérie*, I want so much to touch your breasts."

Her breath caught and her nails dug suddenly into his jacket at the unexpectedly blunt remark.

"I have seen them," he whispered, rubbing his nose over hers, "when you were in the bath, and Maureen asked me to call you to dinner the other night. I knocked, but you did not hear. So I came in." His breath came quickly, like her own, as his hands eased to her waist, her rib cage, in slow, soft motions that were wildly arousing. "You were sitting up in the tub," he whispered unsteadily, "with your back arched, and these," he added, lifting delicate fingers to lightly stroke her breasts, "these were bare, pink and exquisite. Jolana, *ma petite*, I wanted to go to you and put my open mouth here…"

And he did, and through the fabric, she felt the heat and moistness of his mouth and she moaned aloud, giving in to the beautiful sensations he was causing, the heavy shudder of his heart making her all too aware of his hunger for her. And hers for him.

"*Petite,*" he breathed, searching for buttons and hooks. "*Petite*, please, let me see you, touch you…!"

She should have stopped him. Eventually, she would, she promised her whirling conscience. Eventually…

But right now, her body was bare to the cold and his eyes and his mouth, and he was absorbing her with his tongue and his moist lips, and she caught his fair head and held it to her body with trembling fingers.

"Yes, there," she whispered shakily. "There, Phillipe, very hard, all...of...me!"

He took her completely into his mouth, the whispery suction making her ache, making her hungry, making her cry his name with helpless delight.

He lifted his head finally, and his hand cupped her tenderly while he searched her face. His own was dark with emotion.

"I want to marry you," he said huskily.

That was the last thing she expected him to say. She stared at him, gaped at him.

"I want to marry you," he repeated. His hand stroked her warm flesh tenderly. "I want to sleep with you."

"We... We could sleep together... You don't have to marry me," she said, confused.

"No. It is not what I want, a dishonorable liaison. There have been too many of those already." He drew away with a reluctant sigh and watched her fumble with her clothes. "No, it must be marriage. And I have known no other woman who could make me feel as you do. You make me whole."

"But we don't know each other!" she protested.

"We will," he promised. He smiled softly. "From now on we will be together always. I will make you love me and soon you will agree to marry me. I will give you no rest until you agree."

"But I don't want to get married," she protested weakly. Thoughts of Nick were still too vivid in her mind. Marrying anyone would seem a traitorous act.

"You said yourself, *petite*, that your lover will not come after you," he said gently.

That was true. She had to face the fact that if Nick had been going to follow her, he'd have had her address out of Tony by now and been in full pursuit. He wasn't coming after her. He had Margery.

"Don't rush me," Jolana said quietly.

Phillipe smiled. "But of course. I will give you all the time you wish. For now," he added with a rueful sigh, "I think it would be wise if we went back inside. And much safer, for you."

She peeked up at him through her eyelashes. "Afraid I might seduce you?" she teased.

He touched her short, disheveled hair gently. "Afraid I might back you up against the wall and take you, *ma petite.*"

"How exciting," she said with a slow smile.

"Yes, even in the cold, it would be." His eyes narrowed. "If you marry me," he said softly, "I will take you out into the middle of the Mediterranean and make love to you under the sun."

She could almost see that. Her eyes wandered over his tall body. It would probably be muscular, because he was an athlete. Muscular and smooth, she thought, mentally comparing him with Nick's powerful, hair-roughened body. When they made love, Nick's hair had tickled her breasts and her stomach, until it had become a delightful abrasion and finally a harsh, arousing tingle...

"I'll have to carry my art supplies with us to Monaco," she said after a minute, forcing herself back to the present.

He put an arm around her shoulders. "Of course. Come, we will have a glass of wine together before you go to bed." He led her back into the house, and Maureen looked up from her book. She smiled slowly and her eyes twinkled. She could already see the future, if her wicked glance was anything to go by. Jolana only smiled. She was alive, and she wanted Phillipe. Even as they moved apart to sit down, she knew that every step they took from now on would bring them closer together. It was as inevitable as the step that had brought her here from New York. And this time she was going into it with her eyes open and her mind clear. Phillipe was attractive and rich and compatible with her. It would be an advantageous marriage, and having a well-known artist for a wife wouldn't hurt Phillipe one bit. Yes. It was going to be a good life. And if once in a while her mind went back to Nick and she savored the idea of putting herself forever out of his reach, there was no one to know.

Monte Carlo was fascinating. The small, hilly kingdom was gloriously beautiful, and its casinos were places of incredible wealth and elegance.

"We usually go to Saint Moritz for the skiing during the winter," Phillipe told her. "But this year, I felt no such urge, nor did Maureen. So we agreed that we would come here, to the villa. It was fortunate for me that she decided to invite you along, *petite*," he added with a grin. "I would have been alone."

"With all your women, *comte*?" she teased.

He shook his head. "Only one woman, now. Have you forgotten? I am chasing you!"

"I'll have to work on slowing down," she laughed, smiling up at him. He was so handsome. So blond and tanned and utterly perfect. She wanted very much to paint him. And on their third day in Monaco, after the first qualifying race for the motorcar *rallye* was over, she talked him into it.

He wore slacks and an open shirt as he sat for her in the garden. She sketched quietly, hating her involuntary comparison as she imagined Nick in the same pose. Nick, with his massive body and hard muscles, with dark hair covering his body. After all this time, she still missed him so much, despite all her efforts to give her heart to Phillipe. Despite all her denials and resolutions. It was almost a physical agony. Her breasts were sore, and she was tired all the time. It was a mental thing, she told herself. She'd have to get under control or she was really going to make herself ill. Already her period was late, surely a result of her turbulent emotions.

"So thoughtful," Phillipe said with a grin, brushing away a lock of sun-bleached hair from his brow. "What are you thinking about?"

She peeked at him through her long lashes. "Of what you look like under your clothes," she teased.

He cocked an eyebrow and his hands went to his shirt. "Shall I show you?" he taunted.

"Maureen would be shocked."

"Maureen is unshockable, but I think that is not the case with you. Although you try to hide it, I can see you are not a worldly woman. It is part of your charm."

"You have some of that yourself," she told him, and meant it. "Phillipe, you've done so much for me. I want to be able to do as much for you."

"Then marry me," he persisted, and his dark eyes laughed into hers. "Say yes."

She pursed her lips as she worked. "Not today."

"Soon," he said, leaning back with a sigh. "Soon, I will make you say yes. I will seduce you."

"Not if you warn me first," she laughed.

"Will you wager something on that?" he asked drily. "Because it will happen before the week is out."

"Silly man," she said. "Now be quiet, please, and let me work."

"As you wish. But you are caught, *ma petite*. You simply do not know it yet."

She ignored him and kept drawing, aware of his eyes examining every inch of her. He hadn't made any more passes, but she knew it was coming. It seemed inevitable now. Part of her was oddly excited by the prospect of belonging to an appreciative man. And she loved Maureen dearly. If only she could forget Nick!

Just before the *rallye* was run, Phillipe took her to the casino and introduced her to the roulette wheel.

"This is my game," Phillipe told her in a low whisper. "I know it like the back of my hand."

He'd bet several of the chips in his hand on red thirty-six. And as black sixteen was proclaimed the winner, he made a very French gesture with his shoulders. "It appears," he observed, "that I need to reacquaint myself with the back of my hand, *n'est-ce pas?*"

She laughed, beautiful in the white dress she'd worn for Nick, which was the only appropriate one in her wardrobe. Phillipe's eyes touched her body possessively.

"Can't we play the slot machines instead?" she asked, glancing wistfully toward them.

"Peasant," he accused.

She stuck her tongue out at him. "We don't all have thousands to lose," she said haughtily. "Anyway, I have a pocketful of change…"

He sighed. "What shall I do with you, Jolana, *mon ange?*" he asked ruefully.

"I could make several suggestions," she said with a wicked glance.

"Not here," he whispered. "Think how shocked the other patrons would be!"

"The roulette wheel would probably hurt my back, anyway," she laughed, and ran before he could carry out the threat in his eyes.

She won five francs playing the slot machines and thought she'd done something grand. Until Phillipe went back to the roulette wheel and came away with twenty thousand francs.

"You're good!" she exclaimed.

"But, of course," he exclaimed. "Did I not say so?"

Her dark eyes studied him, appreciating the vivid blondness of his thick, straight hair, the perfection of his facial features, the wickedness of his sparkling eyes. He was a handsome man, and he had a unique devil-may-care charm that would easily draw women. Her attraction to him was obvious in her shining eyes.

"Why, *chérie*!" he exclaimed on a grin. "Is that loving look an invitation?"

Was it indeed? Nick was definitely in the past. He was probably married by now. She couldn't very well live the rest of her life mourning him. She was young and alive and Phillipe was interested in her. More than interested, if the masculine appreciation in his eyes was any indication.

She ran a restless hand through her short blond hair. "Maybe," she replied drily, peeking through her long lashes at him.

He cocked an eyebrow. "In that case, I shall double my efforts. So, watch out." He handed her some more coins. "By the way, did you know that the local citizenry are exempt from taxation of personal income but are forbidden the gaming rooms here?"

"Really?" she responded, smiling up at him. "Did you know that the Grimaldis, who founded Monaco in the thirteenth century, were deposed during the French Revolution and that Monaco was annexed to France? It was given its independence again under French protection in 1861." She laughed. "I read up on it when I discovered we were coming here," she confessed at his surprise. "I even know that it's only four hundred and sixty-eight acres big and has twenty-five thousand people. Not to mention," she sighed, "some of the most fascinating places in Europe, all of which I'd like to visit."

"Name them," he invited.

"The museums of oceanography and anthropology and naturally the art galleries and auctions. And the Casino gardens—they're here, aren't they?" she added.

"Oui." He smiled. "I will bring you here in the daylight to see them. Also, the opera and theater are housed in this complex. Do you by any chance like opera, *chérie*?"

"I adore it!" she laughed. "Do you?"

"Yes," he admitted. "It is the only nonsporting event that I can tolerate."

"The ballet?"

He shrugged. "It is not my favorite, but if you like, we can certainly attend."

"I'd love that," she confessed, "if you wouldn't suffer."

He lifted her hand to his lips. "I could never suffer in your company, *petite*. You are so lovely."

She smiled shyly and lowered her eyes. "Flatterer."

"But I mean it," he said softly. "You have brought

such beauty into my life. This is not the place, perhaps, but you cannot know how much it has meant to me, having your company."

She looked up into his eyes and smiled. "Yes, I do. Because I know how much it's meant to me, having yours. I was very unhappy when I came here. You've given life new meaning."

He searched her eyes. "The hurt. It is healing?"

She nodded. "Very quickly."

He smiled. "We will have to pay a little more attention to the balm that heals it best," he said under his breath. "As we did that night in our garden," he added, holding her gaze.

She felt a pleasant surge of warmth at the memory. He was an experienced lover, and she enjoyed his kisses. He'd been rather reticent in recent days, but perhaps he'd been giving her time to adjust. "That particular balm," she said softly, "would never be unwelcome."

His fingers contracted on hers, and his eyes darkened. "I will remember."

She reached up and touched his cheek. "Please do. You must make your guest feel welcome."

"You may depend on my close attention to your comfort," he said drily. "Come."

As they wandered farther into the majestic confines of the casino, Jolana smiled secretly to herself. It looked as if the next few weeks might be more bearable than she'd expected.

And they were. First, Phillipe flooded her with flowers, especially red roses, until she was drowning in their delicate beauty. He took her out to a different elegant restaurant every evening. During the qualifying event for the motorcar *rallye*, which wound around the mountainous roads in a terrifying pattern, he made sure that she and Maureen went to watch.

The Monte Carlo Rally was an international event that drew competitors from all over Europe, and when Jolana found out just how grueling the course was, and how hazardous, she felt apprehensive.

"Oh, *là*, it is not so bad," Maureen laughed. "*Chérie*, you should have been with us in Africa, where the track was fraught with mud and swamps and unbelievable terrain! The drivers are very competent, and very good. Otherwise, they would not compete. And Phillipe has been racing for years."

"Yes, I suppose you're right," she said. Perhaps she'd lived a sheltered life, but it seemed an unnecessary risk to her.

"Phillipe will be fine," Maureen said suddenly, as if she sensed her friend's concern.

Jolana smiled. "Does it show?"

"That you are concerned for him? *Oui*." She smiled. "It pleases me very much. Phillipe has been different since you came to us. I like the change in him, the maturity. I like best of all the way he looks at you. I think perhaps his wild days are over at last."

"Now, don't start speculating!" Jolana laughed, tossing back her hair as she always had despite its short length.

"Oh, not me." Maureen grinned. She turned her attention back to the men who looked like spacemen in their helmets and uniforms in the confines of the odd-looking automobiles. It was noteworthy that complimentary trials were permitted to the top sixty competitors—and that Phillipe was among them. He had to be good.

But Jolana was worried, nevertheless. All her dreams of a new beginning seemed threatened as she let her eyes wander along what was visible of the rugged, rocky coastline. She knew she could never give Phillipe her heart. Despite his devastating treatment of her, Nick was still the only man she truly loved. But Phillipe had become very special to her; he made her happy and made her feel loved and desired. That was all she could hope for and all she really wanted, but now Jolana wondered if she should have allowed herself to care at all for Phillipe. Racing was dangerous. That was being driven home every second. Accidents could happen. What if something happened to Phillipe? It would hurt terribly if something went wrong now, and she was only just realizing it. The night before the race began, she was very subdued. Maureen kept glancing at her over the elegant dinner table, and Phillipe reached out a hand to caress her nervous fingers where they rested on the table.

"Nervous for me, *petite*?" he asked, striking to the heart of the matter. He smiled gently at her shrug. "I am an experienced driver. I know better than to take unnecessary risks. All will be well, you will see. Come. We will go dancing."

"Phillipe, I really don't feel up to dancing tonight," she confessed. She felt tired to death, a nagging malaise that hadn't let up since she left America. She couldn't think why, when she was usually so healthy. Perhaps it was, as she'd thought in the beginning, nothing more than the change of climate.

"Then we will drive around," he said, "and look at the city at night. It is so lovely. Like you, *chérie*."

"That should put you in a good frame of mind for the race." Maureen grinned at him, with a wink at Jolana.

"*Oui*, and it will be necessary. I need badly to win this race."

Maureen's smile vanished momentarily and she glanced at him apprehensively. But the next minute, the smile was back and they were discussing the cool weather and looking ahead to the parties and balls in Paris in late spring and the Grand Prix in Paris in June, when there would be fêtes almost every night.

CHAPTER EIGHT

MAUREEN WAVED THEM off later, and Phillipe laughed as they pulled away from the house in the Ferrari.

"She cannot wait for us to leave," he told Jolana. "Pierre, who is my replacement driver, is exceptionally handsome and also single. She has invited him for cocktails tonight."

"Aha," Jolana laughed. She leaned her head back against the seat, enjoying the cool air as it came in his open window. The view was magnificent. Palm trees were silhouetted against the Mediterranean in the glare of the tall streetlights, and some of the yachts were brilliantly lit in the harbor. It looked like a fairyland, and so different from New York.

"You should see the yachts in Nice," he said as they drove along the shore road. "They are much bigger than these."

"Is that where you keep yours?" she asked.

He looked glum for a minute. "*Oui*. For the present." He sighed. "It is not the size of the one we had before. Like Maureen, I find myself missing the old days when our mother was still alive, before so much of the family fortune was lost. A Ferrari, while a marvelous automobile, is not a Rolls-Royce."

Jolana felt a twinge of guilt. "Phillipe, if things are

hard for you right now, please let me help. At least I could pay for my keep… "

"Jolana!" he exclaimed, astonished. He pulled off the road into a small, deserted parking lot and cut off the engine. When he turned to her, his eyes were dark with concern. "*Petite*, you misunderstand me. Just because I cannot own a Rolls-Royce does not mean that I must limit my companionship to paying guests." He laughed. "I meant only that we are no longer of the class of the superrich, as are these Arabs whom one sees everywhere in the South of France these days. We are more than comfortable. Not that winning purses in the various competitions does not help," he confessed.

"And also what you win at the gaming tables?" she asked slyly.

He shrugged. "All the same, you do not have to pay for your keep."

She smiled at him. "I would, though. You can't know how wonderful it is, to be here with you and Maureen. I think I might not be alive now, but for the two of you."

She hadn't meant to say that. And, sure enough, he pounced on it. He threw a careless long arm over the back of the seat and stared at her, all the humor gone from his face. "That is the second time you have said so. Are you holding something back from me, *petite*?"

She stared at her hands in the lap of her beige jersey dress. "I accidentally took an overdose of tranquilizers," she said after a minute. She felt safe with Phillipe, as if she could tell him anything. "I was so distressed over losing the man I love that I didn't even realize what I was doing. Mixing alcohol with tranquilizers. I was lucky that a friend found me in time."

He caught his breath. "*Mon ange*, no man is worth

your sweet life." He took her hand and drew it to his chest. "I am glad you came here."

"Oh, so am I!" she said heartily. She looked up at him. "Phillipe, I wish I could give you something in return for all you've given me."

There was no smile this time. "How about a kiss, then, *chérie*?"

"So little," she whispered, leaning toward him.

His eyes searched hers. "So much," he corrected softly.

He smelled of spicy cologne and soap and she liked the smoothness of the tanned cheek her fingers touched.

"Where?" she asked, feeling daring.

His eyebrows arched. "Where?" he echoed in a low, sensuous tone.

"Where would you like to be kissed?"

He chuckled softly. "Temptress," he chided. "I could embarrass you quite brutally."

"I dare you," she teased, flirting with him.

He smiled slowly. His fingers went to the open-necked white silk shirt he was wearing under his navy blue blazer. He unbuttoned the shirt slowly, watching her all the while, until all the buttons were loose. He drew it out of his slacks and exposed the whole of his tanned, muscular chest.

"Here," he murmured.

It was true what they said about Frenchmen being sexy, she mused as she bent. Her lips drew slowly over the smooth, clean flesh, and under her mouth she could feel the sudden thunder of his pulse.

"Doucement," he whispered. His hands caught the back of her head and guided her mouth to one hard male

nipple. "Here, Jolana," he breathed huskily. "Do to me what I did to you that night in the garden in Paris."

She remembered. Not only what he'd done, but how it had felt. She was learning that it was possible to desire more than one man and that love took many forms. Phillipe couldn't give her the wild, passionate excitement that Nick had. But he could give her friendship and gaiety and understanding. In return, she could give him her heart, because he couldn't break it. It gave her a wild sense of power, to know that she could arouse him and make him want her, only her, that he had a whole heart to give.

She opened her mouth, letting her tongue tease the rigid nipple, while her hands discovered the strong, hard muscles of his chest and stomach. He had the body of an athlete, and her hands enjoyed the feel of it.

He drew one of her hands down to his flat stomach, guiding her fingers against his body so that his heartbeat increased wildly, so that his breathing became harsh.

"Will you not take pity on me and accept my proposal of marriage, *chérie*?" he whispered at her lips. "I need you so much it hurts."

"You can have me," she whispered. "I wouldn't refuse you."

"But I have already said how it would be, have I not?" he asked, brushing his mouth tenderly over hers. "I want you for my wife, not my mistress. I want everything to be just so between us. So, I will be tormented until you agree to wear my ring."

"Phillipe, I can't love you…" she whispered.

"Non," he whispered. His mouth parted her lips, caressing them tenderly. "Love is a word for less cyni-

cal people. I cannot give you love, either, *chérie*. I have lived too long without it. But I can give you friendship and respect, a life of gaiety and marvelous sex. I can introduce you to a way of life, and a set of people, that you would never know in your own country. I can even give you a title."

She smiled. "I'd rather have you than the title."

"You honor me."

"I think it's the other way around." Her fingers were still against his stomach and as she searched his eyes, she weakened. She had nothing to go back to in New York except loneliness and the horrible prospect of someday running into Nick with Margery. Seeing them together would kill her. But Phillipe was safe. And without the burden of loving, perhaps their marriage would be even better than what she could have had with Nick. Of course it could, her mind insisted.

Her restless fingers began their exploration once more. "Pity me, Jolana," he laughed huskily. "I cannot think when you do that!"

"Can't you?" she asked. Her eyes danced as she looked up at him. She was going to marry Comte Phillipe de Vinchy-Cardin. She was going to become his wife and have his children and live with him all her life. It might not be love that they would share, but then, the pain Nick had given her had far outweighed the small pleasure. She told herself that and someday she might come to believe it.

"All right, *monsieur le comte*," she whispered. "I'll marry you."

"You will?" he burst out. "*Mon Dieu*, she said yes!" He stuck his head out the open window. "She said yes!" he yelled at passing cars, at the top of his lungs.

"Stop that," Jolana laughed merrily and pulled him back inside. "You'll get us arrested, you crazy man!"

"I feel crazy, *chérie*, that is the truth," he said with pure and evident pleasure in his handsome tanned face. It twinkled in his brown eyes like beacons as he studied her slender body.

"I'll try to be a good wife to you, Phillipe," she said with feeling. "I promise, I will."

"Of that, I have no doubt," he said softly. He held out his arms. "Come and kiss me, now that we are engaged."

She fell into his arms, enjoying the warm crush of his mouth. He was never going to be Nick, and probably what she could feel with him would be no match for the wild emotion that Nick was able to draw out of her. But the French were notorious for arranged marriages, and the divorce rate was comparatively low, so perhaps what she and Phillipe would share over the years would make up for the lack of true love. At least, she'd have someone to take care of her and care about her, someone who wouldn't be eternally comparing her with another woman. Despite her efforts to forget, it still stung that Nick had used her as a substitute for Margery. She wondered if the bitter anguish would ever recede completely, instead of just being submerged until something brought it back with blinding shame. At any rate, the door to the past was closed for good. Now there was only the future.

The next day, the grueling motorcar *rallye* began, and Jolana felt herself getting tense all over as Phillipe waved them goodbye and took his place in the driver's seat of the car.

Maureen had kissed Pierre, his replacement driver,

with evident enthusiasm, and waved him off with tears in her eyes.

"I hate racing," Maureen pouted once the drivers were under way. "I hate it!"

"So do I," Jolana said, "but you can't go around changing people to suit your own tastes, I suppose."

She glanced at the taller girl. "You love him, *oui*?" Maureen asked softly.

"I'm very fond of him," came the quiet reply. "Love will come."

"That, I believe. You are much alike. When is the date you have chosen? Phillipe did not say this morning."

"We haven't set an actual date, but I'm sure it will be as quickly as Phillipe can arrange it," she said with a smile, remembering his groan of impatience when he'd finally driven her home last night.

"Marvelous! What kind of dress will you wear? We must go shopping!" Maureen began enthusiastically.

"You'll have to be my maid of honor." Jolana grinned. "So we'll find something gorgeous for both of us."

"*Oui*. And as soon as the race is over, we will have Phillipe outfitted, as well. A morning coat, I think," Maureen said, thoughtfully.

"Yes. When the race is over," Jolana said and stared at what was visible of the route with consternation. It was going to be a long race, she thought. If only Phillipe would be safe. *What am I thinking of?* she asked herself. *He's driving a Ferrari, for heaven's sake!*

But that thought was of little comfort in the hours that followed. One driver was killed on the course on the first leg. Another was badly injured in a subsequent accident and was taken by ambulance to the hospital.

Jolana felt as if she were going to bite her fingernails through.

It was a grueling race. Of course, Jolana reminded herself, that was its purpose—to test to the ultimate limits the reach of an automobile's performance. Everything was under stress, drivers as well as machinery. In this way, car designs were tested before they were mass-manufactured for the public. It was a dangerous thing to do, and it took a special kind of man to do it. Jolana, watching beside Maureen from Casino Square, studied the race cars with wide-eyed fascination. Maureen had told her that Phillipe was competing mainly against German and British drivers who held, with him, the top three places. The German was world-renowned and was driving a Porsche. The British driver was in an Audi, and although Jolana had thought at first that Phillipe was in a Ferrari, it was actually a Lancia with a Ferrari engine. She remarked to Maureen that the cars all seemed to look alike and that she barely understood enough about this type of racing to comment at all.

Watching the crowd that had gathered for the event was almost as interesting as the race itself. A holiday mood prevailed, which sometimes was enough to keep Jolana and Maureen from dwelling too much on the dangers of the race.

When word finally came that the drivers were on their way back into Monte Carlo, the two girls stood near the finish with wide, frantic eyes. The cars came into view minutes later, and Phillipe was in second place. Despite a frantic burst of speed, he wasn't able to place any better than second. But at least he came back in one piece, and Jolana and Maureen hugged him enthusiastically, with tears in their eyes, when he climbed wearily from the racing car.

"Well, I did my best." Philippe grinned. He needed a shave and his face was gray from lack of rest, but he looked wonderful to Jolana.

"What's wrong with second place?" she asked him, reaching up to kiss him warmly. "After all, think of all the crying that poor winner would have done if you'd beaten him, you kindhearted man. I know that's why you let him get in front of you. It was only because you felt sorry for him."

He laughed uproariously. Even quiet Pierre, who had just joined them, burst into laughter.

"Chérie," Phillipe sighed, drawing Jolana close in his arms, shaking his head. "Now I know that I am the most fortunate man in the world. Having a wife like you is going to be so much better than winning races."

"What a sweet thing to say," she sighed, pressing closer. She felt oddly nauseous, but it finally passed and she followed the others into the cameras as the prizes were awarded.

It seemed to be hours before they were finally back in the villa, and even then they weren't alone. Well-wishers, friends of the family, piled in, drinking champagne and chattering all at once. Jolana joined in as best she could, but she couldn't help feeling out of place. Her French wasn't good enough to allow her to join in on technical conversations about racing. There was no one with whom Jolana could discuss art, and she began to realize then just how limited her conversational abilities were. She was going to have to learn the language Phillipe and Maureen's friends spoke, or she'd never be accepted.

She mentioned it to Phillipe later, when he was mellow with champagne and the delicious crepes the cook had prepared.

"I'm afraid I'll embarrass you," she said hesitantly.

"How silly," he laughed, pulling her close as they sat on the sofa and watched a cruise ship come into port out the picture window. "You are so beautiful, *petite*, that no one will notice what you are saying, only how you look." He kissed her softly. "I could have hugged you to pieces when you said that, about letting the other driver win because I was sorry for him. I was so distraught about losing, and here you come and make me feel twice the man I thought I was." He searched her eyes with warmth and affection. "We will make a good match. You are not sorry that you have agreed to marry me?"

She shook her head. "No. I'm very honored to have been asked."

He drew her close to his side and sipped his champagne quietly. "I am honored to have been accepted. It will be well, *petite*. We will be very happy."

She let her cheek slide down his arm until she could see his face. "Care to take me to bed?" she teased with a wicked grin.

"*Mais, oui.* After," he added tauntingly, "we are married."

She hit his chest. "Phillipe!"

"Patience, *petite*," he breathed, grinning as he bent to touch her mouth with his. "All in good time. Right now, I am too tired. And tomorrow will begin the parties. Besides," he said softly, "I want everything to be just right, done properly. Perhaps because as I grow older, I begin to regret all the flouting of custom and convention that I have done. This once, I want everything to be circumspect, you understand?"

"Oddly enough, I do." She studied his face quietly. "Phillipe, I told you I'm not a virgin."

"Neither am I," he answered drily. "Shall we both pretend that it will be the first time?" he teased.

She smiled back at him. *"Oui,"* she murmured. "Let's do that."

And he drew her closer while, outside the window, the ship pulled into port with all its lights blazing.

Jolana and Phillipe were married a week later in a small church overlooking the Mediterranean, with only a few of Maureen and Phillipe's closest friends to witness the rites. Jolana felt as if she were in a dream world, where nothing was quite real. In the space of a heartbeat, she'd put an irrevocable barrier between herself and Domenico Scarpelli. She stared at the white gold band around her finger with a sense of fatalism. Goodbye, Nick, she said silently. Now her life, her love, her body belonged to Phillipe. She was going to be the best wife she could. She was going to make Phillipe very happy. And maybe someday she'd be able to give him more than affection and the gift of her body. Maybe someday she'd even be able to love him.

For their honeymoon, he took her to the Caribbean, to a small French island where the temperature was warm and the skies were blue. And there, at a private villa when the night came softly and covered the island, they became man and wife.

After a light supper, Phillipe led her down to the deserted beach and began slowly to remove his clothing, watching her all the while. She didn't move or turn away. And her eyes found him not only pleasing, but devastating, when the last of the fabric was peeled away. He was smooth and bronzed and as muscular as she'd thought he would be. In the moonlight, with his fair hair moving softly in the breeze, he made her catch her breath. So must the old heroes of Greece have looked in centuries past, as they were sculpted for the appreciation of future generations.

"I do not displease you?" he asked with a knowing smile.

She shook her head slowly. "I was just thinking about the Greeks," she replied drily.

His hands rested on his lean hips. "And now you, madame, my wife."

She removed all her clothes for him. The wine they'd consumed with their meal had made her feel warm and uninhibited, and the pure adoration in his eyes did the rest. She felt the sea breeze brush like a lover's fingers over her nudity as she stood before him in the moonlight, and heard the sigh that left his lips.

"Ma belle amie," he whispered. "Come and let me make love to you."

She moved toward him without fear, without regret. He was her husband now, and he had any rights he cared to take. And in all honesty, the giving was not going to be a chore. He was good and kind and thoughtful. And she would do her very best to love him.

She went against him softly, so that their bodies were pressed tightly together, and she slid her arms around his back and let her hands explore his long, lean contours.

"Slowly, *petite*," he whispered. "Very slowly, so that you do not rouse me too soon."

Her heart trembled with its quick, sharp beat. "Are we really going to make love here?"

His hands smoothed down her back to her hips and

her thighs and back up again, and around to catch her taut, warm breasts. "Here is better than the very narrow-minded approach expected of newlyweds, is it not?" he breathed unsteadily. "Beds are so...mundane, my sweet. This... This is wildly exciting, is it not?"

"Oh, yes," she agreed, burning now with desire.

"I knew you long ago," he whispered as he caressed her, "when Maureen was at school with you and talked of no one but her friend Jolana. She intrigued me so that I had to come and see you for myself. I adored you even then, *petite*. Can you see how much I adore you, little one?"

She could, and it was glorious to be wanted for herself, not as a substitute. It was glorious to be a woman, and wanted, and needed, for only herself.

Grateful to him, she moved, brushing her body up against his so that she intensified what he was feeling and made him tremble.

He caught his breath. His long-fingered hands touched her hips and his thumbs caressed her soft belly as he rocked her gently up and down against him, and his heart shuddered against her soft breasts. Her legs trembled against his as she felt the raging need in his body and wanted nothing but to satisfy it completely.

She brushed the tips of her breasts slowly across his smooth chest and her hands found him and touched him and she smiled as he groaned.

"Phillipe," she whispered, opening her mouth as she lifted it to his.

His breath came heavily as he put his open mouth on hers. His hands lifted her hips against his, higher and higher, until she felt him against her, until he moved suddenly, sharply, and she became a part of him.

She gasped, her nails biting into his shoulders as she met his hot, dark eyes.

"Yes, like this," he whispered with a hot, wild smile. "Like this, standing. It will be better than if I crushed your body under mine into the sand. Rock with me. Lift, rise… *Dieu*, Jolana, *Dieu*, harder than that…hard!" His hands hurt, but she was caught up in the rhythm and the furious hunger and the madness of it, and as she arched back, they overbalanced and went down into the surf.

But neither of them noticed the dampness of the beach, the water crashing against their locked ankles. He was heavy and the sand under her back was abrasive, but her mouth was in bondage to his, and his hands were all over her. She lifted her hands to his hips, matching her wild, frantic motions to his, and the night burned around them. He rolled over with her in the sand, now above, now below, as the pleasure built and built, and she cried out, moaning, biting at him in a perfect haze of mindless motion and agonized sweetness. When the moment came, she felt a symphony of texture and sound and sensation carrying her off like the tide, and she whimpered into his hot throat. It wasn't the incredible pleasure that Nick had given her, but it was more than enough. She held him while he took his own shuddering relief, and then she kissed him and caressed him and comforted him while he regained the strength her body had taken from him.

"*Ma vie*, was it as sweet for you as it was for me?" he finally whispered.

"Oh, yes," she said, and meant it. "Sweet as honey."

"Sweet like you, *ma chère*," he said on a long sigh. He brushed soft kisses on her mouth before he lifted himself away. "*Allons*, we swim! Come!" And, taking her hand, he ran her down the beach with him, into the surf, into the brisk, cool sea. The night had a magic of its own that she knew she'd remember long after she and Phillipe had left to go back to Monaco. Already, she had taken the first step into the future, and found it not at all bitter.

CHAPTER NINE

JOLANA HAD THOUGHT she knew Phillipe very well until they married. Then she began finding out all sorts of things about him.

He was the soul of patience in bed. He could make love to her with a sweet, searing tempo that made music in her body. But if a waiter was a minute late taking his order in a restaurant, he would lose his temper and make a scene. He was meticulous about his clothing, very strict in even his bedtime regimen. He showered first, then shaved, then brushed his teeth. He arose precisely at 6:00 a.m. and wanted breakfast exactly ten minutes later, along with the morning paper. And he was more agreeable if no one spoke to him until he was drinking his second cup of coffee.

Jolana managed to get around his bad moods, or coax him out of them. But as the days went by, she began to wonder if she'd really ever known Phillipe at all. The charming, laughing companion of the past few weeks had turned into a somber, moody boy. And worst of all was his gambling. She hadn't said anything about it in the days before their marriage, thinking it was just a rich man's hobby. But Phillipe thought nothing of betting thousands of francs on the turn of a card, the spin of a roulette wheel.

"Darling, I'm not nagging," she said late one night

when they came in from the casino back in Monte Carlo, where they'd returned after their brief honeymoon. "But don't you think, now that we're married, that you could just cut back a little on the gambling?"

He glared at her from his formidable height. "In France, it is not as in America. Here a woman does not question her husband or his habits. You understand?"

"No, I do not," she said haughtily, glaring up at him. "When you start gambling away our future, I think that gives me a few rights! What about when we have children? How are we going to provide for them if you throw away every penny we have?"

"We have?" he asked with a cold smile. "You forget yourself. The money is mine and Maureen's."

It was the most humbling thing he could have said to her. She'd sworn she'd never wind up in this predicament, being financially dependent on a man.

"So that's how it's going to be," she mused, returning his coolness. "Very well, *monsieur le comte*, I'll go back to painting and make my own money."

He was immediately contrite, in one of the lightning mood changes she was coming to expect from him. He drew her close with a rueful smile. "Forgive me," he said softly. "I am a beast. It is just that, marriage, the confinement of it, is new to me. For so long, I have been a free spirit. Now I have a wife, a lovely wife," he added, bending to kiss her softly, "and responsibilities. I will try to reform, I swear, *petite*. Am I forgiven?"

"I suppose," she answered, and reached up to return his warm, slow kiss. But inside, warning bells were ringing. It wasn't the most encouraging start for married life, to leave a conflict unresolved.

"Now, now, we argue, then we make up," he said softly, smiling wickedly as he kissed her.

"I still want to go back to painting," she said.

"Eventually. Kiss me."

"Not…eventually," she argued between kisses. "Now."

"There is no need. Stop talking, *petite*. I have remembered an appetite that has not yet been fed today," he added with a warm smile and lifted her off her feet.

"Phillipe…!" she ground out, exasperated.

But he was kissing her again, his mouth slow and tender and full of magic. In the end, she gave in without a protest, winding her arms around his neck as he carried her to bed.

Later in the week, he left for a yachting trip in the Mediterranean, leaving Jolana behind. Her stomach was uneasy these days, and the thought of a long sea voyage almost made her lose her breakfast.

She sensed that Phillipe was disappointed in her, but he made no comment. On the other hand, he offered no sympathy. That was the one quality he seemed to lack, compassion. And to Jolana, it was the most important commodity on earth. She'd grown up with a lack of it in her own life. Now she seemed to be tied to a man who had little sympathy for anyone. It didn't make things easier for her.

"He is not used to being married, *chérie*," Maureen told her with a kind smile. "You must give him time to adjust. He cares for you very much, but you must not try to cage him."

Jolana felt shocked. "Have I?"

"In small ways," Maureen confided. "He does gamble, you know. He has done this for as long as I can remember. He is very good at it, and he makes much more than he loses. You know that things are not well with us financially, *n'est-ce pas*?"

"Yes," Jolana agreed. "I even offered to paint. I'm selling quite a lot of canvases these days, internationally."

Maureen's eyebrows shot up. *"C'est vrai?"* she asked with an excited smile. *"Chérie*, I have so many friends... Do you do portraits? *Voilà!* The perfect thing. And it is not considered work in our circles, to paint. It is...how you say, genius."

"I'm not that good," Jolana protested.

"But you are! That painting you did of Nice, it was *magnifique*." She pursed her lips. "Now let me see. A cocktail party, I think. Next week. We will invite all the right people." She smiled and patted Jolana's hand. "You leave everything to me, *chérie*. I will handle it."

"Phillipe might not like it," Jolana said nervously.

"He will," Maureen said offhandedly. "Now, here is what we will do."

Jolana expected the party to be a total disaster, because she was nervous and insecure and uncertain of her ability to please Maureen's titled and wealthy friends. But she learned quickly that most of them were friendly and outgoing and extremely kind. Her beauty intrigued the men, and her bubbly personality and genuine curiosity even gained points with the women. By the end of the evening, she was hard-pressed to manage conversation with all the people who interested her.

"Chérie, you are a sensation," Maureen laughed when they both caught their breaths in the kitchen, where the cook was pouring out canapés at an amazing rate.

"I haven't talked so much in months," Jolana confessed. "I've had an enthusiastic debate on foreign policy with a Greek billionaire and discussed American fashions with a member of the Italian aristocracy. I can hardly believe it."

"Starstruck?" Maureen grinned.

"In the extreme." Jolana held her cocktail glass loosely and her dark eyes were dreamy. "If you could only see the background I had," she sighed, "you'd realize just how fascinating this is to me. They're people," she added, as if she found the fact astonishing. "They're real people. Very intellectual, very involved in all kinds of cultural and charitable projects, and not at all full of themselves. And so—" she searched for the right word "—so regal."

"But, so are you," Maureen reminded her, gesturing toward Jolana's fair complexion set off against the off-white designer gown she was wearing, along with a fabulous emerald necklace Phillipe had given her. Her short blond hair curled softly around her face, and she was slender as a reed—although she'd needed a larger size dress than she normally wore.

Jolana laughed and shook her head. "It's just the trappings," she protested. "A title and designer clothes and fabulous jewelry would make most women look chic. I'm the same nervous coed you used to know at college."

"But now you hide it very well," Maureen said. She hugged the taller girl impulsively. "Come. We must return, or they will think we do not like them."

"I've had two offers already," Jolana mentioned. "The big Greek wants me to paint his wife and son, and that polo player from London wants me to do his prize polo pony."

"Have you accepted?"

She shrugged. "I'm afraid to. I don't know if Phillipe would like having me jet around the globe to paint people."

Maureen considered that. "Mr. Dorianos has a villa in Nice. He could have his wife and son pose there for you. He wouldn't mind. You ask him. And as for the polo player, Jeremy Blaine—it would be better if you did the pony from a photo. He most likely wants more than a painting of a horse," she said. "You watch him, *chérie*. He has wandering eyes and hands."

"Thanks for the warning," Jolana laughed. "I'll just tell him I don't do ponies. In a nice way."

"Good girl. Come."

It was a long evening, but at the end of it, Jolana had lined up enough work to last her at least a month. The commissions were fairly large ones, which should please her absent husband. But when she lay down that night, she wondered at the course her life was taking. When Phillipe had proposed, she'd envisioned something entirely different. She'd seen them going places together, doing things together. They were married less than a month, and already he was cruising in the Mediterranean without her. Somehow, it didn't seem much like a marriage. It was more of a legalized liaison.

Besides the loneliness, she was feeling worse by the day. The mornings were beginning to be an ordeal. She awoke with a sick feeling in the pit of her stomach, and some foods that she once loved were beginning to unsettle her. She was tired all the time, too. But she seemed healthy enough. Too healthy, in fact. Her clothes were all getting tight in the waist. She wondered now if it mightn't be something besides just the difference in climates. Perhaps she was pregnant already.

Her hands went to her waist and she felt a warm glow all over. Could that be it? Could she be carrying Phillipe's child so soon? It had been only a few weeks but they'd taken no precautions. Yes, it was possible. But just to be sure, she'd wait another couple of weeks before she saw the doctor. Meanwhile, it was her own precious secret. When it was confirmed, then she'd tell Phillipe. She only hoped he'd be as happy about it as she felt.

The days passed lazily after that. She commuted once a day to the huge villa of the Dorianos family, where she made sketches of madame and young Stevros. They were a beautiful mother and child. For Jolana, it became more a labor of love than a job, especially when she thought about the tiny life she might be carrying. As a result, the painting, when she started it, had an aura of fascinated affection that shone out of it like sunbeams. When she presented it to madame and Mr. Dorianos two weeks later, it was met with silence.

They gazed at it for a long time, while Jolana held her breath. When Mr. Dorianos looked up, there was a suspicious glaze in his eyes and he seemed speechless.

"It is…most flattering," madame managed huskily, and smiled. It was a wobbly smile. Impulsively, she went forward and hugged Jolana. "It is beautiful. Thank you. In my old age, it will be my greatest comfort. You have managed to capture the very feeling I have for my son."

"Never have I seen anything like it," her husband said, shaking his head as his eyes traced it over and

over again. "Comtesse Vinchy-Cardin, I am awed by
the scope of your talent. You have a rare gift."

"Thank you," Jolana said with a smile. "I'm only
glad you like it."

She left there with delicious elation, rushing back to
the villa to share her praise with Maureen. But Maureen
wasn't there. Phillipe was. And he looked half-angry
when he saw her.

He was suntanned, and his blond hair had traces of
platinum where it had been bleached by the sun. He was
wearing a white suit, and he looked wonderful.

"Phillipe!" Jolana laughed, and flung herself into his
arms. "Oh, Phillipe, I'm so glad you're home!"

"Are you?" He didn't return the embrace. He held
her at arm's length, staring curiously down her slender
body in jeans and a floppy multicolored shirt. "You
look very healthy, *ma petite*. Have you missed me?"

"So much," she said, and meant it. She reached up
to kiss him. "Phillipe, I'm painting again," she en-
thused. "Mr. Dorianos had me to paint his wife and
son, and they had an absolute fit over the portrait! I
was so excited...!"

He seemed to relax. "Ah. So that is why I saw the
Ferrari in his driveway when we sailed into port."

She blinked, staring up at him. "You thought...?"
She burst out laughing. "As if I'd have the energy, after
a month of marriage to you!" she said pertly.

He laughed, too, shaking his head. He linked his
hands around her waist and swung her lazily from side
to side, his lips pursed as he studied her. "I am jealous
of you. Do you mind?"

She wondered. If he trusted her, should he be jealous? On the other hand, it was often said that a husband

who accused a wife of infidelity often did so because he himself was guilty of it. She frowned up at him.

"Who went on the cruise with you?" she asked with narrowed eyes.

He looked startled, then nervous. "A few friends, no one you know. Ah, no more talk of sailing, come and tell me all the latest news! Where is Maureen?"

"Off with Pierre somewhere," she offered. She stopped him at the doorway to the spacious living room that overlooked the Mediterranean. "Phillipe, you aren't sorry we got married?" she asked uncertainly.

"*Chérie!* What a silly question!" He bent to kiss her softly. "Later, when I am rested, I will prove to you how 'sorry' I am!"

But she still frowned, studying him closely. "I think I'm pregnant, Phillipe," she said, unable to put it off a minute longer.

He stood very still, his face rigid, his eyes slowly running down to her waistline and back up. "Have you...seen the doctor?" he asked hesitantly.

"Not yet. But I have all the symptoms." She searched his eyes for some sign of warmth. "We didn't take any precautions," she reminded him. "Phillipe, please say you want it."

Her pleading, hurt look melted him. "But of course I want it," he said, drawing her close. But over her shoulder, his features contorted, his eyes closed. He held her tightly to his muscular body. "You don't know how much I want a child. You have told Maureen?" he asked suddenly, stiffening.

"No, not yet. Why?" she asked.

He sighed heavily. "Let me speak with her first. She

will be as thrilled as I am, I promise you, but I would like to tell her. Is that acceptable?"

"Yes," she said, but she had a nagging suspicion that something was very wrong. She started to ask him, then he abruptly changed the subject, telling her about the trip.

Maureen came home just shortly thereafter, and Phillipe met her at the door. There were quick whispers, followed by Maureen's wildly excited explosion of enthusiasm. She threw herself at Jolana, all laughter and smiles.

"Oh, *chérie*, such a blessing, such a heavenly blessing," she murmured gaily. "I could not be happier."

"I'm very glad," Jolana sighed. "You'll make a lovely aunt."

And while the women were embracing, Phillipe was watching with quiet, confused eyes. He knew the child could not possibly be his. The finest doctors in Europe had been able to give him no hope that he would ever father a child. He was hopelessly sterile. But the de Vinchy-Cardin line needed an heir, and he needed Jolana. Besides, who would it hurt, if he kept his knowledge to himself? Even Maureen did not know the truth about him. He had worked hard to conceal the information from her as well as the rest of the world. He sighed, watching Jolana. A child. That poor, stupid fool in America, her lover of one night, would be the only loser in this. He would spare her the knowledge of her folly.

The more he thought about it, the more pleased Phillipe became. As he stared possessively at his lovely wife, he almost regretted that little brunette he had met on the cruise. He'd have to be much more careful now about his liaisons. He had a feeling that Jolana wouldn't understand or accept them. Well, she wasn't bad in bed. A little reserved still, a little less involved than she should be. He could teach her. And the baby would be nice. He moved closer to her and slid an arm around her shoulders. The future looked very good indeed.

CHAPTER TEN

JOLANA WAS PREGNANT. The doctor confirmed it the very next day, and she felt as elated as she felt afraid.

"This is common," the kindly old physician assured her. "It is a frightening thing, madame, to have the full and awesome responsibility for a child, for raising and feeding and clothing and guiding him to adulthood. But rest assured that we all feel it. You will cope very easily. Your husband, he will be pleased?"

She smiled. "Oh, yes."

"I will refer you to a good obstetrician in Nice, if that is where you will be residing...?"

"Well, Phillipe did say we'd go back to Paris in May..." she answered.

"For good?"

"I assume so, yes."

"Then I can recommend a very good man there," he said, scribbling down something on paper. "I will write to him in your behalf. Since the pregnancy is so far advanced, it would be well if you go soon, madame."

"So far advanced?" she asked.

"Well, it is difficult to say without having you hospitalized for further tests, but..."

Before he could finish whatever he was about to say, the nurse rushed in to tell him of an emergency case that needed immediate attention. Jolana was tactfully and politely pushed out the door, and she went back to the villa frowning.

"Is it so?" Phillipe asked the minute she got in the door. "Is there to be a child?"

"Yes," she laughed, beaming.

"Chérie!" He picked her up in his arms and carried her to the living room, putting her gently on the sofa. "I must take excellent care of you now, my wife," he said softly and bent to kiss her. "Excellent care." He began to unbutton her blouse.

"Phillipe…!"

"Maureen has gone off with Pierre. Cook is in town to buy groceries. The villa is empty," he said wickedly as he eased her out of the soft blue dress and everything under it. "Ah, my wife, how pregnancy becomes you… I find it oddly erotic."

His mouth moved softly over her swollen breasts, and she cradled his head against them as she felt the familiar gentle excitement he created in her body.

"Phillipe, there's just one thing," she whispered as he rose to take off his own clothing.

"Oui?" he murmured, letting his eyes worship her as he got the last of the fabric out of the way.

"The doctor…" She caught her breath as he slid his long, elegant body alongside hers, letting her feel his obvious hunger. "The doctor said that the pregnancy was…advanced…"

He hesitated at her breasts, but only for an instant. "Of course," he said on a smile. "You are past the first week or so, are you not? Now hush, *chérie*, I want you."

He nibbled at her, pleased as he heard the soft moans, felt the hungry pressure of her fingers on his hips. He would have a long talk with her doctor. He would beg

the obstetrician not to tell her just how advanced her
pregnancy was. A few hints about anticipating the marriage vows, and the shame his young, very shy wife
would feel if it were commonly known—yes, that would
silence even the most hardhearted of doctors. And she
would never know. He lifted her silken body, enjoying
the softness of it, the silkiness of her skin under his
fingers. She was so beautiful, his wife. He could almost feel sorry for the idiot who had sent her running
to France after that devastating affair. He had lost more
than he would ever realize. Phillipe smiled as he fitted
her warm softness to him and found her mouth.

"Now," he breathed into the sweet darkness. "Now,
petite, this time let me have all of it, this time…move
with me…and give yourself totally. *Chérie, chérie, je
t'aime, je t'aime, je...t'aime!*"

His voice broke as his movements intensified, and
Jolana clung to him, buffeted by the force of his desire,
glorying in his wild need of her. She wondered what he
meant, but the clouding mist of desire blurred the words.
She was conscious only of the pleasure he could give
her, except for the tiny part of her mind that helplessly
compared his ardor with Nick's.

Afterward she was ashamed. It was Nick she was
thinking of when she gave Phillipe a response that made
him cry aloud with joy. It was remembering how demanding and passionate Nick had been with her that
had wrung the last bit of restraint out of her body and
given it generously to Phillipe and the surging rhythm
of his hips. She'd given him every bit of pleasure she
could, returning his kisses, touching him, adoring him.
And all the while, it had been Nick, in her mind, in her
heart, and she felt as if she'd cheated Phillipe.

He touched her hair lovingly as he lay beside her, damp and sated, his chest shuddering with his heartbeats. *"Merci,"* he whispered huskily. *"Merci.* Today you have given me what you never could before. Now we are truly married. Now, you belong to me."

She pressed close into his arms. "And you're not sorry, about our baby?" she whispered.

"No. I am not sorry." He smoothed her short hair. "We will raise him with every advantage. He will be loved, and needed."

"I hope he looks like you."

"I hope he looks like you," he said in an unusually fervent tone.

Phillipe went with her to Paris when she saw the obstetrician the doctor in Nice had recommended. He managed a private conversation with the kindly middle-aged man before the three of them sat down to discuss the pregnancy and her delivery. She asked for a specific date, but he was vague, mentioning something about the difficulty of deciding exact delivery dates. They would, he said, go from examination to examination and as term approached, he would let her know.

Afterward, Phillipe took her out to eat and they visited art galleries until her feet and strength gave out. They spent the night in the apartment before they were to leave for Monaco the next morning. Unfortunately, there was some unsettling news waiting for her in the form of a letter from Tony.

He was selling his interest in the gallery to Nick. Working in partnership with Nick had become impossible and he couldn't take any more of it. Also, he added, Nick had been demanding to know Jolana's Paris address. Tony refused to give it. The letter closed with a strong plea for her to call him; there were things he could tell her more easily on the phone.

She hid the letter before Phillipe saw it. She didn't want him to know that Nick was looking for her. She wondered why. Surely he was married to Margery by now. What did he want? She thought sarcastically that he probably wanted a little on the side, to make up for what Margery would withhold whenever she got miffed at him. Well, it was too late now. He could find some other poor fool for his extracurricular activities. It wouldn't be Jolana. She had a husband and a baby on the way, and she was finished with Nick forever. Poor old Tony, she was sorry about his gallery. But Tony would bounce back. She stared out the window at the rain and sighed. She wouldn't call him. It would lead to too many questions, and that was a closed chapter in her life.

"You are thoughtful, *petite*. Is something wrong?" Phillipe asked as he pulled her into his arms, resting his cheek on her hair.

She clasped her hands around his where they rested on her thickened waist and leaned back with a smiling sigh. "No, darling," she said softly. "I was just watching the rain."

He turned her slowly. "Suppose you watch me instead?" he said drily, bending.

She gave him her mouth and put her whole heart into showing him how happy she was that they were married, that she was safe from Nick. Thank God Tony had shielded her. She didn't want any complications. Not now. Nick had broken her heart once. She was never going to let him get close enough to try again.

Jolana had hoped that because of the baby, Phillipe

would spend more time with her. But when she was offered a commission painting the family of a wealthy Arab, Phillipe encouraged her to take it.

"*Petite*, the money will be welcome, you know?" he said finally, and he looked so worried that she gave in.

"Are things any better?" she asked softly.

He sighed and wiped the worried expression from his face. "Some," he said. "But we cannot afford to turn down this commission. It will not tire you too much?" he asked.

"No," she said. "I paint sitting down, you know." She kissed his cheek. "All right. But I'll miss you."

"It will not be for long," he said. "The Arab family is only at Beaulieu-sur-Mer. It is not far to go." He grinned. "Perhaps other men will find you all too attractive, *chérie*. I must protect my interests by visiting you often," he added wickedly, touching her rounded stomach, which was just beginning to show her condition.

She laughed. "Well, in that case, I'll have to buy some sexy nightgowns." She frowned a little. "Phillipe, you don't mind the way I look now?"

"Mind?" He let his hands wander down the silky fabric of her dress slowly, and his face changed with the sensation. "I find you wildly sexy, didn't you know?"

That pleased her. She kissed him and tried not to think how it would have been with Nick. Somehow she didn't think Nick would have allowed her to be apart from him during her pregnancy. But, then, he was older than Phillipe. And much more deceitful. She had to keep reminding herself of that, of how he'd hurt her. Because in her heart, his memory was as bright as it had ever been.

The Arab family was fascinating. The children, so

dark and with such huge, liquid brown eyes, were the ideal subjects for Jolana at that particular time in her life. She painted them with love and longing, and marveled at their patience as she sketched.

"*Comtesse*, you are so talented," their mother sighed as she studied the progress of the painting over Jolana's shoulder. "I feel flattered that you agreed to such an arrangement. I cannot believe it would be because you needed the money." She laughed softly when she said that, and Jolana was glad that her financial worries didn't show. Nevertheless, it was so close to the truth that she felt a twinge of hurt pride.

"I enjoy my work," she said quietly, "and such delightful subjects make it all the more pleasant. Your children are beautiful, madame."

The Arab woman studied Jolana quietly.

"There is to be a child for you, soon, I think. I do not presume too far?"

"Of course not," Jolana said, turning. She smiled. "It's our first. But how did you know? My stomach has quieted since I've been here, and I didn't think it showed…"

"A woman almost always knows," came the soft reply. "You have such a glow of beauty. It is one I remember, because my husband often remarked of it when I was carrying our children." She turned away to look out at the ocean, her dark features sad. "They were better days, when there was not so much money. Now, he is so rarely at home and I have very little to occupy me when the children are away at school."

Jolana felt a surge of pity. She felt much the same way herself, because Phillipe seemed to spend far more time away from her than with her. But there was nothing she could say.

"Your husband, *comtesse*. He is a race driver, I am told," the Arab woman said after a minute, turning with a polite smile.

"Yes. I spend much of my time worrying about him," Jolana confessed. She stared at the palette and brush in her hand. "It is something he's always done. I can't ask him to stop. But it concerns me."

"Yes, I imagine it does. Men! I never understand why they enjoy taking risks so much, and never concern themselves with our small feelings."

Jolana laughed. "I suppose it's one of the many differences between the sexes. But in all honesty, Phillipe's devil-may-care attitude was what attracted me in the first place. I've always been so conventional myself that it was fascinating to find someone who liked to break the rules."

"My husband is such a man," the older woman confessed. "But I had no choice in my marriage. It was arranged while I was but a child. I am not regretful, you understand. We have a good marriage. I fell deeply in love with my husband. But our customs are...rigid."

Jolana studied the averted face and wondered what the woman meant. But it wasn't her right to ask personal questions. She turned her attention back to the canvas. "Now, about their hands, madame. Do you like the way I've sketched them in?" she asked, changing the subject.

It was the first of many commissions Jolana accepted. And meanwhile, her husband was drifting further and further away from her. Gone was the carefree man of her early acquaintance. In his place was a restless, impatient man who seemed to have lost interest even in her body.

One night, a rare night when she and Phillipe were both home in the villa near Monaco, she overheard a strange conversation between him and Maureen.

"You should not do this to her," Maureen was hissing at Phillipe after he'd announced that he was going to participate in the international motorcar *rallye* in Grasse. "Not now! And to enter the Grand Prix at Le Mans as well... Phillipe, you take unnecessary chances! It is not fair to Jolana, to put this burden of worry on her now, of all times!"

"I must," Phillipe had replied curtly. "Our finances are worsening daily. The drain of medical bills is tremendous."

"The drain of your wild extravagances is more," Maureen replied sharply. "And the upkeep of your latest diversion is shameful!"

"That is my concern."

"What if she learns of it? Have you considered that?" Maureen demanded. "You fool! She loves you!"

There was a hesitation. "She is...my wife. I give her what I am able to give. But I did not realize how very confining it would be, and the baby so soon afterward..."

Jolana had moved away from the open window, feeling sick and alone and full of regret. She'd suspected for a long time that Phillipe was bitter about their marriage, despite the fact that he seemed to enjoy her company. But he hadn't wanted her in bed for some weeks now, not since her waist had thickened and her stomach was obvious enough to require smock tops. He assured her that he still wanted her but was abstaining "for the baby's sake." Since her obstetrician had assured her that sex was possible until the last month, she knew that Phillipe was lying. What he really meant, she thought sadly, was that he didn't want her anymore. And she was willing to bet that there was more than travel to explain his absences. She began to suspect another woman.

When he left for Grasse, he found her in her studio working on a portrait of yet another child for a vacationing American family nearby.

"Very nice," he said, smiling as he bent over to brush a careless kiss on her hair. He was wearing a navy blazer with white slacks and a white silk shirt with a colorful tie. He looked continental and very handsome.

Jolana, in her flowing red-and-white dress, felt tacky by comparison. Her hair was windblown from a walk in the garden, and her mouth was without lipstick. She looked like a pregnant woman.

"Off to Grasse?" she asked quietly, brushing color on the child's pants on canvas.

"Oui."

"Good luck with the car," she said, glancing up at him.

His eyebrows arched. "What else would I need luck with?" he teased, but his eyes were wary.

She wiped her brush. "Oh, nothing. There. How does it look?"

"The client will be pleased. Jolana..." He knelt beside her and studied her face, feeling a twinge of guilt as he realized how tired she looked. *"Chérie*, perhaps when we are back in Paris, things will be different. It is only another week or so."

She looked down at him. "No. I don't think they will be different. You hate me, you hate the baby, you hate our marriage. That won't change." She put down her brush and got up.

"Jolana!" He caught her, turning her around to hold her close. "*Chérie*, that is not so. I adore you. And I want the baby."

She laughed mirthlessly. "Yes, I can tell. It's why you stay with me so much."

He sighed slowly. "That will change," he said firmly. "When we get to Paris, after the Grand Prix at Le Mans, it will all change. I promise." He lifted his head and studied her wan little face. "I care for you very much. Perhaps I lack the facility for showing it, and my life-style is hard to change after so many years. But I will try harder. I swear it. Forgive me, *petite*, for adding to your worries." He bent and kissed her softly.

She sighed and let him hold her. She liked him very much. But love? She knew now for certain that she would never be able to give him the love she'd given so readily to Nick. As long as she lived, and despite his brutal treatment, her heart would belong without reservation to the dark Italian.

After Phillipe had gone, she wandered around the house like a lost soul. Maureen was away on a cruise with Pierre and some friends, and Jolana was alone. She enjoyed the solitude of the villa, overlooking the rocky coastline, and she wasn't at all afraid. There were servants in the house, and neighbors whom she knew. But being alone with her thoughts was torture at times.

She couldn't help remembering Tony's note. Possibly she should have answered it, but she just couldn't. Why would Nick be searching for her? What could he possibly want? He had his beloved Margery, and her son, and nothing left over to give any other woman. Perhaps

Tony had told him about her stupid accident with the alcohol and pills and he thought she'd meant to kill herself over him. Perhaps he wanted to apologize. She laughed coldly. Why should he care? No man who cared about a woman could actually admit to her that he'd used her to rid himself of his lust for another woman. The thought made her ill, after all these months. Of course, it hadn't been totally Nick's fault. She'd been eager enough, and desperately in love. She'd practically seduced him that night, and he'd been too aroused to stop. But why had he told her the truth? She agonized over it. It would have been so much kinder to let her think he'd been carried away by her, anything except that Margery had stirred him up and he'd used Jolana because of it.

She didn't want to see Nick. She didn't want his apologies or his excuses. She only wanted to try to make the most of her marriage and look forward to having her baby. The past was over. Seeing Nick could only make things harder. If only she understood why he was looking for her. It didn't make the least bit of sense.

By the end of the week, she was feeling deserted and out of sorts. Her painting was going badly, and she needed a diversion. So she dressed neatly in a white linen maternity suit with a red patterned blouse and red accessories and had Maurice, the handyman Phillipe had hired, drive her into town. That small luxury made her feel better. She sent Maurice off to have a drink in a bar while she had lunch at one of the lovely outdoor cafés overlooking the Mediterranean.

In the harbor, boats were everywhere. Sailboats and motorboats and yachts. The weather was lovely and sunny and there was a breeze that carried an almost flowery scent. Jolana felt young and free and able to conquer the world.

She treated herself to a ham and spinach quiche and fresh fruit, with strong black coffee. She'd lost her taste for wine during her pregnancy and preferred the coffee, but sparingly.

As she gazed out over the harbor she heard murmurs around her and felt eyes watching her. That was puzzling. She turned, her hair short and sassy, her complexion faultless, her makeup precise and exquisite, and found a nightmare standing just across the way.

Domenico Scarpelli froze in place as he saw her. She was only partially visible from the waist up, so that her pregnancy wasn't immediately noticeable. But it was her face he was looking at, his dark eyes starving as they searched it. He was thinner than she remembered, and there was a bit of silver at his temples that she didn't recall seeing so vividly before.

Her heart raced, but she fought to keep her poise, looking so elegant and regal that even the waiter smiled at her as he seated Nick.

"Do you mind?" Nick asked huskily before he sat down. The café was crowded. "No," she lied.

He sat down and nodded at the waiter. "Just coffee," he told the man, who quickly left them alone.

"Hello, Nick," Jolana said as carelessly as she could. "What brings you to the South of France?"

He folded his dark, masculine hands on the white linen tablecloth and stared at her. "I could say a conference, if I wanted to lie," he said finally, his voice strained. "But I won't. I came to find you."

She arched an eyebrow as she lifted the delicate cup to her lips. "So?"

"Tony wouldn't tell me where you were," he ground out.

"I asked him not to." She sat up straighter, trying not to notice the black thickness of his hair. Under it, his eyes were dark and full of secrets, his face dark and broad and with new lines in its faultless olive complexion. His mouth was as beautiful as ever, and she remembered so well how it had felt to kiss it and be kissed by it. She dropped her eyes to his navy blue jacket and white shirt. It was open just enough to display the beginnings of his hard, muscular chest with its mat of hair. That brought back even more intimate memories, so she stared at her coffee instead.

"It's taken months to track you down," he said after the waiter had placed a cup of steaming black coffee before him and retreated. "I finally had to resort to a detective agency, but all they could find out was that you'd been visiting the de Vinchy-Cardins and had come south with them on holiday. The French are reticent about disclosing people's movements, aren't they?"

"You make it sound as if we're at war," she commented coolly, smiling at him with a nonchalance that made his expression darken.

"You and I were," he reminded her.

"Were," she emphasized. "That's all in the past."

His dark eyes dropped to his hands around the coffee cup. "Tony told me what happened."

She didn't even flinch. "If you mean the pills, it was an accident, not a suicide attempt. Once I realized you weren't worth such despair, I got better."

The eyes he raised to hers were tortured, anguished. "I messed everything up. I got back to my apartment that night, and Margery was there with the boy, waiting for me." He ran a hand through his thick, wavy hair. "I went crazy. I had too much responsibility, too quickly, I'd given Margery my word that if she got into trouble, she could come to me and I'd take care of her. It was a question of honor, I suppose. I couldn't go back on my word. So I made you hate me, and I pushed you away. Almost too far," he added bitterly. "But I swear to God, all along it was you I wanted, not her. There hasn't been a day that I haven't missed you like hell."

That would have mattered five months before, but she couldn't let it matter now, although she did wish her heart would calm itself. She toyed with her napkin. "You came thousands of miles to tell me that?"

"No," he said harshly. "I came thousands of miles to tell you that I love you."

Her eyes searched his. "Do you, really?" she asked, trying her best to sound unconcerned.

His face froze. "Didn't you hear me?"

"Yes, I heard you." She finished her coffee and put the cup back in its saucer. "Five months ago, after you left my apartment, I might have gone on my knees to hear you say that." She stared at him. "What does Margery think about your sudden change of heart?"

"Listen," he said urgently, dragging her hands into his without looking at them, or at the rings that told her marital state, "Margery's gone back to Andrew. He dried out and he's being good to her. It's what she wanted, what she really wanted. Running to me had just become a habit. When she left him, she realized how much she loved him."

"And what did you realize?" she asked him warily, narrowing her eyes. "When did it come to you that you didn't love her—when she told you she was going back to him?"

He hesitated. "I've known it since the night we shared together." He stared at her face. "For God's sake, listen!" he said harshly, when he saw the indifference in her dark eyes. "Jolana, Margery was my first girl. We were close all through our childhoods. We loved each other. I made the mistake of thinking that I still felt that way about her. The reason I dated you in the first place was to try to show her that there was no future with me, that her place was with Andrew." He laughed shortly. "I felt noble, as if I were making the supreme sacrifice. And then it backfired. She kissed me…dammit, and all I could think of was you. And that night, when we got to the car…"

She flushed, averting her eyes as the erotic memory of that night made her heart go crazy.

"Anyway," he sighed heavily, "I was already beginning to doubt what I thought I wanted from Margery. But she was jealous of you, and Andrew had ignored her. When she showed up at my apartment I remembered you and what I'd told you. And God help me, I was looking for a way out. I was half-drunk… I knew if I told you I'd been thinking of Margery when we made love that it would turn you off. It was the lever I needed. But after I said it, I got sick all over. Especially when you threw me out and I got a look at your eyes." He drew in a shaky breath. "I thought I'd go crazy worrying. When I called Tony, to see if he knew anything, he said you were okay and hung up. I assumed that meant you'd decided you were well off without me. I meant to call you myself… But all at once, I was up to my ears in trouble. Margery moved in with me, with the boy. Andrew was making all kinds of threats. It took time to straighten it all out. Tony said you were okay, so I didn't push it. I… I gave him the portrait you'd done of me, because it was hurting me to see it, to remember what I did to you. I concentrated on Margery. And then it hit me that I didn't love her. That what I felt for her was a kind of brotherly concern with a little leftover passion mixed up in it. I couldn't even kiss her after that night I spent with you." He clasped her hands tighter. "She didn't seem to want that, anyway. She mourned Andrew, she worried about him. Finally, she went to talk with him and he agreed to have therapy. It worked. She and the boy went home. And then I spoke to Tony and he let me have it."

She could imagine Tony doing that. It was oddly satisfying.

"I can't tell you how sick it made me," he said after a minute, the torment obvious in his face. "Knowing you could have died, and I would have been responsible,"

"Don't let your conscience trouble you too much," she replied. "Tony cared enough to come see about me."

"Yes." He studied her face, wondering if it might help his case if he admitted that he'd put Tony up to it. But she looked waxen. Utterly lifeless. She wasn't the lighthearted, laughing woman he'd known in New York. She'd changed in ways that frightened him. It wasn't going to be easy, winning back her respect, her trust. But he was going to do it. He was going to show her how much he cared. He was going to court her. Perhaps in time, she could give him once again the love he'd thrown so carelessly aside months earlier. He'd make sure he appreciated its value this time.

Nick's very presence was sending little thrills up and down her spine, but she schooled her features not to show that pleasure. She owed Phillipe loyalty, if nothing else.

"I'm sorry you had a wasted trip, Nick," she said as she tugged her hands free and finished her coffee. "But I wish you well. No hard feelings. It's all in the past now."

He stared in rigid comprehension as she picked up her purse and left several francs on the table.

"Jolana, please listen to me," he said, feeling almost angry that he should have to plead with her. Didn't it mean anything that he'd relentlessly tracked her down, that he'd cared enough to follow her all the way to France?

She lifted her chin and looked across the table at him.

"I did," she reminded him, glancing past him to where Maurice was coming slowly toward the café. "I even listened to you the night you said you cared for me, that we were going to get married." She smiled coldly. "I even listened that morning when you came back to tell me I'd been a stand-in for Margery in bed. I made a fool of myself over you, and I came to France half-ready to finish what I started in New York," she lied, some part of her enjoying the torment that statement produced in his dark face. "But I had friends here, Nick. And I survived. Even if the circumstances would allow it, I wouldn't be crazy enough to get mixed up with you a second time."

"Circumstances?" he asked warily.

Jolana stared at him with a malicious smile as Maurice came up to the table, nodded at Nick and bowed his head toward Jolana.

"*Comtesse*, the car is ready when you are," he said respectfully.

Nick blinked. His face paled and he dropped his

eyes to her hand, where her rings were displayed. The diamond and gold bands told the story, and he went white as a sheet.

"You're...married," he whispered hoarsely.

"Oh, quite married," she assured him. "To Comte Phillipe de Vinchy-Cardin. And there's something more that you don't know," she added, and got slowly to her feet, watching him.

She knew that as long as she lived, she'd never forget the look on Nick's face, in his eyes, as he saw that she was pregnant. He seemed to have died for an instant.

"Oh, God," he breathed. There was anguish in his voice. Pure, unspeakable anguish.

"You might congratulate us," she said, cocking her head to one side. "Phillipe's very proud of his approaching fatherhood. And I'm rather ecstatic myself. I always wanted a family."

He couldn't seem to breathe. All the light went out of his eyes as she walked slowly away in front of Maurice.

Nick sat as if mesmerized, staring after Jolana long after she had gone. The thought of her with another man was too much for him to bear, and he forced it from his consciousness with an almost painful act of will.

"It can't be," he growled suddenly, his voice low and filled with determination. "It just can't be."

He ordered a whiskey, neat, and drank it down. He didn't know what to do. He didn't feel capable of running his business. He might as well stay in France for a while. Who was the man Jolana had married? he wondered. He would have to find out something about this Comte de Vinchy-Cardin. Later he would call New York and have his research department at the magazine dig up everything they could about him. But now his mind was fogged with misery and heartache. *Jolana,* he moaned inwardly. *Jolana!*

Meanwhile, Jolana was on her way back to the villa, trying her best to hold back the tears she didn't want Maurice to see. She concentrated on the wildly prolific flowering plants along the way, in gardens they passed. But all she saw, felt, heard, smelled, loved, was Nick. She had had her revenge. It had been sweet, too. But how it hurt to see him again, to hear him whispering that he loved her, that it had been her he wanted, not Margery. But it was too late. Months too late. She was married and pregnant, and she could never be with Nick again.

When they reached the villa, she went straight to her room and cried until her chest hurt with racking sobs. As long as she lived, she'd remember the look on Nick's face when she'd stood up, wearing Phillipe's rings and carrying his baby. She wondered if he'd felt as horrid as she had that morning in her apartment. Now there was no hope of going back, as Nick must have seen. *Oh, you fool,* she whispered. *You fool. Why did you have to come after me and ruin my life all over again? How can I let Phillipe touch me now, knowing that you love me and I can never touch you again?*

Well, at least she'd have the memory, she told herself. That would be some small comfort in the long years ahead. And there was the baby. Her fingers touched her stomach lovingly. The baby would be her whole life. She could love it as none of the men in her life had really loved her. She sat up and dried her tears. Perhaps Phillipe would be home today. She needed him now more than ever.

CHAPTER ELEVEN

BUT PHILLIPE DIDN'T come home that day or the next. Neither did Maureen. And Jolana couldn't work, so she paced the floor. Never had she felt so miserable or so alone. Knowing Nick was somewhere nearby only made things worse.

It was stupid to go into Monte Carlo again and risk running into Nick. But she couldn't help it. She decided to have dinner there at the Carlton restaurant. It was almost as if she knew Nick was staying there. It was absurd, but she wasn't even surprised when he walked into the restaurant.

He was alone. She'd been expecting, dreading, to see a woman with him. But he was wearing a light-colored suit and looking handsome enough to sink a ship or two.

His dark eyes spotted her in her becoming lavender maternity ensemble, as she sat by the window overlooking the palm-lined street. He hesitated, but only for an instant, before he came to stand beside her table.

"Isn't your husband with you, Jolana?" he asked quietly.

"My husband is in Grasse, for the race," she said, cocking an eyebrow. "I don't care to watch, if you must know."

"He races?" he asked.

"Yes," she said. "Quite successfully."

Nick didn't have to ask that question. He already knew the answer. Indeed, Nick knew a great deal about Phillipe now. He had placed a call to his magazine, and within a few hours their extensive computerized files had supplied him with more than enough information concerning the Comte de Vinchy-Cardin. Most of what he had learned had been fairly common knowledge, but several items had supplied him with facts that few people were aware of. His attention had been riveted when he heard one of the final pieces of information. It was an incomplete report that had been hushed up very carefully and had never made any of the news media. Apparently, on one of his extended trips to the United States, a woman whom Phillipe had been living with in California had claimed to be pregnant by him and had instituted a lawsuit to force him to acknowledge her child.

The case had been dismissed immediately; in fact, it had never come to trial at all. Phillipe had somehow easily proved he had not been guilty. There were no details available, but the reasons for such a case being dismissed were few: chief among them, Nick knew, was the inability of the accused man to father a child.

Nick had been dazed when he hung up the phone. It had taken several minutes for the meaning of what he had heard to sink in. The child was not Phillipe's. It was his child whom Jolana was carrying. It was his child but he would never be able to acknowledge it. She must hate him very deeply to keep such a thing from him, he had thought—and she had good reason to.

Nick's thoughts returned to the present, and he studied Jolana for a long moment. "May I sit with you?"

She shrugged. "If you like."

He drew out a chair and sat down. It was a hopeful sign, that she'd come into town to eat dinner when she surely had servants at the villa where she was staying. He'd driven by it, impressed by its size. He'd almost stopped, but he was uncertain of his welcome, and he hadn't really fancied running into her husband.

He ordered a beef dish and a bottle of wine, glancing at her as the waiter departed. "Do you drink wine, now?" he asked, nodding toward her waistline.

"No, I'm afraid to," she said honestly.

"How does the *comte* feel about becoming a father so soon after marriage?" he asked pointedly.

She glanced up. "Why, he's delighted. Or he says he is." She dropped her eyes to her plate again with a sigh, "I'm not really sure. He seemed shocked when I told him."

His heart almost stopped. He studied her face with hungry, wild eyes. She didn't know! She didn't know that the baby wasn't her husband's! Incredibly, Phillipe seemed not to have told her about his sterility!

"He does want the child?" Nick asked suddenly.

"Why, of course!" she laughed coolly. "He's overwhelmed that he's to have an heir."

"Then why the hell isn't he here, taking care of you while you carry it?" he asked coldly.

She shifted restlessly. "He races."

"He was off on a cruise just recently, I was told," he added narrowly, neglecting to mention that he'd pigeonholed a member of the local gentry and all but beat that information out of him. "And he spends a good deal of time in casinos as well, in all parts of the globe."

Her dark eyes glared at him from a pale face. "My marital problems are no concern of yours!"

"So you admit that there are problems?" he suggested.

She put down her fork. "I won't sit here and let you upset me..."

"Sit down," he said gently, touching her arm as she started to rise. "I'm sorry. I didn't mean to do that. Jolana, don't go."

Her lower lip trembled as she stared at her plate. Her emotions were haywire, and she didn't know what she was doing here with Nick anyway. She hadn't meant to see him again, she hadn't wanted to. Phillipe would be furious if he knew...!

"Drink some coffee," he said softly, his voice deep and quiet. "We'll talk about other things."

She managed to get some of it down, but her eyes were full of tears.

"He leaves you alone too much," he said. "You need taking care of. You're very pale."

"I'm working on commissions," she let slip.

"Working?" he exploded.

"I paint, remember?" she demanded. "I haven't stopped living just because I'm pregnant!"

He started to speak and then caught himself. He was almost certain that she wasn't painting from choice. He knew the extent of Phillipe's financial problems. No doubt the man had coaxed Jolana into painting for his posh friends...

"You shouldn't take chances," he said finally, pouring a glass of wine. He sipped it. "You mustn't overdo."

She glared at him. It hurt to hear him sounding concerned about her. Now, of all times, when he'd killed the possibility of any kind of future between them. Nick, with his obsession for Margery that had driven Jolana out of the country and into a hopeless marriage and pregnancy. She almost hated him for that. Why had he followed her? Why had he come back into her life to torture her?

"Phillipe can take care of me," she grumbled.

"He could. Why isn't he?" he growled back. "God, I wish that baby was mine," he ground out huskily, without meaning to.

Her heart leaped, but she controlled her features. "I'm glad it's not," she said with momentary venom. "I think I'd throw myself into the Mediterranean if I thought there was the slightest chance of it being yours!"

He went pale and his gaze fell to his glass. She'd hurt him, then. Good, she thought maliciously. Good, let him hurt, let him know how it felt.

"I'm sorry you feel that way," he said under his breath. He took a large sip of wine and felt it melt some of the lump in his throat. He hadn't realized how violent her emotions were, how much she hated him. He'd thought that, because she came into town for dinner, she'd still felt something for him. But obviously it had been only a coincidence. She hated him. He was sure of it now. And he didn't dare tell her about the child, for fear that she might do something desperate. He felt like crying out with pain. He loved her. She was carrying his child, and he wanted it, he wanted her. And she was married to a man who alternately ignored her and used her to make money, and there wasn't a damned thing he could do about it. Because she hated him even more than her present circumstances. His fingers tightened on the delicate wineglass stem and threatened to snap it.

She swallowed her surge of anger and drank some more coffee. "I have to go."

He looked up at her, his face drawn, his eyes hungry. "Will I see you again?"

She felt as if her legs wouldn't hold her. "Don't," she pleaded huskily. "Don't. What happened… It's over. I have a husband and a baby on the way. I can't bear this, Nick."

He caught her hand and pressed its moist palm to his mouth with such urgent fervor that she felt her body ache with response. "Jolana," he whispered achingly. "Oh, God, I love you!"

She drew in a shaking breath and got to her feet, pulling her hand away. "Go home, Nick," she pleaded. "It's too late now. I… I love my husband."

"Not like you loved me," he whispered hoarsely, his eyes blazing with remembered passion. "Not ever like you loved me!"

"I'm glad," she burst out. "He can't ever hurt me like you did!"

He caught at a breath, and his face grew tormented. "Forgive me."

"Will that ease your conscience and make you go away?" she asked. "Then I forgive you. Now, please, go away. Leave me to make some kind of future for myself."

His dark eyes searched hers as he stood respectfully, noticing her regal poise, her beauty as she carried his child. "What kind of future can you have, away from me?" he whispered. "What kind of future can I have without you?"

"You seemed to think at the time that you'd have quite a good one," she reminded him as the hurt broke through. "I'm sorry Margery didn't want you, Nick. But it's much too late to convince me that this isn't just sour grapes. You just want to show Margery you can do without her. I'm sorry. I can't help you. Go home and find someone else."

His eyes darkened as they ran up and down her body. "There'll never be anyone else."

She laughed bitterly. "Noble thought. But I've grown up since I've been in France. There'll always be someone else. Men aren't capable of fidelity. God, how well I know that! Goodbye, Nick."

She turned and walked away, and it dawned on him what she meant. In addition to all his other shortcomings, her titled husband was already straying. Gambling, racing, other women. What kind of life had his stupidity driven her into? He sat back down and poured himself another glass of wine. He didn't know how he was going to go on living. There had been the hope, always the hope, that he could find her and win her back. But today he had learned that all the doors were closed, that he was going to have to go through life without his woman, his child. And that it was his fault. How, he wondered, was he going to live with it?

Jolana walked into the house in miserable silence while Maurice put away the car and opened the door just in time to see Phillipe coming down the stairs.

"Did you win?" she asked.

"Yes. First place." He stared at her darkly. "You were in town. Where? And with whom?"

Here we go again, she thought miserably. She put down her purse. "I was having dinner at the Carlton," she confessed.

"With whom?" he persisted coldly.

She lifted her chin. "With an American I once knew," she said. She knew better than to tell him who Nick really was. "A man in whose gallery I exhibited my paintings."

He glared at her. "Were you lovers?" he challenged.

Gathering her courage, she went close to him. "It was a chance meeting," she said honestly. "Nothing I planned. He was there, and I was alone. He wanted to discuss an exhibit with me."

His eyebrows rose. "An exhibit?" He brightened. "That might be profitable."

"Don't you ever think of anything but money?" she asked. "And you might ask how I feel, damn you! I am carrying your child!"

"Such venom," he laughed, pulling her close. "Stop, you'll hurt the child," he cautioned as she struggled.

She gave up, standing rigidly in his embrace. "Why don't you divorce me?" she asked. "It would give you more time to race and gamble and…"

He cocked his head. "And?" he prodded.

She dropped her eyes. "Nothing."

He kissed her forehead. "Tell me about this exhibit."

She was caught up in her own lie. She made up a wild tale about sending paintings back to New York to be exhibited, about a second one-woman show. Phillipe hung on her every word, interested, absorbed.

"When?" he asked then. "Will you be able to work in Paris?"

She shifted in his embrace. "I suppose so."

"Then, I will call and tell him that you accept. He is staying at the Carlton? What is his name?"

"Phillipe…!"

"What is his name, *petite*?" he asked, already with the phone in his hand. "Jolana, we cannot afford to turn down such an exhibit, *ma chère*," he coaxed, smiling at her. "Come now, it will occupy you when I go to Le Mans. Tell me."

She sat down, waiting for the blow to fall. "His name is Domenico Scarpelli."

"Scarpelli," he said and began dialing the phone.

Jolana paled as Phillipe asked for Nick. Seconds later, he brightened. "Mr. Scarpelli, my name is Phillipe Comte de Vinchy-Cardin! Listen, my wife, Jolana, has told me about this gallery of yours in New York and the exhibit that you want her to do. Mr. Scarpelli, are you there? *Oui*, I think it is a grand idea. Grand! Now, we are leaving for Paris in the morning. You are, too? What a marvelous coincidence. *Oui*, I go to Le Mans in two weeks. Now, suppose we get together say, Saturday, and discuss it? My sister, alas, has sailed to Greece, but Jolana and I can entertain you. You will? Marvelous. Here is the number."

He was giving directions, and Jolana was trying not to faint. What was she to do now? What a hell of a time for Maureen to go on a tour with Pierre and leave her alone like this! Keeping the truth from Phillipe was going to take all her nerve, and she didn't feel up to it at all. *What have I done?* she moaned inwardly.

Thank God Nick had kept his head and gone along with her wild fabrication. But she didn't know how she was going to be able to put on an act in front of Phillipe, who was quite perceptive. Perhaps Nick and her husband would meet and leave her out of it. She managed not to think how ridiculous that sounded and busied herself getting things packed for the trip back to Paris.

The rainy season in the sprawling city on the Seine was over, and everything was in glorious bloom. Jolana was delighted that she could bring cut flowers from the apartment's garden inside and arrange them in the luxury of the living room. Company flooded in the moment they opened the apartment again, and they seemed not to have any time alone. Not that it mattered, she thought with a sigh. They had separate bedrooms now. Phillipe had said that he didn't want to disturb her rest, but she'd reached the point in her pregnancy where she hated being alone. She was a little frightened, a little uncertain, and it would have been nice to have someone beside her in the darkness.

She spent the week dreading Nick's visit and trying not to show it. Phillipe talked of little else.

"It comes at such a good time, *chérie*," he said as she was busying herself with the cook, arranging that night's dinner for the two of them and Nick. "This gallery showing, I mean. The commissions are nice, but you will make much money from a gallery."

She didn't look up from her notes for the cook. "Yes," she agreed quietly.

He stared at her curiously. "You do not mind?"

She stood erect, putting a hand to her aching back, and stared at him. "Have you any idea how long it takes to put together a showing?" she asked quietly.

His eyebrows arched. "Well, no."

"I have paintings in New York, which weren't sold. I need at least ten more. At a couple of weeks per canvas..."

"So long?" he asked.

She glared at him. "I won't do sloppy work, no matter how hard up we are for cash."

He shrugged. "*Chérie*, I was not asking you to compromise your principles," he said placatingly and took her gently by the shoulders. He smiled down at her.

"It was just a chance remark. Besides, did you not say yourself that you wanted to do this show?"

"Yes," she lied. "It's just that…"

"The painting does not tire you, surely. You love it!"

I'm pregnant, she wanted to scream at him. *I have your baby inside my body and it's all I can do to stay on my feet sometimes.* But she simply turned away and started toward the staircase to dress. "Yes," she said. "I love it." And she let it go at that. She had much worse problems than her husband's lack of consideration. Nick was coming here tonight. And she had to watch not only her tongue, but her eyes. She didn't dare let either Nick or Phillipe see how much she was affected by Nick.

She wore a cream silk dress in a shapeless style, with slit sleeves and a V-neckline. It gave her the look of a girl from the Roaring Twenties, and emphasized the becoming flush of her features and the darkness of her eyes in their frame of short, silvery-blond hair. She hadn't let it grow long again, careful to keep it trimmed so that it didn't remind her of the way it had curved around her shoulders when she and Nick were together.

Nick had already arrived when Jolana came back downstairs. She hadn't expected him so soon, and she almost tripped at the bottom of the staircase. But she recovered, grabbing the rail, and was startled to find Nick controlling an instinctive movement toward her. Phillipe merely raised his glass and grinned.

"Careful, *chérie,*" he teased, "you are not so light on your feet these days. You know each other already, I presume?"

Nick schooled his features carefully, but Jolana knew him well enough to catch the glitter of fierce anger in his eyes as he spoke to Phillipe. That fascinated her, that he could be angry on her account. But it didn't bear too much consideration. She had a husband. She was pregnant. She couldn't afford the luxury of letting Nick get to her again.

She moved ahead of them into the living room and sat down. The men were discussing some kind of business, and she waited patiently until they finished.

"Now," Phillipe said after a minute, seating himself beside Jolana while Nick took the armchair opposite, "tell me about this proposition."

"The gallery showing," Jolana prodded, horrified as Nick hesitated.

He searched her eyes quietly for a moment and lifted his brandy snifter to his chiseled mouth. "In addition to the magazine I own," he began, "I own a gallery in New York. At one time I shared it with a cousin, but he and I had a rather bad falling-out." He didn't look at Jolana, but she knew exactly why. It had been over her, she was sure. "The gallery has a wealthy clientele, and some months ago we exhibited some of Jolana's work. It sold well. I'd like to do it again."

Probably he'd like to kill her for that wild idea that had forced him to lie, she thought. But he couldn't. They were both caught in the web of her deception now.

"Jolana would be delighted," Phillipe said for her, lifting his glass in a toast.

"It's a tiring thing, getting ready for an exhibit," Nick remarked, glancing at her. "Are you up to it, *comtesse*?"

She sensed the concern behind the words and hated him because he wasn't Phillipe, who never cared how much she tired herself. She stared into her lap. "I can manage, thank you."

"It wouldn't have to be a large one," Nick continued. "No more than twelve or fifteen paintings. I have in mind featuring another artist in the same exhibit."

Phillipe pursed his lips, and Jolana could see the dollar signs in his eyes. "It will cut down the profit," he murmured.

Nick's eyes flashed, but he smiled coolly. "Better to cut the profit than risk your heir, *comte*," he murmured quietly.

Phillipe had the grace to look ashamed. He touched Jolana's hand where it rested on her lap, and Nick's features hardened so much that she was afraid Phillipe would notice.

"Shall we go in?" she asked suddenly, rising. "I find that I'm quite hungry."

"But of course, *ma chère*," Phillipe said with perfect manners, helping her up. He escorted her, ahead of Nick, into the dining room, where the maid began serving only minutes later.

"Excellent," Nick said as he tasted the delicate soufflé and tender beef and vegetable courses. "Your cook is a marvel."

"We have had her for many years," Phillipe remarked. "She is one of the best." His eyes clouded. "With luck, we may keep her a bit longer." He sighed, and Jolana sensed that something was worrying him very much.

"When can you begin on the canvases, *comtesse*?" Nick asked Jolana with studied carelessness.

"Tomorrow," she said, glancing at Phillipe. "It will give me something to do while Phillipe prepares for the twenty-four-hour race at Le Mans."

"*Oui.*" Phillipe grinned. "She will need occupation, because I go to Le Mans tomorrow."

"So soon?" she burst out, and hated that impulsive query.

Phillipe shifted in his seat. "You know that I must prepare," he said. "Pierre will be there, and we must see to the car. There is much to do. Besides, Maureen will be returning shortly. You will not be alone."

Nick glanced at Phillipe and smiled. "I plan to be in Paris for another few days. It would be my pleasure to keep an eye on the *comtesse* for you while I'm here."

Phillipe brightened. "So kind," he said. "Thank you, monsieur. I do not like to leave her at such a time, but you understand how it is."

Nick's eyes narrowed as he studied the younger man, and Jolana almost believed that he could see right through him. "I understand very well, in fact," he said, and the words were almost a threat.

Phillipe, however, was blissfully unaware of the undercurrents in the conversation. He led the discussion around to racing, and held forth for over an hour. Nick left soon thereafter, promising to discuss further arrangements with Jolana herself.

"A very profitable evening, did you not think so?" Phillipe asked later, smiling secretively. "Perhaps it may all work out after all. You do not mind that I go now to Le Mans?" he added with a frown.

"No," she said. "I don't mind."

He sighed, coming close to kiss her forehead gently. "Jolana, I wish that I could be what you want me to be," he said with a sudden burst of honesty. "I am a rake, and you know that better than you appear to. But if it is any consolation, I am very fond of you, and very proud that you are my wife."

She smiled weakly. "It helps."

He kissed her lips gently. "After the Grand Prix," he promised. "This one last race, and then we will go away together for a few days. We will start over. We will build a good marriage."

She agreed, reaching up to kiss his cheek before she went upstairs alone. But she knew all too well that it wouldn't happen. Phillipe would never change. She would live with him and have his child, and learn to involve herself in other things than marriage. Because Phillipe had nothing to give her. Only his name and his possessions and his title. And she'd have traded them all to be loved.

He left early the next morning, suitcase in hand, pausing to kiss her warmly at the door before he bounced down the steps to his car.

"Will you come and watch me race, this once?" he called up to the apartment.

"Yes," she agreed, smiling. "I'll come."

"For you, I will win. *Adieu, ma petite!*" He laughed and waved and roared away down the street. And she watched him go with a peculiar sense of emptiness. Why had he said *adieu*, and not *au revoir*? A little thing, an insignificant thing, but it worried her.

Nick's visit later that afternoon worried her more. The staff vanished as he walked in the door, and Jolana felt ill at ease with him and a little afraid. He was as big as a house, and his light slacks and the open-necked white silk shirt emphasized both his size and his muscular build. He looked broader than ever, darker, more threatening. She felt tiny beside him, in her green maternity slacks and patterned green smock.

"Suppose you tell me what the hell is going on?" he asked the minute they were in the living room.

"Shush!" she said frantically, and rushed to close the door. She leaned back against it, feeling weak. "The servants don't eavesdrop, but your voice carries, Nick."

"Answer me, please," he continued, glaring at her.

She stared down at her clasped hands and sighed. "Nick, he was home when I got there, and he demanded to know where I'd been, and with whom. He knows too many people, you see. I couldn't have gotten away with lying about it. So I made up the story about a show. It was all I could think of."

He stood in front of her, breathing heavily, staring unblinkingly until she thought her heart would burst.

"He didn't hurt you?" he asked.

It was an unexpected question. She looked up. "No. He wouldn't hurt me, not physically."

"But you were afraid of him."

"I have good reason to be afraid of men," she said wearily, remembering her childhood.

He seemed to remember that, too, because he moved closer and cupped her face in his big, warm hands. She felt the strength in them, smelled the crisp scent of expensive cologne that clung to his deeply tanned skin.

"Nick," she protested automatically. Her hands went to his, but she couldn't remove them. After a minute, she stopped trying.

"How does it feel, being pregnant?" he asked, searching her eyes from an unnerving distance.

It was so unexpected a question that it froze her mind for an instant. "It's... It's not unpleasant."

His thumbs edged toward her lips and traced down to her chin. "Does he move?" he asked.

"Yes, a little," she said, hypnotized by his touch,

by his steady, hungry gaze. "Tiny flutters, like a captive bird."

His breath came heavily, hard. "Let me touch him," he breathed, letting one hand drop slowly, tentatively, to the rounded mound of her belly. His eyes held the question, and his touch was almost reverent as his hand flattened over the contours, warm and oddly sensual.

She trembled a little. Phillipe had never liked touching her since the pregnancy became obvious. He turned his head when she undressed, despite his very early avowal that he found her pregnancy erotic. Once she started showing, his interest vanished altogether. It was as if he found the sight of her distasteful. But Nick... Nick seemed fascinated by her. His dark eyes were watching the soft movement of his hand over the silky fabric of her top, so intent that he seemed oblivious to the world around them.

She swallowed, taking his hand hesitantly and pressing it hard against the side of her stomach where she was beginning to feel the tiny flutters. "Here," she whispered.

"So hard... It won't hurt him?" he asked, lifting his eyes. And at the same time, the baby moved, and he jerked as if he'd been hit. His eyes widened, brightened, his breath caught. "My God," he whispered huskily. His eyes fell to his hand and his huge chest rose raggedly. "My God, I felt him!"

She felt tears sting her eyes. Why couldn't Phillipe be like this? Why did it have to be Nick who made her feel so proud of the baby? It wasn't fair!

"Does it hurt you, when he does that?" he asked, his face radiant, his eyes fascinated as they lifted to hers.

She shook her head, smiling helplessly at the wonder in his expression. "Not at all. It's quite thrilling. I'm not sure he's supposed to move so soon, but the doctor isn't really sure about how far along I am," she laughed nervously.

Nick knew why, and his face darkened, hardened. He looked down at her and wanted her so much, so suddenly, that his body went rigid with the force of it. His woman. His child. Damn Phillipe!

"Nick?" she said softly.

Afraid that she might come close enough to feel what was happening to him, he put her away from him and moved across the room to the window, sticking his unsteady hands into his pockets. "Do you want to do the exhibit?" he asked huskily.

"Phillipe wants me to."

"Damn Phillipe," he said quietly, turning. "Do you want to?"

She wrapped her arms around her swollen breasts. "We need the money. I have to."

He stood still for a long moment. "All right. But you'll work at an easy pace. I won't be responsible for jeopardizing that tiny life inside you."

The way he said it made her go warm all over. She flushed, and he smiled softly at her.

"I find you wildly exciting, like that," he said after a minute. "Are you offended?"

She drew in a steadying breath. "No, I don't think so." Her eyes lifted to his and she felt the staggering impact of his piercing gaze all the way to her toes.

The intensity of the look they shared had an equally disturbing effect on Nick, who felt as if he'd never be able to stand up straight again. He wanted to groan aloud.

"How does he keep his hands off you?" he ground out. "Oh, God, Jolana…!"

She felt young again. Girlish. Uncertain. She managed a wobbly smile. "Thank you," she whispered.

"Doesn't he want you, *amore*?" he asked quietly. "Is that it?"

She closed her eyes. "You don't have the right to ask me such intimate things," she said miserably. "Nick, please go."

"You were mine before you were his," he said, moving closer, closer, until he filled the room, the world. "Look at me."

Her eyes lifted, tear-filled, to find the passion raging in his, making them black and glittery.

His hands touched her stomach, so gently, so tenderly. "If you were mine," he whispered, "and this was my child, you'd never get five feet away from me. You'd sleep in my arms, and I'd comfort you if you were afraid, I'd walk with you and dream with you."

Tears streamed down her face and she pushed at his hands, "I'm married," she whimpered. "I'm married."

"To an idiot," he said harshly. "To a man who doesn't care if you fall down a flight of stairs! Oh, God, leave him. Come back to New York with me! I'll take care of you!"

She forced her legs to take her away from him. She opened the living-room door, her eyes red and swollen, her heart breaking in half. "Please go."

He fought to catch his breath. "No. Please. Please. We'll just talk. Just that. Don't send me away,"

Her eyes closed. "It won't make things easier."

"Close the door and sit down," he said quietly. "We'll talk."

"I can't bear it," she said on a sob, staring at him with pain and torment in her dark eyes. "Please, please go!"

"You mustn't get upset," he said as he realized just how much he was tormenting her. "Jolana, it's all right, I'll go. Please don't cry, darling."

That made it worse. She leaned against the wall, needing the coolness of it against her hot cheek.

He paused beside her and brushed away the trace of tears from her soft face. "I won't be far away," he said softly. "If you need me, I'll be at the Savoy."

She swallowed. "I'm married," she repeated.

His features contorted. "Yes, I know."

Her eyes searched his, dark and accusing. "I don't want you. Go away."

"I brought this on both of us," he said, and he understood her anger, her frustration. "I can't take it back, but maybe we can..."

"Divorce is out of the question. Babies need two parents. I have to make it work, Nick, for the baby's sake. It's too late for us."

"I love you," he said under his breath.

She shook her head. "You're just on the rebound from Margery, Nick, and you don't know it. That's all it is, and maybe there's a little guilt mixed in." She pushed the door open wider, ignoring his surprise. "I'll do you a favor and forget everything you said. Now you'd better go, really. It wouldn't do to start people talking. If you still want me to do the exhibit..."

He glowered at her. "Of course I still want you to do the exhibit."

"Then I'll start at once. Tony can tell you where my paintings are stored."

He sighed. "Tony and I aren't speaking these days,

Jolana," he said. "Perhaps you'd better give me the name of the storage company."

She did, scribbling it on the back of a scrap of paper. "Tony will get over it," she said, "I'm sorry about the disagreement. It was over me, wasn't it?"

He stared at the scrap of paper. "In a way, I suppose so." He looked up, and his eyes were dark and quiet. "Have lunch with me tomorrow."

She hesitated. Part of her wanted to, but the sensible part knew that it was only prolonging the agony to see him, to be with him. "I'd better not. I think Maureen's coming home today."

"Then I'll take you both to lunch," he suggested, smiling.

"Nick…"

"Don't fight me. You can't win, even now."

She glared at him. "I'm a married woman. I'm a pregnant married woman!"

"You're a knockout," he observed, smiling at her flushed, lovely face. "Too bad it isn't a couple of thousand years ago. I'd have thrown your husband to the lions and taken you as my Roman ancestors probably would have done."

"Yes," she murmured absently, "I always thought you had the look of a centurion."

"While you have the look of a particularly beautiful patrician," he said softly. "I was a fool, Jolana. I'll have years and years to regret it all."

"You'll find someone else," she said quietly. "Isn't there a saying about the grass always being greener on the other side of the fence?"

His eyes narrowed. "In other words, I only want you because you got away?" He shook his head. "No. And it's not on the rebound, either. I want you because I love you, Jolana. I'll never stop. Not if you live with Phillipe for the next hundred years. It will be your name I'll whisper on my deathbed."

She turned away, hating the surge of pleasure she felt at the words. "Please, Nick, I can't take any more."

"Join the club." He touched her face lightly. "Phillipe asked me to look after you. As long as I'm in Paris, I'm going to. Will you drive to Le Mans for the race?"

"Phillipe wants me to. I'll probably go with Maureen…"

"You'll both go with me," he said. "I'll arrange it with you later. Meanwhile, plan on lunch tomorrow. Maureen, too, if she comes back in time. So long."

With one long, last look, he walked out the door. When he heard it close behind him, he sighed. What was he going to do? She was adamant about staying with Phillipe. And if he put too much pressure on her, he could endanger the child. His child. Remembering that tiny flutter under his hand made him flush with pleasure. If only he had the right to take care of her, to love her. Oh, God, what a fool he'd been. And it didn't look as if there was a chance in hell of righting things. Well, he'd manage one day at a time. He'd be with her as much as he could. He walked out onto the street and wasn't at all surprised to find it raining.

Jolana was hard at work on a painting of a Parisian street scene when Maureen breezed in the next morning, looking tanned and fit and full of energy.

"Chérie," she laughed, flopping down on the couch with an exaggerated sigh. "I am exhausted with fun! We had such a marvelous time on the cruise. I am sorry you could not come with us."

"I wouldn't have been much help, hanging over the side." Jolana grinned. "Phillipe went to Le Mans day before yesterday to meet Pierre."

Maureen's face gave away annoyance before she erased it. "Did he?"

Jolana studied her closely. "Pierre came in with you today, didn't he?" she asked softly.

The shorter woman sighed heavily. "You are too astute, my friend. Much too astute."

"I've just learned how Phillipe is," she corrected. Her hands carefully structured the street on canvas with gray oils. "You needn't worry. I'm getting used to his women. At least, I tell myself that." She put down the brush and buried her face in her hands. "Oh, God, I'm pregnant, doesn't he care?"

Maureen rushed to comfort her, holding her while she cried and cursing her brother for all she was worth.

When Jolana finally regained her lost composure, she dried her eyes and put away her paints. "My heart just isn't in this today."

"You are painting again," Maureen said, as if she had suddenly noticed what Jolana had been doing.

"Yes. For an exhibit in New York that Phillipe and Domenico Scarpelli decided I should do."

"Domenico Scarpelli?" Maureen said. "Who is he?"

"He publishes a magazine in New York, and owns an art gallery there," Jolana said simply.

She sat down, divesting herself of her paint-splattered smock to leave her swelling contours in their maternity outfit of white and blue. "I had an exhibit in Monsieur Scarpelli's gallery in New York, just before I came over here. He learned from his cousin where I was and flew over to offer me another showing." She smiled carelessly. "Apparently, I made him a good deal of money."

"*Oui*, but you said he publishes a magazine, *n'est-ce pas*?" Maureen asked with a frown. "He also has a gallery."

"He's something of an entrepreneur, I gather," Jolana told her. She stretched. "Nevertheless, it comes at a lovely time. Phillipe says we'll make gobs of money from it."

"And my brother never gets enough money," Maureen said bitterly.

"Oh, it's almost noon! Mr. Scarpelli is taking us out to lunch!"

Maureen's eyes grew large as saucers. "But, how did he know that I would be here?"

"I told him. He's in Paris until the Grand Prix in Le Mans. And," she added with a pretended grimace, "I think he wants to make sure that I produce quickly."

"Should I change?" Maureen asked, conscious of her jeans and green T-shirt.

"You look lovely," Jolana said, "I'm not dressing up."

"*Oui*, but you are married. I am not! And Pierre... oh, *là*! There Monsieur Scarpelli is!" She jumped up, smoothing her T-shirt, to grin over her shoulder at Jolana. "I will let him in."

Jolana's heart threatened to knock her down with its accelerated beat. She hated Nick for doing this to her, for refusing to see reason. She didn't want to be near him. It was pure torture.

There were muffled voices and laughter, and a minute later Nick walked in, handsome in a gray vested suit that emphasized his dark complexion and clung to him like a second skin. He was elegant enough for a magazine ad, sexy enough to make women look over their shoulders. She felt weak at the knees just from looking at him, without remembering how it felt to be made love to by him. His dark eyes skimmed over her possessively and he smiled.

"Comtesse," he said, nodding. "I trust the work is going well?"

"Yes, it is going well," Jolana said. She picked up her purse. "I really should stay here…"

"Nonsense," he said. He took her arm and Maureen's. "I refuse to be deprived of the company of two such lovely ladies. Besides, I've had a special meal prepared."

He took them to a small Italian restaurant, where he apparently was well-known. Someone named Benito rushed out, speaking hurriedly in Italian, and returned with a platter of salad that took Jolana's appetite by surprise.

"It's delicious," Nick told her, smiling at her fascination with it. "Black olives and spinach, sliced eggs and onions, and God knows what else, with a salad dressing that Benito locks in a safe."

"How crisp and cool it looks," Jolana sighed. She let the waiter serve her and smiled as she tasted it. "Marvelous!"

"I thought it might appeal to you. It's nutritious, too."

Maureen laughed delightedly. "You seem almost to know that my sister-in-law's appetite has been poor. It is good to see her eating."

"Yes, it is," Nick said, and for an instant his expression was tender.

"Are you married, monsieur?" Maureen asked with disarming frankness.

"No. Not yet," he said as he dug into his food. "And you?" He smiled.

"No, I have been engaged several times, but each time I broke it off. Perhaps I have just never met the right man," she finished, looking teasingly into Nick's eyes.

Jolana felt a twinge of jealousy. She attacked her salad with renewed vigor, feeling a kind of rage that she hadn't experienced since she learned the truth about Margery. It spoiled the day for her. She had no right to be jealous, of course. But she was, all the same.

Nick took them back to the apartment just an hour later, pleading business as an excuse. He didn't linger, except to arrange a time for the trip to Le Mans the next day for the start of the race. When he left, Maureen raved for the rest of the evening about how exciting a man he was. And Jolana did her best to stay busy and not to notice.

She expected Phillipe to call that night, but he didn't. It was just one more disappointment in a string of them. She didn't sleep well, either. She felt a nagging disquiet, a sense of desolation. Perhaps it was the movement of her child that produced it, she told herself. Finally, she arose at five o'clock in the morning and made breakfast, since she couldn't sleep.

"Chérie," Maureen exclaimed sleepily, with her robe loose around her small, slender body and her dark hair disheveled as she paused in the doorway. "Up so early? I could not believe my ears when I heard the rattle of pots and pans. And where is Cook?"

"Cook doesn't come for another hour," Jolana reminded her. "I was hungry. Want some bacon and eggs?"

"Non!" Maureen exclaimed, making a face. "Just toast and jelly for me." She sat down and watched Jolana pour coffee into a cup for her. "Could you not sleep?"

"Not a wink," the taller girl confessed. She put the coffee pot down with a sigh. "Maureen, I'm worried about the race."

"None of that," Maureen said firmly. "Phillipe is a survivor. He has been in so many races that he is a veteran. This is just one more. You must say that to yourself. You cannot afford the luxury of worry now, *chérie.*"

"Yes, I know. But…"

"Eat your breakfast," Maureen said. She smiled. "We will go to Le Mans with Monsieur Scarpelli and have a lovely time. You can occupy your mind by helping me think of ways to seduce him."

"Maureen!" she gasped.

"Well, as an alternative, you may help me think of ways to let myself be seduced. Is that better?"

"You're impossible," Jolana told her, turning to make toast. "What shall we wear?"

"Something comfortable. It will be a long race, and the seats are hard."

"We aren't going to sit there the whole twenty-four hours?" Jolana asked hopefully.

"No. We will stay with friends overnight," Maureen assured her. "It will be very exciting. You will see. And to watch it with Domenico Scarpelli… *Dieu!*"

It was only a crush, only infatuation, Jolana assured herself. But she felt sick all over. What if Maureen caught his eye, what if they developed a relationship? Could she bear it? And there was Phillipe. Oh, God, what a mess! She finished making Maureen's toast and rushed upstairs to dress, gnawing at her lip.

CHAPTER TWELVE

LE MANS WAS located southwest of Paris, and it seemed to take forever to get there. Jolana's stomach was queasy, forcing Nick to make frequent stops so that she could overcome the nausea. Maureen was as solicitous as Nick himself, and Jolana couldn't help remembering the arduous journey by car from Nice, when Phillipe had refused to stop at all despite her pleas. What a difference there was this time.

She wished that her feeling of apprehension would go away. As it was, she hardly noticed the beautiful countryside they passed on their way to the racetrack. All too soon, they were seated on the benches waiting for the signal that would start the race.

Because of Jolana's illness, they hadn't arrived in time to visit Phillipe before the start. Jolana felt bad about that. She'd wanted at least to wish him luck.

"He'll be all right," Nick said quietly, watching her nervously fiddling with the purse in her lap. "Do you still feel ill?"

She shook her head. "I feel much better, now, thank you." She bit her lower lip as the engines began revving up and the announcer's voice blared out over the stands where people milled in a thick, colorful mass. Her eyes searched for Phillipe's car.

"Which is it?" she asked, searching.

"Number nine, *chérie*," Maureen told her, shielding her eyes from the bright, hot sunlight with her hand. *"Là!"*

Jolana followed her pointing finger, although the cars all looked alike to her inexperienced eye. Funny-looking cars, she mused, with their bumpers almost on the ground, their low-slung appearance making them seem somehow like bugs to her.

"Look, he sees us, he is waving!" Maureen laughed. She stood, waving frantically, and so did Jolana. Grinning under his helmet, Phillipe waved a long arm and his lips moved as if he said something.

Jolana felt strange as she watched him. Her heart began to beat heavily. "Phillipe," she called. "Phillipe, don't!"

"Jolana, *chérie*, what is wrong?" Maureen said worriedly.

Nick held her arm in a firm grip, helping her back down into her seat. "It's so damned hot," he murmured with concern. "Jolana, do you want something cold to drink?"

She swallowed. "Yes, please."

Maureen fanned her with her program, frowning. "You should have worn the sundress, *chérie*, not that suit."

"But it's very cool, really," Jolana replied, nodding toward her two-piece lilac suit.

"Not cool enough, I think."

The engines sounded louder now, and all of a sudden, the race had begun. Maureen paused long enough to watch as the cars sped around the course on the first lap, and Jolana's hands gripped the bench. She should never have agreed to come. Despite all their disagreements, she cared for Phillipe. She couldn't bear it if something happened. It was so hot! Why had she come? *Phillipe, don't do it,* she kept thinking. *Phillipe, please, stop now.*

But he didn't stop. Nick had just returned with something for her to drink as the cars were on their eighth lap. Suddenly, with incredible swiftness, a car spun out. As Jolana and Maureen watched, horrified, it twisted around right into the path of number nine—Phillipe.

Jolana stopped breathing. It happened in slow motion, as inevitably as rain. The car that had gone out of control skidded to a stop just as Phillipe, in the lead, came around the turn. He tried to avoid it, but another car was suddenly beside him. There was a sickening screech of tires, followed by a shuddering crash and the sound of breaking glass. Flames exploded and a woman's voice screamed and screamed, and Jolana realized that it was her own.

Maureen was already running toward the racetrack, only to be stopped by the guards. Jolana tried to go, too, but Nick turned her into his arms and held her fast.

"No," she wailed, "I have to... I have to go to him!"

"Be still," he whispered, holding her closer, his head bent over hers. "Be still, darling, be still. There's nothing you can do. God help him, there's nothing anyone can do," he said, as he saw the tragedy unfolding on the racetrack. The car had become an inferno, and they couldn't get close enough to get Phillipe out. By the time they got the flames under control and the door open, Nick knew there wasn't the slightest hope. Nearby Maureen was weeping hysterically, and Nick called to her. She ran back to him, all tears and anguish, and he folded her close beside Jolana.

"He is dead, Jolana," Maureen whispered pitifully. "He is dead, I saw…!"

Jolana couldn't speak. She tried, but her voice wouldn't come. And as she tried to cling to Nick's great strength, her own gave out. With a tiny cry, she slumped into blackness.

The next few hours were a nightmare of motion and grief. Phillipe had died instantly, they told her. That was at least some consolation. But she kept seeing his face, tanned and handsome, grinning as he waved at her. And she wept until she made herself ill.

Maureen had Pierre now to comfort her, and Nick had said that he would stay at the apartment with Jolana while they made the final arrangements. Jolana had hardly said a word since her collapse. It had been necessary to take her to the doctor, to be sedated. Her obstetrician had examined her and warned her to stay quiet, and he'd given her something to make sure that she did. She was so numb that she hardly heard a word he said. But Nick did. And he never left her, not for an instant.

When she woke, that night, she was lying on her bed, still wearing the suit she'd put on that morning. There was a single lamp burning in the room. And Nick was sitting by the bed, holding her hand.

She turned her head toward him. Immediately, she remembered, and tears filled her eyes.

"No," he whispered. He moved to sit on the bed beside her and draw her up into his arms. He was so tender, so gentle. "No, don't be afraid. I'm here. I'll take care of you."

She buried her face against his shirtfront, feeling his warmth and strength while she cried. "I failed him," she whispered miserably. "I should have gone with him, I should have made sure we got there in time to say good luck to him, I should have…"

He put a finger across her lips. "Things happen as they're meant to happen," he said quietly. "You couldn't have changed it. The risk is something race drivers learn to accept. He knew it could happen. He was ready. You have to accept that he knew what he was doing. All the 'should haves' in the world won't change anything now. You have to go on living, for the baby's sake."

She tried to breathe normally, but every breath hurt. She took the handkerchief that he passed to her and dabbed at her swollen eyes. "He wasn't happy with me," she whispered. "Perhaps if he'd married someone else… or not married at all…he'd still be alive."

"You don't know that. He cared for you."

"I cared for him, too," she sobbed. "Not the way I wanted to, but I did care. And he's… He's dead, Nick!"

He closed her up tightly in his arms and rocked her slowly. "The doctor gave me some tablets for you. I think you should take one."

"No. I don't want to."

"You have to think of the baby, darling," he said at her ear. "You can't upset yourself this way."

At that she gave in and obediently took the pill Nick offered her. She prayed for it to work quickly and take away all the pain she was feeling.

"Poor Maureen," she whimpered. "I should have comforted her…"

"She has Pierre, and she's worried about you, too. Jolana, I know this sounds trite. But grief does pass. It's only a matter of taking it one day at a time, and knowing that each day will ease the pain a little more." He kissed her eyes, kissed the tears away.

"That's what… Tony said," she murmured absently as she wiped away fresh tears.

He stiffened. "Tony?"

"Yes, when I took the pills," she sighed wearily. "He said I had to live one day at a time and not look back. It must run in your family, Nick."

He touched her hair gently. "Yes, it must," he said with faint bitterness. His chest rose and fell heavily. "Was he afraid you might try again?" he asked under his breath.

She shifted restlessly, "I'm so tired," she said.

"Could you sleep?" he asked.

She drew back, her eyes wide and dark and full of pain. "Would you stay with me? Just until I fall asleep?"

He brushed the damp hair from her face. "I'll stay with you all night."

"You can't," she began. "Maureen…"

"Pierre and I are both staying tonight," he informed her. "I won't leave you alone. I think Maureen would be glad to know I'm here."

She felt instantly contrite. "I'm sorry. You're right, of course." She lay back on the pillows. "I'd like my gown, Nick. Can you help me get into it? I feel fuzzy."

"Where is it, darling?"

She gestured toward the chest of drawers.

Her head felt like cotton wool, thank God, and the tears seemed to have dried up for the moment. But she still felt raw inside, festering with guilt and grief and hurt and fear.

He opened drawers until he found the lightweight cotton gown that was several sizes too big, just right to accommodate her swollen stomach.

She dragged herself upright and let him undress her

without a single protest. She was too exhausted to care if he saw her without her clothes.

He eased her out of the suit and her slip and bra, leaving her only in the tiny bikini briefs that slashed across her hips under the swell of her belly. He held the gown for a long moment while his eyes examined her with open curiosity, fascinated by the contours, the textures and the colors of her changing body.

"I'm not a pretty sight these days," she said quietly.

"You are to me, darling," he said, his voice deep and soft and tender. "As lovely as a rose about to bloom. Soft and swollen and quite extraordinarily beautiful. And if the circumstances were different, I assure you, I'd describe your body to you in terms that would make you blush. But for now," he sighed heavily, sliding the gown over her head, "I think I'd better remember how much you need protecting."

She let him put her into the gown and searched his dark, strained features in a deep silence. "You…you don't think I'm…ugly?"

He touched her mouth with a long, trembling finger. "I find you exquisite," he said under his breath.

Her eyes fell and she hated herself for asking the question. It was the wrong time for such things. She shouldn't have led him into that. She lay back on the pillow with a heavy sigh and closed her eyes.

"Go to sleep, little one," he said, easing off the bed to sit down in the armchair beside it. "Sleep now. I'll be here when you wake up. One day at a time, darling. It's what he would have wanted, to know that you were safe and taken care of."

"Don't go," she mumbled as sleep began to overtake her. "Don't go away."

"I won't."

She sighed and drifted off to sleep.

Maureen brought her a tray when she woke up, not at all surprised to find Nick asleep in the chair.

"It was so fortunate that he was with us," Maureen said as she handed Jolana a cup of black coffee and sat down on the bed to drink her own. "I could not have managed, nor could you, alone."

"He shouldn't have stayed there all night," Jolana commented, searching his unshaven face. The hard lines were all erased in sleep, and his mouth seemed relaxed and sensuous.

"Someone had to," Maureen mused softly.

"You frightened us all, *chérie*." She sighed, brushing away a stray tear. "Poor, brave fool. My poor brother. I shall miss him so, Jolana."

"So will I," came the teary reply. She sipped coffee noisily. "If only I hadn't held us up!"

"Nonsense. It was not your fault," Maureen said stubbornly. She brushed back her hair. "Pierre and I have made the arrangements. We will take him back to Toulouse, where our mother and father are buried. It is what he would have wanted, just a simple graveside service. That is all right with you?"

"Of course," Jolana said. She touched her stomach. "At least, there's the baby," she said absently. "I have that of him."

Maureen smiled sympathetically and nodded. She sipped her coffee in silence.

Nick awoke all at once, his eyes opened, black and quiet until he realized where he was. He sat up straighter, hunching his shoulders.

"Your back must be broken, *mon ami*," Maureen said

with a smile. "Come, I will show you to your room. You can shower and shave and then I will feed you."

"Thank you," he said and stood up, looking down at Jolana. "How are you?"

"I'll be all right now," she said, and her eyes dropped to her cup. "Thank you for staying with me."

"No trouble." He ran his arm along his back. "Except that I'm beginning to feel my age. That shower would be welcome about now," he confessed to Maureen.

"*Bien!* Come. Jolana, can I bring you anything?"

She shook her head. "Thank you, no. I'll get up in a minute, when my stomach settles, I'm fine, really," she assured her worried friend.

Maureen agreed reluctantly and led Nick out the door. Jolana finished her coffee and got out of bed. It was going to be another long day.

Jolana walked out the door beside Nick, with Maureen and Pierre right behind as they prepared to leave for Toulouse. There was no sense in delaying the ceremony, and it was generally felt that it would be easier on Jolana in her delicate condition to get it over with as quickly as possible. Friends and distant relatives had been informed, and most of them approved of the arrangement. Whether they did or not, Maureen had stated curtly, it was going to be done that way. The funeral directors had already started for Toulouse, where the service was to be at 3:00 p.m. that day. It was sunny, a lovely, perfect summer day. Except that Jolana felt cold and empty and bitter.

She stepped out the door, to be met with an unexpected and frightening barrage of flashbulbs and loud questions from what was obviously the international news media.

She gasped, stepping back. Nick quickly gathered her close and forced his way through the reporters like a battering ram. His size and strength cleared the path to the car.

The questions burst on Jolana's shocked ears, and as they began to penetrate, she felt sick all over. Did she know, they asked, about Phillipe's gambling debts? Was she aware of his mistress? Had she heard that the whole of his estate was going to be auctioned off to pay his debts?

When they were finally ensconced in the car and Pierre was expertly maneuvering it out of the city, Jolana was white-faced.

"Oh, Jolana," Maureen said miserably as she saw her sister-in-law's expression, "I am so sorry that you had to learn about it in such a way."

"It was true?" she managed.

"*Oui,*" Maureen sighed. She leaned over the back of the front seat, with her small, anguished face resting on her arms. "We were so deeply in debt. And this latest woman of his was very demanding."

Jolana's eyes closed. She was barely aware of Nick's hand searching for hers, locking with it, holding it as he tried to impart some of his own strength to her.

"There was nothing you could have done, *chérie,*" Maureen said softly. "I tried to reason with him, but he would not listen. Phillipe was always a free spirit, you understand. He lived as he wanted to."

"What do we have left?" Jolana asked in a whisper.

Maureen ran a hand through her dark hair. "I am not sure that we will have anything," she said, refusing to lie anymore to protect Phillipe's tarnished image. "He owed much money. Our attorneys informed me last night that we would be indeed fortunate if the sale of all our possessions managed to cover the debts."

Jolana could hardly breathe. She'd expected at least to have a roof over her head. She was carrying Phillipe's child, and there would be nothing left for him. She'd have to paint fast, to manage enough money so that she wouldn't starve. And poor Maureen, who'd never had to work in her life...

Her eyes opened. "If there's anything left, you should have it," she told Maureen. "Anything at all. I can paint. Nick, I can still have the exhibit, can't I?" she asked frantically, looking up at him wild-eyed.

His face hardened. "I'll take care of you," he said. "You won't have to risk the child by pushing yourself that hard."

"I can't let you," Jolana said. "I'm strong. I can take care of myself."

"We'll argue that point later," he said stubbornly. His dark eyes searched her face. "Poor little one. You shouldn't have had this to face, not now of all times."

Maureen, watching them, felt pieces of a puzzle fall slowly into place. This man was the one with whom Jolana had had the affair. She knew it as certainly as she knew her name. Her admiration for him increased tremendously. And if he was willing to take on responsibility for Jolana, that would be one less worry for Maureen to contend with. She was horrified at the prospect of being penniless, although she was certain that Pierre wouldn't let her starve. He'd already offered marriage, and she was reasonably certain that she was going to accept. He was a marvelous lover and she respected him. Perhaps that would suffice.

"It is as well that we get it over with today, *non*?"

Maureen asked gently, reaching back to touch Jolana's hand warmly. "You must not upset yourself."

Jolana nodded. Her dark eyes searched Maureen's. "It's you I'm worried about," she said with a trembling smile. "What will you do?"

"She will marry me, of course," Pierre said with a rakish grin in Maureen's direction. He was dark himself, and his quiet personality was the perfect foil for Maureen's bubbly one.

"Hush, I cannot think of that now," Maureen chided, pouting at him.

"We will discuss it later. But you have no reason to worry for her, *comtesse*," he told Jolana with a wink. "She is provided for."

Jolana sighed, leaning back against the seat. "I'm glad about that, at least." Her eyes filled with tears. Sensing it, Nick pulled her close, relieved to find that she didn't seem to mind his touch. That was a start. But he still had a very long way to go to regain the ground he'd lost so many months ago. His eyes dropped to her stomach possessively. He would have to take special care of her now, so that she didn't risk the baby. If only he could tell her the truth. But it would only make matters worse.

The graveside service was elegant, brief and with a kind of nobility that touched Jolana's sense of propriety. She listened to the words spoken by the priest, her eyes on the coffin, which was made of African mahogany, and hoped that Phillipe's restless soul had found the freedom it always strived for.

She remembered him in so many ways, so many moods. The day she came to Paris, standing in the middle of the street, daring Maureen to hit him and laughing like a clown. Serious, as he had been in the garden of the Paris apartment, the first time he'd kissed her. Passionate, making wild love to her on the beach on their honeymoon. And the last time she'd talked with him, promising to change, promising that things would get better. Grinning and waving from the car as the race began, blond and handsome and irrepressible.

Tears welled up in her eyes as she watched the solemn ceremony come to an end. They wanted her to throw a handful of earth on the coffin. She walked forward in a daze, delicate looking and elegant in her black suit and veiled hat, trembling a little as she heard earth hitting wood with such an empty, final sound.

"No!" she cried out huskily. Realization hit her all at once, that it was over, that she was never going to see Phillipe again as long as she lived. "Phillipe!"

Nick caught her up in his arms and carried her from the cemetery, oblivious to the curious stares, to the murmurs. He held her close, hating himself for starting the chain reaction that had carried her here.

She was weeping silently now, her chest shaking with great sobs. He put her inside the car and climbed in beside her, passing a handkerchief into her trembling hands.

"It's over now," he said quietly. "He's better off. And don't torment yourself by putting him on some kind of pedestal now that he's dead. He wasn't perfect. He was just a man, a part of your life that's over now. He wouldn't want you to grieve forever. And there's the baby to consider now. You can't afford the luxury of putting your child at risk."

She listened silently, her face white under the veil, her eyes stinging and swollen with tears. "It was just so final, you know," she tried to explain. "I was fond of him, Nick. When I needed someone to hold on to, he was there. He made me start to live again."

His face darkened and bent over her hands as he clasped them warmly in his. "I'll always be grateful to him for that," he said enigmatically. "I'm glad you had him to run to. I'm sorry he's dead. But life goes on and you have to start looking ahead now."

"Yes. But not right now," she whispered.

"Not right now." He drew her close against his side and held her until the others joined them.

"Are you all right?" Maureen asked her. Her own face was tear-stained, but she managed a smile.

"I think so," Jolana replied, trying to keep back the tears.

As they drove out of the cemetery, Jolana took one last look back and then buried her face against Nick's already soggy suit coat and cried some more. The tears were hot and burning, but eventually they passed. Eventually she could talk normally and feel the emptiness already beginning to recede. She would make it now. The worst was surely over.

That was what she thought until they arrived back in Paris and discovered an entourage of newspeople lounging at the door of the apartment.

"Turn around," Nick told Pierre. "There's no sense in going through that again."

Maureen thought for a moment. "We can go to a hotel, I suppose. But I will need clothes…"

Pierre grinned. "I have a friend who will go to the apartment for you. He is a gendarme."

Maureen smiled. "Bless your resourcefulness, *mon chère*."

So they went to a hotel, and Pierre went back with Nick to his own. The men had offered to stay, but Jolana shook her head.

"I have to learn to be alone sometime," she told Nick. "It might as well start now. Thank you, but don't make me dependent on you."

His eyes had darkened. "I want to do just that, eventually."

"Don't talk that way. Please. I can't handle any more pressure right now."

He sighed. "If you need me...?"

"I'll call. I promise."

He nodded. "Tomorrow, we'll talk."

"There's nothing to talk about," she said firmly. "I'm going to paint, as soon as this financial tangle is resolved, and you're going to exhibit me."

"How can you possibly support yourself and the baby on what you make painting?" he demanded. "Listen to reason, for God's sake. Maureen will be married. You won't even have the apartment...!"

"Nick, please!" She put her hands to her head.

He took her into his arms and held her gently. "I won't let you put that baby's life on the line, do you hear me?" he asked at her ear. "I'm going to take care of you until it's born, with or without your permission. It's what your husband would have wanted," he added through his teeth.

She drew in a slow, bitter breath. "Nick, he didn't really want the baby," she confessed. "Nor me, after I started showing."

His chest rose and fell raggedly. "I want it," he said huskily. "It, and you."

She felt weak and that wouldn't do at all. She was

still wary of Nick, of letting him close enough to wound her again. She tugged at his arms and he let her go.

"I need to get some sleep," she said. "So do you. Thank you for all you've done."

"We'll talk tomorrow," he repeated. He bent and kissed her forehead with a brief, tender pressure. "Try to rest."

"I'm not your responsibility," she said softly, searching his dark eyes.

He ran a tender finger down her cheek. "Yes, you are. More than you'll ever know, you are." He brought her hands to his mouth and kissed the palms with a slow, terrible hunger. "I don't want to leave you," he whispered gruffly. "I don't want you to have to be alone."

"There are twin beds in the bedroom," she faltered. "Maureen and I are going to share a room."

His eyes searched hers hungrily. "You and I should share a bed," he said under his breath. "And I'd hold you all night. Just that. I'd hold you and if you got afraid, I'd be there."

Tears stung her eyes and she turned away before he could see them. "Nothing's changed, Nick," she said curtly. "My husband is dead, but it's the past that separated us. I won't forget what happened. If you have any idea of picking up where we left off when you threw me out of your life, think again!"

He actually flinched at the unexpected attack. She whirled, glaring at him across the room with eyes that hated him for a moment.

"I thought you might have started to trust me again," he said after a pause.

"I'm grateful for your help," she said. "But I don't

want to get involved with you ever again. You can be my friend, nothing more. Not ever."

She was killing him by inches, and she didn't even know it. Inside, he felt as sick and cold as if he'd been stabbed. She looked so beautiful, with her face flushed and her dark, accusing eyes in that frame of disheveled blond hair. He ran his eyes over her swollen body and wanted nothing more in life than to fall on his knees and beg her to forgive him. But he was a proud man, and she was a stubborn woman. It wasn't going to happen overnight. But he wasn't going to give up, either. She didn't flinch when he touched her, and she'd let him look at her the other night as he put her into her gown, as if she enjoyed the feel of his eyes, his reaction to her pregnancy. Yes, she still felt something. And he was going to fan that tiny ember until it blazed up like a forest fire.

"Then I'll be your friend," he said after a minute, and smiled softly. "Good night."

She watched him go with mixed emotions. She knew that she still loved him, but she couldn't let him know. He wasn't trustworthy, and she couldn't survive another disaster like the last one. Besides, there was still Margery in the background. The thought strengthened her resolve.

The next few days went by in a haze for Jolana. The press kept after them incessantly and finally Jolana and Maureen agreed to one long interview if the media would go away. They answered the questions, withstood the flashbulbs, and finally were allowed to live in peace.

Maureen married Pierre, with Jolana and Nick looking on, and the two of them got ready to fly off to Spain for a honeymoon.

"I don't like to leave you," Maureen said as Pierre waited for her in the car. "The apartment is sold. You have that horrible little hotel room... Oh, Jolana, I feel so guilty that I did not tell you everything in the beginning...!"

Jolana kissed her warmly. "You're my friend. I want only the best for you, always. Be happy. And don't worry about me." She sighed, glancing ruefully over her shoulder at Nick, who was talking to Pierre. "I seem to have a guardian angel, despite all my efforts to make him go home."

"He cares deeply, that one," Maureen said. Her eyes searched Jolana's for one long minute. "Let him take care of you," she pleaded. "You need him now."

Jolana sighed. "I think I'd rather starve than trust him..." She almost said "again" before she caught herself. She smiled. "Maybe I'll become famous and sell millions of dollars' worth of paintings. Anyway, be sure and write me. I'll see you when you come home."

"Okay." Maureen grinned. She hugged her warmly and rushed off to her new husband.

Afterward, Nick took Jolana back to her small hotel room, looking in despair at the shabby furnishings.

"Dammit, I can't leave you in this," he said after a minute, his dark eyes blazing up at her. "Pack your things. You're coming back to America with me."

She glared up at him. "I will not! You have no right to... Nick!"

He had her on her back on the bed. He was careful not to jar her too much, not to hurt her. But she was flat on her back, and he was looming over her, keeping her there with just the threat of his big body.

"If you don't pack," he said softly, letting his eyes drop to her mouth, "I'll take your clothes off, little pregnant beauty, and I'll make such love to you that you'll scream and bring the manager running to throw you out."

Her breath caught as she read the truth of the threat in his dark eyes.

"You screamed that night," he whispered, bending. "Do you remember? You dug those exquisite long nails into my hips and you threw your head back and screamed and screamed..."

"Nick," she moaned helplessly as the memory washed over her like fire, taking her breath, robbing her of will.

His mouth poised over hers, tempting it, teasing it. His fingers went to the front of her smock top and ran possessively over her stomach and up to trace the swollen contours of one soft breast.

She tensed at the feel of it, at the newness after so many months of not being touched at all.

"Shh," he breathed at her mouth. "Lie still."

A tiny gasp caught in her throat, and he bent and fitted his wide, chiseled mouth softly to hers, just brushing it, barely touching it, letting her feel the texture of his hard lips. At the same time, his fingers stroked tenderly around one taut breast, tracing all of it except the hardened tip, in a teasing pattern that made her ache for him to rub his hand across that too-sensitive peak.

"Oh, please," she whispered on a sob, the words going into his soft, searching mouth.

"Where?" he whispered back, his voice unsteady.

She arched her back helplessly. "There," she moaned.

He lifted his mouth, nuzzling her nose with his, and looked down into her eyes. His face was solemn, and his fingers only repeated the same rhythm, torturing her as she writhed sensuously beneath him. Her lips parted, her breath came in wild little gasps. Her dark eyes pleaded with his.

"Now," he whispered, holding her eyes as she lifted and lifted, trying to make him touch her.

The first teasing stroke of his fingers across that hardness made her cry out.

"So hungry," he whispered, watching her. "So hungry and wild, and I want this as much as you do. I want to feel you wanting me. Here. And here." His fingers caught the delicate tip and rubbed it slowly and she bit her lip and moaned achingly.

"Jolana," he breathed into her mouth as he bent. He kissed her with such tenderness that tears stung her eyes, and all at once his hand lifted.

"No," she protested helplessly, trying to catch it, gone beyond shame and pride as waves of desire washed over her trembling body, showing in her wide, pained eyes.

"Shh," he whispered tenderly. "I'm only going to put it under your blouse," he told her, smoothing back her hair with his free hand. "I'm going to touch your skin, darling." His mouth eased back down to hers while she arched, trembling, waiting. And she felt his hard, warm fingers moving under the hem of the blouse, up her taut rib cage, to the soft firmness of her breast.

She made an odd, strangling sound, and opened her eyes to look into his.

"I want to put my mouth there," he told her as his

fingers traced the underside of the hard mound. "I want to taste you."

Hating her weakness for him, her own blazing hunger, she fumbled with the top and, with jerky motions, crumpled it under her chin so that he could look at her.

His eyes misted with emotion, darkened, his hand trembled as it cupped and lifted her to the slow descent of his open mouth. "My woman," he whispered as he took her slowly into the warm, moist darkness of his mouth. "My heart."

Her hands went to the back of his head and buried themselves in his thick hair, holding him tenderly to her body while he searched her with his lips and his tongue. Tears ran helplessly down her cheeks as shivers of pure ecstasy trembled through her body.

Seconds later he turned his cheek against her and lay there, holding her, one big hand spreading over her swollen stomach as he nuzzled her soft warmth, his breath erratic, his heart shaking him.

"Nick," she whispered.

His chest rose slowly. "You are," he whispered, "the sweetest honey in the world. I love touching you and looking at you. I love this," he whispered, running his fingers reverently over her swollen stomach, "most of all, this beauty I can feel under my hands, this tiny life inside you."

Her eyes closed and she was submerged under a tide of tenderness and love.

He put his mouth to her stomach, through the stretching fabric that covered it. And then he sat up with a shaky sigh and reluctantly pulled her top back down.

"You make me tremble," he laughed unsteadily. "I can't take much of that."

Her wondering eyes searched his, and he bent and kissed away the tears.

"Didn't he ever make love to you?" he asked in a deep, tender whisper.

"He...found me ugly...like this," she managed.

"Ugly?" He smiled, slowly, wickedly. "My God."

Her eyes searched his quietly. "You wanted me?" She said it as if it were incomprehensible to her.

"Oh, yes," he replied ruefully. "Another few seconds, and all my good intentions wouldn't have saved you."

"But they did."

"Are you sorry about it, *amore*?" he asked gently, brushing back the damp hair from her face. "Because if you are, we can make love."

Tingles of ecstasy flowed through her, but she forced herself to ignore them. The trap was sweetly baited, but she remembered its jaws.

He watched the wariness come back, felt her tension and fear, and nodded. "Yes, I know. You don't trust me. But we have all the time in the world." He lifted her hand to his mouth. "I want you to marry me."

It was like the past repeating itself. Except that this time, she wasn't crazy. "No, Nick," she said softly.

"All right," he said agreeably. "Then come home and live with me, until the baby comes."

"Your mother would be horrified," she said, grasping at straws.

He ran a finger over her lips. "My mother is delighted. I called her."

She flushed. "I'm a widow. A very pregnant widow. What would your neighbors think?"

"I have a house in the mountains, in Upstate New York," he said with a slow smile. "We don't have any neighbors. There's a lake, and swans, and ducks…a grassy knoll where you can paint, and mountains in the distance."

"It sounds lovely, but what you're offering is to keep me. And I can't let you."

"You'll earn your keep, *comtesse*," he laughed softly. "I'll make you paint, for that trumped-up exhibition you invented."

"You don't have to…"

"I want to." He stretched lazily and got to his feet. "Maybe Tony will forgive me if I take you home."

She studied him for a long moment. "Nick…"

His eyes ran slowly down her body and he smiled. "I want you," he said matter-of-factly. "God, I want you. You make my body sing." He frowned, studying her face. "Jolana, can you have sex?" he asked suddenly.

She swallowed. "I won't…"

"Can you?" he repeated gently.

She shifted. "Well, until the last month."

He was counting mentally, adding up the months since she'd slept with him. That had happened in January. It was now June. Almost July. Going on six months. He smiled slowly, delightedly.

"I'm not going to make love with you," she said stubbornly. "If, *if*, I go back with you, I want that firmly understood."

He lifted an eyebrow and stared pointedly at her breasts.

She flushed, dragging herself into a sitting position. She tingled madly from that scrutiny, from the slight tenderness his mouth and hands had created.

"I don't want to get involved with you again," she groaned.

He went down on one knee in front of her and took her frustrated face in his warm hands. "You can sleep with me," he whispered. "And I'll keep you from having nightmares. I'll comfort you and we'll make plans for the baby. We'll have a nursery added to the house, and buy him lots of toys…!"

Her eyes searched his. "You want the baby," she said suddenly, curious.

"I want you and him both," he said curtly. "I don't have anybody, damn it," he ground out, sighing irritably. "I'm forty years old, and so damned alone, Jolana." He looked into her eyes from an unnerving proximity and she could read the loneliness in them. "I want to marry you. Can't you even agree to think about it? Lie to me, tell me you'll think about it."

She dropped her eyes to his formidable nose and sighed. "I can't lie." She lifted her shoulders. "All right, I'll think about it. But no promises."

"No promises." He moved closer and kissed her trembling mouth softly, warmly. "And you'll sleep with me?"

"Sleep," she specified.

"And let me look at you?" he asked wickedly.

"Nick!"

He got to his feet, laughing, all the hard lines gone, all the irrepressible enthusiasm back. "Get up, or I'll prove to you how hungry I am to have you. On the floor. On your back."

She scrambled up, flushing. "You're a rake!"

"I'm a rake?" he asked with mock astonishment. "You sat in my lap and took me in the front seat of my car…"

She put her hand over his mouth, her face red, her eyes wild.

His own darkened as he pressed the palm to his mouth. "You'll marry me," he said under his breath. "And we'll make lots of babies together. Mama will like that. She'll come and stay with us and help you look after them sometimes."

"And Margery?" she forced herself to say.

He only smiled. "I'll let you find out about that all by yourself. You'll learn to trust me. It won't be as hard as you think. I've had a long time alone to regret what happened. Now I'm going to make it up to you. And you're going to like it, my darling," he murmured, bending to brush a slow kiss over her eyes. "I'm going to make you like every second of it. Now, get packed."

She started to argue, but she knew it wasn't going to do any good. He was a pirate. He'd carry her off if she didn't.

She turned to pack with a tiny smile. Perhaps there was a chance that it might work out. Even so, she had the baby to think of and she had to put him first. Phillipe's baby. How odd that Nick didn't mind that it was Phillipe's. Thank God, she added, because she knew already that living alone and trying to support herself wasn't going to be good for the heir to the de Vinchy-Cardin name. She had to go with Nick, for the baby's sake. But she'd work hard at her painting, and soon be independent again. And then she'd see how things worked out. But this time it would be in her own good time, and on her own terms.

CHAPTER THIRTEEN

JOLANA WAS ENCHANTED by Nick's house. It was a little
over a hundred and fifty miles from Manhattan, near
the Hudson River, and it looked like something out of
the Middle Ages. It was made of massive stones, which
Nick told her had been quarried locally before the turn
of the century and assembled by European craftsmen.
There were graceful arches front and back, and it sat
on a peninsula that jutted out into a lake, giving it more
than adequate privacy. Huge iron fences ensured that
privacy, and there were guesthouses and a boathouse
and dock as well. The main rooms had stone porticos
with iron railings overlooking the lake, and the luxuri-
ous gardens behind the house featured a stone gazebo.
Inside, it was so elegant that Jolana walked around it
awestruck. Even the villa where she'd stayed with Phillipe and Maureen hadn't been this beautiful. There were
leaded glass windows, and crystal chandeliers in every
room. The living room was surprisingly modern, with
modular chrome and white furnishings and an enormous semicircular plush couch. It looked spacious and
open and elegant. And the bedrooms were an education. Nick's caught her eye because of the walls and
the size of the bed. It was paneled with shimmering,
lacquered wood and featured a mirrored ceiling and a
vast, king-size bed.

Nick paused by the door, watching her incredulous expression as she stared at the ceiling.

"I've never had a woman in that bed," he said softly, as if he read the helpless speculation on her face.

She laughed nervously. "Hard to believe," she said.

He caught her shoulders and turned her, missing nothing as his eyes went up and down her body in the velvety beige dress she was wearing. It emphasized her blondness, her creamy complexion and dark eyes. "I've been waiting for one very special lady."

The flush made her wildly beautiful. His eyes searched hers. Slowly, carefully, he lifted her clear off the floor.

"Nick, you mustn't," she whispered.

He stopped long enough to close the door and lock it. "Why not?" he asked gently, smiling down at her as he carried her carefully to the bed. "Don't you want to see?"

She let him put her down, watching as he shed his jacket and tie before he kicked off his shoes and joined her on the brown velvet bedspread.

"Now." He grinned. "Look up."

She did and saw his broad back, and the way he was levered over her, the muscles rippling in his shoulders, his long, powerful legs. She could see the back of his head where her fingers touched the dark waves.

He traced her lips with a lazy finger. "Would you like me to take off my clothes and give you an unobstructed view?"

She laughed, feeling girlish and shy and excited all at once. "You didn't have the mirrors put there, did you?" she asked.

He shook his dark head. "No, the house belonged to

a wealthy European and his young wife. I suppose," he continued drily, "he liked to see everything at once."

She touched his face, tracing the lines, loving him. Afraid that her eyes might give her away, she dropped them to his throat.

"It's a long time until dinner," he said, studying her. "Wouldn't you like to take your clothes off and talk to me for a while?"

"Why would I need to take my clothes off?"

"Oh, we might find something conversational about it," he replied, smiling wickedly.

"I look like a pumpkin," she said.

The smile faded. "Show me."

She blushed. "I can't."

"I want to look at you, the way you let me the night I put you to bed," he persisted. "I want to watch the baby move."

Flashes of pleasure burned her and she couldn't look at him.

He touched her face, her hair, with soft, tender fingers. "Let's make love, Jolana. Let's really make love this time, no more secrets, no more distrust."

She wanted to. She wanted to so desperately. But she looked up at him and remembered helplessly the last morning in her apartment in New York, what he'd said, how he'd looked.

He saw it, and sighed heavily. "Bad memories," he said, nodding. "Yes, I have them, too. I'll tell you about mine one day, about my nightmares. About how I felt the day I finally found you in Monaco."

"I'm sorry," she said, sitting up. "But I had a few nightmares of my own."

"Yes, I know. All my fault." He got to his feet slowly,

standing just in front of her, looking down. He unbuttoned his shirt and ran a restless hand through the heavy mat of hair on his chest. Impulsively, he drew her to stand in front of him and lifted her hands to his body. "This is what drove me crazy," he murmured, pressing her fingers hard into the darkness. "Remembering how you used to look at me when you touched me here, as if you loved the very texture of my skin. I could feel your hands in the night sometimes, and I'd wake up sweating."

Her hands moved slowly over the damp, muscular expanse with remembered pleasure, lingering where the male nipples were hard and distended. "It shocked me, the first time," she said absently, "I didn't know that men were aroused in the same places that women were."

"This, you mean?" he asked, pressing her palm hard against that rough nub.

"Yes."

"Did you know," he asked, studying her face, "that you could do to me what I did to you in Paris before we left, and in the same way?"

Her eyes lifted. "When you touched me…"

"Yes." He searched her eyes, breathing unsteadily as the memory came back full force. "You could tease me until I begged."

That was faintly shocking. She couldn't picture Nick ever begging for a woman's favors. She was almost tempted to see for herself.

"I'd let you," he whispered huskily, his eyes dark and his face hard. "I'd let you undress me and touch me until I couldn't bear it, and I'd beg you with tears in my eyes to take me. Just the same way I could do it to you. And I wouldn't be the least ashamed to let you watch me. Pride has no place at all between lovers."

Her hands stilled on his body. She wanted him to do that to her, she wanted to do it to him. But it was too soon.

"Margery is a closed chapter in my life, Jolana," he said after a minute. "I know how deeply I hurt you. I know the doubts are still there. But I'm going to teach you to trust me again. You're going to marry me, and love me obsessively, just like I'm going to love you. And that baby you're carrying will be the most cherished little human being alive."

She watched his hands lower to cup her stomach, and he smiled.

"I've got you both now," he whispered. "I hold you, and hold him."

Tears misted her eyes. She looked up and he bent and kissed her, tenderly, letting her feel his lips tremble with the longing she aroused in him.

She smiled softly when he drew away, because he made her feel whole.

"I love you," he whispered softly.

She sighed. "Nick…"

"No more of that." He guided her to the door and opened it. "Mama's coming up this afternoon. She's so excited that you're here, she can hardly bear it. She's convinced now that I'm over that insanity about Margery and ready to settle down," he said, grinning.

He made it sound as if it really was over. But she couldn't help wondering.

Later in the day, she and his mother went walking around the back of the house, where the lake spread out beautifully before them.

"You feel good, yes?" The older woman smiled. "The baby, he makes you glow."

"I feel very good," Jolana sighed. She touched her stomach lightly. "I'm still not sure that I should have come here with Nick, though. I don't want to be an embarrassment to him."

"Embarrassment?" His mother sounded horrified. "How could you be?"

"A visibly pregnant widow, living under his roof?" Jolana asked softly. "How must it look?"

"But, it is where you belong," the silver-haired woman said, patting Jolana's hands warmly. "The baby is the most important thing now. There is nothing to worry about. Nick will take care of you both."

"He shouldn't have to, though," Jolana protested, staring miserably at the lake. "If my husband hadn't been killed..." She shrugged, staring down at the ground. "It won't be easy for him, bringing up another man's child."

"He loves you," the old woman scoffed. "Besides, Nick told me it is not your husband's baby. There is no need to pretend, my darling. You love my Nick..."

Jolana turned, staring blankly at the older woman's gently smiling face. "What...?"

Nick's mother sighed impatiently. "Jolana, Nick told me the child is his, that your husband was sterile."

Jolana had gone white. "What are you telling me?" she whispered hoarsely.

"Jolana?" The old woman caught her just as she started to sink, and helped her ease down onto the grass. "Jolana, what have I said? Surely to goodness you knew about your husband?"

But Jolana's eyes were closed and tears were streaming down her cheeks. So that was why. It was all a sham. It was Nick's baby she was carrying, and the deception had been played to its conclusion. He'd brought her here not out of love, but because he was responsible for making her pregnant. It was his child, and he felt obligated to take care of her, and it.

"*Dio*, my tongue will be the death of us all," Mama groaned. "Jolana, you didn't know, did you? Oh, my darling, I am so sorry! So sorry! Wait, you stay here. Right here, you understand? I get Nick!"

As if she could have moved, she thought miserably. Tears were washing down her pale cheeks in a flood, and she'd never felt so hopeless in all her life. The world had gone black.

When Nick got to her, she was crying silently, staring at the lake through a thick mist.

"Jolana?" he whispered huskily.

She shifted, but she didn't speak.

He eased down beside her cautiously, watching her. "Mama said to tell you that she was sorry," he said quietly. "She's gone home."

Her eyes closed. She still couldn't speak. Phillipe had to have known that the baby wasn't his. He'd accepted it, but that explained why he hadn't taken better care of her. Perhaps in his subconscious he hoped she might lose it…

Nick drew in a slow breath, terrified to speak, to try to explain. He didn't know what to say.

"It's your baby, isn't it?" she whispered in a strangled tone. "Everybody…hid it from me. Phillipe was sterile."

"It's our baby," he said after a minute.

She stared down at her lap. "You don't have to marry me," she said harshly. "I won't deny you visiting rights!"

He caught her by the arms and eased her down onto

the grass, holding her there gently but firmly while his chest rose and fell raggedly.

"Let me go!" she flashed, lips trembling, chest heaving as she struggled.

He threw a leg across both of hers and held her pinned there in the sunlight until she stilled.

She hated his superior strength. She hated him. But she was tired, and she was upsetting the baby, and all the fight drained out of her suddenly.

"I could have told you in Monaco," he said quietly, still holding her. "But I was afraid you might do something desperate if you knew. You even told me that you'd rather drown than bear my child."

There was a note in his voice that disturbed her, a huskiness that held a terrible kind of pain.

She didn't want to see it, so she didn't look. "You hurt me badly," she whispered.

"What in God's name do you think it did to me," he ground out savagely, "to find you pregnant with my baby and married to another man?"

He was trembling, and she forced her eyes up to his and was astonished to find a glaze over them.

"Oh, God, you little fool, I love you so," he whispered hoarsely, searching her face with fierce, loving obsession. "I love you and want you, want my child that lies under your heart... And I can't even get near you."

He drew in a shaky breath and slowly let go of her hands. He sat up, running his hands through his hair, staring sightlessly at the lake with a hellish torment on his face.

He pulled a cigarette from his pocket and lit it, shocking her, because she hadn't seen him smoke since they'd been back together. "From the moment I left you all I could see was your face, that horrible agony in your eyes when I told you I didn't want you anymore." He took a long draw from the cigarette. "I called Tony, you know," he said, glancing at the astonishment in her face. "That's right. I was afraid for you. I was already sure I'd made the biggest mistake of my stupid life, and I didn't want you making a bigger one over me. So I called and begged him to go see about you. I knew you wouldn't let me near you, but I was sure you wouldn't turn him away." His eyes closed. "And he made it just in time, just barely in time. Oh, God, I'd have blown my brains out if you'd managed it, Jolana. I couldn't have gone on living if you had died because of me."

She sat up, smoothing her skirt with fanatical meticulousness, not saying a word. He was saying some shocking things, and it occurred to her that no man could admit the things he was admitting without love. By the same token, he couldn't have concealed the knowledge about the baby and his part in saving her life unless he'd cared deeply.

He made a helpless gesture with one hand. "I don't know what to say to you," he said quietly. He glanced at her, loving her with his eyes. "You're carrying my baby. I want it. I want you. I'll love you both until I die."

Pride, he had said, had no place between lovers. And now she knew what he meant. He was baring his soul to her, as he never had before. He was giving her the chance to walk out on him, as he'd walked out on her.

She got to her feet. He sat there, looking up. "I won't blame you, if you go," he said softly. "But at least let me provide for you. Will you do that?"

She turned away from the worshipping, hurting eyes. "Let me have ten minutes, and then come inside, please," she said quietly. She walked away, into the house.

His room was on the ground floor, down the hall from hers. She walked inside, glancing ruefully at the mirrored ceiling, and went on into the spacious bathroom beyond. Without thinking about it, she ran the tub full, stripped off her clothes and stepped into the warm, surging jets of water with a long sigh.

As she bathed, she considered her options. She could leave, hold on to her hurt pride and punish them both, and her baby. Or she could admit that she still loved Nick and try trusting him for a change. If she loved him, she had to trust him. And it dawned on her while she was soaking that Margery no longer bothered her. She did believe that the woman was a closed chapter in Nick's life. She had to believe it, because no man who loved another woman could possibly look the way Nick had out on the lawn.

She thought of Phillipe and felt a twinge of sadness for her young husband. Perhaps in another time and place, they could have made a good marriage. If she hadn't gotten pregnant, or if he'd been more stable… But that was all over now. She had to look to the future. And she honestly couldn't see any kind of future that didn't include Nick. Indeed, at this point she felt as if she couldn't survive without having him near her.

She finished bathing and wrapped herself in a thick, brown towel and stepped out onto the tile. There was a faint noise, like that of a door opening, and she smiled secretly.

She clutched the towel lightly and walked out of the bathroom onto the deep pile of the beige carpet in the bedroom just as Nick closed the door behind him and paused.

He turned his head, spotted her and hesitated, uncertainty touching his hard, broad face for the first time in her memory.

"Hello, Nick," she said softly, and slowly let the towel fall to the floor.

His dark eyes traced every line of her, every curve, from her swollen breasts to her distended stomach and long, elegant legs.

"Well, well, well," he said. "And I thought I was going to have hell changing your mind. I came up here with all kinds of wild ideas, everything from chains to blackmail…"

"You'll have to take your clothes off first," she answered teasingly, feeling more confident by the minute, despite her pregnancy.

He cocked a heavy eyebrow. "Why don't you take them off?"

"Daring me?" she teased. She went close and began to remove his shirt, lingering over the broad, hair-covered muscularity of his chest, touching him with her mouth as well as her hands.

"Just one thing, darling," he whispered, catching her face in his unsteady hands. "I've been without a woman since the night I had you. For God's sake, don't arouse me too much. I couldn't bear to hurt you or the baby."

Her eyes dilated wildly. "It's been months!"

"Almost six of them," he groaned, burying his face in her throat. "Six months, wanting you, dreaming about you." His hands trembled as they ran slowly, tenderly over her back, her thighs, her hips and stomach and breasts. "I hurt like almighty hell."

"Oh, Nick, I never dreamed…" she whispered huskily. She led him to the bed and stretched out on it, avoiding the sight of herself in the ceiling mirror as he finished what she'd started and joined her there.

"Have I shocked you?" he asked softly, watching her eyes run slowly, hungrily over his nudity.

"I didn't think men could go that long without sex," she admitted.

"I could have gone the rest of my life without it, if I couldn't have gotten you back," he growled huskily. "My God, I don't want anyone else. Not anyone."

She touched his chest, running her hands slowly down his body until she made him tense and go rigid, until he groaned and his head jerked down to her shoulder.

"I don't want anyone else, either," she whispered into his ear as she stroked him. "So I think you'd better marry me, Nick."

He said something, but she didn't understand it, because his hands were suddenly at work on her own body. She felt her muscles clench and she cried out.

His mouth bit at her lips, his voice whispered things she only half heard. His hands touched her in ways and places that made her arch and writhe and beg, and when she felt his strong thighs parting her own, she opened her eyes and looked at him as he overwhelmed her.

It had been a long time, and he had to stop quite suddenly when he realized that she was almost like a virgin because of it.

Her hands clenched on his shoulders and she breathed unsteadily. "I'm sorry," she whispered as she tried to make her body relax.

"It's all right," he whispered back, smiling, bending to kiss her very tenderly. "Relax now. Move with

me. We'll do it slowly. Slowly, my heart. Just…rock…
with me. Yes."

She watched his face as the subtle, erotic movement
of his body caused her taut muscles to unlock, as his
eyes holding hers began to twinkle and burn.

He laughed softly as she moved and he felt the sudden ease of his invasion.

"You devil," she whispered up at him, burning with
a sudden, wild recklessness, a fierce need to possess
and be possessed.

His nostrils flared as he dragged at a breath of air,
looking like the Roman conquerors might have over
two thousand years ago, with his dark, curly hair and
his hard, broad face and the eyes that were black with
passion.

"Witch," he accused huskily. "Incite me. Burn me
up. Come on, show me what you want, lift up."

"Watch me," she dared in a whisper, smiling hotly as
her hips moved, her arms reached up, her body arched,
sliding against his in a perfect whisper of provocation.

"I'm going to make you scream," he growled, laughing.

"Are you?" she whispered, trembling with anticipa-
tion. "Make me," she dared him. "Make me…!"

It was fire. Blazing. Burning. She twisted and dug
her sharp nails into him. She bit his shoulder and whispered things that would make her blush in saner moments. She teased him and pleaded with him and lifted
her eyes to the ceiling to watch what was happening beneath it, and at the last her voice lifted to shatter against
it and she thought she might die as her eyes closed on
an edge of ecstasy so sharp that it sliced her into tiny,
exhausted bits when it was over and he collapsed on a
harsh, shuddering groan.

She cried, because it had been the most beautiful experience of her life, because she loved him and she was carrying his child, and instead of the ending she'd expected, there had been a beginning.

"I love you," she whispered at his ear. "I love you, I love you. I want to live with you until I die."

"Not for a long time, *amore mia*," he whispered. "Not for a hundred years, and when you die, so will I, and we'll live forever in our memories. But long before then, we'll raise a houseful of children and every day will be more beautiful than the one before. I love you so."

She held him close, nuzzling her face into his throat. "Do you really think I'm sexy like this?"

He lifted himself so that he was lying beside her and smiled slowly. "Doesn't your mirror tell you the answer?" he asked, nodding toward the ceiling. "Did you watch us?" he whispered wickedly.

She laughed like a young bride. "Yes," she confessed, lowering her eyes.

"Next time, I get to watch." He kissed her softly. "No more regrets? No more secrets?"

"No more." She bent down and kissed him softly. "Let's get married."

His dark eyes searched hers and he nodded. "Let's get married." He pulled her down into his arms, and she closed her eyes, thinking how it would be in the years ahead. Her body tingled like champagne as the baby moved, and Nick felt him, and laughed. The deep, rich sound echoed through the house, like a song of love, endlessly played.

* * * * *

**She vowed to never trust another man...
until she met him.**

*Don't miss this new passionate
Long, Tall Texans romance from
New York Times bestselling author
Diana Palmer!*

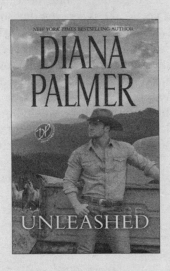

"Palmer knows how to make the sparks fly."
—*Publishers Weekly*

Available now!

True love is in store for one gruff cowboy in New York Times bestselling author Diana Palmer's new Wyoming Men romance!

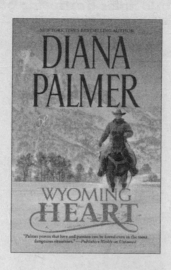

"Palmer proves that love and passion can be found even in the most dangerous situations."
—*Publishers Weekly* on *Untamed*

Order your copy today!

The countdown to Christmas begins now!
Keep track of all your Christmas reads.

September 24

- [ ] *A Coldwater Christmas* by Delores Fossen
- [ ] *A Country Christmas* by Debbie Macomber
- [ ] *A Haven Point Christmas* by RaeAnne Thayne
- [ ] *A MacGregor Christmas* by Nora Roberts
- [ ] *A Wedding in December* by Sarah Morgan
- [ ] *An Alaskan Christmas* by Jennifer Snow
- [ ] *Christmas at White Pines* by Sherryl Woods
- [ ] *Christmas from the Heart* by Sheila Roberts
- [ ] *Christmas in Winter Valley* by Jodi Thomas
- [ ] *Cowboy Christmas Redemption* by Maisey Yates
- [ ] *Kisses in the Snow* by Debbie Macomber
- [ ] *Low Country Christmas* by Lee Tobin McClain
- [ ] *Season of Wonder* by RaeAnne Thayne
- [ ] *The Christmas Sisters* by Sarah Morgan
- [ ] *Wyoming Heart* by Diana Palmer

October 22

- [ ] *Season of Love* by Debbie Macomber

October 29

- [ ] *Christmas in Silver Springs* by Brenda Novak
- [ ] *Christmas with You* by Nora Roberts
- [ ] *Stealing Kisses in the Snow* by Jo McNally

November 26

- [ ] *North to Alaska* by Debbie Macomber
- [ ] *Winter's Proposal* by Sherryl Woods

Harlequin.com

XMAS0319BPA